The Return to Council Grove

Written By
"The Flint Hills Cowboy"
Levi "Doc" Hinck

© 2019 Levi Hinck

All rights reserved.

"The Council Grove Blues" © 2017 Song written by Levi Hinck

Although this book is based on historic events, people, and places, this story is a work of fiction and does not claim historical accuracy. Although accuracy has been sought, artistic liberty has been used in some places.

ISBN: 9781688428294

The Return to Council Grove

Dedication

I would like to thank my grandmother, Nancy Cord, for being my biggest inspiration in life. Whether acting or singing or writing, she has always been my biggest fan and biggest support. I would like to dedicate this book to her.
I have taken bits and pieces of my own personal life and pieced them together in a different era to make this story. I hope readers enjoy it.
Much obliged to you for taking the time to purchase and read this book.
Make sure to look for the next one!

Acknowledgements

I would like to send a special thanks to Nichole P. Conard of RedRock Photography of Wichita, KS, for her expertise in photograph editing and cover design. She brought my dreams to life in the beautiful cover of this book.

I'd also like to thank Holly Sporleder for assisting me as a model for the character Samantha on the back cover. I really enjoyed the photoshoot and shared laughter as we became friends through this journey.

I'd especially like to thank Britta Ann Meadows of Peas in a Pod Editing and Design for her patience and dedication in editing, formatting, and preparing this book for publishing. It was definitely a learning experience for me, but it was so great to be able to work with you.

I'd also like to thank one of my biggest supporters throughout this process: my beautiful fiancée Stephanie Anderson. Stephanie worked a miracle and used her photography talents to conclude the book cover's masterpiece. She also assisted me through many struggles with modern technology (computers) and saw me through many battles of depression and kept pushing me forward. Many a night I said I was through and that I was giving up writing once and for good; however, Stephanie always saw me through and without her help this book would never have been completed.

I also would like to give a shout-out to the citizens of Council Grove, Kansas; the Morris County Historical Society; the Santa Fe Trail Association; and Porter Cattle Company.

I'd like to thank all of those that have stood by me throughout the years. Also thanks to all of those that didn't quite stand beside me through the hardships that life has brought time and again. It took all of you throughout my life to help inspire this book.

Much obliged to y'all.

Chapter 1

His name was Levi Cord. He rode Star, a palomino mare that stood fourteen hands and had a small white blaze on her head. Tied to his saddle were a pair of worn-out leather saddlebags, a duster, and a bedroll with his few possessions wrapped inside. On the left side of his saddle, there at his knee, he had a Model 1866 Winchester carbine. On the stock read the initials L.C. On his hips he wore a pair of the finest nickel-plated .45s that many a man had ever seen. Genuine ivory-handled Colts.

He wore a big black flat-brimmed open-crowned hat made from genuine beaver and tall brown stovetop boots with big silver spurs that jingled along as he rode the dusty trail. He wore a black shirt with white pinstripes and a black pinstriped vest with a black wild rag around his neck. He also wore a black jacket that had sign of many miles traveled on the lonesome trail. Many a gal had said he looked like he'd come straight out of a dime novel.

The year was 1873 when he rode into the little Kansas town of Burlingame, there along the Santa Fe Trail. The chilly October breeze blew stiffly on his face. He had never been to Burlingame before, and was only looking to stay the night. As he rode along the dusty street, citizens passing by glanced at him but quickly looked away, as if they were afraid to make eye contact.

Levi was itching for a good stiff drink to clear the trail dust from his throat. He cautiously rode up to the Santa Fe Saloon and hitched Star to a hitching post. He gazed up the streets to get the layout of every way in and out of town, just in case he had to make a quick getaway.

As he walked up the creaky boardwalk and to the saloon's swinging doors, he took one last glance behind him. He looked inside, and, after studying each face, he entered and headed straight to the bar. The Santa Fe was a beautiful saloon. A longhorn bull's head was mounted over the bar, and the long mirror behind the bar allowed Levi to see every angle of the saloon.

"Right nice place ya got here," he said.

"Thank ya, stranger," the barkeep replied as he wiped the bar with a wet cloth rag. "What'll be your pleasure?"

Levi tipped his hat back. "Whiskey."

The barkeep started to pour him a glass, but Levi stopped him. "No sir, a bottle."

The barkeep handed Levi a fresh bottle of rotgut whiskey and a glass.

Levi reached into his vest pocket and pulled out a pair of shiny silver dollars. "Much obliged." He turned around and spotted an empty table at the back corner of the saloon. It was close to the back door and would make an easy access for a quick escape, if the need arose.

He walked over to the back table and the barkeep followed with his rag. He wiped the table off, then asked Levi, "Ridin' through, or are ya plannin' to stay a spell?"

"What business is that of yours?" Levi replied.

The barkeep wiped his face with the rag. "Are ya lookin' for a room, stranger?"

"As a matter of fact, I am," replied Levi.

"Well, sir, we here at the Santa Fe have the cheapest and cleanest rooms in town. A dollar a night."

Levi looked around the saloon. "Well, do ya, now?"

"Yes sir, I'll have my girl show 'em to ya."

Levi nodded. "Much obliged to ya, sir, as soon as I finish this here bottle." He gave the barkeep a grin and tipped his hat.

Levi was a drifter of the roughest sort. Folks were staring at him and his twin .45s, clearly intimidated. He knew folks were curious about him, wondering who the stranger was, and if he was a bad man. Little did they know, on the inside of his gun belt was carved twenty-four notches, one for each of men that Levi had sent to their maker.

Sitting there alone, Levi sipped his whiskey as the barkeep walked back over to him. "Cigar, sir?"

Levi looked the man in the eye. "Yes sir." The man handed Levi a cigar and lit it for him with a stick match. "Much obliged to ya, sir."

From across the saloon, a very pretty, young dance hall girl in a red dress spotted Levi and came walking over to his table. She leaned over the table, providing him a plain view of her bosom.

"Howdy there, cowboy." She gave Levi a wink and slid over to him close enough that he could smell her perfume. She smelled right nice and her golden hair was curled in the latest fashion.

"Ma'am," Levi replied.

"You lookin' for some company?" She arched her back and ran her fingers through her silky blonde hair.

Levi studied the girl for a minute. "Well, ma'am, I reckon a conversation would be right nice. Trail tends to get mighty lonesome from time to time."

"Where ya headed, cowboy?"

"West...Cañon City, maybe."

She grinned, widening her eyes. "Colorado Territory, huh?"

Levi knew she was probably faking her interest, but it was still working. "Yes, ma'am, sounds nice and sure is mighty purty this time of year."

The girl's soft doe eyes were mighty seducing as she leaned even closer. "So...got ya a gal out there?"

Levi shook his head. "No, ma'am."

"Well, I reckon that means that you'll be lookin' for a li'l romance tonight, huh, cowboy?" She began to run her soft hand along his inner thigh and leaned down to kiss him on the neck. "Oh my!" she gasped with astonishment. "Your neck! Whatever on earth did you do?"

"Accident," he answered bluntly as he pulled his wild rag up to cover the scar that wrapped clear around his neck. "A long, long time ago."

She sat down on his lap and continued rubbing her hand along his thigh. "Well, cowboy...Is that the only part of you that was in this...accident?"

His body begin to tense. "No, ma'am."

"No?" she asked with curiosity.

"It was a long, long time ago."

She looked into his eyes. "Well...shall we take this li'l conversation upstairs?"

He gazed into her soft brown eyes and took her by the hand. "After you." He picked up his whiskey and she led him up the stairs to a vacant room. As she opened the door, Levi gestured for her to enter the room first, then he cautiously inched his way into the room and studied the window and door.

The girl walked over to the brass bed. "So...what's your name, cowboy?"

"What's yours, ma'am?" Levi asked with suspicion. He often would ask other folks their name before giving his, if he even gave it at all. He feared that the wrong person might find out who he was, and, with a past like his, that could end in disaster...not only for Levi, but for them as well.

"I'm Maddie, Maddie Baldwin."

Levi smiled. "Name's Levi, ma'am, just Levi."

"Just Levi?" she asked with a grin.

He gave a half-crooked smile. "Just Levi."

"Well, just Levi," she said. "Are you gonna get outta them trousers or do I have to skin 'em off ya?"

He grinned, then began to take off his dusty boots. He knew she was watching him as he took off his jacket and vest. He unbuckled his gun belt and laid the guns on the edge of the bed. She reached over to touch the ivory-handled Colts, and, quicker than a rattler striking at a steer's leg, Maddie was staring down the barrel of a derringer.

"I'm so sorry!" she pleaded, gasping for air. "I'm so sorry! I only wanted to see!"

Levi uncocked the hammer and placed the small pistol on the stand next to the bed, next to the whiskey. He picked up his gun belt and hung the Colts on the shiny brass bed frame, then continued to undress.

Maddie removed her red dress and feathers, then lay down on the bed naked, watching Levi undress. Levi pulled his shirt over his broad shoulders, and it could be seen that his neck was certainly not the only part of him that had been part of some sort of tragic accident. There were two bullet holes in his right leg, and one on his left arm. There was a scar on his right shoulder, where he had been stabbed in a card game in Abilene, and another scar on his left arm where he was stabbed over eleven dollars in some small town.

On the right side of his back, just below his shoulder, were scars where a man had shot him in the back with a scattergun. The scars showed that Levi had lived a rough and devastating life. He had been through pure hell and back. The stories said Levi had healed quite quickly, out of pure revenge and hate. He was said to have become fearless. When he started carrying two pistols was uncertain. After a tragic night in Dakota Territory, he had sort of let himself go, and for the worst. He stopped attending Sunday go-to-meeting and began to drink heavily and carry a gun. He had no family, nor home, just him and his horse. Some folks had even said that he killed a man in the Indian nation for bringing up that tragic night, though they claimed that man had it coming. If you were to ask Levi, he'd say that fellow needed killing.

As he lay down on the big comfy feather bed, she began kissing his neck and rubbing her fingers down his chest and along his thighs. He kissed her softly and looked into her dark brown eyes and felt his mind drifting back to the past. It had been over eight years since that horrifying night in Dakota Territory.

Maddie kissed Levi's chest, then straddled him, pressing her hands onto his chest. He reached over to the stand beside the bed and picked up the bottle of whiskey.

"Would you like me to pour you a glass?" Maddie asked while continuing to rub his chest.

"No thank ya, ma'am." He pressed the bottle to his lips and began to drink. It tasted so smooth and good, yet a bit strong. It helped him erase the memories of his past. Well, for the time being, anyways. As he drank the whiskey, Maddie straddling him, he closed his eyes and tried to erase the past. He was a strong man, but had a mighty difficult time fighting back the tears. His memories of his past were much worse of a pain than any of the bullets or other wounds he had earned in the past.

Maddie began to make love to him, then reached over to the kerosene lamp.

Levi stopped her. "Only dim it, ma'am. Not all the way out."

"As you wish, Levi."

About an hour after Levi and Maddie had finished making love, Levi began to get dressed.

"Levi?" Maddie asked.

"Yes, ma'am?"

"Would you be willin' to stay a spell?" she asked with lost eyes.

Levi placed two silver dollars on the dresser. "Why should I stay, ma'am?"

"I would enjoy your company. Fact is Levi...you're much more respectable than most the other cowboys comin' in off the trail. You look at a gal much differently, and don't force yourself on her. I admire that about you. No extra charge."

He looked into those sad brown eyes and saw a lovely girl just shy of nineteen. He felt sorry for her lifestyle even though he had been with numerous girls in her profession over the years since Dakota Territory. "I reckon I could stay a spell, ma'am."

She patted on the bed for him to come lay back down beside her. As he did, he reached over for the bottle of whiskey and drank, finishing it to the last drop.

As the night drew on, Levi laid there in the arms of the lovely girl and pictured himself back in the arms of his late sweetheart. He blew out the lamp, and as he did, a tear gently fell down his cheek. Levi had often heard that real cowboys never cry but reckoned that was just a lie. After what he'd lived through, he knew differently.

As he drifted off to sleep, he dreamed of when he was a young boy...the days when his mother's second husband would beat him on a near daily basis, most of the time for no reason. The day when his family abandoned him like a stray dog alone out on the cold prairie. He awoke one morning to find himself alone and lost. He was just a young lad then, and he began to drift across the west at an early age in his life.

In the middle of the night, Levi began jerking and twisting in his sleep. He jumped up soaked in sweat and panting hard.

Maddie, awakened by the noise, said, "Levi! Levi, it's alright! You were just havin' a bad dream. It's alright." She reached to put an arm on his shoulder.

"No!" Levi shrugged away. "I must go. Thank ya kindly, ma'am, for a wonderful evening. I'm truly sorry." He slid his boots on, then strapped his Colts on his hips after making sure they were still loaded. He checked the derringer as well, then placed it into his vest pocket. Putting on his hat and tipping it to Maddie, he said, "Ma'am."

"Goodbye, Levi."

Shutting the door, Levi checked his silver pocket watch. It was just after two. He walked down the stairs of the saloon and out the door. At the livery stable, he saddled Star, then took off out of Burlingame, headed west along the Santa Fe Trail.

He stopped about five or six miles outside of town on Soldier Creek. Getting down off his horse, he leaned down to the creek and took off his hat. He took a drink and let Star graze on the prairie grass. He splashed his face with the cold creek water, then decided to unsaddle Star. He tied her to a nearby willow tree and spread his bedroll on the prairie floor. Coyotes howled off in the distance toward the south, and Star snorted and stomped. Sparkling stars filled the prairie sky and danced on the running creek water below. A pair of whippoorwills serenaded each other, singing a sweet prairie lullaby. Using his saddle for a pillow, he curled up in his wool blanket and drifted off to sleep, keeping his Colts in his hands.

LEVI PULLED HIS hat up over his eyes, avoiding the glare of the morning sun. Staring down at him was Star, holding his tin cup in her teeth. She had been with Levi her whole life. Levi had pulled her from her mother some ten to twelve years back, while he was working as a hand down in the Texas Panhandle for the Bar W Ranch. He raised her from that day on, and the two had become the best of companions.

Levi chuckled. "Well, top of the mornin' to ya." He gave her a grin, then threw his blanket off and got up from the cold, hard ground. He stretched the aches and pains out with each movement of his body, which always reminded him of every injury he had suffered.

A meadowlark called from its perch on top of a bull buffalo's skull, evidence of nearby Indians. Kaw, maybe Osage…the tribe was uncertain, but Indians for sure.

He reached into his saddlebag for the coffee that he kept inside. Star nodded her head and placed the cup at his feet. "Thank ya, girl." She must have been ready to go, because she began to bring brush over in her mouth for him to start a fire for his breakfast coffee. "Purty morning, ain't it, girl? Kinda chilly last night."

After gathering some more brush and some nearby buffalo chips, Levi reached for a match in his coat pocket. Unfortunately, he had used his last one. "Damn."

He reached to his gun belt and pulled out a cartridge. Placing it between his teeth, he bit down on the bullet and pulled the casing free, being careful not to spill the powder. He gently poured the powder into a line along a patch of dead prairie grass. Then he placed the shell at the end of the powder line and, with the hammer of one of his Colts, he began to strike the primer of the shell. Once the primer sparked, it ignited the powder line, which caught the dead grass on fire. Gently fanning the flame with his hat, Levi began to pile brush onto the fire. Once the fire was burning hot, he made himself some of the strongest coffee that a man had ever tasted. He drank a few cups and then lit a cigar with a burning branch he had pulled from the fire.

Shortly after, he picked up his coffee pot and walked to the stream to fill it with water. He walked back over to the campfire and poured the water on the coals, causing it to hiss, and watched as it went out. He stomped the rest of the embers out, then saddled up Star and continued along the Santa Fe Trail.

A COUPLE MILES later, he came to the lovely little settlement of Wilmington, where the Leavenworth Military Road joined the Santa Fe Trail. Wilmington was the home of Levi's late grandfather "Grizzly", also known as Griz. Griz had been born and raised in Wilmington long before it became a town. He had played a very important part in Levi's life. He had taught Levi to respect the land and the wildlife and how to shoot quickly and accurately. Levi was mighty fond of him.

It had been quite some time since Levi had ridden through there since he had gotten word that Griz had passed away. It had devastated Levi and added much more to his depression. His rough past had haunted him, and the better part of his life had been spent running from it.

He was quite surprised at how much the town had grown over the past few years. There were now some thirty houses, two general stores, a blacksmith, two doctors, a wagon shop, and a small hotel. Griz had told Levi stories about when he had helped build the small schoolhouse. Wilmington was a beautiful little community.

As Levi rode into town, he felt the stares of folks studying him. A man walking cross the street made eye contact with Levi, and the man swallowed hard and began to walk a little quicker when Levi slowly reached his left hand back and rested it on the grip on one of his Colts.

He had noticed Star was beginning to favor her left front hoof, so he rode up to the blacksmith and dismounted.

"Howdy!" a voice called from the back of the barn. "What can I do for ya?"

Levi pushed his hat back on his head. "Mornin'. Needin' a new shoe, iffen ya got the time."

The man walked over and studied Star's hooves for a second. "Sure thing. Let me finish up with this here sorrel, then I'll get to her directly."

Levi reached out his weathered hand and shook the man's dirty, rough hand. "Much obliged to ya, pardner."

The blacksmith led the mare to a nearby hitching post and tied her up, then proceeded with tending to the sorrel gelding. Levi gazed up the dusty street, then decided to take a little stroll south of town across the prairie to clear his head.

He came to a hilltop, where he sat down. As he gazed over the prairie, he could see a wagon headed north into town. Pots and pans were rattling as the driver whipped and cussed at the mules that were pulling the wagon. Two little boys chased a little girl beside the wagon and Levi could hear them all laughing. The little girl spotted him and waved to him. Levi smiled and waved back.

After about an hour or so, Levi got to his feet, stretched and dusted off his trousers, then headed back to town. As he walked up to the blacksmith shop, Star let out a snort, then shook her head. He could tell she was ready to hit the trail.

The blacksmith led Star out. "That'll be three bits, stranger."

Levi dug down into his vest pocket and paid the man. "I'm much obliged to ya, sir. I rightly appreciate it, and I reckon Star here does as well."

Levi mounted, then tipped his hat to the blacksmith and headed west out of town along the trail once again. A few miles outside of Wilmington, Levi noticed unshod pony tracks in the mud, a sure sign of Indians. The tracks did not appear to be too fresh, but it still meant they were in the area. As he rode along, Levi spurred Star to a gallop. She was a well-spirited horse and was itching to get out of the area.

A couple hours later, Levi's head started to bob, and he drifted off to sleep in the saddle, knowing Star would continue on.

Star stopped suddenly, causing Levi to wake up. She began stomping and snorting. Levi pushed his hat back and noticed a large herd of buffalo on the trail about fifty yards ahead. "Easy girl," he whispered as he patted her on the neck. "Them ol' shaggies will pass soon." As best as he could count, there were over one hundred buffalo grazing along the trail without a care in the world. Nothing compared to what he had first seen when he'd started out as a drifter.

Levi sighed. "Star, ol' girl, I bet it won't be long 'fore they will all soon just be a thing of the past. Nothing more than a sad memory."

LATER THAT AFTERNOON, the scenery began to turn from flat open prairie to beautiful rolling hills with an abundance of limestone rocks and flint rock. Farms were few and far between in these rolling hills, as settlers were unable to plow the rocky ground. However, there were miles upon miles of open grazing land for cattle. As Levi rode on closer to the rolling hills, his heart seemed to beat with anticipation and joy. He had fallen in love with the

Flint Hills and their beauty the first time he had seen them when he was a boy. It had been a couple years at least since he had been through this country and seen them. Every half mile or so, he would stop Star and just sit in the saddle and admire the prairie grasses. Above, the wide prairie sky was filled with big puffy white clouds that scattered across the sky. The prairie looked just like a sea of grass as the breeze blew strongly across the hills. There was nothing prettier to Levi, and his heart felt something that it hadn't felt in years…a place of belonging and content. He enjoyed the feeling but wasn't sure how to react to it.

In the distance, Levi spotted a herd of elk standing in a small grove of cottonwood trees at the end of a rock bluff. He could hear the bugle of the bull elk echo across the open prairie. Seconds later, a second bull answered. This was gorgeous country…God's country. It was some of the prettiest and most scenic along the whole Santa Fe Trail. There was the most crystal-clear stream that he had ever seen in the whole Kansas territory. It was filled with schools of minnows and largemouth bass. His mouth watered at the sight of a bass, a good four pounds, rising from the water to eat a cicada. Sure would have tasted excellent in a skillet with some fresh prairie chicken or a whitetail steak.

Later on, Levi spotted a small caravan of freight wagons loaded down with store goods most likely headed all the way to Santa Fe. Most of the wagon trains had stopped traveling the trail the past couple of years, but a fellow might still stumble across one or two on occasion. The wagons were being pulled by a team of charcoal black mules that were biting at the bit as they pushed westward. Just ahead, Levi could hear people's voices hollering out, and he spotted several more wagons stopped at a creek crossing. He could hear a man shout, "Hold it up here, boys, looks like we gotta pay a dagburn toll to cross this here bridge."

"That's highway robbery, iffen ya ask me," another man hollered out.

Levi rode closer and noticed a wooden bridge that was built crossing 142-Mile Creek. He had heard some folks in Missouri say a man was charging folks to cross his bridge there, but he hadn't seen it firsthand.

He casually tipped his hat to the folks. "Howdy. Y'all got yourselves quite a load there."

A man with stained yellow teeth looked at him. "Yes sir, we're headed west to Santa Fe and this here feller says we gotta pay him twenty-five cents per wagon just to cross!"

Levi pushed his hat back on his head. "Woowhee, twenty-five cents?"

The man nodded and spit in the dust. "You ain't shittin', mister. We ain't got but forty-five cents between the bunch of us. We ain't gonna have the money until we're on the way back from Santa Fe." The man looked at the fellow running the toll bridge. "Tell ya what, pardner, we'll pay ya in full on our trip back east."

The man shook his head. "I'm sorry, sir, but you'll need the money now iffen ya want to cross here. Otherwise ya can detour north a fair piece and cross the creek up there. Only problem is, the banks ain't as smooth up there as they are here. Steep and rocky as hell, in fact."

Levi looked at the wagons. "Well, maybe I can be of assistance. Y'all wouldn't happen to be carryin' any .44 cartridges to sell, would ya?"

The men on the wagons looked over at each other and one said, "I do believe we just might have a case or two on board." He jumped down from the wagon and went to scrambling through the bed of the wagon. "Here they are, stranger." He pulled out a case of ammunition.

"Well," Levi said. "Seein's how y'all are short on money and how I'm runnin' low on lead, maybe we can make a deal."

The man squinted his eyes. "What do ya have in mind, stranger?"

"Well, sir, how much do y'all need to cross this here bridge?"

"A dollar fifty," the yellow-toothed man answered.

Levi nodded. "And how much do ya get for a box of them there .44s?"

"Well, we get a dollar ninety-eight a box," the man holding the box of cartridges said.

Levi thought a moment. "Well, seein's how we're both in a tight spot, I'll give you a dollar five for a box. That'll get ya across and back on your way."

The men talked it over amongst themselves, then the yellow-toothed man said, "Mister, these here shells cost a heap more than that in any mercantile you'll find this side of Missoura."

Levi grinned. "Well, sir, that's my offer. Thank ya kindly anyways. Good luck on the trail." Levi paid the toll to cross.

"Much obliged to ya, sir," the man said as he took the money.

As Levi proceeded to ride on, the yellow-toothed man hollered out, "Hang on a minute there, stranger! Let's talk about this."

Levi turned Star around. "Change your mind?"

The man looked him in the eye and grabbed the box of cartridges and held it out to Levi. "A dollar twenty-five."

Levi shook his head. "No sir. A dollar eight."

The man scratched his head. "A dollar fifteen and that's my final offer."

Levi pulled his hat down low. "Good day to ya."

As he picked up his reins, the man hollered out, "A dollar ten!"

Levi grinned. The man was quite a haggler. "Alright, sir. Got yourself a deal."

The man handed him the box and Levi handed him a shiny silver dollar and dime and shook his hand. "Much obliged to ya."

As Levi went to cross the bridge, he asked the toll man, "Where's the closest town in these parts?"

The man turned and pointed. "Just over yonder is Allen."

"Allen, huh? I don't recall ridin' through there 'fore."

"There's a dry goods store, a post office for the Kansas City and Santa Fe Stage line, a blacksmith, a hotel…"

Levi decided he would go ahead and ride into town and see if he could pick up a few supplies and just enough grub to fill his saddlebags.

When he rode into Allen, he was met by a woman and her four children as they crossed the dusty street. "Howdy, ma'am," Levi said as he tipped his hat. "Could you tell me where I can find the mercantile?"

The woman studied Levi and his Colts, and, with a mysterious look, she pointed toward the store. "Over yonder just down the street. My husband will assist you."

Levi tipped his hat again. "Much obliged to ya, ma'am." He rode on down the street, studying the town closely. Something came over him, and he could tell that he was on the right trail to finding what he was searching for.

Once he arrived at the mercantile, he tied Star to a hitching post and dusted his jacket and pants off and cautiously walked inside.

"Howdy, stranger," a voice called out from behind the counter. "I'll be with ya directly."

Levi turned his head and saw the store clerk tending to some other customers. He looked around the store and tried to think of anything that he would need along the trail before he would come to the next town. He browsed through the merchandise and noticed that there wasn't very much to offer in this small store. He had heard that back in '66 when the railroad came through to the south it ended the majority of most the traders passing the Santa Fe. Business seemed to have declined except for the locals in the area.

A few minutes later, the store clerk walked over to him. "What can I do for ya, stranger? I don't believe I've seen you in these parts before."

Levi turned. "Just passin' through. Stopped in for some hardtack, salt, coffee, and a box of matches if ya got some."

The gentleman looked down at Levi's Colts. "Might fancy rig ya got there."

Levi nodded but didn't respond.

As he turned to walk to the counter, the man said, "I run the general store here, along with being the justice of the peace and constable."

Levi's heart sank in his chest for a moment as he slowly turned back around to the man. With a past like his, he always got a very uneasy feeling when around a lawman.

"Yes sir," the man went on, "along with running the hotel and mail station and acting as the local blacksmith."

Levi grinned. "Well, now, I reckon that tends to keep you mighty busy, eh?"

"Yes sir," the man answered. "Got four children to tend at home, too." The man walked around behind the counter and started gathering the few supplies that Levi had asked for. "Let's see here…coffee, salt, hardtack…"

"And matches," Levi added.

As the clerk placed the goods into a small burlap sack, he asked, "What color was ya on, stranger?"

Levi looked at the man with a confused look on his face. "Pardon?"

"The war. What side was ya on?"

Levi thought for a second. "Seems like forever ago. I was just a youngster back in them days." Levi was hesitant to answer. Most folks didn't cotton too much to the idea of Confederates in this territory.

"What color, boy?" the man asked bluntly.

Levi could see the curious look on the man's face and could tell right off that he was one of those folks. Levi wasn't looking for trouble. This was a mighty important man in this town, and he didn't seem like the kind of feller to be quarreling with. However, Levi was proud of his heritage and fought for what he believed in. "Wore a gray coat all throughout the Rebellion, as a matter of fact."

The man's face turned pale and his eyes locked with Levi's. Not a sound was heard as the two stared at each other with clenched teeth and hard faces.

Levi's eyes never strayed as he said, "Like I said, I'm just passin' through. Just stopped in for some supplies, then I'll be on my way."

The clerk spit into a spittoon behind the counter. "Ya know what, stranger? We don't tend to agree with vagrants like yourselves in Allen here."

Levi's stomach tightened and he wanted to slap the disrespectful man across the face, but he bit his lip as the man went on.

"Back in '62, Judge Arthur Ingraham Baker had a store about thirteen miles west of here on Rock Creek Crossin'. A few vagrant guerillas like yourself come through. Ol' Baker cussed one by the name of Bloody Bill Anderson, his father, and his no-good brother Jim for horse thieves. Baker managed to shoot the old man in self-defense. 'Bout that same time, a Mexican that belonged to Anderson's gang of cutthroats was hanged by a mob over in Americus. Few weeks later, a gang of four men led by Bloody Bill came back to Baker's home. One of them low-down scum-suckin' bastards called himself William Quantrill. They ordered Baker to go in the store and fetch some whiskey. As he was walkin' down the cellar stairs, they filled him with lead. He managed to draw his Colt and hit Jim Anderson. Only winged him, though. Them damn ruffians shot and killed Baker's wife's brother, George Segur, and threw him into the cellar and set fire to it. Poor ol' Baker died 'fore the fire reached him. Segur escaped out the back window but died a few hours later. Them Rebel bastards stole all their horses and burned everything. Raided all over the damn territory, then found their way here to Allen. They come ridin' into town and placed everyone under arrest and went to tearin' up the saloon. Bastards knocked me down with a Navy Colt to the head and set fire to our house. Thank the good Lord above the lumber used to build the house was green, so it didn't burn. Ol' Jim Anderson had set his Rebel mind to killin' me, but my life was spared through the intercession of Quantrill and Bloody Bill, the former I recognized from bein' somewhat acquainted with them a few years back in Missouri. They shoulda killed me, though, cuz I'd have killed 'em iffen I crossed trails with them again. However, they stole three horses belonging to the Kansas City and Santa Fe Mail Company and my rifle. They took several citizens as prisoners. Rebel scum."

Levi stood there for a moment, taking in everything. The man was wealthy, and he wanted others to know. Levi didn't cotton to rich folks much, especially those that paraded around rubbing it in others' faces. He wanted so badly to put this arrogant man in his place, but he just wanted to pick up his supplies and make tracks quick. After paying the man, he turned to walk out the door.

"Make sure you don't stay too long in Allen, stranger," the clerk said. "We don't need trash like you in town. Get your business done and get the hell out of here. Do you understand me, boy?"

Levi turned around in the doorway and gave the man a look like he was about to come across that store and wring his neck. He knew the man was pushing him and trying to get him to start trouble so he could have a reason for arresting him. As Levi started to walk back to the counter, he saw the man reach his hand under the counter.

"Do it!" Levi hollered out. "Grab that gun and I'll send you to hell with Mr. Baker himself, you Yankee bastard! Bloody Bill musta got soft-hearted when he didn't string your yella ass up."

The storekeeper hesitated when he saw Levi's hands twitch at the grips of his twin Colts.

Levi heard the familiar sound of a hammer being slowly cocked. "Come on, Billy Yank, I'm darin' ya. It's your call."

About that time, the woman Levi had spoken to earlier came walking in the door, her children following.

"Excuse me, mister," said one of the kids as they rushed up to the counter. "Pa, are ya ready to go to the creek to take us fishin'?"

The man's eyes never left Levi's, and Levi returned the glare. There was no backing down. The woman walked past Levi and grabbed a broom behind the counter and started to sweep the floors.

"What's it gonna be, storekeep?" Levi asked the seething man.

The man looked at the woman and children and slowly leaned up and brought his hand back to the counter. Levi knew whatever he wanted to do, he wouldn't do it in front of his family. He bit his lip and then through gritted teeth said, "Good day to ya, sir. Iffen ya find yourself back in Allen, be sure to pay us a visit."

Levi grinned and nodded at the man. "You'd better believe I will do just that." Levi turned to the woman, tipped his hat, and said, "Good day, ma'am." He walked over to one of the children and pinched their cheek and patted them on the head. "You make sure you keep a good eye on your Pa there, alright?" The storekeeper's heart had to be racing, as he was taunting him something fierce now. Levi turned back to him and grinned. "Good day, Yank." He walked out the door and climbed into the saddle.

As he rode down the street of Allen, he studied the buildings. He wasn't sure where he was going to end up, but he knew that he was headed in the right direction. He could feel it in his bones. Once he reached the toll bridge, he tipped his hat to the fellow taking the tolls and crossed the bridge and headed west.

As he traveled along the trail, he kept gazing at the rolling Flint Hills and admiring the beautiful, breathtaking scenery. It was simply gorgeous countryside...some of the finest he had ever traveled. About ten miles west, Levi began to see the small settlement of Agnes City, most of it in ruins.

Griz had often told him stories of hunting buffalo outside Agnes City back in 1857 with the founder Mr. Arthur Ingraham Baker. According to Griz, Baker was quite a handful to hunt with, but a decent man. He had told Levi that the local constable was a man by the name of John Wingfield, who was an honest man and a clean shooter to boot.

As Levi rode on, going over his memories, he felt the urge to shed a tear, but he clenched his teeth and kicked Star to a faster walk. He passed by and wondered what Agnes City had been like a few years back when the Santa Fe Trail was still active and seeing many wagon trains headed west. Sadly, most of what was once known as a peaceful and respectable little community had weathered down, and only a few settlers and buildings remained. He shook his head and continued on.

About four or five miles west of Agnes City, he decided to set up camp just east of Rock Creek Crossing. He remembered that several years back, he had been hunting elk along Rock Creek and had met an old trapper that told him that Rock Creek got its name "Ne-ko-its-as-ba" from the Native Americans. It meant "Dead Men's Creek". Several human bones had been found there, indicating that a great Indian battle had been fought on its banks.

Just six miles ahead on the trail west was the last big stop on the whole Santa Fe Trail...Council Grove. As he spread his bedroll out and lay down, he checked his guns just to make sure they were each on loaded cartridges. You could never be too careful, especially alone on the prairie. As he lay his head on his saddle, he gazed at the stars and thought about his life and the future God above had in store for him. He wondered if he would ever love again and if his heart would ever give another lady the chance to love him. A deep empty feeling came over him as he drifted off to sleep.

Chapter 2

Levi was up bright and early the next morning. The prairie chickens dancing on the prairie reminded him of Indians dancing around a campfire at a powwow he had attended years back. He admired the Indians and how they dressed and danced. He really loved their music. He found it soothing to the soul and rather relaxing.

After saddling up Star, he set out once again, headed west for the Rocky Mountains. As he came to the top of a bluff, he stopped the mare and looked down to see the town of Council Grove. The beautiful Neosho River flowed right through town and made a perfect crossing site for wagons. He studied the town for several minutes, then rode down to the river to find an easy passage into town. Levi had heard stories from travelers that this crossing was one of the best river crossings on the whole Santa Fe Trail. The steep banks and high water sometimes made crossings difficult, but riffles in the stream showed a shallow hard rock bottom that would help make the crossing easier.

Star stopped for a minute, sniffing the water, then, with a little kick, she proceeded to cross.

On the other side of the riverbank sat a couple of older gentlemen with a pair of cane poles. One was wearing a dirty pair of brown trousers that were being held up with black suspenders. The other gentleman was wearing a pair of overalls and a beat-up brown hat. Levi rode through the shallows and one of the men hollered out, "Send some of the dagburn fish up stream here, would ya, fella?"

Levi rode up the other side of the riverbank. "Howdy, gents," Levi said as he tipped his hat. "Much luck this morning?"

The man in the overalls smirked, then reached down and pulled up a woven basket full of channel catfish and drum. "You might say we've had a bit of luck."

The other gentleman chuckled. "New in town, ain't ya, stranger?" He spit tobacco into the dirt at his feet.

Levi nodded. "Yes sir, just passin' through. Figured I'd ride in and rustle me up some sort of grub. Campfire coffee just ain't gonna cut it this morning."

The man in the overalls pointed behind him toward town. "Miss Nancy has some of the finest meals in town. She's quite a looker, too, iffen ya ask me."

Levi grinned and shook his head. He could tell that these gentlemen were about the friendliest pair he had come across in quite some time.

The other man quickly reached down for his cane pole and gave it a fierce tug. "Son of a bitch! Daggum, I missed him again."

Levi looked toward town and squinted his eyes while trying to study the different buildings. It had been quite some time since he had been in Council Grove. He was just a boy the first time Griz brought him. A lot had changed over the years. He pointed at a steeple. "What's that tall building over yonder?"

The men looked where he was pointing. The man in the dirty brown trousers said, "Well, that's the beautiful Methodist Episcopal Church. It was built back in '51. They used it for the Kaw Mission boarding school until '54. The Indians refused to send their young'uns anymore. It then became a school for white young'uns. You know, they say it was the first all-white school in the Kansas territory."

The gentleman wearing overalls pointed across town to the southwest. "A little way down yonder, you'll find a lovely little brick house that our friend and founder Mr. Seth Hays built back in '67. Aunt Sally and he lived there for some time until her death last year. He never married Sally…folks in these parts wouldn't cotton too much to the idea of him takin' up with a colored woman, you know. He took in a young girl back in '67, too, and Sally took care of them just as if she was part of their family just the same. Right nice folks, too. We lost Mr. Hays this past winter."

Levi nodded, interested, but then his stomach gave a growl. "Well, gentlemen, I'm so daggum hungry I could eat a sow an' nine pigs an' chase the boar a half a mile. It's been an honor talkin' with y'all."

Levi turned Star up the riverbank, and the gentleman in the suspenders said, "What did you say your name was, fella?"

Levi turned back to the man and pulled Star to a stop. He hesitated a moment, then answered, "Name's Cord."

The one in the overalls got up on his feet and reached his hand out to Levi. "I reckon I've heard tell of a fella named Cord somewhere before." He shook Levi's hand firmly and smiled. "My name's Linsey. This ugly fella here is Crawford. Pleasure to meet ya, Mr. Cord. Take care now."

Levi chuckled as the gentleman in the suspenders picked up a ball of mud and tossed it at Linsey. Linsey laughed and sat back down on the riverbank and picked up his cane pole. Levi tipped his hat and continued on his way. As he rode along the dusty street, Star stood proud, and Levi sat tall in the saddle. His spurs jingled along as townsfolk curiously watched him pass by. Despite his grumbling stomach, he decided to survey the town before settling in.

Just up the street stood the small Conn Store. Levi knew that when Malcolm Conn built it in 1858, the store had become one of the two most important trading posts in Council Grove.

Further on, he spotted a lovely two-story stone house. In the yard, a young boy was pulling weeds from around the front walk.

"Howdy," Levi called out. "Right nice place y'all got there."

The boy looked up. "Thank ya kindly, sir, but it ain't my folks' place. This here is Mr. Goodson Simcock's house. I just come over now and again to tend to the chores. Did you come to visit him?"

Levi shook his head. "I don't reckon I know this fella you speak of, son."

The boy threw the weeds he was holding in his hand down in a pile and dusted his hands off on his trousers. "Mr. Simcock's been a partner of Mr. Hays for some time. Made himself quite a name here in Council Grove, or that's what my ma says anyhow. Pa said he's fixin' to retire this year sometime."

Levi looked at the boy and then leaned down and rubbed Star on the neck. "Sounds like this Simcock fella is a mighty important man, don't it?"

Star let out a knicker, and the young boy giggled. "Well, sir, if I aim to get these here chores done in time to go fishin' with Slim today, I reckon I better get to it. Good day to ya, sir."

Levi tipped his hat. "Good day to ya, son." He gave Star a little kick and headed on his way.

Once he reached the top of the bluff, he noticed a secluded small cave in the rock hillside. Levi had heard stories told across the trail at many a campfire about a man named Giovanni Maria Augustini that was said to have lived in the cave for a brief time in the spring of 1863. The story he recalled was that this Augustinian fella was an Italian religious mystic. In 1863, he set out with the company of a wagon train and walked five hundred miles along the old trail to Santa Fe, New Mexico. He was later mysteriously murdered. A cold and uneasy feeling came over Levi. He didn't stay long.

Council Grove seemed like a peaceful little town. A lot more peaceful than some of the towns he had encountered over the years. He had seen a telegraph office, an opera house, several other hotels, numerous stores, two banks, a lumberyard, and two saloons.

Back on the main street, he rode past a house where a man and woman in a black buggy with red wheels were parked out front. He rode by and the man called out to him, "Hello, sir, could you tell me where I can find Terwilliger?"

Levi pulled Star to a stop. "What's that?"

The man pointed at the house. "Terwilliger. Would you know where he might be?"

Levi shrugged. "No sir, I can't say as I've had the honor of meetin' this here fella ya speak of. I ain't from these parts…just passin' through."

The man pointed toward the house again. "My lovely wife Mary here and I built this here house in '61. We were downright proud of this place. By the way, my name is Abraham Rawlinson. You see, Terwilliger purchased this house from us back in '70. We just rode in to pay him a visit today. Anyway, iffen ya see him, tell him we stopped by. God be with you, sir." The man whipped his horse and set out down the street.

Levi was beginning to enjoy meeting new folks. They sure seemed friendly here. With his reputation, meeting the wrong man could cost him his life, so he had generally avoided conversation.

He reached the edge of the thriving community, and Levi turned around. He passed by the Last Chance Store, which, for a brief period of the time, had been the last opportunity for freighters bound for Santa Fe to pick up supplies for their long journey.

Just across the street from the Hays House, Levi spotted the Gilkey Hotel. It appeared to be a right nice place. By now he was mighty hungry. He'd heard tell that the Hays House was said to be some of the fanciest dining and the best all-around restaurant west of the Mississippi and, by golly, he was ready to find out for himself.

As he rode up to the hitching post out front of the Hays House and dismounted, a voice called out from behind him, "Howdy, stranger."

Levi turned around and was met by a handsome gentleman carrying a black walking cane. He was wearing a tin badge and a black derby hat.

Levi nodded at the man. "Well, howdy, Marshal."

The man looked him up and down. "New in town, ain't ya?"

Levi's heart began to race, and his stomach tightened. He was always nervous around lawmen. Didn't trust them one damn bit. That probably had a lot to do with his past. Trouble seemed to follow him like a coyote following a newborn calf.

Levi looked at the marshal's badge. "Yes sir, just passin' through."

The marshal's eyes lingered on the guns at Levi's hips. "Where ya headed, stranger?"

Levi fixed his eyes toward the west. "Colorado Territory."

"Rockies, huh? Cold up there this time of year. My name is Vincent…J.S. Vincent."

Levi's heart sank. This was one of the toughest lawmen of the territory.

Levi tipped his hat. "I'm Levi Cord."

Vincent shook his hand. "Well, welcome to Council Grove, Mr. Cord. Ya plannin' on bein' in town long?"

"Only a day or two at most, Marshal," Levi answered as he looked up the street.

"Have ya got a place to stay yet, Mr. Cord?"

"No sir, just rode into town."

Vincent pointed down the street. "Well, they have some mighty nice and comfortable rooms available at the Cottage House iffen you'd be inclined."

Levi gazed down the street toward the Cottage House, then back across the street to the Gilkey Hotel.

Vincent grinned. "Mr. Cord, iffen I was you I'd oblige myself to visit the Cottage House."

Levi stood there for a second considering the options. "I do believe I will check this here Cottage House out."

Vincent smiled. "I'll be making my rounds now." The two men shook hands and Vincent grinned as Levi walked away. "Feel free to stop by over at the jail anytime. My door is always open."

Levi turned to Vincent and grinned. "No thank ya, Marshal. I try to steer clear of such places myself these days iffen I can help it."

Vincent smiled at Levi and tipped his derby hat. "Indeed, sir. Good day to ya, Mr. Cord."

"Good day to you, Marshal." As Levi turned back around, he ran smack-dab into the most beautiful lady he had ever laid eyes on. She had the most amazing blonde hair that flowed down her back so gracefully. Her eyes were a breathtaking sight to behold. They were soft and as blue as the wild Montana skies. They reminded Levi of a crystal blue mountain lake that he had fished for trout in up in Colorado Territory when he was just a boy.

Levi's heart fluttered out of control. "Ex…Ex…Excuse me, ma'am."

As she opened her mouth to speak, Levi gazed at her tender lips and felt the sudden urge to grab her and kiss her right there on the boardwalk. Either that, or just pass out right then and there. "Excuse me," she said with the most beautiful country drawl that he had ever heard. Levi had always been rather fond of ladies with an accent. "I'm so sorry, mister. I wasn't payin' no mind to where I was goin'." She knelt to pick up the basket she had dropped.

Levi knelt also. "Here, ma'am, let me help ya there." At that very moment, her baby blue eyes gazed at him and she gave him a smile that would forever be locked in his memory. Levi's heart just about jumped right out of his chest. "My name is Cord, ma'am, Levi Cord."

The lady gave another heart-stopping smile. "I'm Samantha Parker."

"That's a beautiful name, Miss Samantha Parker…or is it missus?" Levi, heart racing like a wild mustang, was anxious to hear her answer.

"Miss. And it's a pleasure to meet you, Mr. Cord."

Levi studied this amazingly gorgeous young lady and wondered how something so rare and so perfect was not married. He couldn't take his eyes off hers. "The pleasure is certainly all mine, Miss Samantha." The whole world seemed to stop turning as he smiled and returned her gaze. This amazing woman was the woman of his dreams…a godsend.

"Good day to ya, Mr. Cord." Her words brought him back to attention.

"Good day to you as well, Miss Samantha." Levi reached for her hand and gently pressed it to his lips. "Good day, Miss Samantha."

"Why, Mr. Cord…Good day to you." She was blushing as she walked away.

Levi studied her every move as she gracefully strolled up the creaky boardwalk in her beautiful blue dress, that curled, long blonde hair swaying. He couldn't decide if he wanted to tear up and cry or smile. This beautiful lady was simply amazing, a true lady. She reminded him of someone from his past that was very dear to him at one time. In all the cow towns that Levi had ridden into, never once had another woman touched his heart the way a special woman once did years back. That was, however, until today. Looking into the eyes of this beautiful lady and seeing her smile just struck something deep inside him. What on earth could that be? It made all his memories and heartaches seem to just disappear. But what could he do? He was a drifter, and a mysterious one at that. He had a past that followed and haunted him terribly. He had nothing to offer a lady like Miss Samantha. She was an angel sent down from the heavens above. He was sure of it.

Levi shook his head as she slowly faded from sight. He headed for the Hays House. As he walked in and sat down at a table, all he could think about was Miss Samantha. "As purty as a prairie flower," he murmured. She was so petite and graceful, yet so different and exciting. She smelled of the prettiest blue bonnets, and he just couldn't get those blue eyes out of his mind.

He took off his hat and ran his fingers through his dark brown hair. A pretty little waitress about sixteen years old came up to the table. "Mornin', sir, what can I get for ya?"

"Steak and eggs, iffen ya will. I'd be obliged." The waitress poured Levi a cup of hot coffee and then went back to the kitchen to place his order. As he sat there staring into his coffee cup, all he could see were those intoxicating blue eyes. He was lovestruck worse than he had ever been before.

After finishing his delicious meal, he walked outside and mounted Star and set out for the livery stable. As he reached the stable, a short, fat, older man came up and said, "Can I help ya, son?"

Levi patted Star on her neck. "How much for the night to stable Star here?"

"That'd be two bits."

Levi shook his hand and handed him the money. "Much obliged to ya, sir. Take good care of her and load her up on some oats."

"Indeed, sir."

Levi walked toward the Cottage House. He was amazed at how nice the place was fixed up. Much nicer a place than most he had stayed in the past seven or eight years…never mind it was usually the cold prairie ground with a saddle and a blanket. As he entered the lobby, Levi admired the beautiful paintings of the Flint Hills and Indians and such.

The hotel clerk handed Levi a shiny brass key. "Room eight…at the top of the stairs and to the left. Go down the hallway until you see it."

Levi tipped his hat to the clerk. "Thank ya kindly, sir." As he walked up the stairs, he felt ashamed to walk on the red velvet carpet with his dirty boots. Once he reached his room, he unpacked his bedroll and saddlebags, then decided that he could use some cleaning up. Since it was October, bathing in the streams was beginning to get mighty chilly. The Cottage House offered a private room with a galvanized bathtub. A good clean shave and a hot bath would do the body good.

After cleaning up, Levi decided to see about having his clothes cleaned. He headed downstairs.

"Could I have my duds washed?" Levi asked the man at the desk. "They've collected more dust from Liberty to Council Grove than a whole wagon train to Santa Fe."

The clerk chuckled as he took the clothes. "I'll have them washed right away over at Gildemeister's laundry establishment."

Levi went back up to his room and stretched out on the big feather bed. Boy, did that sure feel good, much better than that damn old prairie ground. He could get caught up on some much-needed rest in a real bed for a change. Something he hadn't had the luxury of in quite some time. He had all but worn his mind and body to the core on the trail and was exhausted, to say the least.

He stared at the ceiling, and a smile came over his face. For once in the past eight years, his mind didn't wander back to his horrible past. He was thinking of the lovely Miss Samantha.

BRIGHT AND EARLY the next morning, Levi opened the gates of his pistols to make sure they were both loaded once again. A man in his profession could never be too careful. Some would call it paranoia, but Levi called it wisdom.

He stood and walked across the room and opened the door in his longhandles to call the clerk for his clothes. As he looked out, he spotted his clothes sitting on a wooden rocker right outside his room. He stretched his back and put his shirt on and then his trousers. Boy, they sure smelled nice. They reminded him of a time when he and his past sweetheart had picnicked on a blanket down under a big willow tree along a spring-fed stream, then made passionate love. It was a sweet memory he had failed to remember for some time. He put on his vest, then wrapped his wild rag around his neck. He picked up his silver pocket watch and derringer and put them into his vest pockets. His boots had been shined too, and did they look sharp. He couldn't recall ever looking so nice. At least since that tragic night. Living on the trail, there wasn't any call for fancy duds.

After he dressed and put on his gun belt, Levi walked to the window and drew back the drapes. "Council Grove," he murmured. He studied the streets a moment, then placed his hat atop his head and headed down the stairs.

As he walked out the door and into the dusty Kansas street, he noticed the marshal talking to the blacksmith. As he lit a cigar, he strolled over to the two men.

"Mornin', Mr. Cord," said Marshal Vincent as Levi reached them.

"Mornin', boys," Levi replied, nodding.

"Purty mornin', ain't it?" said the blacksmith.

"Indeed, it is." Levi agreed as he gazed up the street.

Vincent looked at Levi. "Mr. Cord, I'd like ya to meet Mr. Chris Strieby here. Strieby owns the blacksmith shop and has been successful since what, 1862 or so?"

Strieby nodded. "Yes sir, moved to town before the War broke out."

Vincent looked at Levi. "Ridin' out today, Mr. Cord?"

"Well, sir, ain't decided yet. Just come by to check on my horse."

Strieby pointed to Star. "Fine, she's doin' right fine. I took her and gave her a double sack of oats."

Levi shook the man's hand. "Thank ya kindly for that. She's all I got." Sadness filled Levi's heart as his statement sank in. His horse truly was the only thing he had left in this world. He felt his shoulders fall slightly and his mouth turn to a grimace.

Strieby placed a hand on Levi's shoulder. Levi's body tensed, his first instinct to reach for his Colt. However, he turned his head and looked Strieby in the eyes and Strieby gave a reassuring smile with a nod of his head. Levi returned the smile and felt his body relax as he nodded in turn.

"Will you be joining us for this morning's service at the church, Mr. Cord?" asked Strieby.

"No sir, I don't reckon I will be. I don't reckon I'd be too welcome in a place like that. Not anymore anyways." A deep feeling of guilt struck.

Strieby shook his head. "Nonsense, son, everyone's welcome in the house of the Lord."

Levi bowed his head. "Thank ya kindly, sir, but I reckon I'll be a burden somewhere else. Gentlemen." He tipped his hat and walked away.

The sun was now high in the sky and it was a bit warmer than the day before. It was going to be a beautiful fall day. Hundreds of Texas Longhorn cattle bawled from outside of town where they were being driven north to Abilene. A dog come prancing its way up the street and sat down at Levi's feet.

"Howdy there, girl," he said with a grin. He leaned down and scratched the dog behind her ears. She was a real friendly dog and Levi could tell she still had a lot of pup left in her. "Go on home, now," he said, and the dog went on its way up the dusty street, wagging its tail.

As Levi crossed the street, his spurs jingled along and brought a comforting rhythm to his ears as he strolled along whistling a tune softly. He liked Council Grove. The town held many friendly folks and beautiful stunning ladies. Well…one beautiful stunning lady in particular, but she was a real lady and he was a no-good drifter. Besides, what did he have to offer a real lady? The only ladies he was used to these days were not exactly ladylike. They were two dollars a poke at damn near any saloon. And then you were damn lucky if you didn't catch the clap or something much worse.

Levi didn't have anything to offer Miss Samantha. He had no land, no cattle anymore, no home of his own, little money. All he had was a rifle, his twin Colts, saddle, bedroll, and Star. Not to mention a horrible past and reputation that haunted him and followed him everywhere he went. He had sworn off marriage and love anyways.

Once he reached the boardwalk across the street, he strolled his way up to the Last Chance Store. This was one of the nicest stores he had been in since Liberty. They had it all. Fancy hats, dresses, guns, saddles, canned goods, dime novels, farming equipment, brass bed frames, fancy china…After several minutes of admiring some of the most beautiful saddles he had laid eyes on since his ranching days with the Bar W, he asked the clerk for a plug of tobacco.

Suddenly, a gentle voice in a beautiful country drawl spoke from behind him. "Why, good morning, Mr. Cord." He jumped and bumped his head on a kerosene lantern hanging overhead.

Levi's heart began to race, his knees got weak, and his hands began to sweat. As he turned around, he saw that beautiful Flint Hills prairie flower that had not left his mind since his eyes first met hers.

"Are you alright, Mr. Cord?" she giggled.

"Yes, ma'am, I was just…" Levi stopped, knowing he was about to begin stuttering once again, and took his hat off his head.

"Just what?" Samantha asked through her gorgeous and perfect smile.

"You sure look lovely today, Miss Samantha," Levi said, his pulse racing out of control. "You look—"

"Yes?" she asked, biting the edge of her lip.

"You look…well, ma'am…just like somethin' outta Heaven, ma'am." His heart pounded even more fiercely as she began to blush. "That's a mighty purty dress there, ma'am. It reminds me of a rocky mountain meadow in the springtime. It really brings out your lovely blue eyes."

"Thank ya kindly, Mr. Cord," she replied with a shaky voice. "I almost didn't recognize you in those clean clothes and clean-shaven face. I don't necessarily have to stand downwind of ya now." Levi's felt his face redden. She bit down on the corner of her lip. "I'm only funnin', Mr. Cord. You clean up quite well, sir."

He wanted nothing more than to sweep her off her feet right there in the store and hold her tight in his arms and kiss her soft tender lips and never let her go. He cleared his throat. "Well, ma'am, I had better get goin'. I'd hate for folks to get the wrong impression." He turned to the counter and paid the clerk. He then looked Samantha in the eyes and tipped his hat. "Good to see ya again, Miss Samantha."

"Likewise, Mr. Cord," she replied with a smile. As he began to leave the store, Samantha blurted out, "Mr. Cord?"

Levi turned around and gazed into her soft blue eyes. "Yes, ma'am?"

"I was just wonderin'…would you like to join me for a ride sometime? I've got a beautiful spot where you can catch a shockin' view of the Kansas sunset. Maybe we could go and take a picnic some evenin'? That is…iffen you're plannin' on stayin' in Council Grove long…"

Levi's heart raced in his chest. Had he heard her right? A picnic? He took off his hat. "I'd be delighted, ma'am. I'm rather fond of sunsets. I'd be delighted to picnic with ya, ma'am." Levi felt his heart easily falling for this one-of-a-kind, beautiful, prairie lady. "I'd be obliged, ma'am. I'll keep that in mind."

"Wonderful!" Samantha replied with excitement in her eyes. "Well, Mr. Cord, I must be goin' myself. I have to get home and take Dally out for a walk, or she's liable to tear our cottage apart."

"Dally, ma'am?"

"My dog. Danged ol' dog is like a daughter to me. She'll get to throwin' a fit iffen I don't get home soon to let her out. I got to go to a funeral here shortly and don't want her to tinkle on Father's rug. He'd tan my hide for sure."

Levi smiled. "Indeed, ma'am. It was a pleasure talkin to ya, ma'am, like always. I'll be waitin' for that picnic you promised." She smiled as he tipped his hat. "Ma'am."

As he walked out the door, he turned around for a last look at the lovely Miss Samantha Parker. He was shocked to see her turn her head around and look back at him and smile and wink. His heart was pounding rapidly as he smiled back to her and then walked out the door and about broke his neck falling off the boardwalk. Embarrassment overcame him as he got to his feet and dusted himself off hastily. He quickly glanced around and spotted three young girls giggling. Levi pulled his hat down low to cover his face before turning away from them.

He walked over to the saloon and strolled up to the bar.

"Whiskey!" he said to the barkeep. "And one of those fine cigars."

As Levi looked at himself in the mirror behind the bar, he couldn't believe what he saw. A smile on his face? He hadn't seen such a thing on him…well…since he couldn't remember when. It was a rather good feeling too. Levi had suffered from severe depression for the past few years and day by day he had begun to drink more and more. He would have to admit that he was known to get very violent and aggressive on occasion.

He walked over to a table and began to listen to the piano player. He was quite good. Levi loved music, and as a cowhand would play the harmonica and strum on the guitar around the campfires on cattle drives up to Ellsworth and Abilene. The music the piano player was playing was something he had heard before somewhere.

A lovely dance hall girl strolled her way over to the piano and began singing. Boy, she could sing, and was mighty easy on the eyes. Her eyes were a stunning green and she kept staring at Levi. However, his mind was elsewhere, thinking of another yellow rose.

"Any requests, cowboy?" the girl asked with a flirtatious smile.

"Pardon?" Levi replied, his mind coming back to the present.

"Any requests?"

Levi shook his head. "Ma'am, I'm sure you wouldn't oblige my request."

He smiled as she dared, "Try me."

"Well, ma'am, I've always been rather partial to Dixie myself."

She smiled. "Well now, as a matter of fact, our piano player Charlie here just happens to be from Alabamy and most the boys that come in and outta here are Southern cowhands."

Levi nodded along as the piano player began to play the beautiful tune. Several of the cowboys began to sing along. As the song played on, Levi began to think of when he was fighting against the Union army at Pea Ridge, Arkansas. He remembered watching his best friend and uncle both get shot down in a skirmish with Yanks one cold and miserable damp fall morning. So many brave men had lost their lives fighting for what they believed in. Some had said Levi rode alongside Captain Bloody Bill Anderson and Captain Quantrill during the Lawrence Raid, while some claimed he rode with the Jameses and Youngers in Missouri as guerillas. He never admitted it, but he never denied it, neither.

Levi drank his whiskey and gazed around the saloon. Another dance hall girl came up and sat down on his lap. "Well, howdy, howdy, cowboy. Say…I bet you're lookin' for a goodtime, ain't ya?"

Levi shook his head as he looked down at her large breasts pushing out her fancy blue dress and feathers. She had gorgeous long red hair and dark brown eyes. She was pretty, there was no denying that. As he looked into her soft brown eyes, though, all he could think of were those tender blue eyes of the lovely Miss Samantha. Before he had ridden into Council Grove, he would have taken this lovely little gal right up those stairs…and that green-eyed beauty that was singing, as well. But hell no! This time he was feeling something much different. He wasn't quite sure what that feeling was, but he liked it. "I reckon I'll have to pass on the offer this time."

"What's the matter, cowboy?" A pout crossed her face. "Got yourself a purty li'l gal back home?"

"No, ma'am. Don't get me wrong now…you're very purty. I'm just not up for it right now is all."

"Well, then…" She smirked, then got up and walked over to another cowboy at the bar.

Levi just sat there and shook his head and smiled. He thought of his past for a moment and thought about how far he had come in his life since that night in Dakota Territory. Two-dollar whores and rotgut whiskey…that's all he'd had since that devastating night. Weren't much of life by any means.

A couple of hours had passed when three dusty cowpokes that smelled as strong as a sheepherder's stock came strutting in the saloon doors.

"Yee-haw!" one of them hollered as he pulled his six-gun from his side and began firing at the mirror behind the bar. "Hot damn, boys! Where's all the whores at in this godforsaken town?"

One of them was scarcely nineteen and the other two must have been in their early twenties. Each of them wore big fancy silver spurs and batwing chaps that were covered in trail dust, red dirt from down south. One wore a large-brimmed brown hat with the brim rolled up in the front. The other two wore dusty old black slouch hats that had obviously seen better days.

The one wearing the brown hat yelled, "Barkeep! Whiskey and women, and I mean now, damn ya!" He turned to the piano player. "Can't you play that damn thing, you carpetbaggin' Yankee bastard?"

These boys were obviously cowboys that had come up the trail from Texas driving a herd north. They were all proud Southerners and you could tell by the look of them that they were up to no good and looking for trouble. They were probably petty thieves, rustlers, and drifters…ones that gave other cowboys a bad name.

"Hot damn, boys!" said the man in the brown hat. "Look at that li'l green-eyed whore over there at the bar! She's mine!" He strutted his way over to the girl and grabbed her by the arm and swung her around to him. He then shoved his hand down her dress and began grabbing her breast.

"Ow!" she yelled. "That hurts, you bastard! Stop!"

He smacked her across the face and pulled her by the arm, jerking her up the stairs and into a room. The other two boys looked around and each grabbed a girl and made their way upstairs, laughing and hollering and cussing up a storm.

Moments later, one of the girls came running down the stairs crying. Her nose was bleeding. Levi studied the woman and the doors to the rooms where the three men had gone.

One of the cowboys came running out of the room and down the stairs. His shirt was off, and his trousers were undone. "You stupid cheap-ass whore, get the hell back up there now! I ain't done with you yet!" He pointed his .44 Colt at a man trying to stop him from hurting the girl. "Get the hell outta my way, you Yankee bastard!" He hit the man over the head with the barrel of his Colt, dropping him to the floor and leaving him with a cracked skull in a pool of blood. He grabbed the girl by the wrist and began pulling her back up the stairs.

"No, please! No!" she cried in terror.

"Shut the hell up, you stupid whore!" He turned around and slapped the girl across the face not once, but twice. She fell and he yanked her up by her hair and started dragging her, ripping her dress off as they reached the top of the stairs.

Not one soul in the saloon filled with men was helping this poor defenseless girl. Why? Was it the fact that they were all scared of the three cowpokes? Or could it be the fact that the girl was a whore and they didn't want their wives to know they defended a whore in the saloon…even though most of the men in the saloon had treated themselves once or twice a week to the girl while their wives were at a quilting party. Either way, cowardice is how Levi Cord saw it. And he had just about had enough. He waited for the right time to make his move.

At the top of the stairs, the cowboy slapped the girl once more and she fell to the floor on her face. The man came up behind her as she tried to get to her knees. He tore her dress up over her back right on the floor in front of the door to the room. He pulled down his trousers and began to take her from behind right in front of everyone in the saloon. She was screaming and begging him to stop, but he would not listen. An old man who had been playing cards got up from his chair and demanded that the cowboy stop. The cowboy refused and the man begged him to leave her be. The old man drew his gun and it could be easily seen that it hadn't been fired in years. The bullets in his cartridge belt had turned green and corroded and probably wouldn't even fire. The young cowboy pulled a .31-caliber cap-and-ball pocket pistol and shot the old man in the chest. The girl screamed and Levi slid the tie downs off his guns. As the cowboy started to proceed with raping the girl, Levi eased up out of his chair, a cigar in one hand and a glass of whiskey in the other.

"Drop it, cowboy!" Levi yelled through clenched teeth. "Let her go now!"

The cowboy looked up. "Oh yeah, Yank? What the hell ya gonna do iffen I don't?"

Levi's blood filled with anger and hate. He had fought in the War for the South, and these boys were still sucking on the tit when he was killing Yankees. Now to call him a Yank, well that was enough to get a bullet in the belly. "You drop that gun, or I'll send you straight to hell!"

"I say prove it, ya yella-bellied Yank!" The cowboy gave a smile full of teeth stained or missing.

Not a sound could be heard. Levi expected that hearts were beating wildly waiting to see what would happen next…and that everyone assumed he was about to get filled full of holes for defending a two-dollar whore.

Levi stared at the young cowboy's eyes, grinned, and winked. At that very instant, the cowboy swung his gun toward Levi. Quicker than a bolt of lightning crashing down from the sky and hitting a lone cottonwood tree on the prairie, Levi had dropped both cigar and whiskey, cleared leather, and did exactly what he had promised. He filled his stinking miserable carcass full of lead, providing a one-way ticket to the only place the cowboy belonged.

Before the cowboy could hit the floor, the other two came charging out of their rooms with their six-guns firing wildly. One of the boys was naked, with nothing but his wild rag around his neck. The other was still in his longhandles. Lead was flying all over the saloon. Bullets were splattering the walls and windows, and people were dropping to the floor to take cover behind the bar and poker tables. Before the cowboys could make any of their bullets find their mark, Levi shot them both dead. The naked one was hit by a slug in the chest and one in the lower belly, missing his privates by no more than an inch. The other cowboy was hit in the neck just above the collar of his longhandles.

Levi could tell by their faces that all the people in the saloon were astonished. They had most likely never seen anyone handle a gun as fast and deadly as he just had. He enjoyed watching the faces of his less fortunate opponents when he twirled those twin nickel-plated Colts. It would surely make any man intimidated. He knew that he was as fast and blue-eyed as Jesse James, and as deadly and accurate as John Westley Hardin. He was dressed as fancy as Wild Bill. A true pistoleer, if the town of Council Grove had ever seen one. The people in the saloon stood there in awe as Levi ejected the empty casings from his Colts' cylinders and replaced them with new cartridges from his belt.

For several minutes, the saloon was as quiet as a Monday-morning church. Minutes later, two men came busting through the swinging doors, pointing Greener double-barreled scatterguns. It was the marshal and his deputy.

"What in the Sam Hill is goin' on here?" Vincent asked.

One man stood. "It was self-defense there, Marshal, sir. These cowpokes come bargin' in here shootin' up the place and beatin' on poor Lindsay there, and tried to have his way with her without payin', right here in front of God and everyone. Old man Belle there tried to get the cowpoke to let her go, but the boy just beat him over the head with his Colt. Old man Parker tried to stop him, and he shot him in the chest. The cowpoke and the new fella there had some words, then the cowpoke drew on him and, well…this stranger dusted 'em clean. The other two cowpokes come out a-shootin' the place up, and the stranger filled 'em both with lead. It was the damnedest thing I ever seen, Marshal."

Marshal Vincent studied the lifeless bodies, then walked over to Levi. "Self-defense, huh?"

"Yes, sir, Marshal. That fella told ya how it was." Levi was unsure of what would happen next and expected the very worst. He knew if Marshal Vincent were to take him to jail, he would surely be sent to prison or have his neck stretched without a fighting chance.

Vincent took off his derby hat and scratched his head. "Did ya know these boys, Mr. Cord?"

"No sir, can't say I do. Cowpokes, I reckon. Up to no good."

"Well, Mr. Cord, I reckon I'm in debt to ya, pardner." He shook Levi's hand and tipped his hat to him, then went to check on the girl.

A couple of men carried the bodies out of the saloon, and Levi sat back down at the bar.

The barkeep walked over and poured him a new glass of whiskey. "Woowhee, stranger! That sure was some fancy shooting."

Levi looked at the man and didn't even crack a smile. "Sorry 'bout breakin' that glass when I dropped it there. It just seemed like the thing to do at the time."

"No worries," the barkeep said as he came around the bar and swept up the broken pieces of glass from the dusty floor. "Got lots of 'em. I appreciate ya helpin' Miss Lindsay."

Levi looked at the crying girl with a bruised cheek and bloody nose. "It was obvious that no one else was gonna man up and step in. Except for that poor fella." Levi pointed at the old man lying in a pool of blood. "I reckon they man up every payday and take that li'l gal right upstairs and treat themselves on a weekly basis while their wives are home churnin' the butter, don't they? They step right up for a chance at sneakin' away for a good poke. That gal Lindsay there, I reckon, is there for each and every last one of them, hell, even you, I reckon, when you're itchin' for a taste. But stand up for the one they're pokin' when she's in need? I reckon not...miserable, disrespectful..." Levi mumbled the rest of his sentence under his breath and then proceeded to finish his whiskey.

Moments later, Levi walked out of the saloon and to the corner of the street and lit a cigar. The whole town was rather quiet now, except for the undertaker loading the bodies into the back of a buckboard. The air was a bit colder than earlier, and as a rider came up the street, Levi could see the breath of both horse and the rider.

As he stood there smoking his cigar, he pulled his watch from his vest pocket. It was just shy of two o' clock and it looked like most of the townspeople were still at that funeral Miss Samantha had mentioned. What were they going to think of the stranger now? In a way, he could care less, as usual, but something was different this time. What could it be? Was he a cold-blooded killer, an assassin, like most folks said? Or was he a law-abiding man, just a drifting man who wouldn't tolerate a woman being taken advantage of when she resisted? No one for sure knew the story behind Levi Cord, and, hell, even Levi himself was unsure at times. He had loved and lost and was searching for a purpose in life. He was a hard man, but a gentle man as well. You couldn't tell it by looking at him, but he was starving for affection and the true love of a woman.

He had seen and done things in his life, most of which he was not proud of. He knew right from wrong and didn't always make the best choices in life, but, hell, how many folks do? He was human. He was a decent man, honest and sincere. He was a born Christian, but after that night in Dakota Territory, he let himself go. He stopped attending the Sunday services and began to drink heavily and drift from town to town. There was a time when he wanted great things out of life, but life seemed to get him down and he sort of just gave up. He was stabbed in the back by his closest friends and his family. He had lost all trust and made himself an oath never to let anyone close to his heart ever again. These days, Levi had no idea what he wanted out of life. That was, until now. When Miss Samantha Parker's intoxicating blue eyes had met his that morning on the boardwalk, he knew then exactly what he wanted out of life. It was then, that very moment, that his whole life had changed. From that moment on, his heart would be forever in the deepest of love with that blue-eyed prairie angel.

Chapter 3

Levi stood there, still smoking his cigar, as the townsfolk began walking back from the funeral over at the cemetery. Across the street, he could see the most beautiful sight in all Council Grove. Hell, maybe the most beautiful sight in the whole territory. Miss Samantha Parker was walking alongside an older man. Levi assumed he was her father. She looked so beautiful in her Sunday go-to-meeting dress.

As they strolled up the street, Levi felt his heart longing to talk to her. Had she heard about the shooting yet? How would she look at Levi now? Why should it matter, anyway? She was a respectable lady, and he was a no-good drifter.

Once Samantha and her father reached the corner of the street where Levi was standing, Levi lowered his head, covering his eyes with his big hat brim. He was starting to feel ashamed of what he had done in the saloon and feared what Miss Samantha would think. Everyone that was in the saloon at the time of the shootings had seen what had happened and would know that Levi had only done what he had to do. He was possibly a blessing of a new and different sort to the town of Council Grove. He had stopped three outlaws from causing more damage than they had already. Still, he had violently killed three men, and he couldn't bear to have her think that he was a hardened killer. She had to know the truth. Would she even care?

Once Levi thought that Samantha and her father had passed by, he slowly raised his head. Just then, Samantha looked over her shoulder and looked Levi in the eyes and gave him a sweet little smile. He was amazed, and his heart was more than relieved. As they walked up the street, they stopped at the Conn Store and her father walked inside while she waited outside on the boardwalk. She took off her feathered hat, and Levi's heart felt like it had just stopped beating completely at that very moment. Boy, she was a sight to behold. She looked up the street at Levi and he just couldn't take it anymore. He had to talk to her now and tell her the truth about the shootings. He couldn't leave Council Grove with her possibly thinking he was a bad man.

His heart pounding something fierce, he went to the alley that came up alongside the store. He stood where he was sure the people in the store couldn't see him talking to Samantha.

"Miss Samantha?" he called softly.

"Mr. Cord?" she replied with a shaky voice.

"Miss Samantha, darlin', I need to speak with ya, ma'am."

"Is something wrong, Mr. Cord?" Samantha gazed up the street, then looked through the store window.

"Miss Samantha, darlin', I'm not a bad man. I'm no killer."

Samantha turned her head and looked Levi in the eyes. "Mr. Cord, I heard what you did over in the saloon. We're all grateful to ya, sir."

Levi cleared his throat and took off his hat. He ran his fingers through his hair, and she began to blush.

"Mr. Cord, why on earth are ya concerned with me thinkin' you're a bad man?"

Levi stared at the ground. "Well, ma'am…it's just that…" He paused, trying to find the right words to say.

"What is it, Mr. Cord?" Samantha asked.

"Darlin', I just couldn't ride away thinkin' that ya thought that poorly of me."

Levi could see disappointment in her eyes. "Are ya leavin', Mr. Cord?"

He fought for the words to say. "Miss Samantha, darlin', I reckon I've overstayed my welcome here."

"Nonsense! You have earned your welcome here, Mr. Cord. We want you to stay a spell. At least…I want ya to stay." She blushed again, and Levi felt a warmness overcome his heart.

"Ma'am?"

"I would like ya to stay, Mr. Cord. I think Council Grove would enjoy your company. I know I sure would." The store door opened, and Samantha turned. "Oh, Father."

Her father turned his head and saw Levi standing in the alley. He looked at Samantha, then back at Levi, and gave him a look that said he wanted to carve Levi's liver with a dull deer antler just for talking to his daughter. Levi had seen that look from many a time from lots of folks. Levi shifted his weight and nodded toward him.

As Samantha's father took her hand and led her away, he looked back over his shoulder at Levi and tipped his hat to him. Levi knew nothing of her father, but he could tell right off that he didn't stand a chance with the lovely

Miss Samantha for sure now. Just before Samantha and her father had reached the corner of the street, Samantha looked back at Levi and smiled and gave him a little come-and-get-me wink. His heart melted right then and there, and he wondered what exactly she had meant by not wanting him to leave Council Grove.

As they turned the corner, Levi turned and headed toward the jail. Once he reached the jail, he turned around and gazed back up the street. The town had begun to fill up since the funeral service was over. Feeling uneasy, Levi entered the jail.

Marshal Vincent was browsing through a stack of wanted posters on his desk. "Why, top of the mornin' to ya, Mr. Cord. What can I do for ya, sir?"

"Howdy, Marshal, I was just wonderin' iffen ya found anything on them three cowboys from the saloon earlier."

"Well, no papers on 'em, but we're sure mighty grateful to ya. God only knows what might have happened if you hadn't of been there. Say, Mr. Cord, ya lookin' for a job?"

Levi thought a second. "Well, Marshal, not exactly. I'm headed to Colorado Territory for a spell…thought I'd try my hand at some elk huntin'."

"Well, iffen ya ever decide to come back to Council Grove here, we could sure use a hand like you."

"Why, thank ya kindly. Maybe someday. By the way, I'd like to pay for the damages over at the saloon."

Vincent sat in his chair with a look of shock across his weathered face. "Mr. Cord, that's not your obligation."

"I know that, but I'd like to. It's a lovely place and I'd like to pay for the damages just the same."

"Well, iffen you insist, I won't object none. Hell, I'm sure that Ray over at the saloon will be mighty grateful to ya."

Levi dug down into his pocket and pulled out two twenty-dollar gold pieces. "This oughta see to most the damages." He handed Vincent the money.

The marshal nodded and set the coins on his desk. "When do ya intend on leavin' us, Mr. Cord?"

Levi looked Vincent in the eyes. "Marshal, you'd be doin' me a favor iffen ya called me Levi. I reckon I'll be ridin' out in a day or two."

Vincent looked at him for a second, then smiled and stuck out his hand. "Well, Levi, call me Vincent. Sit down and visit a bit, would ya?"

A COUPLE HOURS later, Levi left the jail and headed for the Hays House. Vincent had told him that they served the best steak and fresh hot apple pie in the whole territory, and he was itching to see if the marshal was right. As Levi walked down the boardwalk, he thought about what Marshal Vincent had asked him. Could he really be a deputy? He was damn good with a gun, but could he really go from sitting in a state prison to being an honest lawman? Could he settle down and make Council Grove his new home? He loved this little town and he liked the folks here as well. At least those he had met so far. He could get just about everything he possibly needed over yonder in the Last Chance Store, and if not there, he was sure he could have it ordered at the Conn Store. He had a way with guns, and he also had a way with cattle. Rumor had it, he could break a horse better than any cowboy that had ever lived. He had always loved the cowboy way of life more than anything and had dreamed of owning his very own spread somewhere and starting his own ranch someday. That was, however, until that tragic day in Dakota Territory. After that day, he became a loner, a drifter, never knowing if he was coming or going. He was a heartbroken, lonely dreamer, fighting for a reason to live. Had he finally found one?

As he reached the Hays House, the smell of steak and potatoes frying and fresh apple pie filled his nose. His stomach growled as he entered. As he walked in the door, he was greeted by a young brown-eyed girl who was cuter than a bug's ear.

She grinned. "May I take your coat and hat for ya, sir?" He handed them to her, and she hung them on a rack made from elk antlers.

"Why, thank ya, ma'am." Levi said with a smile.

The girl sat him at a table with a red-and-white-checkered tablecloth and said, "What can I get for ya today, sir?"

"Well, ma'am, I'm really itchin' for a fresh-cut steak and a slice of that apple pie," Levi said as he gazed at the pies on the counter. The girl smiled, then headed back to the kitchen. Levi sat there craving that juicy steak. He hadn't had a good steak since he was punching cows down in Denton County, Texas.

As he waited, he found himself distracted by the thought of Samantha and those stunning blue eyes, and his mind drifted a million miles away. In the midst of thoughts of romance, Levi let his guard down and failed to study his surroundings. All of a sudden, he heard a familiar soft voice behind him say, "Meet me at the bend of Elm Creek, three miles south of town, tomorrow morning at eight. You'll see a big cottonwood tree." He could tell it was Miss Samantha by her sweet drawl. He looked over his shoulder and saw her sitting at the table behind him. Samantha had walked in behind Levi without him noticing. He smiled, happy to see her again so soon.

She whispered, "Don't ask no questions. Just promise me you'll be there."

Levi's heart was racing. "I'll be there, Miss Samantha. I promise it."

The door opened, and Levi turned to see Samantha's father come in. He gave Levi the same look that he had given him before.

"Father," Samantha said, "this is Mr. Cord. He's the man that saved Miss Lindsay from those cowboys at the saloon."

Her father glanced at Levi. "Mr. Cord, are ya plannin' to stay in town long? The last thing we need here in Council Grove is another two-bit gunman like yourself."

Samantha's face turned red. "Father!"

"Well, sir, I don't rightly know yet."

"Well, I hope your stay in Council Grove is very short. We will all rest easier when you're gone." He grabbed Samantha by the arm. "We're finished here!" As he dragged her to the door, she looked back at and whispered, "I'm so sorry."

Levi gave her a smile as her father slammed the door shut.

AFTER LEVI HAD finished what had to be the best steak and apple pie west of the Mississippi river, he headed back out to the dusty street. He strolled over to a nearby bench on the boardwalk and sat down to try to gather his thoughts. He couldn't believe his thoughts had let his guard down, yet he couldn't get out of his head. He wanted to rescue her from her father and take her far away where she would be happy and safe with him forever. He didn't know what it was about this beautiful young woman that made him feel this way. He sat there for the next few hours just watching the townsfolk go by and studying their actions and eavesdropping on their conversations. Several times he overheard a couple of people talking about the gunfight in the saloon, but not once did he hear anything negative about himself. It was quite a nice feeling.

Just before sundown, Levi recognized Mr. Linsey, one of the older men he had met that morning, as he came walking down the boardwalk. "Howdy there, Mr. Cord."

Levi tipped his hat. "Howdy, sir. Mighty purty evening, ain't it?"

Mr. Linsey gazed toward the west at the setting sun. "Chillin' off a bit. Daggum fish quit bitin'."

Levi chuckled under his breath and reached into his vest for his tobacco.

Mr. Linsey turned to him and glanced at his Colts. "I hear tell that you cleared leather quicker than a keg of cider at barn-raisin' time."

Levi spit tobacco on the boardwalk and crossed his legs.

Mr. Linsey shook his head and looked him in the eyes. "They said you bored a hole in 'em big enough to drive a wagon through. Where on earth did ya learn to shoot like that?"

Levi looked up the street at Marshal Vincent making his usual evening rounds around town.

"Mr. Cord, sir, I apologize for stickin' my nose into your business. Didn't mean no harm, was just curious is all. You see, we get all sorts of strangers come through this town…some good, some not so good. From what the folks say in town, you're about the quickest gunhand Council Grove has ever seen."

Levi looked up at him and gave him a crooked little grin. "No need to apologize, sir. I reckon that I've packed iron so long that I tend to feel naked when I take 'em off. I reckon I'll be wearin' these here Colts until I reach those pearly gates—that is, if they see fit to have my kind up there. My grandmother always told me when I was no bigger than a corn nubbin that I was born with a bottle in one hand and a six-gun in the other. I tell ya, sir, a slow draw is a mighty quick way to join the angels, and I never cottoned to the idea much."

Mr. Linsey chuckled and tipped his hat to him and then began walking down the street.

Levi watched Marshal Vincent turn the corner and slowly disappear out of sight. The sun was setting, and a young boy came walking down the street lighting the streetlamps. Levi sat and watched him complete his work.

Finally, the sun set, and the streets were pretty much empty. Levi stood and stretched, then headed toward the Cottage House. He cut through an alley to take a shortcut. The moon wasn't out tonight, and without the light coming through the buildings, it was quite dark.

Suddenly, he heard something walking in the alley behind him. Unafraid, yet even more alert, he cautiously pressed on. However, the noise grew louder.

Levi drew his guns. "Alright! Come on out! Who the hell's there?"

About that time, he saw the same dog that he had come across earlier that morning. "Oh, it's just you, huh, girl?" He knelt and scratched the dog's ears. The dog rolled over on her back, and Levi scratched her belly. She got her leg to kicking something wild.

Levi stood back up and walked up the steps to the Cottage House. Once in his room, Levi took off his hat and gun belt and hung them on the edge of the brass bed frame. He slid off his boots and settled into bed. As he lay there, alone, he thought of why Miss Samantha could possibly want to meet him. He thought of all the hell that he had been through and all the heartaches that he had acquired over the years in the past. His mind went crazy until he finally drifted off to sleep. Tossing and turning, he awoke in the middle of the night and reached for the bottle of whiskey that he had next to the bed.

About an hour later, after drinking half the bottle, Levi drifted back to sleep. He dreamed of Miss Samantha and just what it would be like to have a life with her. He dreamed of growing old together. He dreamed that he married her and raised a son on a large cattle spread somewhere like the place that he had camped at along Soldier Creek after he had left Burlingame. He dreamed of a perfect life.

JUST BEFORE SUNRISE, Levi was up and off to the stable. Once he walked into the barn, Star let out a whinny. He picked up a brush and a curry comb and began to comb her.

"Mornin' girl," he said softly. "Did ya miss me?" She shook her head up and down as if to say yes, and Levi grinned. "Goin' for a li'l ride this mornin'." He knew she would be excited to be going out after having been in the stall all this time. Levi put a blanket on the mare's back and swung up his saddle and placed it softly in place. After cinching the saddle up tight, he put her bridle on and lit out of the barn.

As they rode out of town, the sun began to clear the Kansas horizon. It was a crystal-clear morning and a bit warmer than the day before. As they galloped along, he saw a herd of buffalo off in the distance southwest of town. Riding along, he spotted a whitetail buck standing in a group of cedars with three does. He was a real jim-dandy. He had ten points, and his rack must have spread near forty inches. If he wasn't on the way to meet the beautiful Miss Samantha at Elm Creek, maybe he'd try to take the buck with his trusty Winchester. He had something a bit more important on his mind this time, though.

As they came to a bluff, Levi could see Elm Creek ahead just about a mile. A herd of pronghorn antelope chased each other across the vast open prairie. A flock of prairie chickens danced in the sunlight as a meadowlark sang from his perch on a wild sunflower.

"Gorgeous mornin', ain't it?" Levi said to Star. The sun had just cleared the horizon and was beating down on the rolling Flint Hills. The bluestem prairie grass was beginning to turn from green to a gorgeous reddish brown. The leaves on the trees along Elm Creek were now starting to turn yellow, and the leaves on the nearby thickets of buck brush were turning red.

"Beautiful country," Levi whispered.

Once they reached the creek, Levi spotted the big lone cottonwood tree Samantha had told him about. His heart began to race. His mind ran wild with the things that he wanted to say. Nearing the big cottonwood, he was astonished at what he saw. A picnic basket sat on a quilt next to the creek. Also on that quilt was the lovely Miss Samantha Parker. She was wearing a yellow cotton dress and her blue eyes shined so delicately. The sunlight was gleaming down on her, and the prairie breeze blew through her long blonde hair flowing down her back. She was by far the loveliest sight that Levi had seen since his sweetheart.

"Well, good mornin', Mr. Cord," she said as he dismounted.

"Mornin', Miss Samantha." Levi tied Star to a nearby clump of brush. As he walked over to Samantha, he took off his hat, then knelt and took her soft hand in his and gently pressed it to his lips.

She blushed. "Oh, Mr. Cord, you're such a gentleman."

Levi smiled as he gazed into her baby blue eyes.

"Shall we walk, Mr. Cord?"

Levi stood. "Certainly." He helped her to her feet.

As she rose to her feet, she glanced back at her paint gelding that was tied just a short way from Levi's palomino. "I won't be long, Lightning," she said to him softly.

Walking along the creek, Levi had never felt so right in all his life. That was however, except for a time long ago when he was on a blanket with his late sweetheart in the warm Dakota sun. That felt like a million years ago now as he strolled with Miss Samantha in the Elm Creek bottoms. Not a day went by that he didn't think of that day, yet, walking alongside the lovely Samantha, Levi felt an extreme relief in his heart. What was it about this lady that made him feel so right? He had only met her no more than two days ago. He was beginning to feel that he might have reached the stage in his life where it was time to say goodbye to his past and move on with his life. He would always hold the memory close to his heart and nothing would ever change that, but the feelings he held inside for Miss Samantha were something rare and true and not something easy to ride away from.

Samantha leaded down and picked up an antler a whitetail deer had shed. "Have you ever been married, Mr. Cord?"

"No, ma'am, to be quite honest, I ain't," he said softly as he gazed back up the trail. He could feel the pain inside his heart, and he knew it was probably showing in his eyes. He knew he was a mysterious man to Samantha, but the way she looked at him made him believe she could understand the pain he held so tightly to…even know what it meant to live a rough life and suffer many disappointments along the way. He had always thought a person could tell a lot about someone just by looking in their eyes…that eyes could tell an interesting story if the mind would take the time to listen. And he could tell Samantha was willing.

He looked deep into her eyes, gaining the strength he hadn't realized he had sought, and then stared across the prairie. "There was a girl once…" Levi bit his lip.

She looked him in the eyes. "Go on, Mr. Cord, I'll listen."

Her intense gaze gave him courage. He took a deep breath. "Up in the Dakota territory. She was a beautiful brown-eyed gal that had a heart of gold, and her hair was much like yours. She was a beautiful woman inside and out."

"Where's she at now, Mr. Cord?"

Levi looked up the creek, fighting the tears that were beginning to fill his eyes. The tears began to fill his eyes and he lowered his head. "We were so young and in love."

"That's beautiful, Mr. Cord. What happened?"

Levi gritted his teeth. "One day, we were at a place much like this here spot up in the Black Hills. We put a blanket on the ground under a tall pine tree and had ourselves a li'l picnic. I was young and crazy in love, if you will. I pulled a ring from the pocket of my vest and asked for her hand in marriage. She cried and we laughed. Oh, how we were in love."

Levi paused, but Samantha's wondering eyes encouraged him to continue. "Well, ma'am…we went to the café that evening and had ourselves some supper. We laughed and talked about the weddin' of her dreams. As we walked out the door after finishing our supper, a man was hid out in the alley nearby with a scattergun. I had kilt a horse thief in Abilene some time back. Apparently, this man had been on my trail to avenge his death. Unfortunately, when he found me, I was comin' outta the café with my sweetheart."

Samantha's eyes began to tear up as he went on. "The first shot came with no warnin'. It struck her in the breasts. As she lay there in the street dyin', I reached for her hand as the man fired the second barrel of the scattergun. The buckshot caught me in the back. As I fell to the ground, I crawled over top of her to shield her body. I drifted off, and when I woke up in a local hotel bed four days later, I was told she had left this world. I never got to say goodbye. I was in and out for the next few months, but when I recovered enough to ride, I went out to our barn and dug out a chest that I had buried there when we had first started courtin'. I had thought I could leave my past behind, but turns out I was wrong, and it cost me. In the chest was this here pair of twin Colts and enough cartridges to start a war. I strapped these Colts across my hips, loaded my saddlebags with what li'l money I had, and left that place in search of the murderin' saddle trash that stole my whole world from me. The next few years, I drifted from one cow town to another, checkin' with every jail and marshal in the territory, in hopes of findin' that man. For quite a spell that man had been huntin' my carcass down, but now I was huntin' his."

Samantha swiped a tear from her cheek. "Did you ever find him?"

"I got hot on his trail near Hays City, but the trail vanished in a herd of longhorn cattle. I kept travelin' east and wound up in Liberty. The marshal there was busy huntin' them James boys, but his deputy said that he had had a drifter in jail that just might happen to be the man. When I asked to see the man, he proceeded to tell me that he had been released earlier that morning.

Where he went from there, we don't know. After a few months combin' the Missouri hills, I decided to head back west along the ol' Santa Fe road. That's when I rode into Council Grove here."

Samantha's eyes widened. "You were still huntin' that man?"

"Yes, ma'am, I was and still am. That was, however, until I laid eyes on you."

Samantha placed Levi's weathered hand in hers and looked into his eyes as the tears gently fell down his cheeks. "Mr. Cord, I bet she was a beautiful woman."

"Yes, ma'am, she was at that."

She reached over and wiped a tear from Levi's cheek as it slowly drifted down his face. "Was there ever another girl?"

Levi looked at the ground with shame.

Samantha chuckled, a beautiful sound. "I didn't mean those kinda girls. I was referrin' to someone special to ya."

Levi paused for a minute. "No, ma'am. When she died, I made myself an oath never to love again. I ran every chance I got. No woman could nor would ever fill her spot in my heart. That was however..." Levi cleared his throat. "Until I met you, Miss Samantha."

Samantha blushed and glanced away.

"Miss Samantha." He gently used his hand to turn her face toward him and gazed deeply into her gentle blue eyes. "Darlin', you're a mighty handsome woman. Probably the most beautiful woman I've ever laid eyes on. Yes, I loved in the past once, and she was somethin' that I'll hold in my heart for a long time. However, when I first laid eyes on you, my heart seemed to long for something more. I spent the past eight years mournin' her loss, and I cussed God on more than one starlit night for takin' her from me. When you first smiled at me, though, I knew then and there that my whole world was about to change. I can't explain it, darlin', but I just know that you deserve to be happy and see the world. I don't know much about you, but I can see when I look into your eyes that you are a wonderful woman. Your eyes never stray from mine when you talk to me. That shows me right there that you're an honest woman. I've traveled to danged near every dusty cow town in the West, and I promise you, Miss Samantha, that I have never met another woman like you. You're as purty as the mornin' sun. You are still a young woman and have so much to live for...places to see and dreams to live. Don't waste your life away as I have mine, darlin'."

"Oh, Mr. Cord."

He smiled. "Call me Levi, darlin'."

"Alright, Levi," she spoke softly, staring into his eyes.

Levi pulled her close and wrapped his arms around her soft, tender body. He pushed her blonde hair back from her cheek and pressed his lips to hers as she closed her eyes. She placed her hand on his chest, and he slid his hand down the small of her back.

"Oh, Levi," she whispered. He felt their hearts racing together, and, for the first time, everything seemed to be just grand. Simply perfect. Levi felt passion and want. Love and desire and hope. Could this be the purpose he had been searching for?

Levi ran his fingers through her soft hair and kissed her once again. He prayed to God above that this moment would never end.

She pulled him tightly to her. "Please, Levi…Don't ever let go."

He kissed her forehead. "Never, darlin'," he whispered in her ear. He felt her shiver as he kissed her neck and ran his fingers through her hair.

She moaned. "Oh, Levi."

A crow called from atop a cottonwood tree, interrupting. Levi looked up, and he spotted a whitetail buck foraging through the fallen leaves as a couple of does stood drinking from the stream. Samantha reached down and held Levi's hand, and, out of the corner of his eye, he could see she was watching, too. The warm fall breeze blew across the prairie, blowing a stand of tumbleweeds across the ground, lifting her blonde hair.

As the morning drew on, the two continued to walk along the stream hand in hand. Samantha's hand felt so perfect in Levi's. He never wanted to let it go. For the first time in a long time, Levi was thinking of something besides finding and killing the man who had killed his sweetheart. He was now thinking of how good it felt to be holding the hand of this beautiful and amazing woman of his dreams. Dreams that had arisen after his past sweetheart's death. Dreams that only now he was seeing could actually come true. He hadn't felt this good in years.

Yes, he had had his share of lewd woman over the years, but this was something much different. As he looked into Samantha's blue eyes, he could see something that he had never seen so clearly. He saw himself becoming a husband and a father. The question was, could he give her those things? He'd been a long-time drifter and had nothing to show but a cartridge belt full of notches of the men he had killed, and several scars that would haunt him his whole life. He had been abandoned and had his heart broken and been let down so many damn times that he could not trust anybody. Could he trust Samantha? Would she go and break his heart? When he looked into her eyes, he knew that her love was real and so true.

Once they arrived back at the quilt that Samantha had laid out, she looked at Levi. "Shall we sit and have us a bite to eat?"

"If you wish, darlin'."

She opened the picnic basket and pulled out some cornbread and fresh honey that she had wrapped up in a white cloth, then pulled out a Mason jar full of tea. She handed him a piece of cornbread.

"Doggone, darlin', that looks mighty tasty." He held it as she poured some honey on it, then he waited for her to take the first bite. After she did, he took a bite. "By golly, that's mighty fine cornbread, iffen I do say so myself."

TOGETHER THEY SHARED the cornbread and jar of tea and watched the clouds go by floating in the sky.

Samantha gazed deep into Levi's sharp blue eyes, longing to learn more of this mysterious man. "May I ask you a question?"

"Certainly."

"Why is it that you decided to carry two guns instead of just one?"

She watched Levi as he seemed to be lost in thought. Her eyes traveled once more to his guns.

"Well, darlin', it seems most folks take one look at these Colts and get intimidated, to say the least. I'd hate for folks to take a look at me and not get nervous. They could get to thinkin' they might be a slight quicker than me. A man that don't get nervous while pullin' a gun on a man, now that's somethin' to really get intimidated about." He smiled.

Samantha ran her fingers through her hair. The fact that Levi was a known gunman didn't change her mind about him one bit. She found him to be very charming and handsome and quite interesting. She longed for excitement and adventure in her life.

"Darlin'?"

"Yes, Levi?"

"Iffen I may ask, I know you live with your father, but where is your mother?"

Samantha looked out across the prairie in silence. She swallowed hard. "She took off when I was just a girl. She up and married another man and, Father, well…I just couldn't bear to leave him alone. Truth is, Levi, I love him to death, but lately he's too much for me to handle. The more I am home, the more we disagree on what I should or should not do with my life. I just can't take much more. I'm afraid things are only getting worse. I need to get out of there before I go crazy."

Levi softly brushed her hair away from her cheek. "I'm truly sorry, darlin'. I understand."

Samantha leaned her head on his shoulder.

"Levi, I am saddened to hear about the loss of your sweetheart. I bet she was a fine woman."

Levi lowered his head. "Yes, ma'am. She truly was."

Samantha leaned up and placed her hand on Levi's cheek and smiled. "Smile, cowboy. It looks good on you." Her heart thrilled when Levi smiled. "It's just been me and ol' Dally for some time now. You could say I ain't had the best of luck with gentlemen myself. Dally has been more faithful and devoted to me than any fella ever has. One day her and I will get outta this town and see the country."

Levi chuckled softly.

Samantha took his hand. "Levi?"

"Yes, darlin'?"

"I like you, cowboy." She bit on the corner of her lip.

"Well, I like you too, darlin'."

"I mean, I really, really like you. Somethin' about you captivates me."

Levi blushed and smiled. "I really like you, too, darlin'. You're unlike any woman I've ever known."

For most of the day they sat there, flirting and sharing stories with each other about their past. It was oddly comforting to her to be able to open up to him. The more she talked of her hopes and wishes in love and life, the greater her love for him grew. She watched him as she spoke. He was so attentive, and she felt that he was maybe feeling the same way she did. She hoped it was true and not just her desire deceiving her. They both had shared their numerous heartaches over their lives, and they needed each other. He was her escape from not only depression, but from reality, in a roundabout way. She prayed he felt the same.

LEVI STRETCHED OUT his legs, leaned over Samantha, and softly said, "You have the most intoxicating blue eyes that I've ever seen."

She blushed. "Oh, Levi, you're quite a charmer."

"I mean it, darlin'. When I look into your eyes, I feel my heart just meltin' away. I feel as if there's a wildfire burnin' in my heart. When you smile at me, I feel this feelin' inside that I've never had. You're such an amazing woman, Samantha. When you asked me to meet you out here, I wasn't sure just what I was gonna do. I was tempted to saddle up and ride but the thought of never seein' ya again was…an unbearable feelin'. A pain that I wasn't strong enough to bear."

"Oh, Levi. Kiss me, Levi."

Levi wrapped his arms around her and leaned her back onto the quilt. He then kissed her tender lips. He unbuckled and took off his gun belt and laid it on the ground beside them. Samantha wrapped her arms tightly around him and he kissed her tender lips and the sides of her cheeks and neck. As she began to breathe heavily, she rolled over on top of Levi, leaned down, and began kissing his face. She ran her fingers along his sideburns and began kissing his neck.

"Oh, Samantha, darlin'…" Levi moaned.

"Yes, Levi?" she murmured.

"Oh, darlin', you are so beautiful." His heart was racing, and he craved her soft and satisfying touch.

She continued to kiss him, gently pressing her wet lips to his. "I want you Levi…so bad. Oh, I want you…"

Levi wanted her just as bad as she wanted him, if not even more. He hadn't known her long, but it didn't take long to fall for this wonderful and perfect lady. As bad as he wanted to take her right there on the prairie ground, he looked her in the eyes and said, "Darlin', I care deeply for you. I don't want you to go makin' no mistakes over me."

"Levi, yes, I know. I care deeply for you myself. I'm sorry." She sat up next to him.

He took her by the hand. "Darlin'," he said softly, "Don't you be sorry for one second. You can't help what the body wants. I'll be in town for a couple days." He could see the sadness darken her eyes.

The sun began to work its way toward the western horizon, casting beautiful rays of light across the Flint Hills. Darkness would be setting in soon.

"Darlin', we should be gettin' you back 'fore it gets too dark. You go ahead and ride in and I'll be along directly. I desire you, Samantha, everything about you. The way your eyes sparkle off the sun and the way your hair falls over your shoulders. The way your body feels close to mine. Everything, darlin'."

She leaned up to Levi and kissed him. Her arms encircled him, and as tight as she held him, he knew she didn't want to let him go.

"I know, darlin', I know, but you should be goin'."

A tear gently ran down her soft cheek as she began to fold the quilt and tie it to her saddle. "Will I see you again?"

"If you wish, Samantha." Levi helped her into the saddle, and for a moment the world paused once more as they stared into each other's eyes.

"Goodbye, Levi," she said. He watched her fight back the tears.

"Goodbye, Samantha, darlin'." Levi mounted Star.

Samantha rode toward town, and Levi waited a moment before riding toward the bluff. That had been by far the best day that he'd had in a very long time. Once he reached the top of the bluff, he stopped the mare and threw one leg over the saddle horn and just sat there and watched the sun set across the vast Kansas prairie. It was simply breathtaking and peaceful. The colors across the horizon resembled a painting Levi had seen in a hotel down in Cottonwood Falls once before. They were the faintest pink, with a splash of purple and lavender. Purple cone flowers and other prairie flowers were spread out across the prairie. There were no words that could describe how beautiful it was. The only word that came to mind was Samantha.

Chapter 4

As Samantha rode into town, she had the warmest feeling in her heart and a smile that stretched from ear to ear. She had felt so alone and hopeless for the past two years and now she felt more alive than she ever had. For years she had known what she wanted out of life, but nothing seemed to be going anywhere. She was lonely and tired. And now this stranger had stolen her heart with one simple glance.

She walked Lightning into the livery stable, giving him a good brushing before turning him loose in the corral. She walked home, making her way past the cowboys who were milling about the darkening street, most likely on their way to or from the saloon. When she turned the corner to head to the cottage, her heart fell. Father was standing on the porch.

He crossed his arms as she came up on the porch. "Now where in the hell have you been, girl? Don't ya know supper ain't gonna cook itself?"

Samantha lowered her head and brushed her hair behind her ear. "I'm sorry, Father. I just decided to take myself a li'l afternoon ride."

"Afternoon? Hell, girl, you been gone most the day! I come home and expected a hot meal."

"Yes, Father. I'll prepare somethin' as soon as I wash up."

He turned around and slammed the door behind him as he walked inside. Samantha dreaded going inside and dealing with him. All she wanted to do was just heat herself a hot bath and dream of Levi. She didn't want to have to explain where she had been all day. As she entered the cottage, she lit a lamp and began to prepare supper.

After supper, which had been strained but thankfully quiet, Father stormed to his room. Samantha cleaned up while heating water for a bath.

She reached for a fresh towel and placed it to her nose to take in the fresh scent of lilacs. Once her bath was ready, she began to undress, her mind heavy with thoughts of Levi. He was so stunning and handsome, so strong but yet so tender to touch. Samantha slowly slid into her hot bath. The warm touch of the water upon her skin reminded her of Levi's warm breath upon her neck. Sitting there in the candlelit room, she began to lather a washcloth with soap and softly touched it to her breasts. As she ran it along her tender and delicate body, she dreamed of Levi and longed for his soft touch.

LEVI RODE INTO town, his mind going wild. Was he falling for Samantha? She was everything he had ever dreamed of in a woman. His mind raced with thoughts of her. He rode past the stable and up to the Conn Store. A couple of young girls were playing on the boardwalk, staying within the dim light that came through the window.

Levi cleared his throat. "Howdy, ladies, I was wonderin' iffen you could tell me where Miss Samantha Parker lives?"

The two little girls looked up at him, and one said, "Do you know Miss Parker, mister? Did you come to town to marry her?"

Levi blushed and the other girl in the cutest braids pointed down the street toward a little white cottage with a white picket fence.

"Thank ya kindly, ladies. Miss Parker is sorta a friend of mine, ya might say." He gave them a wink. They giggled, then continued to play.

Levi rode away and looked down the street toward Samantha's cottage. What was she doing now? Was her father home? He could see light from a lamp through the window and many thoughts rushed through his mind. He wanted to race over there and sweep Samantha right off her feet and ride off into the darkness of the night hell-bent and bound for the Colorado Rockies.

As he rode around town, he knew there would be no possible way he would be able to get any sleep in town. It was going to be another long, restless night. He rode out of town and out onto the prairie. The night air was a bit warmer than the night before and he knew that it wouldn't get too cold, so he decided he would sleep on the prairie and clear his mind. It was the perfect place to find himself and do some soul searching. He had a bottle of whiskey in his saddlebags and his stomach was far from being hungry. He was too lovestruck over Samantha to eat.

Levi rode out a few miles from town and spotted a small bluff. That would be a good spot to set up camp. Reaching it, he took his saddle off Star, gave her a handful of oats from the saddlebags, then put out his bedroll.

He settled in, staring at the stars and picturing Samantha in his arms. His heart felt empty. He longed for the beautiful woman of his dreams. He knew he was in no position to ask for her hand. He was hunting a man in order to kill him. Nevertheless, he had fallen for her.

Levi tossed and turned all night. Every time he would close his eyes, his mind would race with thoughts of Miss Samantha in that yellow dress. He had to have her one way or another. He knew her father would never approve, but he was going to wait for her no matter how long it took.

THE NEXT MORNING, Samantha awoke alone as usual, but this time with a smile on her face. She had been dying for the night to pass so she could see Levi. Crawling out of her big feather bed, she stretched out and walked over to the mirror and began brushing her long hair, which looked like a wild mustang's mane at the moment.

She heard Father moving around in the other room. "Where in the hell is my damn coffee?"

She shook her head and tried her best to ignore him. She heard him rustling through the kitchen and hoped he would leave before she came out of her room.

After she finished brushing her hair, she put on one of her favorite dresses. She tied a yellow ribbon in her hair and decided to go for a morning stroll. She just had to see if she could find Levi. But as she walked out of her room, Father met her in the kitchen.

"Damn it, girl, you're just like your mother. I expect coffee first thing in the morning, and I expect it hot."

"I'm sorry, Father. I must have overslept this morning. I'll put some on right now." She began to heat a pot of coffee on the stove, but Father stormed out the front door. Samantha shook her head and put everything back, then left for her walk.

As she walked down the street, Marshal Vincent tipped his derby hat to her and said, "Well, top of the morning to ya, Miss Samantha. Don't you look lovely today."

She smiled. "Good morning to you, Marshal." She walked over to a bench out front of the First National Bank, where she could watch the Cottage House and see Levi when he came out for the morning.

Two hours had come and gone when Samantha looked up at the town clock. "Ten o clock," she muttered. Would a cowboy really sleep that late? She wanted to walk in and go to him, but how on earth would that look? Maybe he had left before she had arrived. She decided to go to the stable to see if he might be there tending to his horse. When she got to the livery, her heart sank as she noticed that Levi's mare was not in the corral. She instantly got a cold, lonely feeling inside. Where was he? Had he left without saying goodbye? Had something happened to him after she left him last night? She feared all the worst possibilities.

She walked out to the corral and saddled Lightning as quickly as she could. She took off for Elm Creek at a dead run. He could be out there hurt or dying, and she would never get the chance to tell him how she truly felt. She just couldn't stand it.

MEANWHILE, BACK EAST of town a few miles, Levi was sitting by a cozy campfire he had started with some dried out old buffalo chips and dead prairie grass. He was drinking a cup of coffee from his old tin cup and preparing to saddle up and ride back into town. After he took his last sip, he swished the now cold coffee in his mouth, then spit it out into the ashes. Stomping out the ashes and coals with his boots, he then took his canteen down from his saddle and poured it over the ashes. After he was certain the fire was out, he saddled up and headed toward Council Grove, thoughts of seeing Miss Samantha on his mind.

As he rode into town, he circled past her cottage in hopes that she would see him ride by if she was home. He rode down the street and circled back once again before heading to the livery. He took his saddle off Star and walked her to the corral.

Walking down the street, he passed by the saloon, and, for some reason for the first time in a long time, he had no desire to go in and have a drink. As he passed by, the Cottage House clerk's wife met him on the boardwalk.

"We missed ya last night, Mr. Cord," she said. "Didn't see ya in town much yesterday, either."

"A bit nosy, are we, ma'am?" Levi asked, hearing the irritation in his voice. He was not pleased with her interrupting his search and he didn't want to waste any time in idle conversation.

The woman lowered her head and blushed. "My apologies, sir. Was only making conversation."

Levi gazed up the street toward the Last Chance Store, hoping to see Samantha. "Just went out for a li'l ride. Purty countryside in these parts." He glanced around again.

"Are ya lookin' for anyone in particular, Mr. Cord?"

"Pardon?" He felt a bit guilty as he realized she probably knew he wasn't paying attention. "No, ma'am."

The clerk smiled. "Do ya plan on joinin' us tonight?"

"Pardon?" He felt his ears begin to burn.

She chuckled. "Your mind is obviously elsewhere, so I'll just bid you good day, Mr. Cord."

"Good day, ma'am." Levi was relieved he remembered to tip his hat as she walked away. He walked to the corner of the street and sat on the bench out front of the First National Bank. From there he could see both the Cottage House and Miss Samantha's cottage to the south.

After about twenty minutes, Mr. Conn came outside and swept the boardwalk in front of his store, then walked back inside after waving to Levi.

Levi watched the streets. While he wasn't watching them, he watched thirty minutes, then an hour, then another thirty minutes tick by on his watch.

Mr. Conn came back outside, carrying a bottle of sarsaparilla, and walked over to Levi. "Howdy, cowboy. Looks like you could use a drink. It's on me."

Levi looked at the man and took the bottle. "Much obliged to ya, sir." He opened the bottle and took a sip. Levi was used to whiskey and cowboy coffee, but, dang, that sarsaparilla had a sweet and unique taste. "Damn, that's tasty! This could be habit formin'." He grinned, then drank a second sip.

Mr. Conn smiled. "Two cents a bottle, iffen ya get thirsty while you're in Council Grove."

Levi reached out to shake his hand. "Thanks again, pardner. I'll keep that in mind."

Shortly after Mr. Conn had went back inside his store, Levi spotted a little girl about nine years old playing with the same dog that he had stopped to pet the day he rode into town. That poor dog was starving for love and affection…just hoping to be wanted.

Levi got up from the bench and walked over to the little girl. "Excuse me, young lady. Would ya do me a favor?" He leaned down and picked some flowers that were growing beside the bank along an old wooden fence near the alley. "Would ya take these over to Miss Samantha?"

The little girl smiled. "Why, certainly, mister. They are very pretty. She will love them."

Levi walked back over to the bench and sat down and waited to see if Samantha came out. The little girl looked so adorable. She was wearing a little green dress and adorable little braids in her hair. He thought how nice it would be to be a father someday.

She skipped up to the front steps, then walked up to the door and knocked. Levi's heart was pounding something fierce, longing to see Samantha. The girl knocked on the door several times, but no one answered. Where could she be? He hadn't seen her on the streets and hadn't seen her leave the cottage.

He walked over to the girl. "Thank ya, darlin'."

She shrugged and handed him the flowers. "She wasn't home, mister."

"Well, why don't you take this shiny silver nickel and go buy yourself a bottle of that tasty sarsaparilla."

The girl smiled. "Thank ya, mister!" She took off running toward the store.

"Hold it!" Levi hollered. "You forgot something!"

She ran back. "What, mister?"

Levi handed her the flowers. "These lovely flowers are for such a lovely lady as yourself."

She smiled again. "Aw, thank ya, mister!" She wrapped her arms around Levi and gave him the biggest of hugs.

He hadn't been around young'uns much. Never had one ever tug at his heart and hug him and make him feel the way this little girl just had.

As she turned around and went running to the store, she hollered, "Ma! Ma! The stranger man gave me a nickel and these pretty flowers!"

A woman who appeared to be the girl's mother looked up the street at Levi and smiled and waved. He tipped his hat to the woman and began to walk up the street. He couldn't figure out where on earth Samantha could be. Maybe her father was home and she went out for a ride on the prairie, but he highly doubted it.

Sick to his stomach from wanting to see her, he walked over to the saloon. Walking through the swinging doors, he went straight to the bar.

"Whiskey," he demanded.

The barkeep poured him a shot. "Havin' a bad day there, Mr. Cord?"

Levi downed it, then slammed the glass on the bar. "Shut the hell up and pour."

Once he had his glass filled, he drank it quickly and demanded one after another. After nine or ten shots, he slammed the glass down and stormed out of the saloon. Levi tended to hold his beer quite well, however, strong whiskey was a completely different story. Give him a few shots and he was singing with the dance hall girls by the piano or fighting mad. Sometimes he would get downright depressed and agitated at every little thing.

As he staggered out of the saloon, Levi's vision had turned quite blurry and his head was spinning something awful. He looked up and saw a man coming up the street looking madder than a pissed off rattler. He wiped and blinked his eyes trying to get his vision to clear up. As the man approached, Levi realized it was none other than Mr. Parker himself. His heart sank as Samantha's father headed for him. He tried his best to stand up straight but kept wiping sweat from his brow. His face felt flushed.

"Good day to ya, sir." Levi said, trying to act unaffected by standing up straight and doing his best to look the man dead in the eye.

"Mr. Cord! Have you happened to see my daughter?"

Levi took his hat in his hand. "No sir, I can't say that I have." Why was he asking Levi? Did he know about yesterday?

"She has been gone all day, and her horse is missing as well." He looked into Levi's eyes and Levi could tell that this man despised him and his very existence.

He looked back into her father's cold dark eyes. "Sir, iffen I happen to see her I will let you know first thing."

The man looked him up and down with a look of pure disgust on his face. "I figured she had gone out huntin', crazy fool kid, but her rifle was still at the cottage." He shrugged his shoulders and gave Levi a bitter look as he continued down the street.

Doing all he could to keep from running to the stable, he attempted to patiently walk back across the street. No need to cause a scene, especially with whiskey strong on his breath. The last thing he needed was something to keep him from his mission. Where the hell was Samantha? Was she alright? He couldn't very well ask her father if she had made it home last night.

As he reached the stable, he quickly saddled up Star and headed out of town hell-bent for leather. Could something have happened to her on her way back? Horrible, terrifying thoughts raced through his mind as he tore across the prairie.

Riding south of Council Grove as fast as Star would carry him, he headed straight for Elm Creek, where he had left her the night before. As he reached the bluff, he spotted the lone cottonwood tree. Spurring Star in the flanks, he tore down the hill as fast as a raging cyclone ripping across the plains. The sun was making its way near the horizon and night was approaching quickly. Levi feared the worst. He had to find Samantha before nightfall. He had to.

SAMANTHA HAD BEEN riding every which way she could trying to find Levi. Her heart was aching for him. What if he had come to his senses about her and taken off? A feeling of emptiness consumed her as she spread a quilt down on the chilly ground. As she sat down, tears began to fill her eyes. She might never see him again, and she hadn't gotten the chance to say how she felt about him.

Her feelings scared her. How had she fallen for him so quickly? What was so captivating about him? She thought back to her first love, Isaac. He had lived a couple houses down from hers and their love had grown slowly as they aged together. When he had finally asked her to be his it had felt like yes was the only possible answer. He had been such a constant in her life that the relationship was comfortable and familiar. But when he came of age, he had been called away by the War and she had found herself alone. She became overwhelmed with loneliness. Isaac had been her first and she had been courted by a few men in the town, but never had she felt an overwhelming pull as she did with Levi. This love was passionate and effortless. It was brave and unknown, and maybe that's why she found herself getting caught up in the excitement of it all. She watched as the sun set once again over the Kansas prairie, but this time it had to be the loneliest one she had ever witnessed. Her heart was breaking, and she was falling apart.

"Beautiful sunset, ain't it?" His voice caught her off guard, and fresh tears began to flow down her cheeks.

"Levi! Oh, Levi! I thought you had left."

Levi walked up to her. "Nonsense. I love you, darlin'. I've loved you since the very moment I laid eyes on you. When you first smiled at me, I knew right then and there that I would love you for the rest of my life."

"Oh, Levi," she cried as he went on. Tears gently fell down her face.

He sank to his knees beside her. "I've never wanted anything or anyone as bad as in my whole life, the way that I want you, darlin'. You are the most beautiful woman I ever saw. Now, I know your father don't like me none and won't approve of us bein' together, but Samantha, darlin', I promise that I will love you the rest of your life."

He wrapped her in his arms and pulled her close to him. Samantha trembled. "Oh, I love you, Levi Cord."

He softly wiped the tears from her cheeks and pressed his lips to her. She closed her eyes and melted into his embrace. As he ran his fingers through her hair, she placed her hand on his chest and began to kiss his neck.

"Oh, Samantha," Levi whispered.

"Yes, Levi?"

He slid off his boots, then unlaced Samantha's boots before sliding them off. She began to slide her dress off slowly. Her heart was racing, but she had never felt so calm.

She reached over and took his hand and slowly ran it along her breasts. "Levi, my love, I seem to have the warmest feeling in my heart since I met you. And I've had the biggest smile on my face that just won't go away. I have felt so alone and hopeless for the past two years, and now I feel more alive than I ever have felt before. I know you rode into town only a couple days ago, but you have stolen my heart with one simple glance."

Levi began to breathe heavily as she placed one finger on his lips and softly said, "It's alright, Levi…I am sure this time. I love you, Levi…"

LEVI TOOK HIS hands and pulled her naked body close to him. Her figure was perfect. "God, darlin', you are so beautiful," he whispered in her ear.

She slid his arms out of his jacket and unbuttoned his vest as she kissed him. After she took off Levi's vest, she slid his shirt up over his head and placed her hands on his chest. She gently ran her fingers down to his gun belt and looked deep into his eyes.

This time, when he looked into those blue eyes, he realized she was sure about what they were about to do. This wasn't just a sexual, lustful romance…it was much deeper than that. They may have only known each other a couple days, and knew nothing of each other, but they were both sure of one thing. They knew they were both in love and had never been more in love in all their lives. What was about to happen was something neither of them had ever felt.

Samantha knelt and placed her hands onto Levi's gun belt. In all his life, he had never once let another person touch his guns. Something had changed, though. He trusted Samantha more than he had ever trusted anyone in his whole life. He knew in his heart that he loved her dearly and, for unknown reasons, she loved him too. He could see it in her eyes. He had to pay attention to the eyes, to stay alive. You never knew when someone was going to be your friend and then stab you in the back.

Still looking into his eyes, Samantha slowly unbuckled the guns and laid them to the side. She wrapped her arms around his waist and then ran her fingers along his waistline. Once she reached the front of his trousers, she unfastened them and slowly pulled them down and off. Both of their hearts were racing, and, though the air was chilly, their bodies were on fire.

They sat on the quilt and she began to kiss him on his chest. She ran her fingers all over his body, causing him to tremble. She touched the scars he had acquired over the years but asked no questions. As she kissed his body, she began to work her way down to his waist. He had never felt so amazing. It wasn't just the physical part that was overwhelming him. The true love he had for Samantha was what made this amazing moment of intimacy so wonderful and special to them both.

"Oh, Samantha…" He moaned. "I love you so much, darlin'…" He laid her down, leaned over her, and began kissing and caressing her body. The warmth of her breath upon his skin sent shivers down his spine. When he got to her breasts, he ran his fingers over places that he had dreamed of since they had met. God, it felt so right.

Moments later, Samantha began to pull Levi closer to her. Kissing his lips, she whispered, "Levi?"

"Yes, darlin'?"

"Please don't ever leave me."

Levi stared into her eyes. "Never, darlin'."

Samantha rolled on top of Levi and straddled him, her long blonde hair flowing down over her breasts. Levi pulled her close to him.

"I love the way you touch me," she whispered. He could tell she had been craving this moment of intimacy.

FOR SEVERAL HOURS, the two made the most intimate and passionate love. Although she had been with a few men before Levi, the intimacy in which he touched her and the softness in his hands made this feel different. It was as if she was right where she was always meant to be. Afterwards, Samantha lay in Levi's arms and stared up at the moon now high in the Kansas sky.

"I love you, Levi," she said softly, her breath catching.

Levi leaned over and kissed her on the forehead. "I love you too, Samantha, darlin'."

They lay in each other's arms, gazing up at the stars while caressing each other's bodies. Samantha sighed. "Did you mean what you said about never leaving me, Levi?"

He looked her in the eyes. "I promise you, darlin', that you can trust me with your heart. I would never lie to you or betray you. I love you dearly."

She leaned up and kissed him and then laid her head on his chest. He ran his fingers through her gorgeous hair. "I have never seen anything more beautiful in all my years. I truly desire you, Samantha."

She looked up at him. "I'll never break your heart, Levi."

"I know, darlin'." He leaned down and kissed her on the cheek, then the forehead. He brushed her hair behind her ears and gently rubbed his fingers along her cheek. Then he got face to face with her and they lay there staring at each other's eyes in the moonlight for several minutes. They began kissing, then she crawled on top of him and the two made love once more.

THEY LAY IN each other's arms exhausted and laughing as they tried to catch their breath. Levi looked over at Samantha and noticed the moonlight reflecting an intoxicating glow in her delicate baby blue eyes. She was so beautiful. Unlike anything he had ever seen before. He had seen some of the most remarkable and gorgeous sceneries over the years, but nothing that compared to the beauty of this prairie rose.

Lying there together that chilly night, Levi asked the question he dreaded the most. "Are ya plannin' on goin' home tonight, darlin'?" He wondered what her father would think when he woke up the next morning and found her gone. Hell, what was he thinking now? Was he out looking for her?

"I don't want to leave you, Levi." She pulled him close.

Feeling guilty, he looked at her and said, "I have some unfinished business to take care of, darlin', before I can return and give you the life you deserve."

"Oh, Levi, promise me that you will be back for me. I can tell you are a very determined man and that nothing can stop you when you set your sight on something. Please let that be me."

Levi softly kissed her forehead. "I promise."

As the moon drew higher in the sky, Levi got up and got his bedroll off his saddle. After tending to the horses, he walked over to Samantha and wrapped her in his wool blanket. "Darlin', as much as this tears me apart, we really should be getting you home."

"But why, Levi?"

"Darlin', someday you will look back and understand. It will all work out, I promise."

"When will I see you again?"

Levi thought a moment, then, looking in her eyes, said, "I will be ridin' out of Council Grove at first light, but I will return for you one day."

She was silent as Levi got dressed and tucked his trousers into his boots, then strapped his Colts across his hips. Samantha dressed herself, then reached over and grabbed her boots at the edge of the quilt.

As she began to lace them, she asked, "When will you be back, love?"

He wasn't quite sure just how long his unfinished business was going to take, but he knew it was going to be a rough trail since he had lost all sign of the saddle trash of a man he was tracking. He turned to Samantha and placed her hand in his. "Darlin', do you think that after tonight I could stay away from Council Grove for too long?" He wrapped his arms around her and squeezed her ever so tight.

Though tears glittered in her eyes, she smiled. "I love you, Levi Cord."

Levi's heart felt more complete than ever before.

AFTER SEVERAL LONG, passionate kisses, Levi helped her up onto her horse. Mounting up, he walked Star alongside Lightning and they headed toward town. Samantha snuggled herself deep in Levi's blanket. She could smell his scent, and it made her feel warm and happy. She wanted to smell this very scent for the rest of her life.

As the two rode with the light of the harvest moon, they spotted a small herd of buffalo along the trail. A pack of coyotes howled off to the east. Shortly later, another pack answered to the south, and then a lone coyote answered ahead of them toward town. This one was much closer. Too close for Samantha's comfort. Levi turned to her as she shivered, and he grinned. She felt something different than before. She felt safe and needed. She felt perfect.

Once they reached the outskirts of town, the two stopped to part ways. Levi, still in the saddle, leaned over and placed his hand upon Samantha's cheek. "I'll be comin' back for you, Samantha. You can bet on it!"

She smiled as a tear gently flowed down her nose. "Oh, I love you, Levi."

Levi wiped the tear away. "I love you, darlin'. Don't you ever doubt that or forget it for one second."

Reaching into a little velvet coin purse that she had, she pulled out a picture and handed it to Levi. "I want you to have this, Levi, and when you're far away and finish tendin' to your unfinished business, remember me and come back to me."

Levi took the picture and looked at it in the moonlight. "It's a beautiful likeness of you. Thank you." He pulled his silver watch out from his vest pocket and opened it up to place the picture inside.

"Before you go, Levi, I also want you to have this." She reached into her saddlebags and pulled out a leather bracelet with beautiful turquoise stones on it. "Hold out your hand, love." As he obeyed, she placed the bracelet on him. "I made this specially for you."

Levi bit his lip, and she could see he was fighting tears. "Darlin', I will think of you often. Every time the sun sets over the horizon, or when I gaze at the blue skies, I will think of you."

She reached into her saddlebags and pulled out a light-yellow wild rag and handed it to him. "I also want you to have this, Levi. It will keep the cold breeze off your neck and help keep the trail dust out of your face." Levi smiled, taking off his dirty old wild rag and tying the new one around his neck.

Kissing for the last time, the two parted ways.

As Samantha began to ride north back into town, she turned back to Levi. "I'll be seein' you, Levi Cord."

Chapter 5

A long and miserable month had come and gone since Levi and Samantha had parted ways. Each passing day, Samantha craved Levi's warm embrace, his kisses, and his crooked smile. She longed to hear his voice and see his mysterious blue eyes. She craved his presence. Every night in bed, she would find herself dreaming of the day he would return to Council Grove on that palomino and rescue her from all her loneliness and heartache. She had fallen in love with Levi so quickly, but she could tell by the way that he touched her and looked deep into her eyes that he had fallen deeply for her as well. She had never felt the way she did with anyone else before. She loved everything about him. Well, except the fact that he was hunting a man that had killed his past sweetheart. Samantha knew in her heart that he was a determined man and that he had to do it, yet she feared for his safety each and every hour that passed. With the passing of each day she wondered if somewhere out there he was thinking of her.

Each night just before sunset, Samantha would ride Lightning out to the very spot on Elm Creek where they had made love. She would spread her blanket out and stare off into the sunset wondering if Levi too was watching the same sunset. She missed him more than anything. She couldn't believe she had fallen so head over heels for this drifting cowboy so fast. Hell, she had only met him some three days before he had left Council Grove like the prairie breeze. The powerful connection between these two hearts was so strong that neither of them could have stopped it if they had wanted too. They were just what each other needed. They were both still young and knew that when they were finally together all their troubles and lonesomeness would go away. Samantha could tell he was an honest man and that he would be forever devoted to her and only her. She knew he had gone from saloon to saloon and had shared a bed with all sorts of dance hall gals and soiled doves along the way. She didn't hold it against him. She knew he had been searching for whatever affection he could find. Samantha was an honest woman and she didn't blame him one damn bit. She knew he had lived a rough life and, like her, was just searching for his purpose in life.

They were both very much alike, Levi and Samantha. She was a true Kansas lady with a heart of pure gold. She loved the outdoors, and, unlike most women of the day, she loved to try her hand at fishing. When she was little, her father would often take her to a nearby field by their farm, and they would lie on the ground and watch the stars. Watching the stars on that quilt with Levi, she had felt the same way she had when she was a little girl...safe and loved and appreciated.

One night as Samantha and her father were having supper at their cottage, Samantha looked across the table. "Father?"

"Yes?" He wiped his mustache with a hankie.

"Do you reckon I'll ever get outta this damn small cottage? I wanna big house with lots of cattle and some of the finest horses in the country. I want a big place where Dally can run and chase rabbits and get into mischief."

Father got a disgusted look on his face. "Damn it, Samantha! That damn man is no good for you! He's a low-down killer! Folks say that he's been to prison! You deserve better than that. I'd hardly call him a man. He's a no-good drifter, to say the least, that will do nothin' but drag you down. You must get him outta your fool head this instant!"

Samantha's heart sank and began to fill with anger. How did he know about her and Levi? She wiped her face with a cloth napkin. "Father, he's not a bad man! You have no right to judge him! He's a caring and soft-hearted man. You can't hold his past against him."

He slammed his fork down on the table loudly. "Damn it! A man like that will never change! Never! That's who he is, and I won't permit you to see him! Is that understood?"

Samantha jumped up out of her chair. "Not hardly!" She stormed out of the room. As she lay on her bed, she closed her tear-filled eyes and her mind drifted off to the thought of Levi. She had been looking for a reason to get out of that tiny cottage and she had found it. She didn't want to go against her father and upset him, but she couldn't change the way her heart felt for Levi. Yet she feared the day she would finally go to her father and tell him she was leaving with Levi.

MANY A LONELY night had passed, and several hundred miles west of Council Grove in the heart of the Rocky Mountains, Levi was sitting next to a small campfire that he had started with some dead branches. He shivered as the cold December wind blew down the draw and down the back of his neck. He tugged at his collar on his coat and pulled it up to block the wind from going down his shirt. It had snowed about thirteen inches during the night and it was bitter cold. As Levi sat next to his fire shivering, he cupped his hands around a hot tin cup of coffee. The steam drifted its way through the mountain air.

Levi had been informed by a marshal in a nearby town that four saddle tramps had robbed a federal paymaster on the stage line, just east of Monarch Pass, two days before. The marshal and a posse were hot on their trail when the snow came up and closed the pass, forcing them to return to town. There was a five-thousand-dollar reward for the leader of the gang, and a thousand-dollar reward for each of the other three outlaws. The marshal in Denver was also offering another five hundred dollars for the three outlaws and a thousand dollars for the leader.

Levi decided he would take a ride up along Greens Creek and up Pass Creek trail and take a look. Having been elk hunting with his father in that area, he knew the territory well and figured a lot of the drainage ditches would make a great hideaway for outlaws. If they hadn't been snowed in, that is. With the pass being snowed off, the outlaws couldn't have gotten far. In some spots up there in the high country, there was close to twenty-five feet of snow.

Once he reached the spot where the stage had been held up, he found where the outlaws had tried to cover up their tracks in the snow. As he got down from his horse and was searching for signs, he noticed that one of the horses was missing a shoe. That was sure going to slow them down for sure. After searching the area for a couple hours, he finally picked up with their trail and rode as far as he could until the sun had gone down behind the pass. He set up camp and prepared a small fire, not wanting to make much smoke that could easily be smelled by the outlaws up ahead on the trail.

As he sat there cupping his hands around his cup of coffee, he heard a lone wolf begin to howl just up the down the trail they had come from. Shortly after, a second one started in, and then a third. Star snorted and stomped the snowy ground and stared into the darkness. With as much snow as the pass had gotten, game was scarce, and these wolves were a pack hunting for some easy food. Levi and Star were the perfect choice on the menu. Levi feared that if they decided to attack, he would have to shoot them, and he couldn't afford to risk the outlaws hearing his rifle and knowing he was on their trail.

"Easy, girl..." he whispered to Star. "Easy girl."

Several minutes passed and the snow began to start falling once again. As the crystal-like snowflakes began to fall on the embers of the fire, Levi watched them melt with a pop and sizzle. Looking up the trail, Star's ears stood straight up as she began to breathe heavily and snort. The horse knew something was out there.

"Easy, girl," Levi said as he prepared himself for an attack. "Two-legged or four?" The horse nodded her head up and down four times and Levi knew then that the wolves were coming closer. Standing up and walking over to Star, he slid the Winchester out of the scabbard. He cocked the lever action to load a loaded cartridge into the chamber, then slid the tie downs off his Colts. Looking up the trail, he heard a wolf howl, much closer than before. The pack had to be just out of the firelight.

A second one howled just behind them, and then, out of nowhere, one of the wolves jumped out of the darkness and onto Star's back hindquarters and sank its razor-sharp teeth and claws into the mare's flesh. Levi swung his carbine with all his might, hitting the wolf against the head with the walnut stock. The wolf hit the ground and scrambled up. As it began to charge the mare for the second time, a second wolf came charging in and began biting Levi's leg just above his right boot. Trying to shake the vicious bloodthirsty wolf off his leg, he could feel the wolf's teeth tearing at his flesh. Swinging his carbine a second time, he struck the wolf in the ribs, knocking it to the snowy ground. Before the wolf could get up, Levi cracked his carbine over its head, crushing the skull.

As the second wolf jumped onto Star's back and went to bury its teeth into her neck, a third wolf jumped out of the darkness and onto Levi's back. Sinking its teeth in Levi's shoulders, the wolf began to go for his neck and for the kill. As Levi dropped to his knees, the wolf began tearing at his back. Levi pulled his bone-handled knife from his boot. He grabbed the snarling wolf by the neck and flipped it over his head and to the ground. As he pinned the wolf to the ground, he buried his knife deep in the wolf's neck. The wolf let out a loud whimper and a yelp that could have been heard clear up the canyon. Pulling the blood-covered blade out of its neck, Levi cut the wolf's throat, and the wolf fell to the freezing snow, lifeless.

Catching his breath quickly, Levi turned around to see another wolf, a big white male, sinking his teeth into Star's neck. His heart racing and his adrenaline flowing wild, he raised back his arm and threw his knife at the wolf. Aiming for the wolf's chest, the knife struck far back and sunk into the wolf's front shoulder. Snarling and growling something awful, the wolf then lunged at Levi's face. Now the wolf was not only hungry, he was injured and madder than hell. Rolling to the ground, Levi wrapped his arms around the wolf and tried to pry its teeth from his arm. As the wolf bit his arm, the two rolled into the snow just feet from the startled mare. Bucking and kicking, Star kicked the wolf right in the face, dropping it to the ground. Levi rolled away as fast as he could just as Star stomped the wolf to death with her sharp hooves.

As soon as Levi was sure that all three of the wolves were dead and that there were no more in the pack, he crawled over to the fire and drifted out of consciousness. Hours later, the fire began to die down and go out and Levi, still unconscious, began to get chilled and started to shiver badly. Star limped her way over to where Levi's blanket was lying next to the fire and picked it up with her teeth. She covered him up to warm him up from the winter cold, then laid down next to him, shielding him from the deadly northern wind as it gusted down from the pass, just as a mare would do with a newborn foul.

As the mountain sky began to crack the first light of dawn, Levi awoke to notice the mare lying next to him. Without her beside him to block the northern wind and share her body heat, Levi would have surely died. No doubt about it. Throughout all the terrifying pain and agony, he attempted a smile. This wasn't the first time that she had saved his life, and more than likely not the last either. Lying on the freezing cold ground, he stared up the snowy trail. There was a new six or seven inches of snow covering the trail now.

He sighed, knowing the snow would cover the outlaws' tracks, and he felt the stinging pain where he had been bitten by the wolf. Moaning as he sat up, he looked around, trying to find his carbine. After digging in the freshly fallen snow where the attack had taken place the night before, he finally discovered it. Anger and hurt overcame him as he noticed the cracked walnut stock. Levi had had it engraved with the initials L.C. when he had bought it new in Ellsworth at Drovers Mercantile for fifteen dollars. That was a good month's wages. The rifle was still useable, however, that wolf's skull had done quite a number on it.

Once he found his blood-covered knife, he went and cut some branches from the base of an old dead pine tree. Clearing the snow where he had his fire the night before, he began to start another fire. After what seemed like forever, he had a nice bed of coals finally going. He filled his tin cup with snow and set it next to the fire. He took out his bottle of whiskey from his saddlebags and laid the blade of his knife in the fire. Once the snow in the cup had melted, he took his wild rag and soaked it in the water. He carefully cleaned the blood from his wounds, then poured whiskey into each bite and claw mark. He had been bitten once each in the shoulder, leg, and left arm, and he had deep gashes down his back from the wolf's claws.

As the whiskey poured into his wounds, his whole body tensed up and he clenched his teeth just like he had done several times before while digging out bullets and patching stab wounds. There weren't any doctors out on the trail, and if there was anything that a cowboy feared most, it was a sawbones of a doctor. Most of them were drunkards, which made it that much more nerve-wracking. That was the reason every cowboy learned to doctor themselves, as well as their horse. A man in this big sky country without a horse was damn lucky if he made it long.

Once he had finished pouring whiskey into his wounds, he took the scorching red-hot blade from his knife and placed it to each wound. The pain was excruciating. After finishing tending to himself, he did the same with Star. She trusted him and didn't put up any resistance. The bond between them was something to cherish and behold. Levi finished tending to her wounds, then put out the fire and tied his blanket back onto his saddle. As he did, he thought about when he had wrapped Samantha in that old worn-out wool blanket while they lay under the full moon. Her eyes had sparkled so lovely in the starlight. He missed her so much. For that moment, all the pain seemed to disappear.

After mounting, he began to follow the trail up the pass. Riding about an hour or so, they reached the high country, just below timberline. The wind was dead calm now, and the whole mountainside was quiet…too quiet. Looking up into the sky, a golden eagle soared over the pass. Levi hadn't been up this high for several years, but he knew most every elk and goat trail around here.

He spotted a place where someone had camped the night before. Riding in a circle around the camp, he picked up some horse tracks, three of them, all shod. Indians didn't shoe their ponies, and that was a sure way for a man to tell the difference between white man and Indian pony tracks. The only reason an Indian would be riding a shod pony was if he had stolen it. When he spotted the three sets of tracks, he wondered if it happened to be the outlaws that he was trailing, or trappers that were hunting this high country. There were four outlaws, and only three sets of tracks. If they were the outlaws, he knew they had split up somewhere, so he circled the camp until he picked up the other rider. Sure enough, the fourth set of tracks was a horse that had lost a shoe.

"That's them, I reckon, girl." Levi said Star.

Following the tracks, Levi could tell they were only a short distance ahead. Not more than an hour, likely. Taking his time, he rode along, watching to see which way they were headed. He knew the only way out of there was back down the trail and right through him. They probably had no idea that he was anywhere around, and he was going to keep it that way as long as he could. There were four of them and only one of him.

He noticed the tracks were starting to get much fresher than they had been when he had first spotted them. That could only mean one thing. They were beginning to run out of trail and were starting to slow up. He looked over the countryside and saw the outlaws were boxed in. He knew if he went any further, he would run out of cover, so he decided to hole up down the trail a piece where there was still plenty of trees for cover. After tying Star to a nearby pine stump, he grabbed the box of cartridges from his saddlebags. Putting them in his coat pocket, he took off on foot up the trail.

About a hundred yards or so up the trail, he knelt and studied the tracks. They were just minutes ahead. They were starting to go in circles, and Levi knew they were now trying to decide which way to go. Studying the terrain and looking for plenty of cover, he sat up in a small grove of aspens that were surrounded by big boulders on all four sides. It was a perfect spot for an ambush. Levi had been a bushwhacker for the South during the War, and he had hidden out several times, preparing for an ambush in a lot less cover than this. The outlaws had to come straight back down the trail, and he would be waiting. He was sure they didn't have enough grub to last them two or three days, and he was prepared to wait them out if he had to.

Once, back in Missouri, Levi and some other guerilla soldiers starved out a group of blue-bellies. The Yankees had only what they had in their pockets, and the Rebs had coffee and two bottles of rotgut whiskey. Levi and his seven companions were all farmers and homesteaders who had their land taken away by the carpet-bagging Yankees. They were experienced hunters and outdoorsmen and were capable of holding out as long as it took the blue-bellies to give up. The Yanks were mostly city folk. School teachers and shopkeepers that had never been out of the big cities prior to the War. Four days went by, and the Yanks began to get mighty hungry and weak. They didn't even have the strength to raise their muskets. On the fifth morning, they tried to make a run for it, charging down the hill, dragging their muskets on the ground. Shortly after the sun had come up that chilly February morning in the hills of Missouri, those Yanks came charging. Levi and the Rebs waited until they were too close to miss and then opened fire. It looked like a turkey shoot. After the smoke had finally cleared, twenty-three blue-bellies lay dead on the Ozark soil. Not one of the Rebs had been even slightly wounded.

As Levi got set up in the grove of aspens, he pulled the box of cartridges out from his coat pocket. Opening the box, he set it on a rock next to his knee so he could get to them quickly. He leaned the barrel of his carbine over a boulder in front of him and aimed up the trail to be sure he was comfortable shooting from that position.

As Levi sat there, he found himself distracted with the never-ending thoughts of the lovely Miss Samantha back in the Kansas Flint Hills. The reward he planned to collect for bringing in the four outlaws would be just what he needed to start a new life somewhere with his beautiful prairie rose. The terms for bringing them in was "dead or alive". That made it that much easier for Levi. He figured if he killed one or two of them, maybe the rest would give up, but he doubted it. You could never tell with men of this caliber. They were desperate, and you could never be too sure just what they would do to escape. This made them extremely dangerous. Some of the most dangerous men in the country had run these canyons a time or two.

About half an hour later, Levi began to hear crunching in the snow up ahead on the trail. He could hear the outlaws' horses' hooves clashing on the rocks as they came riding back down the trail right toward him. Levi had been in well over twenty shooting engagements and was perfectly calm as he waited.

Minutes later, Levi heard a horse snort some fifty yards up the trail. It came closer, straight toward him. It was a shaggy strawberry roan. On her back sat a tall man wearing a buffalo hide coat. He had a mean weathered face and sandy blond hair. He wore a ten-gallon gray hat with his wild rag wrapped over the crown and tied under his chin to keep the freezing cold northern air off his ears. At his side was a Winchester carbine that was stashed away in its scabbard. The other three men followed closely behind him, shivering, and probably wishing they had chosen another lifestyle working in a warm saloon or shop somewhere with a big potbellied stove, instead of running and hiding out in the hills with empty bellies and near-frostbitten hands and toes.

One of the men was riding a tall gray stud that was limping on his left hoof. Levi could tell right off that this was the horse that was missing a shoe. If there was anything that he couldn't stomach, it was two things. One was a man laying a violent hand on a woman or child, and the second was a man riding a lame horse. There just wasn't any call for it. Levi had a great love for horses and respected them. This man obviously didn't, and Levi decided he had it coming.

The other men rode mustang ponies that looked like they had been ridden hard for weeks. Levi's stomach turned as he saw how poorly treated these horses were. Pure hate and anger flowed through his veins as the men rode closer. He had half a mind to just unload his carbine into the four of them right then and there and fill them with hot lead. If it had been a year or so back, he wouldn't have thought twice. It was easy money.

When the first man, wearing the gray hat, came to within thirty yards, Levi pulled his knife from his boot and removed the tie downs from his Colts. When the man got to within ten yards, the others about twenty-five yards behind him, Levi took his bowie knife and took careful aim at the man's face, then threw the knife as hard as he could. The man never saw it coming. The antler handle of the knife struck him hard in the face, making him fall off the back of his horse.

Hitting the ground, the man grabbed his face. "What in the Sam Hill was that?" the man yelled. "Son of a bitch!"

Levi sat back, hunkered down below the boulder where he had his rifle rested, and chuckled to himself. Poor bastard.

"Somethin' broke my damn nose!" the man yelled in agony.

One of the men laughed. "Did that tree jump out and bite ya there, Jim?"

"Shut the hell up, you stupid bastard!" Jim yelled, still holding his face.

The other three men laughed and joked as he stood and tried to get back on his horse. Before he could mount, Levi lined down his trusty carbine and put his sights on the man's chest. As he pulled the hammer back, he took a deep breath, and as he exhaled, he gently squeezed the trigger. The bullet tore through Jim's buffalo coat and dropped him to the ground.

As his horse took off, Levi jumped from the rocks and grabbed the reins. Before the men could reach under their coats to draw their guns, Levi was behind the horse, firing one of his Colts under the horse's neck. As quickly as he could fire that Colt, he let the lead fly as he led the horse to the rocks. Tying the horse to a fallen aspen, he ran behind the boulder and grabbed his carbine. The men had scattered for the brush, but Levi knew they couldn't get far.

He reloaded his Colt, then put a shell in the carbine to replace the one he had shot. As he reloaded, the outlaws fired wildly all over the rocks.

"Jim?" one man called out. "Jim!"

"He's dead!" another voice yelled.

Levi snuck down low and crawled through the snow to another boulder along the trail about ten yards out. From there he could see one of the men staring up into the rocks where his fallen comrade lay. Levi leaned his carbine on top of a fallen pine and squeezed the trigger. The shot rang out, echoing down the trail. The bullet struck the tree next to the outlaw, inches from his face.

Two shots rang out from the left, and Levi saw another man firing from behind a rock. He spun his rifle toward the man and began firing wild from the hip. Bullets splattered the rock he was hiding behind. Levi began to run toward a clump of brush some fifty feet away then slipped on a frozen rock and fell to the ground. Using the stock of his carbine, he lifted himself up and headed for the brush. A shot fired from the left. Another from the right. When he reached the brush, he laid down on the ground and crawled a couple of feet further to a large boulder that would provide him with more cover.

Shots were firing from both sides of him. As he looked to his left, he saw one of the outlaws' horses standing alone. Its rider had taken cover when the shooting had started. Levi thought that if he could get to the horse, he would be able to tie it up and pack its dead rider belly down over the saddle. That is, however, after he killed him.

Levi spotted movement to his right. It was one of the men trying to circle around behind him. He took aim with the carbine and put the bullet right into the man's right leg. Spinning around, the man fired wildly. Levi loaded another shell into his gun and sent the next bullet right through the man's temple. Taking some cartridges from his belt, he reloaded his carbine. Two men were dead, and that meant there were only two more to go.

"Ben?" one of the men yelled out. "Ben, where the hell are ya?"

Levi listened to where the man was shouting from and spotted him trying to get to his horse. Levi knew that if he reached the horse, he had a good chance of getting away. He shot at the man, making him stay down the hill and not get a chance to reach his horse. As Levi shot, another shot rang out. The bullet tore through Levi's coat, just under his armpit. Amazingly, the bullet missed Levi by less than an inch. He took off running, both of the men firing their pistols at him. As he ran, he fired his carbine from his hip just as fast as he could jack out the shells.

Just before he reached the rocks where he had first set up, he saw one of the men running for his horse. Spinning his rifle around as fast as he could toward the man, he pulled the trigger, only to discover the carbine was empty. He let it fall, and, grabbing for his Colts, he drew and fired them both, hitting the man in the shoulder and in the cheek. As the man fell to the ground, Levi spun to see the other man aiming a Winchester right at him. He lunged for the ground just as the man fired. The bullet struck him in the back. Dropping to the ground, Levi tried to crawl to cover, but the man had run up and now pointed the rifle to the back of his head.

"Hold it, you son of a bitch!" the man yelled. "Make one twitch and I'll send you to hell directly!"

Levi lay there in the cold snow, as the man ordered.

"Charlie?" the man hollered. "Hey, Charlie? You alright?"

"Yeah!" the second man replied. "Dodgasted bushwhacker got me in the shoulder!"

"I got him!" the man replied as he put the barrel of his rifle against Levi's head. "Where's Jim and Ben?"

"Dead," Charlie answered. "Both dead."

Charlie, who had been shot in the shoulder, caught his horse and came running up the hill to where Levi lay. "You sum bitch killed my brother! I'm aimin' to cut you in half!"

He pulled out a knife from his boot and leaned over Levi when the other man hollered out, "Hold it! Let's find out who the hell he is first." The man with the rifle looked down and kicked Levi over on his back with his boot.

"What in the hell are ya, mister, some kinda law?" He pressed his rifle against Levi's temple.

Levi's heart was racing, and he could hardly breathe.

"Damn it, mister, I asked you a damn question!" the man shouted.

When Levi refused to answer, they began to kick and beat him with the butts of their rifles. They took off his gun belt and noticed the twin Colts.

Charlie put his knife back into his boot and began twirling the guns. "Woowhee, Arch, lookie here at these fancy Colts." He put the gun belt on and tightened it up.

Arch took Levi's hat off his head and put it on his, then he leaned down to take off Levi's boots, which he then put on his own feet.

Levi could feel a sharp burning pain from where the butt of the rifles had hit his head, and blood was trickling down into his eye. Blinking his eyes, he saw the Charlie walking over to his horse and getting a rope of the saddle. Levi had been beaten several times with the men's rifles and had taken several kicks to the ribs and face. His head was spinning, and he couldn't hardly see anything beyond a blur. He was pretty sure he was on the verge of passing out.

After Charlie fetched his rope, he walked over to Levi and rolled him over onto his stomach. He tied both of Levi's hands behind his back and gave him one last kick to the head, nearly knocking him out. The two men went through his pockets, taking his watch and the twelve dollars he had in his money belt.

As he picked up his watch, Arch opened it. "Woowhee! Lookie here, Charlie." He took Samantha's picture from the watch and turned it over. "It says here, 'to my dearest Levi Cord, love, Samantha'." He guffawed. "Ain't she purty?"

Levi winced as the man tossed the picture aside. Samantha's image lay on top of the snow next to his head.

About half an hour after trying to catch the other horses, the two men spotted the horse that Levi had tied in the grove of trees earlier.

"Charlie, over here!" Arch yelled. "Here's Jim's horse."

Charlie ran down the trail to where the horse was tied and mounted the horse. He rode over to Levi and pointed Levi's Colt at him.

"Lookie there, you sum bitch. I'm gonna send ya to hell with your own damn gun!" Charlie said.

"No!" Arch yelled. "Leave him! There's no way in hell he's gonna make it, and besides we need all the lead we got!"

As the two men turned to ride away, the one yelled, "I'll see you in hell, you sum bitch!"

As they rode on down the trail, Levi could hear them talking. "Well, well, well, what have we got here?" He knew they had spotted Star tied where he had left her. He begged for his body to move, to get up and save her. That horse was his partner and he'd be damned if he had to live this life without her. Levi urged his body to rise but his limbs were too weak.

As Levi lay there on the freezing cold mountain floor, Samantha's picture blew up to his cheek. Just before he closed his eyes, he saw clouds beginning to darken the Colorado sky, a sure sign a snowstorm was working its way toward the pass.

LEVI AWOKE TO find himself in horrific pain. His entire body felt as tight as a worn-out piece of cowhide. He was frozen stiff and had no strength to even move his head. About an hour went by before he gained enough strength to raise and turn his head. As he opened his eyes, his head began to spin something fierce. Once he began to regain his vision, he noticed something was sticking up out of the snow next to him. Lying there for several more agonizing minutes, he began to gain some of his strength. As he tried to move his arm, he felt where the bullet had broken one of his ribs. Easing his arm up away from his back, he could feel the rope that the outlaws had tied him up with. As he looked to see what was laying in the snow, he realized it was the picture.

"Samantha!" he whispered. His heart began to pump the frozen blood through his veins. He felt more strength at that very moment when he laid eyes on that picture than he could ever imagine. He closed his eyes and laid his head on the cold ground. "I love you, Samantha, oh, how I love you," he whispered. His whole life flashed before his very eyes as he lay there freezing and weak. He thought of that day he had ran into Samantha in front of the mercantile. The first time their eyes met and she smiled at him, the day at Elm Creek when she held his hand, and the first time he had kissed her. He thought of the night they had made love and how soft her skin felt. He thought of the way her eyes sparkled in the starlight and how they never strayed when she talked to him. He thought about everything he had told her and how she was going feel when he didn't return to Council Grove for her. A tear gently rolled down his cheek and his heart sank in his deep in his chest. He couldn't hurt her like that. She had been hurt too much in her life and he had promised her that he would never leave her. He had to fight. He couldn't let go now. For the first time in his life, things finally made perfect sense. He had met the woman of his dreams, the one whom he wanted to share the rest of his life with. He wanted to give her everything she dreamed of. He wanted to wake up next to her every morning for the rest of his life.

Chapter 6

"Good day, Miss Samantha," the teller said as Samantha entered the bank. "What can I do for ya?"

Samantha smiled. "Good day, Mr. Harvey. I would like to visit with Mr. Hennson, if I may, sir, regarding our mortgage."

"Yes, ma'am. He'll be right with ya shortly."

"Thank ya kindly." As she waited, her mind fluttered back to when she and Levi had made love alongside the creek. A small smile crept across her face and she felt her cheeks flush.

"Miss Samantha, how can I help ya today?" came a voice from behind her. She turned around to see Mr. Hennson, the bank president. "By golly, ma'am, you seemed a thousand miles away just now."

She shook her head, trying to focus on the reason she was at the bank. "My apologies, sir."

He smiled. "What is it I can do for ya today, ma'am?"

"I would like to discuss matters regarding our mortgage."

"Certainly. Let's just step here into my office." Mr. Hennson opened the door to his office. "Please, Miss Samantha, have a seat."

Samantha smiled and took a seat across from Mr. Hennson's big shiny oak desk. The chair behind the desk was made from a beautiful black-and-white-spotted longhorn cowhide and had shiny black horns for the legs and arm rests. She looked at Mr. Hennson as he sat down. "I would like to withdraw twenty-five dollars to pay off our mortgage this month. That should be enough to cover the past three months."

Mr. Hennson looked at her and scratched his head, and she could tell by the look in his eyes that something was wrong. Dread filled her. "Ma'am, I hate to be the bearer of bad news, but it's the thirtieth of November."

Embarrassed, Samantha said, "I'm truly sorry, sir. It's just that since we lost the boardinghouse, things have been rather rough."

Mr. Hennson took off his spectacles and laid them on his desk. "Have you ever considered getting yourself a job, ma'am?"

Samantha drew back, trying to hide her disgust. To ask a woman to work was disrespectful, distasteful, and downright plain rude. She imagined if Levi had heard Mr. Hennson ask her that question, he more than likely would have shot him right there. "No, I have not considered it. My father wouldn't cotton to the idea." She really didn't have the slightest idea how her father would feel about the idea of her taking a job, and, honestly, she didn't care much neither, but she felt her dignity begin to return as she offered the excuse.

"Ma'am," Mr. Hennson said. "If ya don't have enough to pay your mortgage from June through December by the end of the year, I'm afraid you and your father will be losing your cottage. The twenty-five dollars that you wish to withdraw from your account to pay for the past three months will leave you at four hundred and seventy-five dollars. If you don't have the full amount by the thirty-first of December, you will lose the cottage. You've missed too many months as it is, which is in breach of the contract your father signed."

Samantha sat there in that tiny little bank office with tears in her eyes. "Not again…" she whispered. They had already lost their boardinghouse, and she couldn't stand the thought of failing once again.

"I'm sorry, ma'am, but my hands are tied."

"How much do we have left in our account?"

He looked at the ledger. "After you withdraw the twenty-five dollars, you will have thirty-five dollars and thirty-two cents."

Samantha did the calculation in her head. "That's still four hundred and fourteen dollars." Her heart sank.

"Four hundred and fourteen dollars and sixty-eight cents to be exact, ma'am." He settled his spectacles on his nose.

"There's no way," she cried.

He shook his head. "I'm sorry, ma'am. I'm truly sorry. You and your father are good folk. Times are mighty hard these days."

Samantha bit her tongue. What in the hell did this stupid bastard know about hard times? She looked through her coin purse and counted all that she had inside. Two dollars and twenty-four cents. Looking back up, she asked, "Could we get a loan of some sort to pay the back months till now?"

"I'm afraid not, ma'am."

Struggling to keep her composure, Samantha got up from her chair. "Well, Mr. Hennson, thank you for your time."

He looked at his watch. "I'm sorry, ma'am. I am truly sorry."

Samantha left the bank. She had to figure out just how they were going to come up with enough money to pay the mortgage and not lose their cottage. When they had moved back to Council Grove, everything had seemed to be just perfect. Now it was all falling apart, piece by piece. She couldn't wait until Levi rode back into town to her rescue and take her away to start a new life.

Walking across the street, she decided to check at the café to see if there was any possible way she could work. It was no time to let pride or disgust get in the way, and she knew her father wouldn't have any better ideas. Washing dishes or waiting on tables to try to make a little extra money to help pay their mortgage would be worth it.

As she walked by the saloon, she gazed in the windows and noticed the dance hall girls all sitting at a table. They were all wearing fancy dresses and feathers, and each one of them wore black lace and garters on their legs. A thought that she had never even dreamed of considering came to her. She was broke and desperate. She was young and attractive. She was shaped as well as the other girls, if not better. Girls in that profession usually were young, desperate, lonely girls that had nowhere else to turn. And they made darn good money tending to the cowboys coming into town off the trail. Could she be one of those girls?

As she gazed through the window, she felt someone's hand rest on her shoulder. "Miss Samantha, ma'am?"

Startled, she jumped, then turned to see the owner of the boardinghouse. "Oh, Mr. Schmidt, you startled me."

"I apologize, ma'am. Is everything alright?"

Samantha looked at the old man. He was in his mid-seventies, and he wore a white mustache and always combed his white hair to the side. He was a handsome man for his age. "Why, yes, yes, it is."

"Ma'am, I know we didn't get started on the right foot when I first came to Council Grove. I want you to know that I never meant to put you and your father out of business. I'm sorry for the inconvenience that I have caused."

Samantha looked him in the eye. "Mr. Schmidt, sir, it's not your fault. You have a beautiful boardinghouse. I know you never intentionally tried to put us out of business. My father may not see it that way, but I do. You're a good man, Mr. Schmidt, and the Lord has blessed you."

He looked up the street toward the church. "Ma'am, I have noticed lately that you haven't been to church on Sundays. Is everything alright?"

Samantha wanted so badly to open up to somebody, but who would even understand? "Yes sir. Everything is alright. It's just been a busy week."

"Since I come to Council Grove, you have always had a smile on your face. If ya don't mind me sayin', ma'am, the past year or so you seem really down and depressed. You look like a lost soul, Miss Samantha. I know it's none of my business, ma'am, but I've been told on numerous occasions that I'm a mighty good listener, iffen ya ever need someone to talk to sometime."

Samantha looked into his brown eyes and knew he was an honest and decent man. She hadn't talked to him much before. When they saw each other in church on Sundays, she would always talk to his wife Sue. When they had lost the boardinghouse, though, she had found herself avoiding her out of discomfort from the situation. "Thank ya kindly, Mr. Schmidt. It's just been kinda rough lately since we lost the boardinghouse. Our mortgage is way past due and I haven't the slightest idea how we're going to pay for it. It's just that…" Her voice began to crack, and she paused.

"What is it, dear?" the old man asked.

"It's just that, things have really changed. They're not what they use to be, not at all like I had pictured." A tear fell down her nose and Mr. Schmidt pulled out his handkerchief from his coat pocket and wiped it away.

"Miss Samantha, you're young and got the whole world in front of ya. Ya got your whole life ahead. Sometimes we fall, but that is when we just get right back up and pull up our bootstraps. We shake off and start over. We are never too old to change. We all make mistakes in life, ma'am, and that's how we learn. Life is much too short to waste it away being sad and blue. You should get out of Council Grove for a while. Go relax somewhere special and try to forget about your worries."

"It's so hard," cried Samantha. She took the handkerchief he offered and wiped her eyes.

"I know, dear. That's why we have the good Lord to comfort us with his love and help us back up when we fall. He cares, ma'am. You have such a beautiful smile…that is, when you do smile. In the past two years I hadn't seen much of that smile, until about a month or so ago."

Samantha looked up. "A month ago?"

Mr. Schmidt grinned an ornery little grin under his white mustache. "When that stranger fella rode into town."

Samantha thought she was about to have a heart attack. Could he know about her and Levi? Her hands began to sweat, and her pulse raced out of control. She had no idea what to say.

He chuckled. "It's alright. I was in your shoes once myself. When I was a young lad in St. Louis, I was workin' at the telegraph office when the 12 o'clock stage come in. The most beautiful woman I ever laid eyes on in my life got down. She was something out of a Tennyson poem. So graceful she was with her long brown hair and soft green eyes. She was comin' from Denver to work at the Silver Dollar Saloon."

Samantha's eyes widened.

"Yes, ma'am, she was a dance hall gal. My pa wouldn't stand for me to be a-courtin' such a gal, and my ma would tan my hide just to think of it. However, I became deeply in love with this young woman and we struck up a friendship that has been strong for more than fifty years."

"Your wife?"

The old man grinned and nodded. "We've been married for over fifty years and we couldn't be happier. You can't let others' thoughts and words keep you from goin' after what your heart desires and your own happiness." He smiled and dipped his head toward her. "Good day to ya, Miss Samantha."

He walked down the street and Samantha stood there for a moment, thinking about what he had said. She found herself daydreaming once again.

As she smiled from ear to ear, she headed toward the Hays House humming a tune to herself. She walked down the boardwalk and felt a huge weight had been pulled off her shoulders and her heart. She was feeling much better than she had felt a half hour ago. As she walked inside, the hostess, Miss Nancy Cooper, greeted her. "Well, hello, Miss Samantha, how are you on this fine day?"

"Good, thank you."

"How can I help ya today?"

"Well, Miss Nancy, I was just stoppin' in to see iffen by chance y'all could use any help in here. Maybe tendin' to dishes or waitin' tables? I bake a delicious pie as well."

Smiling as she cut a piece of fresh blueberry pie, Miss Nancy said, "Well, Samantha, as a matter of fact, one of our girls will be leavin' us Thursday. She is gettin' married and movin' back East. We're sure gonna miss her, but at least she finally found a good decent fella who will love her and care for her. We will be needin' someone to wait on tables and such iffen you'd be so inclined."

Samantha felt a spark of joy. "Oh, Miss Nancy! I would love to."

"Well, if you're here by 10 o'clock on Thursday, you got yourself a job."

Samantha smiled. "Thank ya so much, ma'am. You're a lifesaver."

Miss Nancy grinned and shook her head. "I don't know about all that, unless you're starvin' to death."

If Miss Nancy only knew. "I can't thank you enough."

As she left, she had a smile from ear to ear that wouldn't go away even if she tried. As she walked toward the cottage, she passed by the Conn Store and had a sudden idea.

As she walked inside, Sarah, Malcom Conn's wife, said, "Well, Samantha, how can we be of service to ya?"

Samantha walked up to the counter. "I was just curious to know if you'd be interested in purchasing some of my fine jewelry and some fresh baked pies…to sell here at the store."

"What sort of jewelry are we talking of here?"

"It's just some things that I have put together in my spare time."

Sarah smiled "We'd love to see them, if you would like to bring them in."

"Why, certainly. I'll go straight home and fetch them."

When she got home, she dug down into the wooden chest where she stored her belongings. Down underneath some dresses and bonnets, and even an old fiddle her father used to play at night after supper. Her mother had loved hearing him play, but since she had passed, he had kept it tucked away. Deep toward the bottom of the old oak chest, wrapped in a Confederate flag, was a small wooden box full of earrings and bracelets she had made during the long, lonely nights. When they had lost the boardinghouse, she had found herself spending most of her time alone. Making the jewelry had given her mind something to focus on and her hands something to do. Taking the box of jewelry, she walked into the kitchen and grabbed a fresh peach pie she had baked earlier that morning. She headed back over to the store, praying the Conn family would agree to buy her jewelry and pies.

Back at the store, she placed her offerings onto the counter.

Sarah opened the box and her eyes lit up as she saw the jewelry made from beads and porcupine quills. "Oh, my, I declare. These are absolutely beautiful. You made these yourself?"

Samantha grinned. It was so nice to have someone appreciate the hard work and craftsmanship that had been put into them. "Yes, ma'am, I did."

Sarah was clearly impressed with the jewelry. "How much for each of these? They are simply breathtaking. You have a wonderful talent."

"How does a dollar each sound?"

"We'll take 'em all," Sarah replied, and Samantha just about fell over in shock.

"Now what have we got here?" Malcolm looked over her peach pie.

"I made it this mornin'. I was hopin' that if ya liked it, maybe you would like to buy one or two of them every week to sell here in the store."

Malcolm took a slice of the pie and bit into it. "Oh my! It's absolutely delicious. We'll give ya fifty cents a pie every week. What all sorts of pies can ya make?"

Samantha smiled. "Peach, pear, apple, blueberry, blackberry, cherry, you name it."

"Well, what would you say to three pies a week at fifty cents each? That'd be a dollar fifty a week. If we sell more than we expect, would you be willing to bake some more?"

"Why, certainly," she replied. "I really appreciate it. You have no idea just how good this makes me feel. God be with you both."

When Samantha arrived back at her cottage, she was exhausted. It had been a rather long day. The day had started out fairly bad, but after her conversation with Mr. Schmidt, she had begun to feel much better. She and Mr. Schmidt were so much alike. He had met the greatest love of his life and ran away and married her and now they had been together for fifty years. She thought about all he had said and realized that everything Levi had told her was very much like everything that Mr. Schmidt had said...not to waste her dreams and life away. She feared that if she stayed with her father, her dreams would never come true. She had fallen more in love with Levi than she had been in love with anyone in her whole life.

Samantha figured she would work at the Hays House waiting on tables as well as selling her jewelry and pies to the Conn Store. This way she could start making money to help pay for their mortgage and help her father get some of their bills paid off before she left. She wanted to help him out all that she could. She would do everything in her power to help those she cared about, no matter what the circumstances. But she had spent way too long being depressed and alone. It was time for change.

Later that night, Samantha filled a tub with hot water and began to undress. Sliding her baby blue dress off, she slid her way into the tub. As she lay there enjoying the hot water upon her skin, she began to think of Levi. Where was he at? Had he thought of her lately? Had he found the man he was hunting? When was he coming back to Council Grove? Would he be back before the end of the year? So many thoughts flooded her mind.

As she massaged her body, she thought of the night they had made love. She craved his body against hers, wishing he could hold her tight and they could gaze into each other's eyes. She longed for the warmth of his breath on her neck as he kissed her and ran his fingers through her soft hair...the way that he held her tight and gently caressed her body with his fingertips and tender wet lips. Nobody had ever touched her the way he did, and she knew nobody else ever would either. Only him, whenever he came back for her.

Once she had finished her bath, she slid into her cotton robe and went to throw some logs on the fire. It didn't take too much to keep their little cottage heated, thankfully. The stove they had in her bedroom was enough to heat the whole place, even her father's room that was across from hers. After she had the fire going nice and hot, she slid into her big empty bed and her mind raced with thoughts of Levi.

Later that night, she had a sick feeling come over her stomach and a feeling of worry in her heart. Something was wrong, she could feel it. As she got out of her bed and got dressed, she paced the cottage. She stoked the fire, then she walked back and forth, staring at the windows. Could Levi be in trouble? There was no way of knowing, and it drove her insane. She knew he was a strong man and was probably just fine, but something felt wrong. She didn't know what it was, but she knew something wasn't right.

LEVI WAS BEGINNING to catch a chill. He had been laying there on the snowy ground for, at least by his clouded calculation, close to four hours. Drifting in and out of consciousness, he kept thinking of Samantha. If he gave up, it would break her heart. He knew she was a very strong woman, but her heart was still very fragile. She had been through a lot in her life and had suffered many disappointments. He couldn't stand the thought of him being one of them. He loved her. Oh, how he loved her. He had laid there for hours since the outlaws had left him, beaten and tied up, trying to recover the strength to crawl over to where he had shot the leader of the gang. He knew that his bowie knife was still there in the snow where it had fallen after striking the man in the face. He figured that if he could crawl over and find it, he could somehow cut his hands free.

After lying there for several hours, his circulation slowed down. He couldn't get the strength in his legs to stand up, and every time he would try to sit up, his head would spin something fierce. About two hours after the sun had set behind the divide, he began to regain strength in his legs by rubbing his knees together to warm them. After several minutes, Levi was finally able to get up to his knees. Hunkered over, he looked down and could barely see Samantha's picture lying in the snow.

"I'll be back, darlin'," he said to the picture.

Once he managed to get to his feet, he limped over to the trail where his knife lay hidden somewhere in the snow. As he got to where the leader of the gang lay dead, he noticed something that took him by complete surprise. When the two surviving outlaws had left, they had taken the horses but seemed to have forgotten to take the leader's Colt. Through all the brutal pain and agony, Levi somehow began to smile. He knew if he somehow survived, he would kill the men that got away.

Scraping the snow away with his feet, he searched for his bowie knife. After several yards of scraping with his boots, his feet began to get feeling back into them, and as the blood started pumping, he began to feel his toes ache from the cold. The moon reflected off something shining brightly in the snow. It was the blade of his trusty knife. Kneeling, he rolled over onto his back, then tightly gripped the bone handle of the knife with his fingertips. He slid the rope around his wrists up and down the blade.

After several minutes, the blade finally cut through the thick frozen rope. As soon as his hands were free, he limped over to where one of the outlaws had discarded his boots after stealing Levi's. Levi knelt to slide the man's boots on, and he was amazed that they fit somewhat. They were a bit snug, but they beat being barefoot in the snowy Rockies.

He limped his way back in agonizing pain and picked up Samantha's picture. "I love you, sweetheart. I will always love you." Looking at her image, he began to have the biggest urge to survive. He had to see Samantha again. He had to rescue her from her lonesomeness and heartaches…he just had to!

As he put the picture into the lining in his hat, he headed back up the trail to the fallen outlaw. He strapped on the dead man's gun belt and took the buffalo coat and put it on himself. It was heavy and big, but it sure was warm.

He limped up the hill to where he had killed the second outlaw. He leaned down and unbuckled the gun belt and strapped it across his hips over the other one. They were both right-handed holsters, so he spun the one around and wore it backwards to wear the left-handed Colt facing butt forward.

As he turned to walk back down the trail, he spotted the man's Winchester laying in the snow. Picking it up, he began to load it with the cartridges he found in the gun belts.

After loading all three guns, slowly limped his way down the trail to where he had tied Star. Once he spotted the tree where he had tied her, he remembered that the other two outlaws had stolen her. His blood began to flow with pure hate and anger. Not only did these men shoot him in the back, beat him after he was down and tied up, and take his watch, but they had stolen his companion. His loyal horse. He cherished his Colts and his carbine, but stealing his mare was bounds for death! They had signed their own death certificates for sure.

Levi searched the snowy trail and finally picked up the outlaws' tracks. As he began to head back down the mountain, he could tell that the outlaws were taking their sweet time leaving the mountain. Their leader had been killed, and the pass was snowed off, leaving them only one way out.

About an hour later, the sky began to cloud up, covering moon. Levi couldn't see more than a foot in front of his face. Knowing it was nearly impossible for him or the outlaws to travel with no light, he decided to hold up and try to regain some more of his strength. Breaking some branches, he cleared away a spot in the snow and began to start a fire the same way he had the night before with his bowie knife and the powder from a cartridge.

Once the fire was burning hot, he pulled his knife out and laid the blade in the fire to tend to his wounds. He didn't have too much trouble until trying to clean the wound on his back where he had taken a bullet. Reaching the blade of the knife around to his back, he could feel where the bullet had broken one of his ribs. As he held the scorching hot blade over the bullet hole, he gritted his teeth and cussed something awful.

After finishing, he lay down next to the fire and drifted off to sleep. He dreamed of Samantha. The way she felt in his arms was unexplainable. He had to see her again. All throughout the night, as he lay there drifting in and out of sleep, Levi fought a fever that would have been the death of most other men. He was strong and a fighter, though, and he had something on his side that was stronger than anything…the true and undying love of a woman.

Once the first crack of daylight struck the Rocky Mountain horizon, Levi awoke to feel well rested. The few hours of sleep did him good. His fever had broken, and the pain seemed to subside just long enough for him to get ready to go after the outlaws. After he was sure the fire was out, he grabbed the rifle and set out.

Following the two outlaws wasn't all that hard at all. Not only were they following the same way back, but one of the men was leaving a fairly nice blood trail, which made tracking them that much more convenient. Levi smiled as he recalled having shot the man in the shoulder.

The sun came out from behind the clouds, and the mountainside began to warm up a bit. After about an hour of trailing the two men, Levi noticed the blood in the snow getting fresher, which meant the outlaws were starting to slow up. After studying the trail, Levi decided the best thing he could do was to try to get up ahead of them and cut them off. The outlaws were riding slow enough now that he thought he could get around them and set up an ambush.

His body ached something awful, and every step down the mountain reminded him of the vicious wolf attack and the skirmish with the outlaws. He was strong and determined, though, to make it back to Kansas to be in the arms of the lovely Miss Samantha. He just clenched his teeth and limped down the mountain, thinking up more colorful cuss words. Getting off the trail, he began to work his way over the ridge and down the other side.

About four hundred yards down the mountain, he began to get extremely sharp pains shooting up his back. He realized the bullet that had been lodged in his back was rubbing on a nerve and kept sending sharp spasms up and down his back. He had hoped closing up the wound would have helped until he had gotten to town. After dropping to his knees from the excruciating pain, Levi tried to pull himself up using a nearby pine tree. Reaching into his pocket, he pulled out Samantha's picture.

He gazed into her eyes, remembering their intoxicating blue. "Your love is the only thing that keeps me goin'." He tucked the picture back into his pocket and continued his way down the mountain.

About thirty minutes had come and gone when he came to a small clearing along the trail. There was a stand of piñon trees just off the trail that would give him plenty of cover to hide in. As he looked up the trail, he spotted some dead, fallen aspens. Gathering a bunch of them, he fought through the excruciating pain and did all he could to pile them up, covering the trail in order to make a barricade. It took him much longer than he had wanted, but he still went rather faster than most men would have in his condition. This would stop the outlaws for a few minutes. The brush was so thick along the trail they would not be able to get through it with the horses. They would have to get down off their horses and move the trees to allow them to go along their way. That's when Levi would make his final move.

Several minutes later Levi could hear a magpie calling from his perch on a small aspen just up the trail. As he looked up to see the bird, he could tell that the magpie had spotted something. Levi cocked the rifle, loading a live cartridge into the chamber. As he sat there patiently, a Stellar's jay began to call up the trail. He knew then that the outlaws were just around the bend. As he sat there quietly, not moving a hair, he could hear the men laughing. They were close, maybe fifty yards. Seconds later, the two men came riding around the bend. Levi spotted Star being led by Arch, the man that had stolen his hat and boots. His blood flowed with anger and hate. The only way they were getting off that mountain was slung over the saddles of their own horses.

Levi took a couple deep breaths and let them come right to the barricade. Once they reached it, Arch said, "What in the Sam Hill?"

Charlie scratched his head. "That weren't there before, were it?"

As Arch crawled off the palomino, Levi snuck out of the piñon behind them. As he leaned down and grabbed one of the dead trees to move it off the trail, Levi raised the rifle and said, "Ya know, pardner…you ought not mess with another man's horse."

Arch turned around quickly. "How in the hell?"

He drew for his gun, but Levi shot him right in the chest. As he fell to the ground, Charlie spun around on his horse, pulling his rifle out of his scabbard. Levi sent three slugs into him before he could get his rifle free. One slug struck him in the elbow, another in the left breast, and the third in the throat.

As Levi walked over to Arch, he spotted his watch hanging out of his vest pocket. Arch, blood trickling out of his lips, looked up. "Mister, who in the hell are you?"

Levi looked down at him. "I'm the man who's gonna send you straight to hell, you worthless son of a bitch." Levi took his hat and boots off the man and put them back on. He unbuckled the twin Colts and put them back across his hips after taking off the pistols he had taken off the other two dead outlaws.

As Levi went to put his watch into his vest pocket, he opened it up and reached for Samantha's picture in his pocket. He pulled it out and gently placed it back inside the watch.

The outlaw, covered in a pool of his own blood, smiled a nasty, crooked smile. "Hey, mister, that your gal? Iffen ya ask me, she looks like a whore! I bet she can suck—"

Before he could finish, Levi drew his Colts and unloaded all twelve shots into Arch's chest and face. After he reloaded, he pulled out his carbine from a scabbard on one of the outlaws' horses and reloaded it as well.

He walked over to Star and scratched her head. "Howdy, ol' girl. Did ya miss me? We got 'em, girl." It took all he had to lift the lifeless bodies of the outlaws over their saddles, but he managed to do it. Once he had them belly down, he took some rope and tied them to their saddles.

As he rode back up the trail to where the other outlaws lay dead in the cold snow, he began to feel extremely exhausted. As he reached the location where the bodies lay, Levi recovered the box of cartridges he had put on the boulder while hiding and waiting for the outlaws. He searched the area over well to be sure he had recovered everything that was worth a damn.

After Levi had the other outlaws tied up on their saddles, he began to head down the mountain. After riding several hours, they reached the beautiful Pass Creek and spotted an old cabin Levi had stayed in a few times with his father when they were hunting elk. The cabin was built somewhere around the early 1820s by some mountain man who had an eye for beautiful scenery. It lay at the corner of a big meadow along the stream and was surrounded on all four sides by mountains. Elk, mule deer, black bear, and beaver were plentiful here, and the stream was full of fresh cutthroat and brook trout.

Levi knew in just a couple hours more he would be in town, but this cabin was a very special place to him, and he decided to stay there for the night. There were a lot of precious memories there for him. After starting a fire, he unloaded the dead men from their saddles to relieve the horses' backs and legs.

As he sat beside the fire next to the old cabin, he gazed at the aspens in the meadow and watched a herd of elk as they ate the bark of the trees. He watched a large six-point bull as he ran a younger bull away from his cows.

The bull was majestic, and Levi could feel his mouth water just thinking of a fresh-cut elk steak.

The sun was setting behind the mountains. The sky was clear, and the mountains turned the most beautiful blue as the sun began to disappear over the horizon. The colors in the sky reminded him of the sunset that he and Samantha had watched back in Kansas on the prairie. The dark blue mountains made him think of that gorgeous blue dress she wore the first time they had met in front of the mercantile. He missed her so much. As he sat there watching the sun set, he made himself a promise. Someday, when he and Samantha wed, he would bring her to this very spot and show her just how beautiful and breathtaking a Rocky Mountain sunset can be.

THE NEXT MORNING Levi was up with the sun. Loading the four dead men back onto their saddles, he turned to see a sight that he wasn't expecting. A paint horse was standing in a grove of aspens about one hundred yards away from the cabin. Atop its back was a Ute Indian brave wearing an elk hide robe and a coyote skin on his head. Levi's heart skipped a beat.

As he studied the Indian, he noticed movement in the trees beyond the paint mare. After closely observing the movement, he could see three other Indian braves riding toward a game trail that was at the other end of the meadow. As they rode through the leafless aspens, Levi could see the breath from their ponies. It was an eerie sight, but a relieving one. He knew they knew he was there. There wasn't denying that one bit. He knew, however, that if they had wanted to kill him, they wouldn't have had any problem doing just that. There were more than just the four of them in the area, he was sure of that. This appeared to be a small hunting party. Splitting off into groups of three or four allowed them to surround the herds of elk and mule deer, or the great buffalo herds, giving them more of a chance to kill several rather than just a few.

Levi had been nursed back to health once by a small Ute tribe in those mountains across the river to the north. They had found him after he had been shot and left for dead by a jealous husband. The Ute had a great deal of respect for him. He was known to them as "The Great Hunter". After he recovered and left the tribe, he would often return with pelts from beaver, coyote, elk, and even sometimes buffalo or bear. Other times he would bring meat to the tribe just to show his appreciation.

As the Indians reached the edge of the meadow, they stopped and turned around to look at Levi. He raised his hand in the air for a moment, and he could see one of the Indians repeat the gesture. Soon the other Indians joined in. As they rode into the dark timber, Levi mounted his horse. He planned to reach the marshal's office in less than two hours. As he headed down the trail, he passed several beaver ponds on the crystal-clear mountain spring. He felt his heart long for the time he could bring the lovely Miss Samantha up there to catch some trout and watch the magnificent sunsets.

Just before nine o'clock, Levi and his load came riding into town. People rushed outside when they saw Levi leading the lifeless bodies into town. The sun was out and shining bright, melting the snow in the street and making it a muddy mess. A black three-legged dog came limping its way through the puddles to investigate Levi and the dead outlaws. Off in the distance, a rooster crowed as the sun came out behind the clouds. Icicles melting from the rooftops trickled water into the street, making a small flowing stream along the boardwalks. In this little stream, a young boy splashed a stick he was playing with.

As he reached the jail, Levi leaned over to dismount. As he pulled his boot out of the stirrup, he collapsed in the mud. He was exhausted, and his fever had returned.

As the marshal came out of the jail, he yelled, "Quick! Get the doctor!" The marshal motioned for a man standing nearby to come over. "Give me a hand here!"

The man hurried over. "Sure thing, Marshal."

"Let's get him to the hotel," the marshal demanded.

Carefully lifting Levi up, the two men carried him over to the hotel. Levi drifted in and out of consciousness.

A while later, the doctor, a short black-haired older gentleman, arrived. Levi didn't much care for doctors. Most he had met in his time happened to be drunkards. He approached Levi, scissors in hand. Levi was groggy and barely conscious, but he raised a hand and grabbed the doctor by the wrist to stop him. He was weak, though, and the doctor grabbed his hand and released his hold. "Easy now, cowboy. Let me take a look!"

As the doctor cut Levi's shirt from his body, the marshal said, "Good Lord! This man's been through hell!"

After cleaning his wounds on his head and face, as well as his arm where the wolf had bitten him, the doctor rolled him over on his stomach. "Mercy sakes alive! This bullet hole has been there for some time. This man must be as strong as an ox and as tough as a grizzly."

As Levi lay there in that big feather bed fighting consciousness, the doctor picked up a bottle of whiskey and took himself a drink. "You best not be thinkin' you're workin' on me while you drink yourself into a state." Levi tried to sit up, but the pain was terrible. He needed to get the hell out of there, but his body wouldn't cooperate.

The marshal held him down. The doctor pulled out the tools he needed then cut the skin on his back and went inside to try to carefully pull the bullet out. Levi winced and groaned in a haze of pain. The doctor grunted. "He's broken a rib."

"Poor bastard's lucky to be alive," said the marshal.

"Hmm…" the doctor said as he dug around searching for the slug. "He wouldn't have been if he had waited any longer to get here."

Levi felt the pliers as the doctor worked on his back. The pain was unlike anything he had ever felt before. He felt weaker than ever and as he tried to see where he was, his head began to spin something awful. His vision was blurry, and he couldn't make out anything but the light shining in from the windows. As he drifted out of consciousness, he drifted into a deep dream. He dreamed that he had died and when Samantha found out that he was never coming back to Council Grove for her, she just fell apart. All the love that had grown between them had all just tragically ended and now all her hopes and dreams would never come true. He had promised her he would return for her and now he had done just what he said he would never do: break her heart or leave her. He wanted to be her husband and the father to her children. He wanted to give her everything she had ever dreamed of. To share a lifetime of love and trust, passion, and romance with her. If he let go, how could he ever give her all he had promised her? He had to hang on.

Chapter 7

It was a cold and lonely winter day back in Council Grove. Samantha had heard nothing from the man she had fallen so in love with. Not a day had gone by these past two months that he wasn't on her mind. She had been working at the Hays House every day but Sunday, and she enjoyed it for the most part.

She was ready for her knight in shining armor to come riding back into town and rescue her. She had been making jewelry out of beads and porcupine quills she had bought from the Kaw back in the spring. The Conns claimed many of the customers said she made some of the most beautiful jewelry on the whole prairie. She had been bringing in a steady three dollars a week, working her fingers to the bone. Miss Nancy said she was a friendly, easy-going lady and that everyone enjoyed her company. She hid her feelings for the stranger behind a smile as she waited tables.

Samantha would catch herself watching the west road that came into Council Grove…sometimes with a feeling of loneliness and other times with hope. She hadn't known him for long, but she knew in her heart he would someday be coming back for her. She would often wake up at night feeling something was wrong. She would get up and pace the little cottage, and sometimes she would find herself sitting alone in the dark crying and drinking whiskey.

She had been so lost for the last few years. For the first time in a long time she had felt some meaning in her life. She felt wanted and needed. Loved and desired. Everything she had been longing for. Now she just found herself waiting and wondering. Would Levi rescue her from her loneliness and heartache? Would he really take care of her and give her children? She would find herself doubting their love, but then she would dream of his gentle blue eyes and knew he would do all those things and much more. She had a lot of hope and faith in him, and she hoped that somewhere out there in those Colorado Rockies Levi knew that.

That morning, Samantha was up with the dawn, unable to lay back down because her body ached so much. She had been working every hour of the day, and she would be up all night tossing and turning. She was so stressed. No matter how hard she worked to get ahead, there was always something to pull her back.

As she crawled out of bed, she thought she would work on her beadwork, or possibly a quilt. Maybe she would read a new book. When she sat down to read after breakfast, she became distracted by thoughts of Levi. She had to get away. She was going insane. It was Sunday morning and most of the town was at the church, including her father. She walked over to the stable and saddled up her horse and set out for Elm Creek.

Once she arrived at her favorite spot—where she and Levi had made love for the first time—she tied her horse to a nearby stand of buckbrush and began to walk. She followed the creek. It was a chilly clear day and the wind was blowing tumbleweeds across the prairie. A rooster pheasant crowed off in the distance. She spotted a spot in the creek where a family of beavers had made a dam. A large male beaver stood up on the dam and dove down deep into the crystal-clear stream below. She wished Levi was there to share this gorgeous day with her. As she paused by a tall old cottonwood tree, she could hear the soft rippling of the stream as it trickled its way down the rocks. Up ahead, a large mule deer buck lowered its head to drink from the stream. He was a magnificent creature.

Samantha's heart longed for escape from Council Grove and all that was causing her such grief and turmoil. She desperately needed a change of scenery. She wished Levi had taken her with him to Colorado, but she knew he had to find the man he had been hunting for. He'd be back soon, though, and then everything would be the way it was supposed to be. She would never again feel the way she did now. She would be happy, and everything would be perfect. She was so anxious to be back in Levi's strong arms. He made her feel like an angel, beautiful and loved and cherished. She knew that never again in her life would another man ever make her feel so special. She had found her true soulmate. She aimed to be Levi's girl for the rest of her life. Totally devoted to each other and lost in love forever. All he had to do was come back to her.

Samantha had hidden from her true feelings for far too long, and things were starting to seem clear to her. She knew she would be trapped for the rest of her life if she didn't get out. As Levi had said, she shouldn't punish herself. She dreaded the day it would come, and she didn't want to feel as if she had failed her father. But she knew what she had to do, and with the passing of each long and lonely day, leaving her father only got easier.

She walked along the banks of Elm Creek for the better part of the day, thinking of the past and what the future held. Was everything finally changing and getting better? Was everything she was doing really worth it? Could this man love her and be forever faithful to her for the rest of her life? She cast her doubts aside. She knew he could and would. She just had to get by until he returned.

BACK IN THE Colorado Rockies, Levi lay in his warm feather bed in the hotel fighting to recover fully. As he awoke, he looked up and saw a lovely dance hall girl bringing him in a tray of hot breakfast.

"Well, good mornin', sleepy head," said the girl. "I was wonderin' if you was ever gonna wake up."

He reached up and felt the whiskers on his face. "How long have I been here?"

"Well, let's see here," said the girl. "You rode into town on Tuesday, so it's been goin' on a week now."

Levi tried to sit up, but he had no strength. He looked toward the window. "Where's my horse?"

"The marshal had it taken over to the livery, mister."

Levi looked the girl in the eyes. "My name's Cord, ma'am. Where's my guns and duds?"

The girl pointed to the chair in the corner of the room. "Over there, Mr. Cord. I hope ya don't mind…I had your clothes washed for you."

"Much obliged to ya, ma'am," Levi said as he attempted to smile despite his stiff and aching body.

There was a knock at the door, and the girl answered. The marshal stepped into the room, standing with his hat in hand. "Howdy, Bessie."

"Howdy, Marshal," she replied.

"We were startin' to wonder about ya, pard," the marshal said to Levi. "You musta took quite a beatin' up there in the hills."

Levi nodded. "Not as bad as them that done it."

"Yes sir, I reckon you're right about that. They were all full of holes, and the one fella had thirteen in him. Shall I ask how that come to be?"

Levi grinned. "Man ought not mess with another man's horse."

The marshal shook his head. "Well, sir, we're sure grateful to ya. The stage line is sure gonna be mighty grateful too. We all thought that money was long gone. I took the bodies over to the jail and sent out a telegraph to the U.S. Marshal in Denver the day that you rode in. The men were also wanted for robbin' a bank up in Montana Territory back in September. Once you're up and around, just stop by the jail and I'll get ya the reward ya got comin'." He tipped his hat and left.

The girl walked over to him. "You gotcha a girl, Mr. Cord?"

Levi looked at the girl. She was very pretty, and she wore a lovely baby blue dress. Her hair was long and brown, and her eyes were as blue as her dress. She was well built, and her breasts were large and filled her dress out perfectly.

Levi managed to give her a smile. "As a matter of fact, ma'am, I do. She is the most beautiful woman I have ever laid eyes on. Her eyes are the most intoxicating blue, much like yours, ma'am. Her hair is long and soft and flows down her back, waving like the prairie grass across the Kansas Flint Hills."

"Where's she at?"

Levi looked toward the window. "She's back in Kansas in the little town of Council Grove, waiting for my return. She is truly a piece of heaven if I've ever seen one. Her skin is as soft as velvet and her smile is as lovely as a misty mornin's sunrise over the divide."

Levi pointed at his jacket and vest, which were hanging over the back of a chair. The girl brought them over to him, and he pulled his watch from the pocket of his vest. He opened it up and showed her Samantha's picture.

"She's beautiful," the girl said with a smile.

"This here picture has saved my life. I was lyin' up there in the snow, wantin' to just give up. I was attacked by a pack of wolves one night, then the next I was shot in the back and tied up and whipped after I was down. I was on the verge of lettin' go when her picture blew up to my face. As I looked into Samantha's eyes here, I got an extreme amount of hope. I just had to make it. I ain't known her all that long, but that very moment I laid eyes on her, I just knew she was the girl I wanted to spend the rest of my life with. I promised her I'd be back for her and I couldn't bear to think of breakin' her heart."

The girl's eyes began to fill with tears. "That's so romantic, Mr. Cord."

"Well, I don't know about all that, ma'am, but I do know that the power of true love is strong enough to work miracles."

The girl gazed out the window. "I wish I could find me a love like that. That Miss Samantha is a very lucky gal."

Levi looked into her eyes. "You will…just be patient. Someday, when you stop lookin' so hard, he'll find you. Trust me, a gal as purty as you…you'll have cowboys fightin' each other to win your heart. Have faith. Just don't settle."

The girl smiled, then gently gave Levi a hug. "I'll let you get dressed if ya feel up to it, Mr. Cord."

Levi struggled through the pain and managed to slowly sit up. "Yes, ma'am, I reckon I'll be ridin' out directly."

Levi crawled his way out of bed and began to get dressed. His body now felt rested, but he was stiff and sore all over. Carefully inspecting his Colts, he made sure no one had messed with them or unloaded them on him, then strapped them across his hips and put his hat on his head.

After he left the hotel, he limped his way across the street to the jail. Before he walked in the door, he turned around and gazed at the mountains and the pass that he had come down from a week earlier. There was a haze that lay over the valley that was simply breathtaking.

As he walked into the jail, the marshal said, "Well, howdy, Mr. Cord. I didn't expect to see you up and movin' around so soon…I figured you'd stay in bed today."

"I'm much obliged to ya for all ya done for me, Marshal."

"Well, I didn't have too much to do with it. Miss Bessie done the most part. She stayed right there by your side near every danged minute."

Levi smiled. "She's a mighty sweet gal."

The marshal winked. "Very purty one, too, ain't she?"

"Yes sir, she is at that."

The marshal got up from behind his desk and walked over to the window. "How the hell did ya find them boys up in that pass, pardner?"

Levi shook his head. "It weren't that hard. The pass was snowed off and there was only one way in and one way out. I just picked up the trail and followed 'em up the pass. I slipped back and set up in a grove of trees and waited for 'em to come back down the trail. There was some shootin', and I kilt two. That's when I took one in the back, and the other two roughed me up a bit while I was down. They stole my horse, and the next mornin', I tracked them down the trail and kilt 'em."

The marshal twisted the edge of his mustache, then turned, and Levi could see him study his guns. "Why in the Sam Hill did one of those boys have thirteen holes in him?"

Levi gave the marshal a crooked grin. "Like I said 'fore. Ought not mess with another man's horse. The rest was between me and him."

The marshal shook his head. He dug into a drawer on his desk and pulled out four wanted posters. He laid them out on his desk, and Levi recognized the images of the four outlaws.

"Wanted dead or alive," the marshal said. "The first one here is Jim Allen. Second one is Ed Cahill. He was workin' on the Jackson spread until he run off with ol' man Jackson's horse and wife. The other one here is Charlie Dunbar. He's the one ya tried to cut in half. He was the gang's so-called leader. I don't know who the other man was. Must have been a drifter that fell in with 'em."

Levi spit in the brass spittoon in the corner. "That Charlie fella kept callin' him Arch. I couldn't tell ya his last name, though."

The marshal leaned over his desk and handed Levi a stack of crisp greenbacks. "This is the twenty-five hundred that the marshal in Denver had up for the reward. The rest is over at the bank. I'll go by there with ya and ya can pick it up. You've got quite a deal of money comin' to ya, Mr. Cord. I'm not sure if ya heard or not, but the stage line also put up another five thousand for the four outlaws."

Levi's eyes widened and his heart just about jumped right out of his chest. He hadn't heard anything about it. That extra money would go so much further than he had planned. He slid it into his pocket.

Once the marshal and Levi arrived at the bank down the street, they walked up to the teller, who said, "What can I do for ya today, Marshal?"

"We're here to pick up the reward for the outlaws that held up the stage."

The teller smiled. "This must be the famous Levi Cord that everyone's talkin' about."

"Pardon?" Levi asked, confused.

"You're the man who single-handedly took down four bloodthirsty outlaws up Monarch Pass."

Levi sorta nodded. "Yes sir." His mind was miles away in the sleepy little town of Council Grove. All he wanted now was to collect his money and be on his way.

The teller walked back to the vault and pulled out two bags. As he set them on the marble counter, Levi's heart began to race. The teller began pulling out stacks of money and counted, "One thousand, two thousand, three thousand, four thousand, five thousand. This is the five thousand for the stage line reward." He opened up the second bag and counted once more. "Two thousand, four thousand, six thousand, eight thousand. That's a total of fourteen thousand, Mr. Cord." The teller placed the money back in the bags and slid them across the counter to Levi. "Well, sir, what are ya plannin' to do with all that money?"

Levi picked up the bags. "I reckon I'll ride over to Cañon City for a spell and then back to Kansas and start me a li'l ranch."

They left the bank, and the marshal looked at Levi. "That sure is a mighty large amount of money to be ridin' with there, Mr. Cord."

"Well, Marshal, I reckon I'll manage."

The marshal shook his head. "You know what, pardner, I reckon you will."

As they reached the livery, Levi saddled up Star and threw the money bags into his saddlebags.

After he saddled up, the marshal shook his hand. "Good luck to ya, Mr. Cord. May God be with ya on your journey."

Levi tipped his hat. "Much obliged to ya for everything, Marshal."

After saying his farewells, Levi rode out of town and pulled the money the marshal had given him from his pocket and stuck in inside his socks. He figured that if he were to get ambushed, they'd have a harder time finding it this way. He rode along the Arkansas River. He wasn't planning on really heading south to Cañon City, though. He knew that wherever he told the teller or the marshal where he was headed, he wouldn't be safe. He was carrying more money than most folks would ever see in a lifetime. Every two-bit gunman in the territory would be looking for him. He was planning on heading north. He rode south most of the day, riding in circles several times in order to try to break up his trail, then circled back, crossing the river and riding into the hills.

RIDING ACROSS COUNTRY, the jingle bobs on a cowboy's spurs made a sweet lullaby, and the steady rocking motion of the horse could put a grown man to sleep like a baby. He let himself doze on and off in the saddle, though he stayed alert for unwanted company. He couldn't be too careful carrying that much money on him. It was a very dangerous plan to try to travel alone, especially in his current situation. Rumors of Levi Cord and the Monarch Pass showdown had surely spread far and wide within the past week. He decided to lay low and camp outside of town in the hills. He didn't even make a fire that night. He didn't want to chance someone seeing it and come around. He just laid his blanket down on the ground and used his trusty saddle for a pillow.

The next morning, just after sunup, he set out again. Soon after, he rode into a mining camp. People milled about. He could see tents and rough wood buildings set up for gambling and saloons, along with other various types of business. Stopping in front of a wooden building, he crawled down out of the saddle and lit himself a cigar before entering.

A man with a sandy blond beard came barging out of the swinging doors and ran right into him, nearly knocking him off his feet. "Watch where ya walk, ya stupid bastard!" the man slurred in Levi's face.

"Excuse me, pardner." He looked into the man's eyes as he shoved passed him, and Levi thought he recognized the man. As he watched the man walk down the street, he tried to figure out where he had seen that man before. He tried to picture the man without a beard but struggled to place just who he was. There was something about the man's eyes that looked familiar, though.

As he walked into the saloon, the piano player was playing a familiar tune. Levi was rather fond of the song, and it reminded him of the beautiful girl back in the Flint Hills that he had fallen so in love with. He walked up to the bar and noticed in the mirror that he needed to shave. He was starting to look like a regular mountain man. "Whiskey," he said to the barkeep. "A bottle."

A blonde saloon girl came walking over to him, wearing a beautiful pink dress. She had gorgeous blue eyes and curls and white feathers in her hair. Levi smiled and said, "Howdy, ma'am."

"Howdy, cowboy. Lookin' for a good time?"

Levi looked the lovely girl up and down and grinned. "Well, as hard as it is to turn down an offer like that, I reckon I'll have to pass it up, thank ya."

The girl gave him a look of shock then tossed her hair and walked away. "As you wish, cowboy."

Levi poured himself a glass of whiskey, then stood there at the bar and smoked his cigar. Who was that man he had just run into? He could swear he knew him from somewhere.

He looked around the saloon. This place had obviously done quite well for itself in this mining camp. There were polished brass spittoons at the end of the bar. There was a large six-point bull elk head mounted over the bar, and one wall was covered with all sorts of animal mounts from deer to ducks and even an antelope and mountain lion. Levi thought that this was a right nice place to relax.

"Right nice place ya got here," he told the barkeep.

"Thank ya kindly, stranger," the man replied.

After about an hour and two cigars, Levi left the saloon and headed to get a place to sleep for the night. Levi undressed and stretched out on the bed in the dimly lit room. He pulled his watch from his pocket and placed the picture of Samantha to his lips. He could still recall her scent, and he felt a deep loneliness in his heart. He missed her more than he had ever missed anyone.

As he lay there staring at her picture, he began to think of just what it was he was going to do with all that money he had gotten for bringing in the outlaws. He wanted to give Samantha the best life that he could…a big home, children, happiness. He had always wanted to own his own cattle ranch somewhere, and this was the perfect chance for him to fulfill his dreams. He decided that once he had finished taking care of his unfinished business, he would ride back to that lovely little spot he had camped at that night on Soldier Creek after he had left Burlingame. It would be the perfect place to build his ranch and start a family. The land was rich, and there was a spring-fed creek and plenty of prairie grass for cattle and grazing some horses. He could see it all in his mind. A big cabin with a big barn or two, a stable, Samantha's hand in marriage, and two or three little ones running around the farm. Game was plentiful there and it was a beautiful place for a new start.

THE NEXT MORNING, he made his way over to the barber. When he walked in, the barber, who was an older fat man with a curled mustache that had turned white over the years, said, "What'll it be for ya today, stranger?"

"Shave and a bath." Levi took off his hat and hung it by the door.

After his shave, he soaked in a tub the barber had heated for him behind a partition. As he was sitting there enjoying the hot water, he heard someone walk in the door. Thinking nothing of it, he continued to wash himself.

He lit a cigar, and he heard the barber talking to the man that had just walked in.

"Howdy, pardner, what can I do for ya today?" the barber asked.

"Got anything that'll cure a hangover?"

Levi listened closely. There was something about the other man's voice that made his stomach turn.

The barber chuckled. "I can run ya a hot bath, sir. Got another fella back there, but I got another tub ready."

The man groaned. "I got drunker than a peach-orchard sow."

Levi's eyes widened as he remembered exactly who the man was. His cigar fell from his lips and splashed and hissed as it hit the water in the tub. That voice belonged to the evil coward Levi had been hunting.

Levi reached for his Colts, which hung on a nearby chair, and his heart began to race wildly. Goosebumps stood up on the back of his neck as he listened to the man, just on the other side of the partition. For nigh on eight years, Levi had been hunting the man that had killed his sweetheart and left him there to die at her side with a round of buckshot in his back. He had trailed him from Dakota Territory to Kansas and lost his trail outside Hays City. He had picked it up back in Missouri, before he met Samantha. Now, after all those rough and lonely miles, and all the long and miserable heartbroken years, here in this little barbershop in Colorado Territory, was the man that had changed Levi's whole life. His blood flowed with rage and anger and pure hate, and he thought about busting out from behind the partition and shooting the gutless coward in the face.

The water had cooled, and Levi eased his way out of the tub, dried off, and got dressed. He was shaking so much he could hardly even button his shirt. After he slid his boots on, he buckled his gun belt on across his hips and put his hat atop his head. After waiting for several minutes, he heard the man walk out the door. Walking back out from behind the partition, he watched the man walk over to the saloon.

"Who was that fella?" he asked.

"Some drifter in for a shave. He coulda used a bath too, iffen ya ask me."

Levi tipped his hat. "Good day to ya, sir. Much obliged for the shave and bath." He headed across the street to the saloon. Staring through the swinging doors, he spotted the man sitting at a table with a saloon girl standing at his side while he was playing stud. He had been wondering for nigh on eight years what possessed this man to take away his world.

Levi entered the saloon and walked up to the table. "Ya boys reckon ya have room for one more?"

The man looked up and said, "Sit, stranger."

Levi did so, and the dealer dealt out five cards each.

Levi picked up his cards. He had a full house, three queens, and two eights.

A man wearing a derby hat looked at his cards. "Dealer, I'll take two."

Levi watched the other men. The one in the derby hat picked up his cards. "Hmm…well now." He tapped his fingers on his cards. "I reckon I need to find a new occupation, fellas."

The other two men at the table studied their cards.

"I'm stayin' in, boys," one of the men said as he took a shot of whiskey.

The other man looked at his cards for a minute and then laid his cards down on the table. "Boys, I reckon I gotta fold this round."

The men laid their cards on the table and Levi placed his cards down last. Levi held the winning hand. "Looks like today is my lucky day, eh boys?" He eased his hand to his hip and slid the tie downs off one by one from his twin Colts. His trigger fingers were itching to finish the deed that he had set out to do so many years ago. He picked up his winnings from the table and gave the men a grin. "I reckon I've been waitin' on this day to come for quite some time."

The man he had been hunting glanced up from the table. "Say, stranger, you mind passin' some of that luck over here?" He chuckled and then looked at Levi with curiosity in his eyes. "Have we met somewhere, pardner?"

Levi looked the man dead in the eyes. "Ya ever been to Ellsworth?"

The man scratched his nose. "Yes sir, I have, but that ain't where I've seen ya, I know it. Maybe it was Wichita."

Levi shook his head and then stretched his neck. "No sir. Not Wichita."

The man returned his gaze. "Damn it, mister, I know I've seen you somewhere. What you say your name was again?"

Levi glared at him. "I didn't say." His fists were balling up and his fingers were itching to reach for his Colts.

The man twisted the ends of his mustache.

Levi eased his hands back to the table to deal the next hand of stud. "It'll come to ya sooner or later."

After several hands, a saloon girl came swishing over to Levi in her red dress and garters. She sat down on his lap uninvited and began rubbing her hand up and down his thigh. Reaching down, he grabbed her hand. "I reckon that'll be just about enough of that, ma'am."

The so-called man raised his eyebrows. "What's the matter there, stranger? You object to a fresh whore?"

"Reckon I'll pass, thank ya." Levi tipped his hat to the woman.

The man laughed. "Ya married or something?"

Levi bit the side of his lip and felt the blood start pumping through his veins rapidly. His face grew red with anger. "Or something is right." Levi was livid by this point. For the murderer of his first love to ask if he was married was more than enough to send him straight to hell.

The man shook his head and laughed again. He pulled the girl standing next to him by the arm and kissed her. "Woo doggie! I'm out, boys. This girl here's got me harder than—" Before the man could finish his sentence, the girl grabbed him and kissed him and led him upstairs. The other men began another hand of stud.

Levi sat at the table observing the saloon, waiting for his move. As the girl he had turned down walked by, he said, "How much?"

The girl smiled. "Two dollars, cowboy. I knew you'd come to your senses sooner or later." She reached down for Levi's crotch, and he grabbed her by the hand and led her up the stairs.

"Which room is yours?" he asked.

She led him to her room, then began to undress.

"Hold it, ma'am," Levi said. "I just wanna ask ya a few questions."

The girl looked him up and down and glanced at his twin Colts. "What are ya, some kinda law?"

"No ma'am, I just wanna know about the man that was playin' cards. The one that come upstairs with that other gal."

The girl looked at Levi for a minute. "He's been here since yesterday."

"Where did he come from?"

"He said he'd come from Missouri way. Said he killed a man for killin' his brother sometime back and—"

"Who was his brother?" Levi interrupted.

"I don't know his name, mister, but he said he was shot in Abilene and that he had chased the man to Dakota Territory and finally caught up with him and shot him down in the street after he finished his last supper."

Levi's heart was racing, and he was furious. "How do you know all of this?"

"A man will tell a girl anything, if she'll truly stop and listen."

"Did he tell ya that he also shot a woman?" Levi said as he gritted his teeth and fought back the tears.

The girl's eyes widened. "Pardon?"

"Well, ma'am, I was in Abilene sometime back and a man tried to steal a horse from the livery. Unlucky for him, that horse belonged to me. It was dark that night, no moon at all, and I was sleeping in the stable when he came in and tried to steal my mare. We fought for several minutes and then he pulled his gun, but mine cleared leather first. I shot and killed him then left town. Three years later I was comin' outta a café with my fiancée in Dakota Territory, when that man here came steppin' out from the alley and fired a scattergun, brutally killing her and shooting me in the back."

The girl held her hand over her mouth as the tears filled her eyes. "Oh, dear God."

"Sometime later, I recovered and set out after the man. It's been nigh on eight years I've been trailin' him and now I've found him, and I aim to kill him. I'd be obliged ma'am, iffen you'd keep this quiet."

The girl nodded her head. "You kill that son of a bitch! Give 'em what he's got comin'!"

Levi paid the girl, giving her an extra five dollars. He had never known why the man had tried to kill him, but now he did. The man in Abilene all those years back was the man's brother. In a way, he felt sorrow for the man. He knew how he must have felt. He took away someone that the man must have been close to, so that man took his sweetheart. And that man thought that he had killed Levi.

Levi walked back down the stairs and outside. He walked across the street and sat down where he could watch the saloon doors. He was waiting for the man to leave so he could make his move. It was cold and windy, but Levi wasn't going to miss his chance to finish this fight and go back to Kansas to rescue his new love. He had gotten overeager countless times at the poker table to just draw his Colts and murder the coward in cold blood just the way he did his past sweetheart, but he was waiting for the right time to make his play.

Several hours had passed when the man finally came out of the saloon. Levi studied his every move. Following him slowly, he watched him go to the stable. Looking through the cracks of the barn, he could see the man saddling his horse. Cautiously opening the door, he snuck in and then let it slam.

The man jumped and turned around fast with his hand on the butt of his six-gun. "That's a good way to get a belly full of lead there, stranger."

Levi smiled. "You wouldn't shoot a stranger now, would ya there, pardner?"

The man raised his eyebrows. "You know, mister, I just can't seem to figure you out."

Levi gritted his teeth and prepared to make his move. "Dakota Territory come to mind?"

The man's face turned pale and his eyes widened. "No…It couldn't be."

"Your brother was a horse thief. I caught him stealing my horse. I didn't want to kill him, but he drew first."

The man spit in the dirt. "You're a damn liar!"

"No sir."

"But I killed you!"

Levi grinned. "Ya shoulda made sure I was dead. Now I'm here to finish this. I aim to send you straight to hell, you worthless son of a bitch!"

The two men stood there for a moment and Levi saw the man's eyes twitch. His face squinted and he drew for his Navy Colt. Levi pulled his Colts and sent two slugs into the man before he could even clear leather. One slug hit the man in the gut, just below the belly button, and the other struck right under the left breast. As the smoke began to clear from the stable, the man lay on the ground in the hay, taking his last few breaths.

Levi walked over to the man. "There. Now it's over."

The man tried to reach for his pistol, but as he did, his riddled body began to jerk. Seconds later, he took his final breath. Levi stood there holding his guns, smoke still coming out of the barrels. Tears filled his eyes as he began to shake uncontrollably. He dropped to his knees and wept for several minutes. He placed one of his Colts back in the holster.

Levi walked over to the jail. "Marshal, there's been a shootin' over at the livery, and I reckon you oughta come now."

The marshal jumped out of his chair. "What in the Sam Hill do ya mean, there's been a shootin'?" He grabbed his coat and hat and then grabbed his pistol off the desk and placed it in his holster on his hip. "Come with me."

Levi led him to the body. "I've been trackin' this son of bitch for many years now," said Levi. "He killed my fiancée and shot me in the back. Been a rough trail leadin' up to now, but finally caught up with him here. You can wire the marshal in Dakota Territory and he'll verify my story."

The marshal looked over the body and scratched his head for a moment.

"Well, son, help me take this body over to the jail and I'll see if we can reach this marshal you speak of."

They carried the body to the jail and laid it on the cot in a vacant cell. The marshal walked over to his desk and dug inside the drawer and pulled out a stack of wanted posters. "Have a seat there. I want you to tell me the story you told me again about this here fella and how you know him."

Levi sat down and began the story once again, adding more of the details. After he finished his story, the marshal shuffled through the stack of posters and raised one that had the dead man's image on it. "By God, son, I was 'bout to toss your ass in that cell with him, but I guess I oughta shake your hand instead. Seems that the man was actually wanted down south for killing a piano player in a saloon. There's a five-hundred-dollar reward out for him. You come by tomorrow, and I'll get it to ya, alright?"

Levi couldn't believe his ears. It sure was turning out to be his lucky day all the way around. "Alright, Marshal. I'm sure obliged to ya. I apologize for causin' a ruckus in your town, but the deed is done."

The marshal reached out his hand. "I'm obliged to you, son. If you ever need a job, I could sure use a man like you to help me keep peace in this ol' town."

Levi smiled and tipped his hat. "I'll keep that in mind." He walked out the door and then headed back to the hotel.

It was finally all over. A world of stress had been released from his heart. He would get a good night's sleep tonight, and after he awoke in the morning and fetched his reward, he would be on the trail and closer to being back in the arms of the love of his life.

Chapter 8

The bright sun was shining high over the lovely little town of Council Grove. Samantha was working long hours every day but Sunday, and when she wasn't waiting tables at the Hays House, she was home working on her jewelry or her quilts. Often, when the weather was nice, she would ride out to Elm Creek Dally and spread her blanket out on the prairie floor and waste her Sundays away reading stories of romance and adventure. It helped ease her mind and escape from all the stresses at home.

She wondered where Levi was and if he had found the man he was hunting. How long would it be before he returned for her? She had no idea how they were going to survive together, but she didn't care. All she knew was that she loved him dearly and that things would work out somehow. She knew in her heart that he needed her just as she needed him. She kept their love affair secret and not another soul knew anything about it. That was, however, except for Mr. Schmidt, but she knew her secret was safe with him.

Many nights, when she and her father sat together to eat their supper, she would find herself wanting to tell him that she was leaving, but she just couldn't stomach the thought of hurting him. He should have been able to see it coming, but he was too wrapped up in other things. Levi had shown Samantha more love and passion than she could ever remember. She needed a man like him in her life…someone to show her she was beautiful and special. Someone to treat her like an angel. She needed it, and she would never be truly happy until she got it. She needed to be true to herself. She was believing that more with the passing of each long day.

She often imagined what life with Levi was going to be like. Would they marry? How many children would he give her? Would he settle down and hang up his guns? She dreamed of a big house with a swing on the porch, where she could sit outside and read her books and work on her quilts and jewelry. She dreamed of having a big barn with a corral and lots of horses and chickens to give her fresh eggs each morning. A big herd of cattle grazing in the pasture and little ones playing with a baby goat in the yard. She and

Levi and a little boy and a little girl, all sitting on a blanket under a sycamore. She could see it all so clearly in her mind.

A MONTH HAD passed since Levi had finally killed the man he had been tracking for so long. He had left the mining camp and was headed east toward Abilene. While riding the trail, he kept searching for the perfect place to build his cabin and start his own cattle ranch. He was ready to stop drifting and rambling and finally settle down and plant some roots. He spotted several places that looked rich in land, but his heart was really set on that little place where he had camped on Soldier Creek after leaving Burlingame. It was only a few miles from town and had everything that he needed to give Samantha the life that she deserved.

He passed a small group of buffalo grazing in a nearby cottonwood creek bottom. He had bought himself a packhorse and a trusty new rifle. It weighed a ton, but anything within a thousand yards was a goner when Levi pulled the trigger. When Levi spotted the small herd, he thought he would treat himself to some fresh buffalo steak. There was enough meat on one of them big old shaggies to last him a fair piece. Levi figured he could sell the hide in Abilene and fill his packhorse with all the meat he could get.

As he approached the herd, he dismounted and walked on the opposite side of Star. This way the buffalo wouldn't spot him. The mid-January air was mighty cold, and the wind was blowing from the north, coming down from Canada. A thin sheet of powdery snow had fallen overnight, and it was now overcast.

As he walked alongside the mare, he could see the small herd of three cows and one big bull standing in the grove of cottonwoods. A couple times they would look up at the mare but didn't pay her any mind at all. When Levi got to within three hundred yards, he slipped the gun out of the buckskin sleeve he had bought to protect its beautiful wood stock. As he cautiously walked closer, he could begin to see the breath of the bull as he grunted to his cows.

"This oughta do, girl," Levi whispered to Star. He lined the barrel of the rifle over his saddle and began to take careful steady aim. After he pulled the hammer back, he gently squeezed the back trigger to set the front trigger. Just before he squeezed the trigger, he saw the buffalo quickly throw up their heads and look back across the prairie. Just behind them was a Pawnee hunting party: eleven Indians, all in war paint and riding painted ponies. They were armed with Winchesters along with bows and lances.

Seconds later, those Indians were charging down off the bluff, running the buffalo straight toward Levi. There was nothing between them but open prairie. Jumping on Star as quickly as he could, he gave her the reins and gave her a kick with his spurs.

"Hyah!" he yelled. "Get the hell outta here, girl!"

The Indians' rifles reported just behind him. The snow was flying up from under the mare's hooves, and as Levi looked back over his shoulder, he could see them getting closer and closer. After riding several hundred yards at a full run, Levi pulled the reins back, stopping Star in her tracks. He jumped to the ground and pulled her quickly to the ground. Quickly, he lined the barrel of his rifle over his saddle and fired. The slug roared across the prairie, sending one of the Indians flying off the back of his pony. As quick as lighting, Levi had another shell in the chamber and was taking aim at another charging Indian. He fired, and the second Indian went flipping off the back of his pony and one of the pony's hooves kicked him in the face. The Indians were firing their rifles and bows and closing in on him. A bullet flew right by Levi's head. Loading another shell into the chamber, he took aim at another Indian that was just about to shoot his rifle at him. Levi sent the slug into his chest.

By now, they were circling all around him about one hundred yards out. There were eight of them left, and, after circling him, two of them came charging right at him. They were whooping and hollering and waving their bows and lances in the air. They were closing in on Levi, and he pulled out his trusty Winchester '66 carbine from the scabbard. Jacking a shell into the chamber, he fired, sending one of the Indians off the back of his pony. Before he could fire a second shot, the second Indian came crashing down off his pony and onto Levi. Pulling his Colt, Levi tried to shoot the Indian, but took a blow to the face with a tomahawk. His adrenaline was flowing something fierce, so he didn't feel much pain at first. Rolling the Indian over and pinning him to the ground, he pulled his other Colt and shot him in the belly.

All at once he heard something coming like a twister across the plains. He looked up to see the other seven Indians coming full speed right at him. Wiping the blood from his eyes, he holstered his Colt and grabbed the carbine and started firing as quickly and accurately as he could. The first shot went wild across the prairie and the second struck one of them in the shoulder. The

Indians' rifles were firing all around him now. Arrows were flying from every direction. One Indian came to within ten yards behind him when he was shot in the chest by Levi's carbine as Levi whirled around. Dropping to the ground, he unloaded his carbine. Drawing his Colts again with pure intent to kill, he started firing at every Indian that came in close. Smoke was all over the prairie and dead Indians would soon freeze to the prairie ground.

As one Indian came soaring off his pony, Levi filled him with lead. After several minutes the Indians began to fall back and regroup to prepare another charge. There were five left, and Levi was lucky enough that he hadn't been struck by one single arrow or bullet. How long would his luck last? He was outnumbered but he didn't dare doubt or second-guess himself. His blood was pumping, and his heart raced as he tried to remain calm and keep his scalp. His face was now throbbing from the blow of the tomahawk, but he had to keep calm and focused if he wanted to stay alive. As the Indians regrouped, he loaded his guns as quickly as he could. They began to charge once again as he slid a new shell into the chamber of the rifle. Taking careful aim, he sent a slug right into the windpipe of one of the Indians. The Indian did a backwards somersault off his pony.

The other three Indians came charging in, and Levi drew his Colts. For less than a minute, shots rang out across the prairie and it sounded like the Battle of Mine Creek all over again. Firing those faster than ever before, he sent two of the Indians flying off of their ponies, full of lead. The last Indian turned his pony west. Kicking up dust, he put distance between him and Levi in no time.

Picking up the rifle, he slid a shell out of his belt and into the chamber. Pulling back the hammer, he set the back trigger and raised the sight. Wiping the dirt and blood from his eyes, he saw the Indian on a dead run about five hundred yards out. Taking a deep breath, he lined the sight with the Indian's back. He squeezed the trigger as he softly exhaled, and the report of the rifle shook the prairie ground. About two seconds later, the slug tore through the Indian's buckskin robe and into his back. As soon as he fell to the ground, a big hush came over the whole prairie. Eleven dead Indians lay on the cold prairie floor.

Levi fell to his knees and sighed. He looked around at the lifeless bodies. "Whupped 'em again, girl, didn't we?"

After several minutes, he reached into his coat pocket and pulled out a flask of whiskey. Pressing it to his lips, he tipped his head back and drank. It tasted so smooth and warm on his lips. He walked over to Star and gave her a drink of the rotgut and patted her on the head. "Atta girl." He poured some on his wild rag and cleaned his head wound from the tomahawk. It was a fair blow, but it hadn't been a direct hit, so it had only chipped his cheek and forehead. It had almost severed his nose, but he cleaned it the best that he could. It was starting to hurt like hell, but it was a long way from the heart. All he had to do was try to keep it clean and pray it would heal on its own.

Saddling up, Levi headed on down the trail toward Abilene. He had been in a number of gunfights and had learned to handle himself extremely well under pressure. Nevertheless, he was amazed that he hadn't been hit by a single bullet or arrow.

Once he reached Abilene, he rode past the livery stable where he'd killed the coward's brother for trying to steal his horse. He was glad all the miles of trailing the man were over. No more bounty hunting, no more killing. He was ready to hang up his guns and settle down with the greatest love of his life. All the miles he had traveled and all the fights that he had been in over the years sure took their toll on him. He felt like he was an old man already.

As he rode down the street, a herd of longhorn cattle came around the corner, led by eight cowboys wearing wide-brimmed hats and batwing chaps. They had on big wild rags, and each wore a six-gun on his hip. They were obviously cowboys up from Texas reaching the end of their long drive. Levi supposed they were headed to the stockyards to sell the stock and collect their paychecks.

Tipping his hat as they rode by, Levi got an idea. Why couldn't he buy himself a herd of cattle and drive them back to that little spot of Soldier Creek and build a ranch? He could hire himself two or three good cowboys, and within a few months he could have his cabin built and ready for his new sweetheart. He wanted so badly to ride down to Council Grove and get her right then and there, but he knew that the trail was no place for a lady. He aimed to go back and build his ranch, then, when he was settled, he'd go and fetch her.

Levi decided to go back and talk to the cowboy in charge of the outfit. He rode up to the outfit on the outskirts of town. "Howdy. Which of you boys is the ramrod of this outfit?"

A middle-aged man with sandy blond hair said, "I'd be that man, pardner. What can I do for ya?"

"Well, sir, I'm lookin' to buy some beeves and saw ya boys ride through and figured I'd ride over here and see iffen you was in the market to sell these head or if ya already had yourself a buyer."

The man studied Levi. "Well, pardner, we're drivin' up to Montana Territory for eight dollars a head. Market up there is sky high."

Levi took off his hat and scratched his head, thinking for a moment. "I'd give ya ten dollars a head iffen you'd drive 'em east of here a spell to Wilmington."

The man looked toward east. "How far is this Wilmington?"

"A heap closer than Miles City, I reckon. I'd say around a hundred miles, give or take a few. I'll pay ya half now, and half when the job is done."

The man turned to his cowhands. "Well, boys, looks like we got a li'l change of direction here. We're headed east."

Levi smiled. "I reckon we got ourselves a deal, mister?"

"The name's Allen Renner." The man stuck out his hand. "You got yourself a deal…"

Levi shook the man's hand. "Levi Cord."

"You that fella that caught those four outlaws that held up that stage out there in Colorado Territory?"

"Yes sir, I reckon I am. How in the hell did you know about that?"

"By God, pardner, you're the talk all along the trail. Folks talkin' 'bout you clear down to Denton County. They say you're a match for ol' Jesse James himself."

Levi chuckled. "Now, I don't reckon I know 'bout all that. You boys thirsty? How 'bout we head up yonder to the saloon and I'll buy y'all a drink?"

Once they got to the men began to hoot and holler.

"We'll set out an hour after sunup, so don't have too much fun," Levi said. "Don't want ya boys feelin' poorly in the morning."

About that time, a bunch of soiled doves walked into the saloon, and the boys all got silent. It sounded like a Sunday morning service. Levi smiled and reached into his pocket, then laid twenty dollars on the table. "It's on me, boys. Now remember, we're off early in the morning."

The cowboys began whooping and hollering again as they each grabbed a girl and headed straight upstairs.

The barkeep walked over to Levi. "Can I get ya a drink, sir?"

Levi turned to him. "A sarsaparilla would do just fine." He shook his head in disbelief. For the first time in years he had turned down a glass of whiskey. He was changing. He didn't have the urge to kill or drink anymore. The only desire he had now was to build his ranch and then go get his girl.

As the barkeep brought him a bottle of sarsaparilla he said, "Cigar sir?"

"Ya know, I don't mind if I do."

The barkeep handed Levi a cigar then lit it for him. Levi reached into his pocket and pulled out his watch. As he opened it up and looked at Samantha's picture, he felt a great deal of joy. He was really doing it. All his dreams were slowly but surely coming true.

BEFORE THE SUN cleared the horizon the next morning, the men were up and ready for a full day's ride. Tying their bedrolls and dusters to their saddles, each one checked their horses' feet. After a full breakfast, the sun had cleared the horizon across the Kansas prairie, and the cowboys began to gather the cattle and drive them east.

The sun was shining bright and the wind was calm. The smell of the horses and cattle flowed through Levi's nose. It was a smell he had smelled several times before when he was ranching down in Texas. He enjoyed the aroma of horses and cattle and leather. It reminded him of a better time and a better life. It was the smell of the country, and country he was to the core. Country was all that he had ever been and all that he was ever going to be. He was far from being a carpet-bagging Yankee.

As they rode the trail, they jumped several flocks of ring-necked pheasants and Levi thought one would taste mighty good. About ten miles east of Abilene, the boys decided that they would press on a few more miles before setting up camp for the night. As they continued along, Levi spotted a couple of rooster pheasant running into a ditch and decided he would try to sneak up and shoot a couple for supper.

Cautiously dismounting, he snuck up to the thicket he had seen the pheasants run into for cover. Levi took the tie downs off his Colts and prepared for them to come busting out of the thicket. As he walked closer, one of the roosters came cackling and jumped up right under his feet, raising all sorts of racket. Levi drew his right Colt and dusted him right out of the air. Instantly, two more roosters jumped up, and Levi drew the Colt on his left hip and started firing. Smoke filled the air and feathers flew.

Off to the left, a rooster took off running and one of the cowboys drew his Winchester from his scabbard and shot. The first shot missed its mark, and the rooster jumped and took off running even quicker. The cowboy fired a second shot and nailed him. Within minutes, a total of six pheasants were dead.

The cowboys laughed and joked and exclaimed over Levi's shooting. As they settled down for the night, Levi cleaned the pheasants.

"Boy, oh, boy, pardner," the camp cookie said, smiling. "I'll cook them birds up with some carrots, taters, and beans, along with some of the best biscuits known to man."

Levi chuckled as he handed him the pheasants. "Sounds like a right fine meal iffen ya ask me."

"Then I aim to fix y'all up some huckleberry pie and put some calf slobbers on top."

Levi's mouth watered as he pictured a fat piece of pie with a slab of melting butter on top.

Later, as they sat around the campfire eating and telling stories of soiled doves and cow towns, one of the cowboys pulled out an old, beat-up guitar and started picking a couple songs.

After a few songs, Levi reached out his hand. "May I?"

The cowboy passed the guitar to Levi. "You know your way around a guitar, pardner?"

Levi grinned and started picking a song he had written some time back. The cowboys all sat around and watched and listened.

THE NEXT MORNING, they began to see deer and even an occasional turkey along with a few small herds of elk. The vast open prairies were beginning to turn to rolling hills and draws of timber were full of game. Riding east of Fort Riley, they began to angle their way south toward Alma.

"Beautiful country," Levi said to the trail boss as he spotted a herd of buffalo grazing off to the west.

As they got closer to Alma, they decided to set up camp close to a stream where they would be close to water and down out of the cold winter wind. Most of the snow had melted off and turned to slushy mud and muck. They pulled the chuckwagon up along the edge of a sandbar and started a fire. The cookie placed two big Dutch ovens on the coals and began to cook some delicious venison stew. After supper, he treated them with a piece of hot apple pie.

The cowboy pulled out the guitar again, and this time another pulled out a fiddle and joined in. It was some of the best music Levi had ever heard. Levi pulled his old harmonica from his saddlebags and played along. Two of the cowboys got up and started to dance together. The others laughed and joked.

It was a beautiful clear night, and the moon shone brightly. A barred owl called from his perch atop a sycamore tree. Shortly after, a second owl responded up the creek. This was the most enjoyable night Levi had had since he was with Samantha.

EARLY THE NEXT morning, the sun was shining bright as the men saddled up and began driving the cattle onward toward Wilmington. Several hours after leaving Mill Creek, they came to the top of a big bluff that overlooked a ranch. As they rode down to the ranch, Levi noticed a dozen thoroughbred horses that were some of the finest horses he had seen in a long time. Riding up to the corral, he looked them over.

A stocky man wearing a worn-out pair of overalls walked out of the barn. "They're all for sale."

Levi turned to the man. "How much?"

"Fourteen dollars a head."

Levi shook his head. "I'd give ya twelve dollars a head."

The man laughed. "Son, I wouldn't part with my three-legged egg-suckin' dog up there on the porch for fourteen dollars. I might take thirteen dollars a head."

Levi looked the horses over good then said, "Pardner, I'd give ya twelve dollars a head and not a penny more."

The old man looked at him for a minute. "Twelve dollars a head?" He sighed. "Got yourself a deal, son."

Levi pulled out the money from his saddlebags and paid the man, then shook his hand. "Much obliged to ya, sir. Could ya tell me how far the next town is?"

The man pointed east. "Eskridge is just over the hill a couple miles. Where y'all headed?"

"Wilmington. Fixin' to start a li'l piece of a ranch up there and run us a few cattle and thought some good horse flesh would help."

The men shook hands once again and then they set out once again on the trail. They were only roughly twenty miles from Wilmington now. Levi figured to reach it in a couple days.

When they reached Eskridge, there was something familiar about this town to Levi, but he couldn't place it. He had been danged near to every boomtown and cattle town west of the Mississippi over the years, but something about this one caught his attention. As they rode down the street, he saw a big brick building on the corner and instantly he remembered why this little Kansas town had caught his attention. The brick building was the local bank. About thirteen years ago, Levi had fallen off the beaten path and started riding with a few boys that weren't exactly Sunday-go-to-meeting kind of folks. Levi and those boys held up that bank one fall and Levi had been shot off his horse but managed to get away with a busted nose and a broken elbow and a little over four thousand dollars. Nothing had ever come of that robbery. He hadn't heard tell of anyone being caught and didn't wait around the area long enough to find out either. He sure wasn't aiming to attend a necktie party in the near future.

They quickly pushed the herd through town and right before sundown, a drifter came riding up. Levi took the tie downs off his Colts as the man approached. He was wearing a large-brimmed black hat and a pair of brown chaps with a gray duster. He had sandy brown hair and clean-cut sideburns, and his eyes were blue. He had obviously been a drifter for some years. His face was weathered, and his tall black boots were covered in dust.

As he rode up to Levi, he said, "Howdy!"

"Howdy," Levi replied.

"My name is Bud Christopher."

Levi nodded. "My name's Levi and this here is Allen Renner. We're pushin' this herd over to Wilmington."

The man reached out his hand and both Levi and Allen shook it. Levi knew right off that this Bud Christopher was a decent man. He could tell that he had been mixed up in some sort of trouble somewhere, but when the two shook hands, a friendship struck up from the start.

"Where ya headed, Bud?" Levi asked.

"No place in particular, I reckon. Anywhere besides Manhattan," Bud said with a look of uneasiness in his eyes.

"Well, sir," said Levi. He could tell Bud was obviously running from something in his past, very much like himself. "You know cattle?"

Bud smiled. "Yes sir, I know a few."

Levi nodded to the cowboys. "Well, pardner, you can throw in with us iffen ya want to."

"I reckon that's about the best damn thing I've heard all day." Reaching out his hand to Levi, they shook hands again and Levi knew he had just hired on a good man. He didn't ask what he was running from in Manhattan. It didn't matter. Everybody was running from something, whether it was a woman, or the law, or civilization.

They stopped to rest their horses. Levi wanted to check with the mayor to see about buying the land outside of town on Soldier Creek. They were now only a few miles from Wilmington.

A man came up the street and said, "Howdy. Where ya boys headed?"

"Over yonder on Solider Creek," Levi answered.

"Ah, Wilmington way, huh?"

"Yes sir," Levi replied. "Who would I need to talk to about buyin' a piece of land out there?"

The man smiled. "Well, sir, that'd be me."

Levi explained the location of where the land was that he wanted to purchase.

"Fine li'l spot of land there," the man said. "A dollar an acre."

Levi's heart was overwhelmed with joy and excitement. This was it. His dreams were finally coming true. Before long, he would have his cabin and barns, and then he could ride back out west to Council Grove and fetch the lovely Miss Samantha.

After concluding the deal, the men decided to set up camp for the night and get a fresh start to finish their journey at first light. Just after sunup, the boys gathered the herd and pushed them south toward Soldier Creek.

Levi rode a little taller in his saddle that morning. A couple miles south he fixed his eyes on a spot. "That's it, boys, right there. She's perfect. That little grove of trees over there is where I'm gonna build myself a cabin." Pointing over to a clearing, he said, "There's gonna be my barn, and some stables over yonder."

The cowboys hooted and hollered. Climbing down off their horses, they set up camp and then the cookie treated them to a fresh veal stew. It was simply delicious.

As they sat around the fire, Levi said, "Well, boys, I reckon I'm gonna ride into Burlingame and fetch me some lumber, iffen y'all be lookin' for work."

The cowboys looked around at each other. "Mr. Renner, sir?" one of them asked. "Whatcha got in store for us now?"

"You boys are done with me, I reckon, so that's in your hands now."

Levi looked at them. "I'll pay ya boys thirty cents a day."

The cowboys talked it over and then one of them said, "I'm with ya, Levi." Then another one said, "Hell, count me in." Before the men were through with their dinner, every one of them had decided to stay and hire on with Levi.

Levi smiled. "Boys, I can't thank y'all enough for this."

As they finished eating, Levi pulled his bottle of whiskey from his saddlebags. He tossed it to Bud. "Take ya a swoller of that."

Bud smiled and did. "You gonna be needin' any hands once your cabin's built, Levi?"

"Well, Bud, whatcha got in mind?"

"I can break any horse with four legs, and I'm purty handy with a six-gun and a rope."

Levi smiled. "Pardner, iffen ya cotton to good ol' country livin', I reckon I could use a good hand like yourself."

Bud nodded. "I'm a man of my word, Levi."

Levi looked him in the eye. "I reckon you are at that, Bud."

Bud looked around for several minutes. "Why this spot here? To build your ranch, I mean?"

Levi looked out across the prairie as he smoked his cigar. "You ever been in love?"

"Once," Bud answered.

"Well, this here place is a right purty place and would be a fair place to start a family. I've drifted for many years. I lost someone I held dear to my heart some time back and I swore that I'd never love again. That was till I rode into Council Grove a few months back."

"What happened?" Bud asked.

"Well, I just happened to meet the purtiest gal I ever laid eyes on. The moment her blues eyes met mine, I knew exactly what I wanted outta life and who. I promised I'd be comin' back for her. She is so..." Levi gazed over the land that would soon be a working ranch. "She was so perfect. I figure to finish building the cabin in a month or so, then I'll ride out to Council Grove and bring her back."

Bud shook his head. "Ya know what you're getting yourself into?"

Levi looked up at the moon, then pulled his watch from his pocket and opened it up. Looking at Samantha's picture he said, "Damn right I do, pardner."

Not a cloud covered the sky, and the wind was rather warm for this time of year. Spring was just around the corner. It was the last week of January, and perfect weather for building the cabin. Not too hot, not too cold, just right.

The men loaded up in the buckboard and headed to Burlingame. They passed a settlement that had at least six small empty buildings. Levi pointed over toward an abandoned stone building and shook his head. "My grandfather Griz once told me he helped build this here settlement back in '58."

Bud shook his head. "Damn shame to see a town like that go under."

As they rode on, Levi spotted the empty building were the Havana Stage Station once was. "I hear tell that the station here was quite a stop on the mail stage line."

Bud looked over at Levi then looked back toward the building. "Why's that, Levi?"

"A fella once told me that they served some of the best meals around. They quit lodging folks back in '69, after the railroad came through Burlingame."

Levi whipped the team and proceeded down the trail when one of the hands pointed to the south. "What's that over yonder?"

The men all looked to see what he was talking about. As they did, they spotted a large three-story stone building.

Levi shook his head and gave a soft chuckle. "I'm thinkin' that was the brewery I heard tell of a while back. I guess the fella had big plans for the place, but while it was under construction his plan seemed to fall through due to lack of money, not to mention the town closing down."

Bud shook his head and spit in the dirt. "Sure a waste for a buildin' like that to go unused. Surely someone 'round here can use it for somethin'."

Levi took out his tobacco and put a chaw in his lip then spit. "It's a shame, ain't it? Place musta really been hoppin' a few years back."

About four miles up the trail, they reached the lovely settlement of Burlingame. The streets were wide enough to allow a wagon and a team of horses or oxen to turn around. Located at the intersection of the two-block main business district was a public well that was often used by travelers on the Santa Fe Trail. Levi liked Burlingame; it was a lovely little town and he just knew that Samantha would enjoy it.

In town, they pulled the wagon up in front of the store. As they got off their horses, a tall man came up to them. "You boys passin' through?"

Levi walked over to the man and said, "I just bought a spread up yonder on Soldier Creek."

"Wilmington way?"

"Yes sir. Fixin' to build myself a li'l piece of a ranch up there."

"I own the store here and run a fair business, if I do say so myself. I came here in '54 and have been here ever since. Got myself a fine little cottage down yonder on Switzler Creek. Fairest place in all Burlingame. Built in '67, and she's a beauty." It seemed like the man liked to brag. Levi could tell right off he was a Yankee, a carpetbagger. He was friendly, though, and Levi was fixing to stay in the area, so he figured he'd learn to like him.

"I expect you boys are needin' some lumber, eh?"

"Yes sir." Levi replied.

After several trips in and out of town, the men finally had enough lumber and tools to start building the cabin. Levi rolled his sleeves up and said, "Well, boys, reckon it's time to get to it. She's gonna be beautiful."

OVER THE NEXT few weeks and several more trips to town than Levi had planned, the cabin was just about ready. "You boys have been doin' a heap of work here. I'm right proud of ya. Here in a day or two, we'll have that roof on and she'll be finished."

As they continued to build, Levi kept catching himself daydreaming of Samantha. Would she be happy here? Is this what she had dreamed about? Could he give her the life she truly deserved? He'd get so distracted that he'd miss the nail he was hammering and hit his thumb. He'd cuss, and the men would laugh.

February came and was gone in the blink of an eye. There was still a hint of chill in the air and all the snow had melted and caused the creeks to fill up and flow wildly. Soon the spring showers and thunderstorms would be rolling in.

One morning, just after breakfast, the men crawled on top of the cabin to put the finishing touches on the roof. A few hours and several nails later, Levi crawled down the ladder and walked over to a tree in the front yard.

Looking back at the cabin, he said, "By God, boys…I reckon she's done. Ya think she'll do?"

The cowboys laughed and one of them said, "Boss, if she don't cotton to it, I'll marry ya!"

Levi laughed. Not just any usual laugh either. This was a different kind of laughter. One that soothed the soul and cleansed the mind. It felt mighty good too. Everything was falling into place in his life. The cabin was finished and now it was time to ride back west to fetch his sweetheart.

"When ya ridin' out, Boss?" Bud asked.

"I reckon I'll be out at first light."

"Could ya use some company?"

"There's plenty of work to be done here yet. I'll be back in a week or so, and then we'll get started on that barn."

Bud nodded "Sure thing, Boss."

Levi pointed to the cattle. "They'll be calving any day now, and I need a good hand here to tend to 'em."

Bud smiled. "I sure can't thank ya enough for takin' me on. Times have been kinda rough on my hide lately, and you have sure been awful kind."

"Don't mention it, pard, you woulda done the same for me," Levi said as he handed Bud a cigar. "Now let's you and me take one last trip into Wilmington before tonight."

LEVI AND BUD returned as the men sat around the campfire out front of the cabin, playing that sweet-sounding cowboy music and dancing the night away.

One of the cowboys saw them pull in with the wagon. "What the hell? Who the hell is with 'em?"

Levi smiled as the cowboys realized the wagon contained a bunch of saloon girls in feathers and fancy dresses. Taking their hats off, they began to hoot and holler.

"You boys deserve a good time," Levi said. "I brought y'all a li'l gift to say thank ya. I appreciate all your hard work the past couple of months. I never could have done it all without y'all." Reaching into the back of the wagon, he pulled out a bunch of bottles of whiskey and tossed them to the cowboys. "Drink up, boys. This here is Sally, Katie, Dixie, Maddie, Daisy, and Becky. I told 'em you boys were getting mighty lonely out here, and they were just sittin' out front of the saloon gettin' mighty lonely themselves, so here they are! Have fun!"

They all had quite a little party that night there on Soldier Creek. In all the music and laughing, though, Levi never once touched a bottle or a woman. He had changed. His heart was devoted totally to Samantha. He had finally parted from all his rough and rowdy days. No more rambling, no more drifting, no killing…unless the need be, of course. As the party carried on, Levi decided to take a walk along the creek by himself. The moon was reflecting off the water, and he could picture Samantha's eyes sparkling as she walked alongside him. The sound of laughing and music began to fade out as he got further away. It was a beautiful night, and tomorrow was going to be a beautiful day for riding. The anticipation to be with her was driving him so wild that he was mighty tempted to take off right then and there and head toward Council Grove. Morning couldn't get there quick enough.

Chapter 9

One morning, while Samantha was waiting on tables at the Hays House, she saw two men wearing batwing leather chaps and tall dusty boots and spurs come in. She overheard them say they had just ridden in from Abilene.

Mr. Schmidt and his wife were seated at a table behind the two cowboys. As she was handing Mr. Schmidt his plate of steak and eggs, she heard one of the men say, "Did you hear 'bout that feller west of Abilene that got jumped by that Pawnee raiding party?"

The other man answered, "I hear tell there were a dozen of 'em!"

"Yeah, they jumped 'em there on Gypsum Creek and gave him a run for it, they did. He gave quite a fight too. Carried a rifle and a pair of nickel-plated twin Colts."

Startled, Samantha's hand shook, and the breakfast on the plate dropped all over Mr. Schmidt's lap and onto the floor.

"I'm so sorry!" she exclaimed.

Mr. Schmidt took her by the hand. "Dear, it's no trouble at all."

As she cleaned up the mess, she listened as the men continued their conversation. "He took down eight of them bloodthirsty savages before one of 'em cracked him over the head with a tomahawk."

Samantha's heart felt as if it had stopped beating. Tears filled her eyes.

"He was a tough feller," one of the men said.

Samantha paused her cleaning. *Was* a tough feller?

The man went on. "He single-handedly whupped the whole dozen. Arrows and bullets were flyin' all over. He kilt 'em all."

The other man spoke. "I saw the feller in Abilene, and he bought us all a round. He told us how he fought them savages off. Didn't even break a sweat."

Samantha's heart raced. Surely Levi was alive, then. This man they spoke of just had to be Levi. Most men carried a gun, but not many were known to carry a pair of them…let alone a pair of nickel-plated twin Colts. It had to be him, but what was he doing up in Abilene? He was supposed to be in Colorado Territory. Had he finished his business? Was he on his way back to

Council Grove? Her mind ran wild. She looked up to see Mr. Schmidt watching her, compassion showing on his face.

Mr. Schmidt turned to the cowboys. "Excuse me for asking, but this man in Abilene…do you know where he was headed?"

"Well, sir, he bought a herd of cattle from some drovers that were headed up north. He was headed east with 'em, but I couldn't tell ya where he was bound from there."

"Do you happen to recall his name?" Mr. Schmidt asked.

"What are ya, mister…some kind of law?"

"No sir, I ain't. He just sounds an awful lot like a fella I once knew."

The man nodded. "Hell, mister, everybody knows him. He's gotta be one of the fastest shooters in the territory. Some say he's faster than Jesse James and Billy Bonney. They say he's fearless and deadly as Doc Holliday. He's killed more men than typhoid, and, hell, that was just durin' the War. They say he rode with Jesse himself back in Missouri until Jesse got tired of him always outshootin' him. They say when a man looks into those cold blue eyes, he gets the shakes so bad he'll shake right out of his boots before he even draws his guns."

Samantha was overwhelmed with anticipation.

"Hell, mister," the other cowboy said. "Everyone knows Levi Cord."

Samantha's heart went wild with excitement. It was him! Her cowboy.

Mr. Schmidt smiled. "That's just the man I figured." He looked at her and winked.

She smiled as she went back to her work, but she couldn't focus. She broke two cups and one plate in all the distraction.

"Land sakes, child, where is your mind today?" asked Miss Nancy.

"I'm truly sorry, ma'am," Samantha apologized. "I don't know what has got into me this morning."

Thoughts of Levi ran through her mind all day. Was he still in Kansas? Was he on his way to Council Grove to get her?

After she got off work and headed home, she ran into Mr. Schmidt in front of the Conn Store.

"Good day, Mr. Schmidt," she said.

"Beautiful day," he replied, taking off his hat. "How is your father, Miss Samantha?"

"He's been workin' a lot and is hardly ever home."

Mr. Schmidt looked her in the eyes. "Give it time. One day you'll look back on everything and it will all be like it was just a dream. That stranger fella will come ridin' back through town, and when he leaves, we'll all miss the company of the lovely Miss Samantha."

She looked up at him, tears threatening to spill out of her eyes. "How do you know?"

Mr. Schmidt placed her hand in his and smiled. "Child, I wasn't born yesterday. I saw the way you looked at him and the way that he looked at you. He reminds me of me when I was a young lad. If he knows what's good for him, he'll be back for you." He shook his head. "What do you see when you look at the future?"

She thought for a minute. "Levi. I see Levi." Her lip quivered.

"Be true to yourself, child. Go after all those hopes and dreams of yours. Take that beauty of true love and live it. Never look back. Make each other happy."

Samantha gazed into the old man's blue eyes. "What…what about my father?"

"Child, I know he loves you. He'll always love you. And if he really loves you, he will understand. Yes, he might be angry and hurt and confused, but in time he'll be alright. If he really cares for you the way he should, he will be happy for you. He'll want you to be happy. He may not see that himself, but in due time, he will. He's a strong man and you are a strong woman, Miss Samantha. Life is much too short to live it unhappy. Go live life to the fullest. Be happy."

Samantha stood there, staring down the street. She thought about everything Mr. Schmidt had said and realized she knew just what she had to do. She'd known it for a long time now, but now she could see it more clearly. "Thank you, Mr. Schmidt."

"You think about what I said, Miss Samantha. Have yourself a splendid evening, ma'am." As he strolled up the street, he turned back and gave her a little smile. She smiled back at him and then headed to the cottage.

When she walked through the gate, she could see that her father was home. As she walked inside, she said, "Hello, Father."

He turned to her. "Where ya been?"

"I was working with Miss Nancy."

He gave her a look of disgust. "If you have any notions at all of runnin' off with that two-bit gunman, I reckon I'll have to beat some sense into you. I won't allow you to see that man, do you understand? He is no good. Never will be. A man like him cannot be trusted."

Samantha felt her face turn red with anger and her whole body began to shake. "Father, you have no right to judge that man! He's kind and caring and I love him!"

He jumped out of his chair. "Love him? What in the hell do you know about love?"

"A lot more than you, obviously!"

He raised his hand to smack her across the face, but she glared at him and yelled, "If you do it, it will be the last time you ever see me! I can promise you that!"

"Well, don't let the door smack you on the ass when you go!"

Samantha rushed out the door of the cottage and ran to the stable and saddled Lightning. As soon as she mounted, she took off out of town as quickly as the old gelding could run. Once she reached Elm Creek, she laid her blanket down on the ground. She buried her face in her hands and wept. "Why, God? Why does life have to be so damn hard? What did I do to deserve this pain?" She pounded the prairie floor with her fists. "Come back to me, Levi!"

MANY MILES EAST of Council Grove, Levi had left Bud in charge of the ranch and started out west toward Samantha. He followed the Santa Fe Trail, and as he pushed west, he had the best feeling he had ever had…at least that he could remember. It was a feeling of pure happiness and excitement. The tragedy in Dakota Territory now seemed like a lifetime ago. All those years of being alone and miserable, drifting from cow town to cow town, killing if the need be, had passed. He had been a hopeless cause, a lost soul. Now all that had changed. He had met the most amazing woman that had ever walked the earth. She brought out the real him. She didn't care what he had done in the past. She knew that she could change him from his wicked ways and give him the life and love that he so very long needed. Levi knew that his whole life was taking a turn for the better.

As he rode along the old trail, the March spring air was cool and the grass was beginning to turn green. The breeze was blowing the tails of his coat as he rode at a gallop, his spurs jingling along. The sun was shining bright as it cleared the Kansas horizon and sparkled on the blades of grass. It was a gorgeous morning, and Levi was smiling from ear to ear. He had bought himself a new black jacket and vest and a new white starched tailored shirt. He had shined his boots and cleaned and polished his Colts. The wild rag Samantha had given him was around his neck.

Along the dusty trail, he saw several herds of buffalo, elk and pronghorn. He had the hunting fever badly, but something else was stirring in his blood and nothing was going to get in his way. There would be plenty of time for hunting when they returned to the ranch. All he cared about now was rescuing the love of his life. He could see her lovely face with those gorgeous blue eyes and that ornery little come-and-get-me grin. He wasn't wasting anymore time.

His anticipation was growing stronger and stronger with every mile. As he rode along the trail, he spotted something on the trail ahead of him. He couldn't tell what it was for sure, but he knew it was something alive. Maybe a deer or an elk. Thinking nothing of it, he just kept the mare at a steady gallop along the trail. Once he reached the spot where he had seen whatever it was on the trail, he noticed it had vanished. Looking at the ground, he stopped Star in order to investigate. He noticed horse tracks, five sets of them, all shod. They had headed off the trail for the brush up ahead. Levi's smile disappeared and he began to feel very uneasy. Who were these men? Why did they take off for the brush so suddenly?

Continuing along, he kept a cautious eye out, inspecting every bush along the trail. It looked like a perfect place for an ambush, but why would anyone want to ambush him? Still, you could never be too careful. When you least expected it, someone could be hiding in a thicket, ready to bushwhack you. They could be horse thieves, cattle rustlers, or just petty thieves that would steal your watch or the money you had in your poke.

Looking up the trail, he began to get a might edgy. Star began to switch her tail and snort. She was nervous about something, and so was Levi. "Easy girl," he said softly. Inspecting his surroundings, he began to spur Star to a trot.

"Hold it!" a voice called out from nowhere. "Hold it right there, mister!"

Two men came riding up from his left and three men came up from the right. All of them were heavily armed with carbines and one had a scattergun. Each wore a six-gun on his hip.

A tall man wearing a big brown hat with the brim flipped back said, "Drop them Colts in the dirt, mister!"

Levi looked the man in the eyes. "What seems to be the problem here, boys?"

The man spit in the dirt. "You sir…you're the problem. Now I said drop them Colts in the dirt, or I'm gonna bury you in it!"

Levi looked at the five men and knew that there was no way that he could draw and kill each one before they got him. They had five guns on him, and he could tell by the looks of them that they were prepared to use them.

"Mister, I'll tell you one last time." The man reached back and cocked the hammer on his Colt in his holster.

Levi slowly unbuckled his gun belt and dropped it to the ground. An empty feeling came over him the second those Colts hit the ground. He was now unarmed, except the carbine in the scabbard. His hideaway derringer was in his vest pocket, and his bowie knife…

"Drop that knife too," the man said.

Levi pulled the knife from his boot and dropped it to the ground. He thought about throwing it at the man, who appeared to be the leader of the outfit, but he had a strong feeling that he'd have been shot dead before he could spur Star.

"Now get down off that horse there, mister," the man said.

Levi eased his boot out of the stirrup and slid down off the mare.

"Woowhee, boys, get a look at them fancy duds. That's a right nice fancy horse ya got there, mister. In fact, I believe I'm gonna have to have that horse."

Levi's blood flowed with anger at the outlaws. He was in a bad position. There was cover about twenty yards off the trail if he could get to his Colts and break for it, but there was no way.

As the leader climbed down off of his horse, Levi said, "Stranger, I'd be much obliged iffen you'd reconsider."

"Excuse me?" the man asked with a grin.

"It's just that, this ol' mare has been with me many years now, and she don't cotton to no one else but me."

The men laughed and the leader said, "Well, now…ain't that a sweet li'l story? I'd say that almost made me cry. Then I'd have to shoot ya, sure's shit. No, mister, I don't reckon I will reconsider. I'm takin this horse and I'm gonna take these purty Colts here too. Now, what do ya think of that?"

Levi clenched his fists. "You worthless, miserable, cotton-pickin' Yankee bastard!"

As the man grabbed the reins of the mare, Levi looked down at the Colts, too far out of reach to get to them before the outlaw did. Levi breathed heavily as he watched the man lean down and picked up the Colts then buckle them over his own gun.

The men put their guns at ease, and the leader walked over to Levi. "I'm much obliged to ya for this purty horse. It's a long walk for ya from here, I reckon." He looked down and saw Levi's watch chain hanging out of his vest pocket. "Hand over that there watch, mister, and whatever else ya got there in your pockets."

Levi looked at the men and then looked down at his Colts on the leader's hips. They were both tied down, but the other one that the man was wearing was not. He looked down at the bowie knife on the ground a couple feet beside him and then looked back up to the carbine in the scabbard on the mare.

As the man reached for his watch, Levi slid his hand into his vest pocket and grabbed his derringer. Cocking the hammer back, he drew it out and shot the man right under his right eye. The bullet crashed through the back of his skull, and before he could hit the ground dead, Levi drew the man's gun from its holster and began to fire at the men as he rolled to the ground.

Shots were firing from every direction. Star reared up, kicking and bucking. One of the slugs Levi sent from the six-shooter struck one of the men in the chest, sending him off the back of his horse. Quicker than anybody had ever seen, he fired all six shots from the gun, sending three of the men to the ground. Two of them were dead and the other was hit in the arm. Smoke filled the air, and the prairie echoed with gunfire. In all the commotion, Levi managed to get his carbine out of the scabbard. He turned to fire it at the man, and a bullet struck him in the right leg just below the knee. As the bullet penetrated the skin, he could feel the flesh burn like someone had pressed a scorching branding iron to his leg. Another bullet struck him not an inch from the other bullet. Spinning, he began to fire wildly. One of the bullets struck one of the men's horses in the neck, dropping it to the ground, falling on its rider's leg. The man screamed in agony and Levi turned and shot him in the throat.

Shots rang out behind him and he could feel a bullet sink into his hip. Dropping to the ground, he fired the carbine from his hip until he had emptied it. Seconds after the first shot was fired, four men lay dead. The fifth outlaw had a slug in his shoulder, and Levi had one in his hip and two in his leg.

The man walked over to Levi. "Damn, mister, you're a tough son of a bitch!"

Levi lay on the ground, burning with pain. The outlaw rolled him over with his boot and pointed his gun right at Levi's face. Out of the corner of his eye, Levi could see his bowie knife lying right by his hand.

The man cocked his gun. "I'm sendin' you to hell, stranger!"

Just before the man pulled the trigger, Levi swung his arm under the man's feet as hard as he could, dropping the man to the ground, and the gun fired into the sky. As the man hit the hard ground, Levi grabbed the knife and lodged it into the man's chest, piercing his heart.

Blood trickled out of the man's mouth and down his cheek and made a pool on the prairie floor. Levi rolled over onto his back and breathed heavily as he stared up into the big open sky. Once he caught his breath, he tried to get to his feet, only to realize the bullet had broken his hip. He couldn't stand up, much less get into the saddle. He was in serious trouble once again.

Reaching up to Star as she walked over to him, he unbuckled the cinch and pulled the saddle off her back.

"Come here, girl," he said through clenched teeth. "Come down here."

The mare leaned her head down and he took her bridle off. Pulling his bedroll from the saddle, he curled up in it and laid there in agonizing pain, trying to figure out what he was going to do. He had told Bud he'd be back in a week at the latest. He had only been gone two days now. Bud wouldn't have any idea he needed help. As usual, he was all on his own.

After several hours, the sun began to set, and the air began to chill off. The whippoorwills were singing, and off in the distance a lone wolf began to howl. Levi drifted off to sleep.

THE MORNING SUN drew high in the Kansas sky. Levi had been shivering, fighting a fever, and in excruciating pain all night long. All that day and into the next night, he drifted in and out of consciousness. He hadn't eaten anything, and the only thing he had to drink was some whiskey from the flask he kept in his coat. He held his watch with Samantha's picture and her bracelet close to his face.

On the afternoon of the third day, Levi began to shake something terrible. His body was fighting all it could to keep from getting blood poison or gangrene. He poured whiskey into his wounds to purify them the best that he could, which probably saved his life once again as it had many times before.

Sometime just before sundown, the sound of hooves coming across the prairie jolted Levi awake.

"Hold it, boys!" a man yelled. "Good Lord Almighty! What in the hell happened here?"

Levi barely had the strength to open his hazy eyes. He heard a groan escape from his lips.

"By God! This one is still alive!" As the man slowly pulled the blanket off Levi, he softly said, "Easy, pardner, easy now."

Levi didn't move, though he wouldn't have been able to if he'd tried.

The man's voice broke through the darkness again. "Get that mare and saddle her up! We gotta get this man to a doctor and quick! Wayne, Lobo, you two give me a hand here. We gotta get this man in the wagon."

Levi felt them lift him up and carry him a bit before laying him on blankets. He was burning with a fever, but he tried to focus on what was happening. He saw one of them tie Star to the back of the wagon.

"Lobo," he heard a voice say, "check out these Colts. I'd say these are 'bout the purtiest pair of hoglegs I've ever seen."

Another voice spoke. "Reckon we oughta pick all these guns up and throw 'em in the wagon. Hell, these boys won't be needin' 'em anymore."

He watched them pick up his Colts along with all the outlaws' guns. They looked and saw Levi's scabbard empty, so they picked up the carbine and slid it inside the scabbard.

Levi groaned and pointed toward the spot where he had been laying, and one of the cowboys said, "Here's a watch!" He opened it up and looked at Samantha's picture. "She's beautiful."

He looked up at Levi, and through all the pain and agony, Levi gave a half-crooked grin and nodded. He walked over to him and handed him the watch, and Levi held it tight in his hand as he held it close to his heart.

"You alright, mister?"

Levi nodded. He didn't have the strength to talk or even hardly move.

"Well, boys," the foreman said. "I reckon we oughta give these men a proper burial. Grab a shovel off the wagon and let's get some holes dug. No matter what breed these men are, outlaws, whatever…they still deserve a decent burial. We gotta get this man to a doctor, so let's get to it."

The men got to digging five holes about four feet deep. Once they had the men properly buried, the foreman said, "Well, I reckon we oughta say something. Grab me my Bible from the wagon."

One of the men brought it to him, and he flipped through the pages. The men took off their hats as he began to read. Levi hazily recognized the twenty-third Psalm.

As soon as the foreman finished reading, he said, "Mount up, boys, and let's press on. We gotta push 'em on to the nearest town."

They all mounted up and, whoopin' and hollerin', they gathered the herd. "Alright, boys, let's move 'em out!" the foreman hollered.

As they rode along the trail, Levi heard one of the cowboys ride up to the foreman. "Dan? That poor fella, you think he's gonna make it?"

"Well, he's purty shot up, but I think if we get that lead out of him and he gets some rest and food, he'll have a chance."

Levi groaned as the wagon hit a bump and a fresh jolt of pain went through him. He welcomed the darkness as he slid off into unconsciousness.

LEVI AWOKE TO see it was just before sundown. The wagon was stopped, and he could hear the bustle of the men setting up camp.

"Jethro, gather some bush and start me a quick fire," shouted the man Levi remembered was the foreman. "Cookie, as soon as the fire is hot, boil me some water! We gotta tend to this man. God only knows how long he's been like this."

A while later, a man came over with the water. "Here you go, Dan."

Sitting in the back of the wagon in the dim light of the kerosene lanterns, Dan carefully undressed Levi. "Jethro, go heat this knife on the fire till it's hot, and then we'll try to get these slugs outta this fella." Levi felt vulnerable, but also realized this man was his only chance of staying alive.

Once the man brought back the knife, Dan said, "Wayne, hold that lantern up here close...Right there. That's good. This slug has torn through his hip. It's broke clean through." Feeling along the skin on the opposite side of the bullet's entrance, Dan felt the bullet lodged in the skin a couple inches from Levi's scrotum. "Damn, that sure was a close one!"

Levi cussed in agony. His faced was sweating something fierce and he had come down with a dangerous fever. He thought that his time had finally come. Tears filled his eyes at the thought of never making it back to Samantha.

The cowboys all huddled around the back of the wagon, their eyes as wide as silver dollars as they watched their foreman digging around Levi's riddled body with a scorching-hot knife. Levi squirmed and kicked and cussed.

"Found the bullet," Dan said. He held up a bottle. "Cowboy, you might wanna take yourself a swoller or two of this before I go to cuttin' on ya."

Levi opened his lips, and Dan gave him a long drink. The rotgut whiskey sent a welcome warmth and numbing sensation. Dan held up a stick. "Alright now, bite down, cowboy. This is gonna hurt like hell."

Levi braced himself for the coming pain. As Dan cut the skin where the bullet was lodged, it just popped right out in his hand. Dan chuckled. "That was a might easier than I reckoned."

After he cleaned the wound, he laid the blade of the knife back over the fire to get it good and hot again. Then he placed the scorching blade over the entrance and the exit of the wound.

"Lobo, grab me a strand of hair from this man's mare's tail."

Using the strand of hair, he stitched up the wounds. Then he looked over the rest of Levi's body. "There's a bullet hole just under his knee. The bullet tore clear through the front of his leg and stuck in the calf about an inch deep. I reckon the best way to get that bullet out is to cut the wound a heap wider and pull the bullet back out the same way it went in."

As he began to cut the skin, Levi drifted in and out of consciousness and dreamed of the lovely blue-eyed Samantha back in Council Grove. He had come so far. He was through hunting men down and drifting. He wasn't out looking for trouble, but trouble sure seemed to find him. He couldn't give up now. He wasn't going to be able to walk for quite a spell, if he did make it and he didn't get blood poisoning.

LEVI STARTLED AS a hand touched his shoulder.

"Wake up, pardner, you need to get some grub in ya." Dan gently shook Levi's shoulder. "One of ya boys get this man something to eat."

Levi relaxed, realizing he wasn't in danger.

Dan sat on the end of the wagon bed. "Here, pardner, eat ya some of this son of a bitch stew Cookie fixed up. It'll do ya a heap of good. Reckon you're too tired to lift your arms, so I'll just feed ya."

Levi, wrapped up in a blanket that smelled of horse sweat, said, "Yes sir, I do reckon I could eat a bit."

Dan watched Levi's face as he puckered up his lips.

"Boy, this sure is tasty." He burned his lip and cussed under his breath.

"Sorry, pard, might be a tad hot. Once ya eat up here, you need to get yourself some more rest. We're headed up the trail to Ellsworth. We should be there sometime in the next couple of days. We'll get ya to a doctor there."

Levi thought a moment. Ellsworth was north. He had to get to Council Grove, which was west. Ellsworth was out of the way, but he didn't have much of a choice either. If he didn't go with them, he'd be all alone and stranded on the prairie. He couldn't walk or even ride. He had to go wherever the cowboys were taking him. There he could get his rest and heal his wounds. Once he recovered, he'd leave for Council Grove.

Levi looked at Dan and softly said, "My horse?"

Dan grinned and nodded. "She's just fine, pardner. We fed her some oats and tended to her."

Levi smiled. "I'm much obliged to ya, mister, for everything. My luck sorta ran out on me quick."

Dan looked at him. "Those men we buried back there…They friends of yours?"

Levi rolled his eyes. "Not hardly. Damn horse thieves."

"All five of 'em?" asked Dan.

"Yes sir, every last one of them egg-suckin' bastards."

Dan had a look of shock on his face. "There were five of 'em, and only one of you. How…?"

Levi saw his eyes light up and his jaw drop. Levi squinted his eyes in pain as a terrifying shooting pain shot through his hip.

Dan watched him with sympathy. "Easy, pard, breathe now."

Levi took a slow, deep breath and tried to wait for the pain to pass.

"Where ya from, pardner?" Dan asked.

Levi thought for a minute. For the first time in years, he actually belonged somewhere. He had been a drifter for several years. Now he had a home and a ranch of his own. "I got a spread back on Soldier Creek outside of a li'l piece of a town called Wilmington."

"What in the hell ya doin' way out here?"

"Well, sir, I was trackin' a man I'd been after for a spell and stopped over there in Council Grove for a night. Little did I know that I'd meet the most handsome blue-eyed gal this side of the Mississippi."

Dan chuckled. "Oh, one of them dancing gals, huh?"

"No sir, she ain't! She's a true lady. The moment those blue eyes met mine, I knew I had to have her. She's a lovely little country gal and the sweetest woman you'd ever meet. I aim to give her the life she deserves."

Dan looked at him with a half-cocked grin. "My apologies, pard. She must be the girl in the watch. You ain't let that thing go since we picked ya up."

Levi smiled. "If ya only knew…"

Once Dan had helped Levi finish his plate of stew, Dan said, "Alright, pardner, you should get yourself some shut-eye. We're gonna push on up the Chisholm Trail and get you to a doctor. We got near two hundred head of Spanish Mustangs and right around two thousand head of longhorn cattle we're drivin' up from Texas. Might take us a spell to make it, but we'll get ya there one way or another."

Levi's body was stiff and sore, and he couldn't argue. "Thank ya kindly. I'm much obliged to ya boys."

"Call me Dan, pardner. I'm the ramrod of this here outfit." He looked at Levi waiting for a response, but Levi just nodded. "Alright, Dan, thank ya kindly." He appreciated that Dan didn't try to pry for his name.

Dan tipped his hat. "I'll be checkin' on ya, pard."

SEVERAL DAYS PASSED by, Levi bearing the pain and trying to rest as the wagon jostled him around. Just before sundown one breezy evening, Levi awoke to the sound of cheering.

"There she is, boys!" Dan said. "Ellsworth. We'll ride in and get this man to a doctor."

Levi lay on his back and watched the clouds go by as they pressed on. He could see the dust kicking up from under the cattle's hooves and tumbleweeds blowing across the prairie.

Levi heard a cowboy ride past the wagon. "Hey, Dan, you know what this means?"

"What's that, Jethro?" he heard the foreman answer.

"A town means a saloon, and a saloon means bug juice and dancin' girls."

Levi chuckled to himself, then grimaced as the wagon hit yet another bump.

"Jethro," he heard Dan say. "Y'all have earned it. I'm gonna have ya stay with the cattle about a half mile outside of town, and me and Cookie will take the wagon in and get this man to the doctor. Then we'll see about gettin' you all some rest."

Levi sighed. A bed would sure be nice. Until then, he might as well try to get a little more sleep.

LEVI WOKE UP as the team pulled to a stop.

"Howdy, Marshal," said Dan. "We need a doctor."

"You boys run into some kinda trouble?"

"No, not ourselves," replied Dan. "But we came across a feller on the trail 'bout thirty miles back or so."

Levi could hear the marshal's spurs jingling as he walked over to the wagon. Levi pretended to be asleep as he carefully looked through his nearly closed eyes. The marshal looked Levi over. "Who is he?"

Dan came over to the side of the wagon. "He's been shot twice, one of 'em through the hip. He can't walk none. He hasn't said his name, but I'll tell ya this, there were five rustlers that jumped him, and he kilt 'em all hisself."

The marshal looked at Dan. "Killed 'em all himself, you say?"

"Yes sir, we found 'em all full of lead near this feller."

Levi's stomach tightened. He tried to reach for the derringer in his pocket but was unable to move due to the pain.

Dan reached into the wagon and pulled out Levi's twin Colts. "These were on the ground by him when we found him. All the rustlers were wearin' guns. This man didn't, so I figured they was his."

Levi's heart raced but his strength was gone. He feared what the marshal would do if he realized who he was.

The marshal looked over the Colts. "I only know of one man that carries a pair of Colts like these." He looked at the inside of the cartridge belt and saw the notches that Levi had carved. Levi made a note to remember to add five more when he could.

Dan turned to the marshal. "I heard tell down in San Antone 'bout a fella in Colorado Territory that single-handedly took down four outlaws. That man was known all over the west for his nickel-plated twin Colts. The pair of Colts that we picked up were a matching description. They got some of the most beautiful ivory grips that a man had ever laid eyes on. They call this fella a two-gun pistoleer."

The marshal raised his eyebrows. "What was this fella's name you speak of?"

Dan took off his hat and scratched his head. "Ya know, I can't recall. They say he's the quickest gunman in the territory."

Levi feared the outcome of the marshal knowing his name, but something seemed a bit different. He didn't quite know how to describe the feeling, but he felt a bit safer than he had before. He wasn't sure why. He wanted nothing more than to change his lifestyle and go straight and hang up his guns for good.

The marshal turned as another man joined them. "James, go get Doc Anderson." The man nodded and left.

"We got his horse back with the herd," Dan said. "She's quite a horse. A palomino mare. He's got a '66 carbine too."

The marshal looked at Dan. "Why don't ya send your man to fetch that horse and the rifle when we get him settled. I'd like to find out just who this man is for sure."

"Marshal, I talked a spell with him, and he seems to be a decent fella. Said he's from back Wilmington way somewhere and he was headed to Council Grove to fetch a gal."

"Well, I'll wire the Marshal J.S. Vincent there in Council Grove and see if he can tell us anything about him or the gal he was goin' to fetch. She oughta know what has happened here."

Dan nodded. "Yes sir, Marshal. He never said her name, but maybe the marshal in Council Grove will know something."

LEVI LAY AWAKE in the dimly lit room, fighting the pain. It felt good to finally be in a bed, but a throbbing pain kept shooting through his head, making it hard to sleep.

The doctor sighed as he finished looking Levi over. "Boys, this fella looks like he's taken on the whole Yankee army himself. Whoever did the patchin' on him done quite well, but I'll need to check in often and clean the wounds."

Dan walked over to the bed and looked down at Levi. "Do you think he'll pull through alright, Doc?"

The doctor covered Levi with a blanket. "It's really hard to tell at this time. It appears he has been through way more engagements than just this one. Fella has bullet scars and what appears to be bite marks or something damn close to it all over his fool body. It's gonna be hard to tell for some time. I won't promise that this man will ever be able to walk again."

Levi's eye filled with tears as he groaned and covered his eyes with his hand. He imagined Samantha's face if he could never walk again. He felt like giving up right then and there, and he wished he had just died out there on the prairie instead of possibly being a cripple the rest of his life.

The doctor dug through his bag and pulled out a small blue medicine bottle.

"What's that, Doc?" asked Dan.

"Laudanum. It'll help this poor fella with the pain and help him rest, which is just what he needs to do for some time."

"Ain't that habit formin', Doc?"

The doctor shook his head and poured Levi a spoonful. "I reckon he has more to worry about right now than bad habits."

Levi sipped the laudanum. The taste was downright horrible. He couldn't understand how someone could make something so disgusting a habit.

The doctor left as Lobo entered the room, holding Levi's carbine. He handed it to Dan and then left.

Levi watched Dan hand his gun to the marshal. "Here ya go, lookie here at this stock."

The marshal rolled the gun over and inspected the engraved walnut stock.

Dan squinted his eyes in curiosity. "L.C.? What ya figure that stands for?"

The marshal grinned. "Well, by God, that's just what I figured. This man here has himself quite a reputation. That's the famous two-gun pistoleer, Mr. Levi Cord, for sure."

Levi was in more pain than he could recall encountering for quite some time. At this point he was so focused on the thought of never walking again that he couldn't care less if anyone knew his name.

Dan looked over Levi's rig. "That's sorta what I figured with those fancy Colts. You figure he's wanted for anything?"

The marshal shook his head. "This man is good friends with a marshal in Colorado Territory who happens to be one of my close acquaintances. He's quite a fighter, and you're right, he is a decent man to hear tell. You say he's headed to Council Grove to call on a girl?"

"That's right. He says she's quite a gal. Some blue-eyed country gal that stole his heart. You know how that goes."

The marshal smiled. "Unfortunately, I do. This man has been what most folks call a drifter. A ramblin' man of the sort. If you and I knew his whole story, I'm right certain we would understand this mysterious man. I hear tell he's got quite a story."

Levi slowly started to drift in and out. He saw Dan look at him. "Poor fella."

The marshal took off his hat and leaned Levi's carbine against the wall in the corner. "You say he had a spread back where?"

"Yes sir, Wilmington area."

The marshal smiled. "Well, by God, that's sure good to hear. This gal in Council Grove must be one hell of a woman to trip this boy's trigger."

"Yes sir, I reckon she must be."

Levi felt the laudanum taking effect. He fought for enough strength to open his eyes. He softly cleared his throat and the two men looked at him.

"You're damn right she is, boys."

Chapter 10

Back at the ranch on Soldier Creek, Bud began to get mighty worried about Levi. Levi had told him that he'd be gone for no more than a week or so, and now it had been over a month. It was the first part of April and the cows were dropping calves nearly every day. The spring showers had started, and all the creeks were full. Every evening, Bud would sit outside the cabin and gaze across the horizon hoping to spot Levi and Samantha returning.

As the sun went down, a strange and peculiar feeling came over Bud. Something was just not right. Levi should have returned weeks ago. Something had to have happened, but what? Indians, outlaws, wolves? Anything could be wrong. Levi could be lying out there somewhere alone needing help, or he could be out there in a patch of weeds shot dead. There was no way of knowing.

He decided that come morning he would set out toward Council Grove in search of Levi. Just before sunup, he saddled up his horse and tied his bedroll on the back of his saddle along with his duster and rifle. He filled his saddlebags with some bacon, salt, pepper, jerked beef, hardtack, and a bottle of whiskey. He also packed away two boxes of cartridges and made sure his sidearm was loaded, as well as his rifle.

As he set out on the Santa Fe Trail, his spurs jingled and his saddle creaked as his gelding galloped along. A prairie rattler lay out across a bleached buffalo carcass, sunning itself in the warm spring air. He gave it a wide berth.

He pushed toward Council Grove, praying everything was alright. However, he had a strong feeling in his gut that it was not. He came to a small cottonwood grove with five graves that appeared to be somewhat fresh. With all the rain the prairie had gotten, all the tracks that Levi would have made would be long gone. He rode up to the graves, then got down off his horse. Surely there would be some sort of sign as to what had happened there. As he looked around, he came to a spot where the brush was thicker than anywhere else on the trail in the area. It looked like a perfect place for an ambush. Pulling his rifle out of the scabbard, he jacked a cartridge into the chamber and cautiously proceeded. A strong stench filled the air. He spotted a rotting horse carcass. The smell was extremely rank, and Bud could tell it had been dead for some time. Wolves had pretty much cleaned everything out but the hide and bones, so it was hard to determine the cause of the animal's death.

Pulling his wild rag over his face, he got down on his knees and carefully searched the ground for some sort of sign. About ten feet away from the carcass, he found a shell casing. As he looked around, he began to find several more and a couple Colt cartridges. He knew there had been a fight, but he couldn't determine over what, or if Levi had been involved. There was no sign of Indians anywhere, so he was sure it was white men.

As he continued to look over the area, he came across an area where a large herd of cattle had been driven north. The rain had washed most of the tracks from the horses away, but there were several cow tracks still visible. He could tell there were several hundred head pushing north, probably to Abilene or Ellsworth. Bud couldn't find Star's tracks anywhere. Questions still unanswered, Bud mounted and resumed his journey.

The blue skies began to turn to clouds and the wind began to pick up. Thunder crashed, and it sounded like cannons echoing across the plains. Off in the distance, lighting made a crack and then came zigzagging from the big dark thunderhead clouds to the prairie ground. Bud's gelding, Shiner, snorted and let out a whinny. A big storm was brewing over the plains and it was going to make traveling across the prairie mighty rough…not to mention dangerous. The creeks would soon begin to fill up and rush with rapid white water and crossing them would almost be suicide. Cowboys always loved the spring weather for driving cattle, but they dreaded the thunderstorms the warm weather brought with it. Up in the mountains, the snow would begin to melt and cause the streams and rivers to flood. A lot of cowboys didn't know how to swim, and they feared reaching river crossings. Many of them drowned along the way. Bud knew how to swim, but not well enough to fight through moving water.

The storm got closer. Thunder crashed almost every second now. Rain began to fall, and in seconds it came pouring down harder and harder, falling on Bud's hat brim. He untied his duster from the back of his saddle and put it on to keep himself dry. He flipped the collar up around his neck to protect from the wind and continued on. The raindrops began to form puddles.

Across the soggy prairie, a herd of buffalo stood enjoying the spring shower. It helped keep the flies and other insects away and cooled them off tremendously.

The further Bud rode, the harder the rain began to fall. The wind began to howl something fierce as tumbleweeds bounced and rolled across the prairie. Bud's gelding began to switch his tail and shake his head. He stopped in his tracks, still shaking his head.

"Whoa, boy! Whoa. What in the hell's got into ya? Easy, boy! Easy, now! Settle down!"

Suddenly, Bud heard a commotion back down the trail. It sounded like a train that was hell-bent for leather across the prairie. However, there were no train tracks anywhere nearby.

Bud turned in the saddle. "What in the Sam Hill?!"

The clouds were a greenish gray color and forming a huge funnel shape that stretched out over the trail for at least a half mile wide.

"Oh, hell!" Pulling on his left rein to pull his horse around, he kicked with his spurs. "Hyah! Let's get the hell outta here, boy!"

Giving Shiner the reins, he leaned forward in the saddle and gave him hell. That horse took off faster than he had ever run before. Mud was kicking up into the air, flying up from his hooves.

As Bud looked over his shoulder, the sound of the storm brewing became eerie and petrifying. He saw the funnel spreading its way out and to the ground. As it touched down, it began to pick up the dark prairie soil and grass and turned it from a light gray color to a dark black. It was headed straight east toward Bud and it was coming fast.

"Hyah!" he yelled. "Hyah, boy!"

The twister was gaining on them, and the closer it got the quicker it came. Bud had never heard anything like it before. It was gurgling and roaring as it picked up tumbleweeds and yucca plants, along with everything else in its path. He could hear the sound of trees breaking in half. This twister was growing by the second and becoming very violent. It was now nearly a mile wide. Anything in its path was in serious trouble. There were only a few trees around, and that left very little cover for Bud to hide in. He was in terrible trouble.

He turned his horse at an angle, cutting northwest now, trying to get out of this deadly storm's path. Kicking that horse as hard as he could, he began to wonder if they were going to make it. The winds were blowing so strong that if he hadn't had his hat tied down, he would have lost it for sure. He had never felt such strong winds before. He had heard of homesteaders going through these violent storms but had never been in such a one himself.

"Hyah! Hyah, boy! Hyah!"

Up ahead, he could see a ravine that bordered a creek. He thought that if he could get to it in time, he could possibly get down out of the storm's path. Once he reached the ravine, he pulled back the reins and jumped from the saddle to the ground. "Down, boy! We gotta get down!"

He pulled the horse down to the ground, and, holding his head down, he huddled next to his horse, covering his face with his wild rag and his hat.

He heard a crack. As he turned to look, he saw a cottonwood tree bowed over. The winds were so strong that it was pulling up from its roots. He tucked his head down as the tree came breaking free from the ground. He felt it fly right over him, not two feet above his head. He looked to see it bounce a few times on the prairie floor and then all at once it was sucked straight up into the black sky. Water from the creek was forming a funnel and shooting straight up into the sky. It looked like it was raining from the ground to the sky. The twister was directly over them as it cleared the ravine. It passed over the creek within less than five seconds, but it felt like an hour.

The twister went along its deadly path, and Bud stood and pulled his horse up with him. "Easy, boy, easy." He patted him on the head as he watched the storm head its way west, terrorizing the prairie. It was unlike anything he had ever seen before.

As the twister faded out of sight, Bud took off his hat and ran his fingers through his dark brown hair. "Whew. That was a close one."

He climbed back into the saddle, shook his head, and continued on the trail, following the twister. Excitement tugged at his chest. He loved storms, especially twisters. They fascinated him and he often would chase them just to watch them curl and change form like a threatened rattler.

Riding along, he observed the damage from the storm. Trees had been ripped from the ground and carried miles from where they once stood. Mounds of dirt appeared every couple of yards where the twister had ripped the buck brush from its roots. Just down the trail, Bud came across a small sod house and what appeared to be a small barn. The twister had destroyed it, along with a corral and a small ten-acre crop. It had caved the roof of the soddy in, and one of the walls was blown down.

Jumping off Shiner, Bud called out, "Hello? Is anybody in there?" He tried to dig his way into the soddy, but there was too much debris and it was impossible to get inside. He searched the debris for any settlers. As he pulled back a large wooden table covered in fallen sod, his heart sank deep in his chest. He saw a man's leg covered in blood. The bone was sticking out just above the ankle. He carefully tore his way through the rubble, trying to free the man. Once he got the table and sod cleared off, he gently picked him up and carried him outside. The man was unconscious, and Bud wasn't sure if he was even alive.

He lightly tapped on the man's cheek. "Mister? Mister?" He leaned over and put his ear on the man's chest to see if he could hear his heart beating, and that's when he noticed the man's rib cage had been totally busted, most likely from the roof caving in on him.

Realizing the man was dead, Bud once again entered the destroyed soddy. He thought he heard someone crying, but when he turned around, he realized it was just a shutter squeaking as it blew against the fallen wall. His heart was filled with relief that it wasn't a human. As he continued to search, he came across a woman's dress and a cornhusk doll. His stomach sank and he now feared the worst. He knew that somewhere in all this rubble that was once a family's home was a woman and possibly a small child. He leaned over and picked up the doll, and when he turned around, he saw what he feared the most. It was a tiny hand sticking out from under a potbellied stove. The wall had crashed in and knocked the stove over, pinning the child on the ground.

Quickly, Bud cleared his way through the rubble to the stove. Once he finally reached it, he lifted it and discovered a small girl about five years old. He leaned down and picked up the little crushed, lifeless body. As he carried her outside, he noticed what must have been the mother buried under the sod wall. He shook his head. "My God." He placed the little girl on the ground next to the dead father and went back inside to dig the mother out. Once he got her out, he noticed her neck had been broken. He had no idea if there might be more, so he continued to search for the next couple hours.

After he was sure there were no other settlers, he wrapped the three bodies in blankets that he had found and began to dig three graves with a pitchfork that he dug out of the collapsed barn. Once he had buried the bodies, he took his hat off. His voice interrupted the now-quiet prairie air.

"Dear Lord, today has been a tragic day here in Kansas. These three settlers lost their lives for a reason I'll never know. What they done in your eyes to deserve this will forever remain a mystery. I ask you here today, Lord, to please look over the souls of this family. Give them everlasting life up there in the beautiful heavens with you and your angels above. Let them live in peace eternally in the hereafter, Father. In Jesus' precious name I pray. Amen."

Bud wasn't much of a praying man, but he spoke his heart. Once he finished, he began to sing the hymn "Shall We Gather at the River", his voice low and solemn.

He placed his hat back on his head and turned toward his horse. He had witnessed one of Mother Nature's deadliest tragedies firsthand. His heart ached for those that had lost their lives, and he feared that he might come across more demolished farms along the trail. He would stop at each one and search for survivors no matter how long it took. He took his horse by the reins and walked him down the trail a couple hundred yards and then began to set up camp. The sky was still covered in a blanket of dark black clouds. In the distance, thunder crashed, and Bud could see lightning flash in the west. It had finally quit raining.

All throughout that long and miserable night, Bud kept drifting in and out of sleep. He couldn't get the image of that poor little girl out of his mind. Her little blonde hair in braids and her dress soaked in blood. It just tore his heart in two. She was so young. Now her life was suddenly all over because of a devastating storm. It didn't even seem real to him. That was by far the worst night of Bud's life.

The next morning, Bud awoke and was amazed to see the sun shining bright. The storm had passed, and only a few clouds of dusty gray floated in the baby blue sky. It was going to be a beautiful day, much more beautiful than the day before.

Bud saddled up and continued his way toward Council Grove. Mud puddles covered the prairie floor and robins splashed wildly in search of their morning breakfast. Other than the prairie being soggy and muddy, it made for a good day to ride. About three hours after he'd set out, Bud began to see the building tops of a distant town. He realized he had finally reached Council Grove.

As Bud rode closer to town, he smelled an old familiar aroma blowing in the breeze. He rode over the hill and spotted a herd of longhorns being driven by a dozen or so cowboys. Some of the cattle had moss-covered horns that spread four feet wide. They were bawling and shaking their heads as they pushed up the draw just east of town. Bud was glad to see that the storm had left Council Grove untouched. He had feared that he'd be riding into another devastating disaster.

Riding into town, he turned onto the main street and rode past the Hays House to the marshal's office. As he got down off his horse, he stretched his legs and gazed over the town. It was a lovely little town, just as he had heard Levi brag about numerous times. This was his first time coming here.

As he walked up onto the boardwalk, a man walked out of the jail. "Howdy, stranger. The name's Vincent and I'm the marshal here. Is there something I can do for ya?"

Bud reached out his hand and pulled his leather glove off before shaking the marshal's hand. "Howdy there, Marshal. My name is Bud Christopher, and I'm from Wilmington way, back east a fair piece. My boss rode out here to Council Grove a month or so back and never returned." Bud didn't know who would know Levi by name, so he figured his title would do just as well.

Vincent's face got a look of interest as Bud went on. "You see, sir, he came here to fetch a girl and said he'd be back in a week at the latest, but he never returned. I set out to search for him and came across five fresh graves back yonder. There appeared to be a fight and I could see that a herd of cattle had been drove through headed north."

Vincent leaned on his cane. "I got a wire 'bout a month ago, give or take a few days, from the marshal up in Ellsworth. It seems some man was ridin' toward Council Grove here when he was ambushed by five rustlers. There was a shootin' scrape and the five rustlers all met their maker."

"What happened to the man they ambushed?"

"Marshal said the man took a slug in the leg and one to the hip. He's a tough son of a bitch, I'll tell ya. Some cowpokes driving a herd to Ellsworth found him a few days after the shootin', curled up in a blanket and barely still suckin' air. They took him up to a doctor in Ellsworth. I reckon he was in purty bad shape."

Bud gazed up the street and then looked back at Vincent. "Ya wouldn't happen to know this fella's name there, would ya?"

"Why, sure I do, stranger. He's the famous two-gun pistoleer the whole territory is talkin' of these days. The one and only man I know that can outgun five rustlers without getting kilt. He's Levi Cord."

SAMANTHA WAS WAITING tables at the Hays House when a group of dusty cowboys came strutting their way through the doors for supper. They all wore big leather batwing chaps and ten-gallon hats. They wore big fancy spurs on the heels of their tall stovepipe boots. They all could have used a shave and a bath, to say the least. They were rather polite and friendly, and Samantha could tell they were all Texas cowboys by the way they dressed and talked. As she walked over to their tables, they all looked up at her in amazement.

"What'll be your pleasure today, gentlemen?" she asked with a smile.

One of the men's jaw dropped. Taking his hat in his hand, he said, "Eyes as lovely and as blue as a Rocky Mountain lake. Hair as purty as a wild mustang runnin' down a canyon with the breeze blowin' in its mane. Smile as purty as a misty mornin' sunrise over the divide, shinin' on a grove of yellow aspens."

Samantha knew she was blushing something awful. All the cowboys had taken their hats off and were staring into her eyes. One of the cowboys said, "By golly, boys, she is!"

"Excuse me?" Samantha said, shifting nervously from foot to foot.

"You're her, ain't ya, ma'am? You just gotta be her."

"Her who?" Her eyes narrowed slightly.

"The lovely prairie rose that everyone's talkin' 'bout all over the territory."

Samantha began to grin and blush something terrible. She couldn't control herself. "Whatever do you mean?" In her heart she knew exactly what they were playing at, but she didn't dare let herself get excited before she had heard it for herself. She prayed she was right and that they had crossed paths with Levi…that he was keeping his word and truly coming back for her.

One of the other cowboys grinned. "You're the purtiest gal this side of the Mississippi. The sweetest thing outta the Flint Hills."

Another added, "Ma'am, they talk of you all the way up to Abilene and over to Ellsworth."

"What in tarnation are you boys talkin' about? Y'all must have got me confused with someone else." She placed a hand on her hip as she shook her head a little. She wished they would just say what she wanted to hear!

"I beg to differ, ma'am." The cowboy shook his head. "My name is Dan, and I'm the ramrod of this outfit. You see, we just happened to meet a handsome fella east of town here a fair piece that just went on and on 'bout you."

Samantha's heart raced wildly.

"Ma'am, we was drivin' a herd north to Ellsworth when we come across a creek bottom. As we crossed the creek and rode through the brush, we came across five dead rustlers and a man curled up in a blanket. He was clinging to a watch with a picture of a lovely woman inside it. The man had been shot once in the leg and once in the hip." His eyes drifted down from hers as he played with the brim of his hat.

Samantha's heart now sank deep in her chest as he went on. Her eyes filled with tears. She began to shake all over, and one of the men got up from his chair. "Here, ma'am, sit down." He took her hand and helped her sit. As the man—Dan?— went on, she felt as if her whole world was slipping away.

"Ma'am, this Levi fella kilt all five of them rustlers by hisself. We found him a few days after the shootin', clingin' to that watch and picture. He was in mighty poor shape. We took him with us to Ellsworth. Our foreman dug the bullets out of him on the trail and we put some grub in his gut. He was mighty weak, and we all feared that he'd die 'fore nightfall. We took him to the hotel and got him all cleaned up. The bullet in his hip broke the bone so he couldn't walk. He was in bed for quite a spell, but within a couple weeks he was well rested and eatin' good. He still wasn't able to walk none, but he's quite a fighter. Never once did he part with that watch. He held your picture close to him every second. He bragged and bragged from the moment he came to about how he was on his way to Council Grove to fetch the most amazing gal in the Flint Hills. He told us all about you, Miss Samantha. He showed us your picture and said that as soon as he could walk, he'd be on the trail to Council Grove to come and fetch you and make you his girl. He has been well tended to, ma'am. You shouldn't worry none. The first chance he gets, he'll be ridin' this way. You can bet on it."

Samantha couldn't believe what she was hearing. "I need to go to him!"

"Ma'am, don't take this the wrong way now, but we believe it'd be best if you didn't. Ya see, Levi's a very prideful cowboy. It'd tear him in two for you to see him in his condition."

"Nonsense," she replied.

"It's true, ma'am," one of the cowboys said.

"Give him some time, ma'am, and he'll be along. He's strong, and the love he has for you has kept him alive this long. He'll be fine. Just give him time and he'll be along directly. Trust us."

Samantha sat there for a moment and everyone was silent. After a few minutes, Samantha got up from the table.

All of the men stood as she did, and one of them said, "Ma'am, we hate to bring bad news to ya. Just know that Levi is just fine. He wouldn't want ya worryin' yourself none over him."

Tears began to pour down her face. "I'm so sorry, excuse me." She covered her face in her apron and ran out the back door into the alley.

Moments later, Miss Nancy walked up to her and handed her a soft white hankie. "Heavens, child," she said, taking her in her arms. "Easy, child, easy. It's gonna be alright."

"I'm so sorry," Samantha cried.

"Nonsense. I wondered what was goin' on inside that li'l mind of yours. The stranger, huh? He's sure a handsome drink of water, ain't he? You have nothing to be ashamed of, child. I've been there before. I know just how ya feel. My pa didn't cotton none too much to my first love. He was a gambler, and a poor one at that. I fell in love with him at first sight, but Pa wouldn't let me marry him. One day I woke up and I just knew what I had to do. He cared for me as much as I cared for him, so we jumped the first stage headed west and here we are in Council Grove near fifty-five years later."

Samantha looked up at her and smiled through her tears. She wiped her eyes. "How did you get the nerve to leave?"

Miss Nancy took her hand. "One day, I just packed my bags and said goodbye and then we took off. I loved Pa so, but leavin' was the best choice I ever made in my life."

Samantha hugged her. "Thank you so much, Miss Nancy."

"Child, I want you to take the rest of the day to find your inner self. Take some time to find out what it is that makes you happy and go for it! That stranger fella is a right handsome man. Hell, child, if I was a might younger, I'd be chasin' after him myself."

Samantha smiled. She really liked Miss Nancy. She made her feel comfortable. Mr. Schmidt made her feel the same, but hearing it from a woman's point of view really helped ease her mind and make her decision. She feared that her father would never speak to her again if she ran off with Levi, but her heart was telling her to. Folks were giving her advice without her even asking for it. They were understanding her true feelings without even hearing a single word.

Samantha looked into Miss Nancy's eyes. "What on earth will my father think if I run off with him?"

"Child, it's not what your father thinks or feels. It's how you feel. Don't go frettin' yourself over what your pa or others think or might say. This is your life, not theirs. Happiness that comes between a man and a woman, like that of you and that stranger fella, now that just don't come along every day. You could go spendin' your whole life livin' like ya do now, unhappy and just plain miserable. Or you could go live life to the fullest. There'd be no one to blame for your unhappiness but yourself. Sure, this fella has killed God only knows how many men, but iffen you ask me, they probably had it comin'. Ain't none of us God's precious angels. However, this stranger must think that you are."

Samantha smiled.

"Child, you have the grit and savvy that I once did at your age. I ain't no spring hen anymore, or you'd have yourself some competition. You can better that fella. Hell, child, you can better each other. Go for it! Rescue each other from loneliness. Live life and be happy."

Samantha smiled as she looked into Miss Nancy's eyes. She thought about everything she had said to her and everything that Mr. Schmidt had said previously. They were both right. She gave Miss Nancy one last hug. "Thank you so much for everything."

The woman patted her on the shoulder. "Child, you take the day and go think about what I said." She headed back inside.

When Samantha walked in, the cowboys all became quiet. She looked across the café to Miss Nancy and smiled. One of the cowboys said, "Ma'am, we apologize for upsettin' ya. That wasn't our intentions a'tall."

"I'm fine, boys…just a li'l shook up, but that's all."

Dan cleared his throat. "Ma'am, Levi would tan our hides raw iffen he'd knew we'd done told ya about him bein' all shot up and all. He's a prideful man. He cares a great deal for ya, you should know that. He intends to call on you just as soon as he can. You shouldn't worry none. He's a good man and he's got quite a surprise waitin' for ya."

"A surprise?" she asked. "What on earth could it be?"

"Well, ma'am, we'll just let Levi tell ya that hisself."

"I want to see him!" Samantha demanded.

"Miss Samantha, ma'am, Levi wouldn't cotton too much to that. I tell ya, it's just a man thing. If ya want to get in touch with him, he is stayin' at the hotel there in Ellsworth. You could send a wire to him. I'm sure he'd be obliged to hear from ya. You could even write him a letter iffen ya had a mind too."

Samantha felt a great deal of excitement come over her. A letter! She would write to him and tell him her true feelings and just what he meant to her.

"Splendid idea!" she said. "Do ya reckon he'd write me back?"

"Ma'am, iffen he don't, we will ride up there and give him a lickin'."

The cowboys all agreed, and Samantha smiled. As she walked out the door and headed toward the cottage, she had a smile from ear to ear. She knew where Levi was at and that he hadn't forgotten or changed his mind about her.

When she arrived at the cottage, she went to her desk and picked up a quill and a bottle of ink and a notebook of paper. She threw them into a basket with a blanket and headed down to the livery. Once she had saddled up, she headed toward Elm Creek. The sun was shining bright and there wasn't a cloud hanging in the sky as far as the eye could see. The breeze was blowing warm and strong. When she reached Elm Creek, she spread her blanket out on the ground.

She reached down into her basket and pulled out her notebook of paper and her quill and ink. As she tried to think of what to write, her mind raced with thoughts that had flowed through her heart each and every day since he had ridden away. Picking up her quill, she dabbed it into the bottle of ink and began to write.

Once she had finished the letter to Levi, she rode back into town and to the post office. As she walked in, she held her head up high. "Good day, Mr. Simcock."

"Good day, Miss Samantha. What can I do for ya?"

Samantha handed him the letter. "I'd like to send this letter to a friend who is staying at the hotel in Ellsworth."

"Her name, please?"

"Mr. Levi Cord."

The postman looked up with a look of amazement on his face. "I beg your pardon, ma'am?"

Samantha smiled, remembering what Miss Nancy had told her earlier. It wasn't about what others thought or felt. It was about what she felt.

"Yes sir...Mr. Levi Cord."

Chapter 11

A few days had passed since Bud had left Council Grove to find Levi. The weather was excellent for riding. A warm spring breeze blew in his face as he galloped along under sunny skies. Marshal Vincent had told him where Levi was staying to recover.

When he arrived in Ellsworth, he rode straight to the livery and paid the gentleman to stable and feed his horse, then he went directly to the hotel. When he walked in the door, he was met by a beautiful woman with long black hair and stunning dark brown eyes.

"Howdy, ma'am," he said as he took off his hat.

"Why, howdy," she replied with a sweet southern drawl.

"Ma'am, my name's Bud Christopher. My boss is said to be stayin' here somewheres."

"Who's your boss, Mr. Christopher?"

"His name is Levi Cord."

The lovely girl smiled. "So you're the cowboy he left in charge of his ranch while he returned to Council Grove to fetch his sweetheart?"

Bud stood there in shock. "Excuse me, ma'am?"

"Why, mister, I've heard all about you. My name's Cheyenne. I've been tendin' to Mr. Cord for the past few weeks." Bud's surprise must have shown on his face, because she quickly said, "Why, Mr. Christopher, I'm ashamed you'd even think such a thought. Mr. Cord is a gentleman. All he speaks of is his lovely prairie rose. I've just tended to his bandages and meals and such."

Bud ducked his head. "Why, certainly, ma'am. It's just that…" Bud looked up into Cheyenne's lovely brown eyes and lost his train of thought.

"What is it, Mr. Christopher?"

"You have such gorgeous eyes, ma'am."

Cheyenne smiled and blushed. "Why, Mr. Christopher, you are quite a charmer. Mr. Cord is in room eight, at the end of the hall on the left."

"Thank ya kindly, Miss Cheyenne. It's been a pleasure makin' your acquaintance."

Cheyenne winked. "The pleasure's all mine."

As he walked up the stairs, he turned to get one last look at Miss Cheyenne as she walked out the door. She was by far the most stunning woman he had ever laid eyes on. He knew exactly how Levi must have felt when he first met Samantha.

Reaching room eight, he knocked on the door and heard a man's voice say, "It's open." When he entered, he saw Levi lying on a big brass feather bed. His face was pale, and he had grown a full beard.

"Well, by God Almighty!" Levi said. "Bud! How the hell did you find me?"

Bud walked over and shook Levi's hand. "Well, Boss, you said you'd be back in a week at the latest, and when ya never showed up, I figured you was needin' a hand, so I set out to find ya. I came to a spot on the trail back east of Council Grove, where I found five fresh graves and enough empty cartridges to make a man figure a war was fought."

Levi grinned under his whiskers as Bud went on. "I come to a homestead that had been hit by a twister. Had to bury a man and a woman and…" Bud gritted his teeth. "And a li'l girl…Anyways, later I met the marshal in Council Grove."

"Vincent?" Levi asked.

"Yes sir. He told me he got a wire from some feller here in Ellsworth that told him you were laid up here, and I hopped on the trail north and here I am."

Levi smiled. "Well, pardner, you're quite a tracker. How's the ranch?"

"Well, Boss, some of the boys decided to stay on and tend to things so's I could come find ya."

"How's the herd?" Levi asked.

"Terrific! We had more calves than I had figured on. Still had a bunch nearly ready to drop when I set out west. The boys are tendin' to 'em just fine, though, so there's no need to fret. The week you left, we started building the barn and got 'er done and, boy, she looks right nice, iffen I do say so myself. We got up a corral and some cattle pens as well, so she's looking mighty purty."

Levi was silent for a moment. "By God, Bud, you're quite a cowboy, you know that? I don't know what to say, but I'm obliged to ya for everything. You're a true friend."

The two men shook hands again and shared a chuckle. Levi leaned over to the nightstand and picked up a box of cigars. Pulling two out, he passed one to Bud and then lit them both. They sat there smoking their cigars as they caught up on things.

After a while, the men were distracted by a knock at the door.

"It's open," Levi said.

As the door opened, Bud jumped to his feet. "Why, Miss Cheyenne!"

"Howdy, Mr. Christopher," she said with a little grin and a wink.

"You two have already been acquainted, I see," said Levi.

Cheyenne and Bud smiled at each other.

Levi cleared his throat. "I've been telling her some about ya the past couple weeks."

"So I've heard," replied Bud.

Cheyenne walked over to the bed and placed a tray of food on Levi's lap. "Thought you might be getting hungry by now." She turned to Bud. "Could ya stand a bite yourself, Mr. Christopher?"

"Call me Bud."

"Here, Bud," Levi said. "Take this lovely young lady on over to the café and treat her to some grub." He reached for his vest, which was hanging on a chair by the bed, and pulled a ten-dollar gold piece from the pocket. He threw it to Bud. "Go on now."

Bud smiled, excited at the thought of being in the company of a woman as beautiful as Miss Cheyenne. "Shall we, ma'am?"

Cheyenne smiled. "Why, certainly. I'd be delighted. Could you use anything else, Mr. Cord?"

Levi shook his head. "I reckon I'll get along just fine."

LATER THAT WEEK, the stage came rolling into Ellsworth carrying the mail. Levi could hear the creak of the wheels and the driver urging his horses to a halt. He peered out the window and watched the stage drivers unload the sacks of mail and carry them inside the post office.

Roughly an hour had passed when suddenly he saw a blur of motion outside the post office. The postman was running toward the hotel.

Levi could hear the commotion as the postman entered the hotel. "Mr. Cord! Mr. Cord! Which room is he in?" Apparently getting an answer, feet pounded on the ground like a heard of buffalo, and a knock sounded at the door. "Mr. Cord! Mr. Cord!"

"Who in the hell is it?" Levi had readied himself for the arrival as he heard the scene, but he still reached and drew his Colts from the holster hanging on the bed frame. It was likely just a letter, but one could never be too careful. After all, why would there be such a commotion for a simple letter?

"Postman, sir! You got a letter!"

Levi kept the Colts pointed at the door and cocked the hammers back. "Come on in, it's open."

The door opened, and the postman and the hotel clerk came rushing in.

Levi uncocked his Colts and laid them in his lap. "You say I got a letter? That's awfully funny. I ain't expecting no letter. Who's it from?"

The postman looked at the clerk and smiled. "It's from…from…" the man paused.

"Well, damn it, who in the hell is it from?" Levi demanded.

"It's from Council Grove, Mr. Cord."

Levi was confused. "Marshal Vincent?"

The postman shook his head. "It's her."

Levi's jaw dropped. "Samantha?"

His heart raced as the postman handed him the letter and he read the envelope. He pressed it to his nose. It smelled of the sweetest lilacs.

The clerk cleared his throat. "What's it say, Mr. Cord?"

Levi tore open the envelope and unfolded the letter. He looked up at the two gentlemen. "Sorry, boys, but would ya oblige me to a bit of privacy for a moment?"

"Why certainly, Mr. Cord," the postman said. "We'll be right downstairs."

As the men walked out the door, he began to read, his heart racing with anticipation.

My Dearest Levi,

I miss you so much it's unbearable. Your amazing eyes have my mind mesmerized every second of every day. You have haunted my dreams, yet in a good way of course, my darling. I fall asleep picturing you holding me close and whispering sweet nothings to me and making me feel indescribably wonderful. I wake up every day with a huge smile and lingering thoughts of you. I love you, Levi, so much. You are special in every way to me and it seems as if my whole world revolves around you. It's so hard to explain the feelings that you arouse in me. They are honestly like nothing that I've ever felt before.

My heart aches for you more and more with the passing of each day. Missing you is hell. I've never missed anyone as much as I miss you. God, it's killing me. You're simply amazing. I haven't been myself for the past few years, but when you rode into Council Grove all that changed. I don't know what it is that you did to me, but I am liking it. I love you, sweetheart, and, plain and simple, you make me happy. I need you in my life.

There are so many things that I want to say that I don't even know where to begin. You don't know how good you make me feel. When you held me in your arms, I felt like I was floating away on a heavenly cloud. I felt more comfortable with you than I have ever been with anyone before in my life. I felt like I could melt away in your embrace and stay there forever. I wish I could hug you like that and never let you go. I can't begin to tell you how amazing I felt in your arms, so loved and safe. I can't begin to explain the capacity of feelings that I have for you. I swear I can still feel your embrace and your kiss upon my cheek. You are truly amazing. I'd love to be your girl. Right now, I'd just about give anything to be snuggled up in your arms. The suspense and anticipation of that moment is killing me.

You have the most gorgeous blue eyes ever. The kind that seduce me without even really trying. I can't get them out of my head. Hell, I can't get you out of my head. You're always on my mind, making me smile just by thinking of you. You haven't the slightest clue what you truly do to me. I fall asleep every night with thoughts of you plastering a sleepy smile on my face and every day seems to be consumed with you. I miss you more than I ever thought possible. My life feels so joyful and enriched with you in it, and if I died tomorrow it would be just fine because you've made me happier than I've ever felt before. I love you, Levi Cord, and I promise I will until the very day I die. You deserve the world, and my biggest fear is that I may never be able to give it to you. I can't predict the future, but I will do anything in my power to make you happy and fulfill your life.

Many a night, I go out to Elm Creek, where we shared the most amazing night of my life. I pretend that, if only for a moment, you are with me, the summer breeze blowing ever so slightly. Crickets chirping, and the big sky full of beautiful big stars looking down on us. I promise you right here and now, Levi, that I'll do my best to make every day of your life worth living. Don't ask me what that means exactly. I reckon we'll just figure out together what makes life worth living as we go along. I'm no miracle worker, but I'll do my best to make you happy and be the best friend that you could ever have.

You're just the sweetest man alive. You make me feel so special, loved, wanted and desired. I feel as if I'm a giddy little schoolgirl. You fill every void that I have in love and in life. You make me melt inside just by saying hello. So far, my dreams have started to come true and I'm loving every second of it. You are a dream come true. My dream come true. I love you so, so, so much, cowboy. Your eyes, how they captivate me. I know there is a lot I don't know about you and all the things that have occurred in your life. Those blue eyes don't share anything with me. They are like a big wall of clouds that I can't break through, but yet I still walk toward them. I just get lost in them and fall deeper and deeper for you. You see something in me that I don't see in myself. I see something in you that you don't see yourself as well. That's what makes our relationship so amazing. I long for your kisses, your touch, your embrace. That stunning smile and your cowboy charm. Hell, Levi, I just long for you!

I heard of your misfortune on the trail. My heart aches for your recovery. Always know that you are in my prayers. My heart is eternally yours. I pray for the day that you recover and return to Council Grove. I'll be waiting for your return with anticipation. Take care of yourself, love, and if you need anything in the least, your girl will always be here. I love you, my dearest and most handsome Levi Cord.

All my heart,

Samantha

Levi sat there in shock and amazement. More joy overcame his heart than he had ever felt before. Never in his wildest dreams had he imagined he'd get a letter from her. How had she heard of his misfortune? How did she know where he was staying?

Carefully folding the letter, he placed it back into the envelope. He pressed it to his nose and smelled the intoxicating scent and smiled.

He sat there for several minutes, just staring out the window. He thought of Samantha and wondered what she would think of the ranch. Would she be happy there? Could he give her all that she deserved? He knew he could. Much better than her father could. He would love her and honor her for the rest of his life. Cherish her and care for her and all her needs and wants. He would settle down and give her a family. He had traveled many a lonesome mile, drifting and rambling. Drinking and killing. Saloons and dance hall girls had kept him company for the past several years, but no amount of whiskey or lewd women could ever satisfy his heart the way that Samantha would.

Levi had been in bed since the cowboys had brought him into town. He hadn't been out of bed on his own one single time. He was feeling a hundred times better than he had when they first brought him in, but his legs were extremely weak. He hadn't put any weight on his hip or tried to walk at all. His wounds were healing really well, but the wound where the bullet had torn through his hip was extremely sore.

All he could think about was getting back to her and he knew he had to heal quickly. She was waiting there in Council Grove. He had completed his unfinished business and bought some land and built his ranch. Now all he needed was Samantha's hand and a family of his own.

After several minutes, he leaned over to the nightstand and pulled out a piece of paper and a quill and a bottle of ink. He sat there for a moment, then began writing a letter, conveying his love and affection and praying they would be together again soon.

Shortly after he had finished, Bud and Cheyenne returned.

"So, Boss," Bud said. "I hear tell you got yourself a letter?"

Levi smiled. "Damnation, don't anything happen in this country without the whole daggum territory finding out?" He chuckled. "Yes sir, I did, as a matter of fact."

"Is everything alright with Miss Samantha?" asked Cheyenne.

"She's just fine," Levi answered.

Cheyenne picked up the tray. "Could I get you anything, Mr. Cord?"

Levi smiled. "No, ma'am. Thank ya kindly, but I reckon I'm gonna get myself a bit of exercise today."

"You shouldn't be getting outta bed just yet. You need your rest."

"Ma'am, I reckon I've got just about all the rest a man could get. Besides, I'll get plenty when they lay me in the ground in a pine box."

Bud stepped forward. "Ma'am, Levi here is a purty stubborn breed of cowboy. I reckon he could use some exercise."

Cheyenne shrugged her shoulders and rolled her eyes. "Men."

Levi and Bud both chuckled, then Levi slid his left leg over the side of the bed. Bud and Cheyenne walked over to him.

"Could you use a hand there, Boss?" Bud asked.

"Help me up, would ya?" Levi replied.

Cheyenne set the tray down and gently took Levi's left arm as Bud took his right. Levi slid his hands under his right leg and lifted it up and slid it off the bed and to the floor. "Damn!" he cussed.

Samantha bit her lip. "Are you sure about this, Mr. Cord?"

Levi gritted his teeth. "Yes, ma'am, I am." He had to get up and get back to his normal self. Samantha was waiting for him. He couldn't stand to think of her living the lonely and miserable life she had, stuck in Council Grove in that tiny cottage with her father. He pressed his weight onto his left leg and began to stand up. "Son of a bitch!"

Bud and Cheyenne held his arms and he stretched his back out straight. "Woowhee, y'all. That sure feels better."

It took several minutes for Levi to regain the strength in his legs to even try to walk a single step. His first step was hell. He felt as if he was a newborn child learning how to walk for the first time. After his first step on his left foot, he eased his right foot forward a few inches.

"Easy, Boss," Bud said calmly.

"That's it, Mr. Cord," Cheyenne said softly. "One foot at a time. Easy now."

"You're doin' great," Bud said. "Miss Samantha would be so proud of you. If she could only see you now."

Levi smiled through gritted teeth as he slowly slid his left leg forward a few inches, then his right. After his fifth step, his legs buckled.

Bud's gripped tightened as he lifted him up. "Easy, Boss! Easy."

"Nonsense!" Levi shouted. "Just hold me up, damn it!"

They held Levi up by his shoulders, and once again he began to relearn to walk. Step by step, inches at a time, he limped around the hotel room with the help of his friends. After about an hour on his feet, Levi's legs grew tired and he decided that he'd had enough, so he crawled back on the bed.

"You done good, Boss. Damn good." Bud chuckled. "You're as strong as an ox, Boss. You're quite a fighter."

Cheyenne smiled. "I didn't reckon you was gonna ever walk again, but I declare, you'll be back on your feet in no time a'tall. I'm right proud of ya, Mr. Cord."

Levi was feeling more pride than he had in years. His whole body ached, but he figured he'd get some rest and then give it another shot in the morning. He'd already come a long way, and he was determined to get to Council Grove.

Cheyenne picked the tray up once more. "Mr. Cord, I'm gonna go get ya some supper, alright, hun?"

"I'd be obliged, ma'am," he answered.

She turned to Bud. "Could I bring you something?"

"No, ma'am, I reckon I'll manage just fine. Thank ya."

"Alright then, boys. I'll see ya after bit. You just lay there and rest, Mr. Cord."

"I reckon to. Much obliged, ma'am."

As she walked out of the room, Levi looked at Bud and gave him a little grin. "What do you think, pardner? Mighty sweet gal, ain't she? Purty, too."

Bud smiled. "I reckon she is at that. I wouldn't mind havin' myself a gal like that someday."

Levi chuckled. "Well, what in the hell are ya waitin' for?"

Bud looked at Levi curiously. "What do ya figure, Boss?"

"She's a good gal, been through a heap of heartache in her life, but she's strong. Mighty good cook too."

Bud smiled and began to blush.

"She deserves a man like you, Bud. She's been walked on and treated poorly for way too long. I'm sure she'd just 'bout give anything for a cowpoke like yourself."

"You really reckon so, Boss?"

"Pardner, I've seen the way you look at her and she at you. I can see it in your eyes. She's been waitin' for a man like you for some time now. Hell, it'd do ya both a heap of good. She deserves a family and so do you. Think about it. Go take her for a li'l stroll."

Bud grinned. "I reckon I'll do just that."

THE NEXT MORNING, Levi awoke to a soft knock on the door. It was Bud and Cheyenne. "How ya feelin' today, Boss?" Bud asked as they entered.

"A might better, I reckon. Did y'all get my letter to the postman?"

"Yes sir, Mr. Cord," Cheyenne said with a nod.

"I'm much obliged to ya. I hope she gets it soon." Levi stretched his arms and sat up in bed. "So, Miss Cheyenne, ma'am, what's on the menu this mornin'?"

She grinned. "Got some fresh eggs and fried taters with a side of grits."

Levi's mouth watered as she placed the silver tray over his lap. "Sure looks mighty tasty, ma'am. Much obliged to ya."

"Weren't no trouble a'tall, Mr. Cord. Are ya feelin' up to gettin' yourself some more exercise today?"

Levi smiled. "You're damn right I am! Just as soon as I get through eating this magnificent breakfast."

Cheyenne blushed and shook her head.

There was another knock at the door, and the doctor stuck his head in. "Howdy, Mr. Cord."

"Well, howdy, Doc," Levi said. "Top of the mornin' to ya, sir."

The doctor walked in the door, carrying his black leather bag. "How ya holdin' up this morning? I heard ya was up walkin' around yesterday."

Levi nodded. "Yes sir, a li'l bit. Gettin' there. Damn hip hurts like hell, though."

The doctor shook his head and laughed. "Well, son, a slug'll do that. I brought you a li'l something that'll help ya walk when your legs are a might stronger." He handed Levi a black walking cane with a shiny brass handle on it.

"Thanks, Doc."

The doctor shook his finger at Levi. "You should still take it easy for a spell, though. Every two hours or so you should try to walk some and gradually put more weight on your right side there. You've seemed to heal quite well, considering the hell you put yourself through. You'll be just as good as new before too long, I reckon."

"That's my intention, Doc. Gotta be ridin' out soon."

The doctor smiled. "Yes sir, I reckon that gal has just 'bout given up on ya by now." He laughed at Levi's glare. "Well, I hate to run, but I got to be headed over to the Carter farm. Mrs. Carter should be havin' that baby anytime now. Gonna be awful funny if that baby don't look like Mr. Carter. Gonna be a heap more funny if it looks more like Deputy Gray. Take care of yourself, son, and don't overdo it, ya hear?"

AFTER BREAKFAST, LEVI swung his legs off the bed and on to the floor. Cheyenne and Bud held him up by his shoulders as he cautiously stood up.

"Easy there, Mr. Cord," Cheyenne said. "We've got all day…no need to rush."

He shifted his weight from one leg to the other and felt much stronger than he did the day before. Carefully, he took one step forward on his left leg.

"That's it, Boss," Bud said excitedly. "That's it. Easy now, you got this."

Levi slid his right leg forward and began to put some weight on it gently. It hurt like hell, but he placed all his weight on it and slid his left leg forward again.

"That's it, Mr. Cord, you're doin' great!" Cheyenne said with a huge smile.

Levi smiled through his gritted teeth. "Over to the door and back." Holding his shoulders to give him balance, they followed him across the room to the door then back to the bed.

A tear trickled down Cheyenne's face. "Oh, Mr. Cord, Samantha is gonna be so proud of you. She's gonna be so excited to see you!"

Levi nodded. "Now back to the door again."

After three times of the same routine, Levi decided it was time to try something different. "Alright, now hand me that cane."

Bud looked at him with wide eyes. "Are you sure about that, Boss?"

"Hand me the cane, Bud."

Bud reached over and handed him the cane. He took hold of Levi's shoulder, but Levi shrugged and said, "No. Let me try it on my own."

Levi stood up straight and then began to place his weight on his left leg. Pressing down on the cane, which he held in his right hand, he took one step forward with his left foot. As he dragged his right leg forward, he held tight to the cane. He was very shaky, but he kept at it. It took him nearly half an hour to go from the bed to the door on his own, but he was showing progress.

Bud shook his head. "Damn, Boss, you're 'bout as stubborn as a mule."

His legs were still very weak, especially his right one, but he was getting stronger. His hip was stiff and sore, but it wasn't going to stop him much longer. Each day he spent there in Ellsworth was one day less that he had to spend with her. He couldn't have that.

After dinner, he continued the same routine. He spent the whole day exercising and growing stronger.

Just before supper time, Cheyenne said, "Mr. Cord? Would you like me to heat a tub for ya?"

Levi considered her offer. "Ya know, ma'am, I reckon a hot bath would be right nice."

"Certainly. I'll get you boys some supper, then I'll heat ya two a couple of tubs." She smiled as she looked at Bud as he smelled under his arm and rolled his eyes.

Bud smiled and looked at the floor. "I reckon I could use a bath myself."

"Yes, Bud, I reckon you could at that," Cheyenne said with a grin and a wink. "You could also use a shave, too, iffen ya don't mind my sayin' so."

Bud felt his whiskers. "Indeed, ma'am, I reckon I could."

AFTER SUPPER, LEVI and Bud soaked in the tubs, cigars in hand.

Levi sighed. "Oh, hot damn, that feels mighty good."

"I'm right proud of ya, Boss. You've come a long way. You'll be in the saddle again 'fore ya know it."

"I reckon I will be. It's been a rough road, but I reckon once I get back on my feet and get Samantha back to the ranch everything will get better in due time. Pardner, I never thought I'd ever love again. After that day up in Dakota Territory, I sorta let myself go. I tell ya, I've been shot and stabbed and broken damn near every daggum bone in my body, but there is no pain that will ever equal the pain I felt when I lost her. I began to bury my sorrows in the bottle and dance hall gals, driftin' from cow town to cow town huntin' down men that weren't any worse than me for blood money. I did damn near anything to make a dollar in those days.

"Pardner, I was a lost soul, just a driftin' cowboy with no real destination in mind. There was a time I'd gotten purty mean and quick on the trigger. Hell, I'd shoot a fella just for lookin' at me crosswise." Levi stared ahead at the wall as he paused to smoke his cigar. "After the War, I strapped on that pair of Colts and set out west. I was still a young lad then, full of wildness. I headed south to Texas and took a job on a ranch breakin' colts. One night durin' the roundup, we all went into town and started drinkin' it up and havin' us quite a time. A few ol' cowpokes came in yellin' and cussin' and beatin' on a few of the girls, and I tell ya, pardner, I don't cotton one bit to no one beatin' on a horse nor a lady. I stood up from my chair and hollered at one of the cowpokes to remove his hand from one of the girls. He walked over to me and slapped me right across the damn face. He knocked my hat off my head and stomped it to the floor. I drew my Colt and sent a slug right through his upper lip. The slug sent three of his teeth out the back of his skull. All hell broke loose then. The three other cowpokes threw down on us and there was lead flyin' all over the damn saloon. One slug tore through my wrist and sent my Colt flying. I pulled the other one and began shootin' at one that was aimin' his hogleg right at me. I sent a slug right through his cheek. He fell to the floor holding his face and I turned and shot another man right in his jugular. After that things happened so fast. The other cowpoke was hit in the chest by six slugs, but I don't recall who shot him. I walked over to the man I'd shot in the cheek and he begged me not to shoot him again. I leaned down and picked up his Colt and placed it to his forehead. He was begging for me to have mercy on him, but I couldn't. 'You should never lay hands on a lady!', I told him. Then I kilt him. His brains splattered all over the floor. It was a ghastly sight if I ever saw one. I was only seventeen years old then, but no man could match me. I was forced to leave Texas. The marshal was friends with the men we killed, and though it was said to be self-defense, he didn't quite see it that way. I took off, and that's when I met the gal I was to wed. You know most of the story from there."

Bud looked at Levi. "Is it true you killed those Pawnee out there by Abilene? Was there really a dozen of 'em?"

"Yes sir. There was eleven of 'em, to be exact, but I fought 'em all myself."

"How in the hell did you survive?"

Levi looked him in the eye. "Prayer."

Bud shook his head and grinned. "What about those outlaws up there that held up the stage? Did you really kill all them, too?"

"Yes sir."

"They say you killed sixty men. Is that true?"

Levi looked him in the eyes and then looked out the window. "Pardner, I only kilt men that needed killin', or at least I thought they did." He looked back at Bud. "Times have changed."

Bud cocked his head. "How do you figure?"

"Bud, I have changed. The love of that beautiful woman has changed the way I look at life. That's why I bought that spread back yonder on Soldier

Creek and built the ranch. I can't change the past, but I can change the future, and I intend to do just that. I'm done huntin' men and killin'. Done driftin' and drinkin'. No more lewd women and lonely nights for this ol' cowpoke. I aim to marry that set of blue eyes and settle down. Start us a family and sit on the porch on our swing and watch the sun come up every morning cuddled in a blanket with her, drinkin' a cup of coffee."

Bud smiled as Levi went on. "Pardner, I love that gal, and I'm gonna give her the life she deserves iffen I have to die doin' it!"

"I reckon you will, Boss."

"Bud, I've seen the way that you act around that lovely Cheyenne. I ain't blind and I sure's hell ain't dead. You ought to settle down yourself and ask for her hand. Bring her back to the ranch and give her a family of her own. You're a good man, pard. A fine man. You'd make her a good husband."

Bud shrugged. "But, Boss, she's a…" He stuttered for a moment. "She's a whore, Boss."

Levi shook his head. "Pardner, these days a woman's got to do what she can to survive out here. That's a whole other reason you should take her away with ya. Don't hold her occupation against her. Take her with ya and love her and make her happy. You both deserve it."

BUD SAT THERE, feeling the water beginning to cool. Could he be a good husband to Cheyenne? Would she even want him? He could tell there was a strong connection between them, but asking her to go off with him was a bit different. Should he? What on earth would she say? He'd been married twice before, but he didn't have the best of luck with womenfolk. He was nervous, but he felt really comfortable around Cheyenne. She was unlike any of the other girls that he had courted in the past.

At that moment, Cheyenne walked into the room.

"Ma'am?" Bud shouted as he grabbed his hat and covered himself.

"Could you boys use some hot water?" Cheyenne grinned as she peaked into Bud's tub. "It sure looks like you could."

Bud's felt his face begin to burn. Levi laughed as she poured some hot water into Bud's tub.

"What's that matter there, Bud?" Levi asked. "Water gettin' a mite cold?"

Bud reached over the tub and picked up his boot and threw it at Levi. Cheyenne and Levi laughed, and Bud felt embarrassment overcome him.

"When you boys finish up, I'll have your supper ready."

"Much obliged, ma'am," Levi replied.

Cheyenne poured some hot water into Levi's tub. "Mr. Cord? How ya feelin' this evening?"

"Just dandy, ma'am. I could stay here for days."

Cheyenne headed for the door, then turned around. "Oh, I almost forgot, here's a razor and a mirror for ya, Bud." She walked over and gave them to him and as she did, she kissed him on the cheek. He felt his eyes widen and it felt as if his heart would gallop right out of his chest. He was growing mighty fond of Cheyenne.

Levi turned to him and smiled and shook his head. "Remember what I told you now."

After Bud had shaved and cleaned up, he dried off and got dressed, then helped Levi get out of the tub. As they got back to the room, Cheyenne brought them their delicious supper. Bud helped Levi get back into bed and together they sat and ate.

"She's sure a fine cook, Boss."

"Indeed, she is." Levi answered. "It'd sure be nice to have a cook like her around wouldn't it?"

Bud grinned with a mouthful of juicy buffalo steak. "I reckon it would be right nice."

Later that night, as he left Levi's room, Cheyenne was coming up the stairs. "Is there something else I can do for ya, Bud?"

Bud shook his head and grinned. "No, ma'am." He placed his hat in his hand and worked the band in his fingers nervously. "I was just headed out to take myself a moonlight stroll. Would ya care to accompany me?"

Cheyenne smiled and blushed. "I'd be delighted to, Bud."

"So would I, ma'am." He took her arm in his and together they left the hotel and headed down the street.

After a few minutes, she asked, "So, Bud, have you ever been married?"

"Yes, ma'am, twice actually."

"What happened?"

"Well, ma'am, let's just say we didn't see eye to eye. How 'bout you? You ever been married?"

"Me? Lord, no!" she answered with a laugh. "There have been men, but none of them stayed long. They'd always get what they want and then I'd wake up one day and they'd be gone."

Bud took her by the hand and looked her in the eyes. "I'm sorry."

She gazed up the street. "Sometimes I wonder if there even is a man out there for me."

Bud felt sorrow in his heart for this beautiful young woman. He couldn't understand why she didn't have men fighting for her hand. Even though her line of work had her courting any man passing through, he wished to take her away from that life. She was a true lady as much as he had ever seen. "Cheyenne, you're a wonderful woman. How any man couldn't see that I'll never know. I'd purt near given up on the whole love thing myself. That was, however, till I saw you. I want you to come back to Soldier Creek with me. I ain't got a damn thing to offer in this world but my horse and saddle, but Levi has started his ranch and I tend to help him run it as long as he'll have me on. I might not have much yet, but I promise that I'll do my best to take care of you and love you for the rest of your life."

Cheyenne's eyes filled with tears. She wrapped her arms around him. "Oh, Bud, I will go with you in a heartbeat."

He wrapped his arms around her and kissed her. They held each other for several minutes before continuing their stroll. How could a woman as beautiful and kind as her be a whore? She deserved the world and maybe he was the one to give it to her.

Bud and Cheyenne returned to the hotel and headed back to Bud's room. Once inside, Cheyenne turned to Bud and took off his hat. He unbuckled his gun belt and dropped his Colt to the floor. He slid his boots off as quickly as he could, and she unbuttoned his trousers and pulled them off. Bud unbuttoned his vest and slid it off with his shirt. He reached around her and slid his hands to the back of her dress and unbuttoned it. He gently tore it away from her body and cupped her breasts in his hands.

"Oh, Bud," she moaned softly. "I need you. I need you now."

He threw her onto the bed and took off her bustle. She wrapped her legs around him and pulled him as close as she could to her. Moments later, he leaned down and began kissing her breasts as he took her. Their bodies were shaking and sweating as they made passionate love.

As they lay in each other's arms, Cheyenne laid her head on Bud's chest and he brushed his fingers through her hair and kissed her on the forehead. "You are truly amazing, Miss Cheyenne."

"You're truly an amazing man, Mr. Christopher." She leaned up and kissed him.

Bud wrapped his arms around her and held her naked body close to him. He kissed her neck. "I'm so glad I met you."

"I've been waitin' for a man like you for what seems like forever, Bud. Mr. Cord has said such great things about you. He was right, you're quite a gentleman." She rolled over and began kissing him once again, and, just before the sun came up over Ellsworth, they made sweet, passionate love once again.

Chapter 12

It seemed like forever since Samantha had sent the letter to Levi. She counted the days as she went through her routine, the hours rolling by slowly. Every time she would pass the post office, or her father would bring in the mail, she would find her heart racing, but no letter ever came.

She had been at the café since morning, the foot traffic slow but steady. When the door opened again, she looked up and smiled at the familiar face.

"Good afternoon, Mr. Simcock," Samantha said walking up to his table once he was seated.

"Good afternoon, Miss Samantha."

She sat down at a corner table, feeling sweat trickling down her forehead. "What can I get for ya today?"

Simcock smiled. "How 'bout a cup of coffee and a steak with some onions and taters?"

"Will that be all?"

"For now, I reckon. Forgive me for sayin' so, but you look mighty purty today, Miss Samantha."

She blushed. "Why, thank ya kindly. I reckon you just earned yourself a piece of blackberry pie." She smiled. "I'll have your steak out to ya directly."

"No hurry, ma'am."

She rushed her way through the café taking orders and cleaning tables while Simcock sat there patiently at his table.

Samantha soon came out with a pot full of hot coffee and a plate of fried taters and onions on top of a juicy slab of steak.

"Mmm," Simcock said. "Looks delightful. Thank ya, ma'am."

She poured him a cup of coffee and then went on waiting and cleaning tables. The Hays House slowly began to clear out. When he finished his plate, Samantha brought out a piece of fresh blackberry pie. "How was your supper? Everything alright?"

"Ma'am, that steak was the best I've ever sank my teeth into."

"Well, I'm glad you enjoyed it, Mr. Simcock."

"I saw your father today."

"Oh?"

"He came into the post office this afternoon to fetch your mail. I told him you hadn't received any today, but as a matter of fact, ma'am, a letter did come for you."

Samantha's heart began to race wildly. She sat down at the table across from Simcock. "A letter for me?"

He reached into his jacket pocket and grabbed the letter. As he handed it to her, her hands were shaking. "I didn't tell your father," he said. "I didn't want to—"

"Thank ya for that," Samantha interrupted. "Thank ya so much!"

"No one else knows that it came for ya neither. The way I see it, it's none of their business. I figured you'd probably want to open it later after you finish here. I hope it brings you some good news."

Samantha nodded, slipping the letter into her apron pocket and heading back to work.

Simcock ate his pie, then wiped his gray mustache. He paid for his meal and gave her a nickel tip. "I thank ya. That was a right fine meal."

"Thank ya, Mr. Simcock. You come back now, ya hear?"

"Will do, will do." He looked at Samantha and gave her a little grin.

"Thank you so much," she whispered with a smile.

After the Hays House finally closed, Samantha helped clean up and do the dishes. She was anxious to get home so she could read Levi's letter.

"Land sakes, child, you look exhausted," said Miss Nancy. "You go on home and get ya some rest. We'll finish up here."

Samantha wiped the sweat from her forehead and her cheeks with her apron. "Are ya sure, Miss Nancy?"

"Yes, child, go home and relax a spell. You need it."

Leaving the Hays House, she hurried down the street to the cottage as fast as she could. The sun was going down and the beautiful red and orange painted itself across the sky. When she walked inside, she quickly made herself some lemonade and changed her dress. Her father was out somewhere, so she had the cottage to herself. She took her lemonade outside on the porch and sat down on the swing to read the letter. Her hands were shaking wildly as she opened the envelope and pulled the letter out. She took a sip of lemonade and began to read.

My Dearest and Most Lovely Samantha,

I was so grateful to receive your letter. I send my deepest apologies for not returning yet. I have thought of you every second of each passing day. Your love has kept me alive, when the Devil thought otherwise. It's been a rough and miserable journey without you. I miss you terribly. I long for your company. I long for your breath upon my skin.

I finally succeeded at my unfinished business and am ready to settle down and start a new life. I want you to be there by my side. I have a surprise for you, my love, and I hope you'll like it. I have been getting stronger and better every day. I'm not in the shape I was when you last saw me, by all means. I hope you won't be disappointed in my appearance. As I said, it's been a rough trail.

My heart longs for you. I promise with all my heart that I will return to Council Grove for you the very first chance I get. I love you, Samantha. Oh, how I love you. I've spent many a lonely night on the trail, watching the golden sun set over the horizon and thinking of you. You are always on my mind. You are truly the most amazing woman I've ever met. I love you dearly. You truly stole my heart the moment I looked into those soft, delicate blue eyes of yours. You have brought out a side of me that I never thought I'd see again. You are the most stunning, most handsome woman alive. I long to spend the rest of my life with you. I hope I can make you the happiest woman ever. I'll do my very best to give you the life that you deserve and make all your hopes and dreams come true. I desire you, darling. Keep being beautiful and keep being you. You are one of God's greatest creations, and I stand by my word on that. One day soon I'll be riding back to Council Grove and calling on you. When I ride out, you'll be going with me. We'll start a new and better life together and live happily together for the rest of our lives. I will always cherish you, my love. I love you from the depths of my soul.

Your Dearest Cowboy,

Levi Cord

Her eyes filled with tears as she folded the letter up and placed it back in the envelope. They were tears of joy. She had never felt so loved and wanted in all her life. She knew Levi would forever make her feel just the way that she felt now. She knew he would love her and take care of her. Nobody had ever made her feel as special and wonderful as he did. He was such a charmer, even through a letter. She pictured him holding her in his arms and telling her each line as she got lost in his piercing blue eyes.

After several minutes of staring at the flowers she had planted in her garden, she decided to write another letter to Levi. As she sat on the porch swing, she tried to think of what she should write. She had so many things she wanted to say to him. As she set down her glass of lemonade, she began to write what she was feeling in her heart.

After she finished her letter, she went inside and grabbed a pair of scissors from her sewing box. She cut off a small lock of her hair and tied a small yellow ribbon around it and stuck it in the envelope with the letter and then sealed it up. She kissed the back of the envelope and then went inside to run herself a hot bath.

BRIGHT AND EARLY the next morning, Samantha drank herself a cup of hot coffee, then dressed and headed for the post office. As she walked down the street, she began to hum one of her favorite songs. It was the lovely southern ballad "Dixie". As she strolled along the boardwalk, she could hear the cattle bawling in the stock pens just outside of town. Robins were singing and splashing in mud puddles, evidence there had been a spring shower sometime during the night. A rooster crowed just up the street. Chickadees called to each other from a plum thicket behind the Hays House, and a male cardinal called from his perch atop a cedar tree by the jail. Seconds later, a female answered his call, and the two flew over to the banks of the Neosho. The sun was shining bright, and, off in the distance, Samantha could see the dark rain clouds that had passed over Council Grove just hours before. It was going to be a warm and lovely day.

Once she reached the post office, she noticed that Simcock hadn't yet arrived. She decided to sit down on the bench out front and wait. She had the day off from working at the Hays House and as she sat there waiting, she enjoyed watching the birds splash in the puddles and sing their lovely songs. She loved the outdoors and nature. She was about as country as a girl could get. She loved animals and dreamed of raising her own someday.

About twenty minutes had passed by when she spotted Mr. Simcock walking up the street. Once he reached the post office, he tipped his hat. "Why, Miss Samantha, top of the mornin' to ya."

"Good mornin', Mr. Simcock."

"I expect you've got another letter for me, don't ya?"

She smiled. "Yes sir, I sure do."

As he unlocked the door he said, "So, ma'am, how's Mr. Cord?"

She grinned. "He's gettin' better, I reckon. He's a strong and prideful man."

"So I hear tell. Does he intend on ever returnin' to Council Grove?"

Samantha nodded. "I expect he will."

He turned to her. "Ma'am, he would if he knew what was good for him."

Samantha blushed as they walked inside.

Simcock took off his jacket and hat and hung them on a coat hanger by the door. He took down the closed sign and went behind the counter. "So, ma'am, the letter?"

Samantha handed it to him. "When do you expect he'll get it?"

"I expect sometime near the end of next week. The stage headed to Salina will be here 'round ten today. I'll see to it that it gets on there."

"Thank ya, Mr. Simcock. I sure do appreciate your help."

"No worries, ma'am, it'll be our li'l secret."

"Good day, Mr. Simcock," she said as she opened the door to leave.

"Good day to ya, ma'am."

As she left the post office, she stopped by the cottage and changed into a yellow-and-white-checkered dress. Even though wearing yellow meant you were a soiled dove, it was still her favorite. Most folks frowned upon those types of womenfolk, but Samantha just admired the color and loved the dress. She didn't cotton too much to what other folks thought when it came to her attire.

Samantha braided her hair and tied two little yellow ribbons at the end of her braids. She gathered her basket and a quilt and set out for the livery. After she had Lightning saddled, she rode south of town a few miles in search of some wild prairie flowers.

As she rode along, the warm spring Kansas breeze blew in her face. She smiled as she watched a couple jackrabbits chase each other. "Hey there, li'l ones," she said. "Y'all are so stinkin' adorable."

Just ahead, she spotted a small grove of trees surrounded by the most beautiful blue wild indigo patch. She crawled out of her saddle and grabbed her basket and began to pick the flowers. She placed the first one in her hair and began to hum.

After about an hour, she spread her quilt down on the prairie floor and stared up at the white puffy clouds that spread across the Kansas sky. It was so peaceful out there, surrounded by rolling hills. The breeze was slightly blowing through the grass and making it look like waves across the ocean. A meadowlark sang his lovely tune as a pronghorn grazed in the distance. Lightning grazed on the prairie grass nearby without a care in the world.

She found herself gazing at the northern horizon and daydreaming of Levi riding tall on his gorgeous palomino. She could see it so clearly…his big black coat with its tails blowing in the breeze, that big flat-brimmed hat protecting his face from the hot sun. A smile covered her face as she drifted off to sleep.

Several hours later, Samantha awoke and decided to head back into town. After she took Lightning to the livery, she took her basket of wild prairie flowers and headed to the Hays House. As she walked inside, Miss Nancy looked up from behind the counter and smiled. "Land sakes, child, can't you get enough of this place?"

"Yes, ma'am," Samantha said with a grin. "I just wanted to bring ya these flowers I picked." She reached into her basket and pulled out a small bouquet.

"Why, child, bless my soul. Those are lovely! Thank you." She grabbed a porcelain vase and poured some water into it, then placed the flowers in it and set it on the counter. "They sure brighten up the place, don't ya reckon?"

"Yes, ma'am, they sure do."

"You truly are a blessin', sweetheart."

After she left the Hays House, she headed over to the Cottage House to see Mr. Schmidt. "Well, howdy to ya, Miss Samantha. Don't you sure look lovely today."

"Howdy, Mr. Schmidt, and thank ya kindly."

Mr. Schmidt walked out from behind the desk and took Samantha by the hand and gently kissed it. "It's always a sweet pleasure to see you, ma'am."

Samantha blushed. "Thank ya."

"Any word from you-know-who?"

"Mr. Schmidt, who are you speaking of?"

He smiled. "Well, I declare, girl, that stranger fella."

"Oh, him. As a matter of fact, iffen ya should know, I received a letter from him just yesterday." She giggled and smirked.

"Yes? How is he recovering?"

"Slowly, but he is getting stronger each day."

"That's wonderful news. He should be ridin' back this way soon then, shouldn't he?"

"I'm prayin' so."

"He will, he will. Just give him some time to heal properly. So, Miss Samantha, what brings you to the Cottage House on this beautiful day?"

She reached into her basket and pulled out another small bouquet of wildflowers. "I thought you might like some prairie flowers I picked today."

"They're right purty. I'll set them right here on the counter." He took a glass of water and put the bouquet in it and set them on the walnut desktop. "Thank ya, ma'am. That stranger fella has no idea how lucky he is."

"Well, Mr. Schmidt, I should be on my way. I just thought I'd say hello and drop these flowers off for ya."

"Well, thank ya, ma'am. You have a good evening, Miss Samantha."

"Same to you sir." She headed over to the post office.

"Why, Miss Samantha," Simcock said. "I didn't figure to see you back so soon. I'm afraid there's no mail for you and your father today."

Samantha smiled and reached for another bouquet of flowers. "I just wanted to stop by and give ya some flowers that I picked today. To say thank ya for...well...you know..."

Simcock smiled. "Bless you, Miss Samantha. You didn't have to do that."

"I know, but I wanted to."

"I'll give ya a holler when your letter arrives."

"Thank ya, Mr. Simcock. Thank ya so kindly."

"You have a blessed day, ma'am."

"You do the same. Tell your wife hello for me."

"I will."

When she reached the cottage, she knelt to pick a couple of daisies that grew along the walk. Inside, she placed the rest of the flowers along with the daisies in a vase on the dining room table and filled it with water. She went to her room and sat down at her desk and began to unbraid her soft blonde hair. Once she had unbraided it, she ran a comb through it and splashed her face with water to wash away the dust from her ride. She took off her dress and slid into her robe. She loved the way it felt against her body, so soft and comforting.

After she had eaten supper, she gathered some porcupine quills and beads and began to make a bracelet. She thought she would make one for her cowboy. She'd been in a good mood ever since she had gotten his letter. She had needed to hear from Levi for so long. She had been so stressed out for the last few months. When she received his letter, a tremendous amount of hope and joy came over her. She now knew he thought of her and was still coming back for her. She had been so worried about him, but now she knew he was alright. She was so relieved and would rest easier at night. Once she finished making Levi's bracelet, she went to her room and crawled into bed. Shortly later, her father came in and she acted like she was asleep. She didn't want to argue, and lately that's all they seemed to do.

BACK IN ELLSWORTH, Levi awoke feeling much stronger than he had felt since the ambush. He sat up and wiped the sleep from his eyes, then swung his legs out of bed. Outside his window, songbirds sang their familiar lovely melodies as the sun rose over the horizon. A dog barked up the street as it chased a squirrel up an oak tree. Levi reached for his cane and then slowly stood up. He stood there for several minutes and then started to ease his way around the room, one step at a time.

After about an hour, he got dressed and stuck his derringer in his vest pocket. He put on his hat and walked out the door and leaned on the balcony.

"Good morning," he called down to Bud and Cheyenne, who were sitting downstairs drinking coffee.

"Well, top of the mornin' to ya, Boss," Bud replied. "You look a heap better today."

Levi grinned. "Yes sir, and I feel a heap better."

"How's the ol' hip holdin' up, Mr. Cord?" Cheyenne asked.

"Well, ma'am, it's mighty stiff this mornin', but I reckon it's getting a lot better than it was."

"You cotton to gettin' some more exercise today, Boss?"

"Well, pardner, I'm thinkin' I might catch me some fresh air, iffen you two don't object to helping an ol' cripple down those damn stairs."

Cheyenne looked at Bud with a grin. "What do ya think, Bud? Should we help him down the stairs?"

Bud grinned at Levi. "I reckon we can help him get down 'em, but he's on his own gettin' back up."

Levi shot Bud a dirty look. "You damn ornery cuss, you can keep it in your britches long enough to get me back up those damn ol' stairs, can't ya?"

Cheyenne blushed, and Bud chuckled. "Well, Boss, I reckon we can get you back up there iffen we have to hog-tie ya and throw ya over my shoulder."

They all laughed, and Bud kissed Cheyenne. They walked up the stairs and each of them took Levi's shoulders and helped him down the stairs.

"Easy now," Levi said through clenched teeth.

"What do you think, Cheyenne, should we push him?"

Cheyenne giggled. "Bud, I declare."

"Your eyes just melt me right out of my boots," he said.

"Oh, Bud, you're talkin' foolish."

"No, it's the gospel truth."

Cheyenne blushed, and Levi said, "Y'all are 'bout to make me sick."

Once they got him to the bottom of the stairs, he walked toward the door on his own with the use of his cane. Cheyenne opened the door and the sunlight hit Levi right in the face. He squinted his eyes and took a deep breath. This was the first time he had been outdoors or even out of his room since he had arrived in Ellsworth. As he walked outside, he took another deep breath and started to limp his way toward a bench that was outside of the marshal's office.

"Well, howdy, stranger," a voice called from inside the jail. "Didn't figure to see you up and at 'em so soon."

Levi sat down on the bench and the man inside the jail came out the door. He was a tall drink of water with a big handlebar mustache and was wearing a black frock coat. He wore a big flat-brim black hat like Levi's. He walked over to Levi and offered him a cigar. "Cigar, stranger?"

Levi said, "I'd be obliged, Marshal. Say, I've been thinkin' about this, and ain't I seen you somewheres before?"

"Stranger, I hear tell you was in the War with my brothers, James and Virgil."

Levi thought for a moment. "That don't ring a bell, Marshal."

"Well, from what I hear tell, you was on a different side than they was."

"Was they Yanks?"

"Yes sir. Fought at Pea Ridge there in Arkansas."

Levi scratched his head. "Hell, I was at Pea Ridge. I suppose you'll be wanting my kind out of town then, eh, Marshal?"

"Stranger, the War's been over for goin' on, what, seven years now? The past is the past…I've got no quarrels with you. I've heard all about you, but, hell, who hasn't? They say you killed near sixty men and that you can draw them twin Colts as fast as ol' Wild Bill himself, if not a heat faster. They say you killed a dozen Comanches all single-handedly up near Abilene."

"They were Sioux."

"Pardon me, a dozen Sioux Indians. I've heard tell of you, Johnny Reb."

"That's it!" Levi said. "You're Wyatt Earp, ain't ya? I mighta known."

The marshal reached out his hand. "Yes sir, and you're Levi Cord."

"Yes sir, Marshal." Levi shook the marshal's hand. "Mighty fine cigar."

"So, Johnny Reb, you still bounty huntin'?"

Levi looked the marshal in the eyes. "No, Marshal, I reckon those days are over for me. I got myself a spread back near Wilmington and I reckon I'm gonna head back there after a spell and work my ranch and retire my guns."

"After you head back to Council Grove for that lovely gal of yours, I expect," the marshal said with a grin.

Levi couldn't figure out how the marshal knew about Samantha, but he smiled and said, "Yes sir, Marshal, I'll be swingin' through there first."

"I wish you the best of luck, Johnny Reb."

"Much obliged to ya, Marshal."

"Iffen you need anything, just holler."

"Thank ya kindly, Marshal."

The marshal tipped his hat. "Good day to you, Mr. Cord."

"Good day to you, Mr. Earp."

As Levi sat there on the bench, he watched the people walk up and down the streets. They all seemed friendly and happy. He liked the little town of Ellsworth. A herd of longhorn cattle came around the corner, pushed by a dozen dusty cowboys that had just ridden in along the Cox trail. The cowboys were whistling and hooting and hollering as they pushed the cattle up the street to the nearby Union Pacific Railroad. Their spurs were jingling, and Levi smiled as he looked at one of them closely. It was a young boy, maybe twelve years old. He reminded Levi of himself when he was that age. All he ever wanted was to be a real working cowboy. He remembered his first drive north from Texas, up the Chisolm Trail. He was young then, but he could do the work of a grown man.

As the cowboys passed by, Levi gazed up the street and saw a man playing with an adorable little boy around three or four years old. He thought about Samantha and wondered if they would have a little boy, or maybe even a little girl. He dreamed of becoming a father and teaching his little boy to rope and ride and to hunt and fish. He had never thought about children before, but once he met Samantha that all had changed. Now that was all he could think about…ranching and babies and marrying Samantha.

After a couple hours of enjoying the fresh air and watching people come and go, he decided to head up the street to the saloon. As he limped his way through the swinging doors, the piano player quit playing and everyone turned their heads toward Levi. They stared quietly as he walked up to the bar. "Barkeep, sarsaparilla."

"Certainly."

Levi reached down to his hips and noticed something different. This was the first time he'd ever been in a saloon without his twin Colts. A slight sense of fear flowed through his blood as he felt inside his vest pocket and felt for his derringer. He might not have the Colts, but at least he wasn't completely unheeled.

As he stood there sipping his sarsaparilla, the barkeep wiped the bar. "Well, Mr. Cord, we didn't expect to see you walking so soon. How are you feeling?"

"Just dandy," Levi replied.

Everyone in the saloon began to gather around Levi and ask him all sorts of questions. "Mr. Cord, Mr. Cord, are you going to be heading to Council Grove soon? How are you feeling? Why ain't you healed, Levi?"

Levi grinned and sipped his drink. "I'm feeling quite a bit better, y'all. A lot better than I was lying out on the trail with that slug in my hip, I'll tell you that much." The people smiled as he went on. "I plan to head toward Council Grove in a week or two."

"To get Miss Samantha?" a voice asked from the crowd.

Levi smiled. "You bet. I tell y'all, I only saw her one time when I fell head over my bootheel for that lovely blue-eyed gal. When I left her and headed to Colorado Territory, that love I felt for her grew stronger and stronger with every mile I rode west. I was attacked by a pack of bloodthirsty wolves one night and shot and licked up purty bad by those outlaws I was chasin'. As I lay there thinkin' I was never gonna make it off that cold and snowy pass, I kept her picture close to me, and, I tell ya, as I stared into those gorgeous angel eyes of hers, I got the most strongest will to live. I had to survive. Had to fight the pain and the cold. I couldn't let her down. I'd promised her I'd be back for her, and I couldn't bear to break that angel's heart. I hung on and got through it all thanks to her. I tell y'all, there's nothing stronger than the power of true love."

A lovely blonde saloon girl, wearing a green dress and feathers in her hair, smiled as a tear fell softly down her cheek. "That is so romantic! Are you going to ask her to marry you, Mr. Cord?"

Levi blushed for a second. "Well, ma'am, I reckon I'll go to Council Grove shortly and take her to this little spot on Elm Creek. I reckon I'll ask her to marry me there and then start a little family and raise our cattle."

Everybody in the saloon smiled.

A few moments later, Levi turned to the piano player. "It sure is quiet in here, ain't it?"

The barkeep hit the piano player in the shoulder with his towel. "It sure is, Levi. Billy, why ain't you playin' that damn thing? I didn't buy it to sit there and collect dust."

The piano player walked over and began playing. Instantly, Levi recognized the tune. It was one of his favorites, "The Yellow Rose of Texas". He limped his way over to the piano and sang along with two saloon girls.

A couple hours later, Levi decided he had been up and moving around long enough. He was getting sore, and he decided to head back to the hotel and eat some supper, then get some rest. Once he entered the hotel, Bud and Cheyenne greeted him with ornery grins. "Well, howdy, Boss, you look all tuckered out."

Levi looked them both in the eyes. "What in the hell are you two grinning about? You been up to no good?"

Cheyenne smiled. "Mr. Cord, whatever do you mean?"

Levi replied, "By God, girl, you two look like a pair of foxes just come out of a henhouse."

Cheyenne blushed. "Are you hungry? I was just about to rustle up Bud something to eat."

Levi nodded. "Why, yes, ma'am, I reckon I worked up quite an appetite today out there. Some supper would be right nice, iffen y'all don't mind getting my crippled ass up those damn neck-breakin' stairs."

"Sure thing, Boss," Bud said as he stood and pinched Cheyenne on the rear.

"Bud!" she shouted, blushing.

Bud laughed. "Come on, let's go get this worn-out ol' cripple up to his bed."

Levi smiled and shook his head. "Boy, you're askin' for a whoopin'."

As they reached the top of the stairs, Levi began to get tired and weak. He had been on his feet for most of the day and was ready to relax. In the room, he took off his vest and shirt and Cheyenne and Bud helped him get his boots and pants off. Once down to his longhandles, he gently slid his way into bed and let out a huge sigh of relief as his head rested on the feather pillow. "Damn, that feels better."

"You gonna feel up to ridin' soon?" Bud asked as Cheyenne left the room.

"Well, my hip hurts like hell still, but I reckon by next week or so I should be back in the saddle again. Let's hope, anyways."

Bud looked Levi in the eyes. "Boss? I want to thank you for all you've done for me. Takin' me in, and givin' me a job and home and all. I'm sure obliged for everything. I've had a spell of bad luck for the past nine years or so and was runnin' from life itself when you found me."

"I know you'd been running from somethin', pardner, but I wasn't sure what. Hell, we're all runnin' from something. I didn't know and I didn't care to know just what it was you were runnin' from. I figured if you wanted me to know, you'd tell me when you had the mind to. Pardner, I've seen and done a lot of things myself, most of which are kept unspoken. I'm no angel neither. I don't hold a man's past again him."

Bud nodded. "I rightly appreciate that, Boss. God only knows where I'd be now if it weren't for you taking me on."

Levi smiled. "Pardner, I've met all sorts of men in my time on the trail. Lawmen, outlaws, rustlers, horse thieves, you name it. Hell, I've rode with both a time or two. When I first laid eyes upon you, Bud, I could see in your eyes I could trust you. Yes, I could tell you'd had a rough past, but so have I, and I couldn't hold it against ya. I knew my herd was safe with you."

Bud smiled. "How did you know you could trust me?"

"Pardner, in all my years and miles, you get to learn people and who you can trust."

"Well, Boss, I'm sure glad I happened to be ridin' that same trail you was that day. I'll be forever in your debt, Boss. I'll never let you down."

"I know, Bud, I know."

"You're the only person I would truly call a friend, Levi."

"Bud, you have helped me more than I could ever ask. You have given me what I have always dreamed of. You helped me build my cabin and ranch. Pardner, you came lookin' for me and you found me. You are a true friend, and I'm proud to say that."

The two men shook hands as Cheyenne walked in with their supper.

"Hope you boys are hungry," she said with a smile. "Am I interrupting something?"

Bud looked at Levi and then at Cheyenne. "No, darlin', I was just about to tell Levi here that we plan to get hitched."

Levi's eyes got big as he smiled. "Well, congratulations. When are y'all plannin' on this big weddin'?"

Bud looked at Cheyenne. "Well, we ain't talked about it quite yet. But I reckon just as soon as Cheyenne here wants to set a date." He pulled her down onto his lap and kissed her. "What do you say, darlin'?"

She smiled. "Oh, Bud, whatever you wish."

"No, whatever you wish."

Levi smiled and picked up his supper. "Looks delicious, Cheyenne, right delicious."

"Well, thank ya, Mr. Cord. I hope you boys enjoy it. I'll be downstairs if y'all need anything."

AFTER THEY HAD finished their supper, Bud and Levi sat and chatted about the past and their futures and a little bit about anything and everything that crossed their mind. They came to learn a great deal about each other and bonded exceptionally well that night.

It wasn't long before Levi had drifted off to sleep. Bud looked at him and smiled. He walked over and picked up the dishes from Levi's lap and tucked him into bed.

"Good night, pardner." He blew out the lamp and carried the dishes downstairs to Cheyenne.

"Is Mr. Cord still hungry?"

"No, he's asleep...he's had a long day. Let me help you with the dishes, love, then let's head off to bed ourselves."

"So early?"

Bud gave her an ornery little grin, and she looked him in the eyes. "Bud, you behave now!"

"You know you want it."

"That's not the point, you ornery little cuss! Besides, you've already proven you can't handle it."

He pinched her on the butt and kissed her soft tender lips. They laughed and joked while washing the dishes, then chased each other up the stairs.

Chapter 13

Levi had been up and exercising every single day the past week. Each day he stayed out a little longer and walked a little further. He was healing wonderfully, getting stronger and stronger, though his hip bothered him something fierce after being on his feet all day.

He was getting dressed when he heard a knock at the door. Limping over to the door his hand gripped the knob and pulled it open slowly, the bright smile of the hotel clerk greeting him. "Mornin' sir, the postman dropped by and left off a letter addressed to you." He held the letter out to Levi and gave him a wink.

"Good day to ya, sir," Levi smiled as he took it. "Much obliged to ya." He closed the door and limped back to the bed where he sat on the corner and tore open the envelope. Unfolding the paper, he began to read.

My Dearest Levi,

I was so excited to get your letter today. I miss you terribly. I long for your presence. How are you holding up, my love? I pray you are recovering quickly. My heart aches for you so. Not a single day goes by that I don't get lost in thoughts of you. You are by far the most amazing gentleman I have ever met. Your charm just sweeps me off my feet and takes my breath away. I love you so, Levi. I wish you could be here holding me tight and never let me go. I dream of the day that you return to Council Grove and back to me. I've pictured it in my mind near a million times over. I am so ready for your return. I want to spend the rest of my life in your arms love. I want to start a family with you and love you unconditionally till the day I die. You mean more to me than you'll ever know. You stole my heart from the first time that I looked into your gorgeous blue eyes. I lie awake every single night, thinking of you. You truly do something to me that no one has ever done before.

Do you know when you might be coming back to Council Grove yet? You've got a lot of folks praying for your recovery. You are in my prayers both day and night, and constantly in my thoughts. I hope you are feeling well and getting the proper care that you need. I wish I could be there to take care of you. Things haven't changed all that much here. I took a job at the Hays House. It's stressful as a dickens, yet it keeps me busy and keeps my mind occupied. Things with Father tend to just get worse every day. I reckon that will help me when I leave. I pray you mean everything you have said to me. I have fallen so hard for you, love, and there's no turning back now. I'm so ready for a life with you. I hope this letter finds you well. I have enclosed a small gift for you, until we can be together again. I love you, Levi Cord, with all my heart, and I always will. I look forward to getting your next letter if you don't return before then. You are much a stronger person than I have ever been. I love you, cowboy.

All My Heart,

Samantha

He pocketed the bracelet she had made for him. Having read the letter, the urge to get on the trail toward Council Grove was overwhelming. He couldn't wait any longer. As he left the hotel, the warm breeze blew his coat tails up. He squinted his eyes as the wind formed a dust devil and blew it up the street. He favored his right leg, leaning on his cane, as he strolled his way up the street to the livery stable.

Once he reached the livery, he walked inside and grabbed a handful of oats. He walked over to Star and softly said, "Hello, girl, how ya doin'?" He fed her the handful of oats and picked up the curry comb and a brush. She snorted and shook her head as he scratched her forehead. After he spent several minutes brushing the mare, he slid a blanket over her back and swung his saddle onto her and cinched it tight.

"Easy, girl," he said softly. "Easy, let's just see if we can do this here." He put his left foot in the stirrup and hung on to the saddle horn. For several minutes he bounced up and down on his feet, getting used to the feel of jumping back into the saddle.

"Easy, girl, easy." He reached up and grabbed onto the cantle. "Here we go." He held tightly onto the saddle and prepared to give all he had. As he jumped up off the ground, he pulled himself up, but he didn't have enough strength to swing his right leg up and over. He struggled for a moment before falling to the ground. "Son of a bitch." He got back up to his feet and dusted himself off before trying again. This time he got closer but still was unable to swing his leg over the saddle. Once again, he fell to the stable floor and felt his pride being crushed. His eyes filled with tears as he gritted his teeth and tried to mount up another time. This time he hit the floor harder than before and landed directly on his right hip.

"Damn it! Why, God? Please help me. Please, God, I'll do anything. Just let me ride again." He stayed there on the floor in the hay and wept for several minutes, letting out all the bottled-up emotions.

Moments later, the door opened and in walked Bud. "Levi!" he yelled as he ran over. "Levi, what in the hell are you doing?"

Levi quickly wiped the tears from his face. "Don't look at me, Bud, I ain't fit to be seen right now!"

"Aw, Boss, everyone falls apart now and then. We're only human. There's nothing wrong with shedding a tear or two sometimes. Hell, I've shed enough to fill the Neosho River ten times the past few years. Sometimes I just ride off alone to break down and cry."

Levi looked Bud in the eyes. "Really?"

Bud smiled. "Yes sir."

Bud reached down and helped Levi get to his feet. The last fall had bruised Levi's hip something awful. Bud took him by the arm and helped him walk back over to the hotel and up to his bed.

Levi felt as if he would never be strong enough to ride again. "Damn it, Bud, why in the hell can't I just get into the damn saddle? If I could just get in the damn saddle I could ride!"

Bud took Levi's hat and laid it on the table by the bed. "Boss, you'll be on the road soon enough, trust me."

Levi gave a look of disgust. "I've been here in this damn godforsaken bed for too damn long. I've gotta get to Samantha."

ABOUT A WEEK later, Levi and Bud walked to the café for breakfast. It was a chilly May morning, but warmer than the week before. As they walked in the door, Levi limped his way over to a corner table. He was still relying on his walking cane.

As they sat down and took off their hats, a lovely lady in her early twenties walked up and asked what she could get them. They both ordered coffee with steak and eggs.

"So, Boss," Bud said. "What are you grinning about?"

Levi's smile widened as he wiped his hair to the side of his forehead. "I reckon I'll be riding out of here in a day or two. I figure I'll be able to get in that damn saddle by morning, then I'll be off at first light. I reckon it's been long enough. Too damn long."

"Would you like me to ride along with you to Council Grove, or would you rather me head back to the ranch?"

"Pardner, I'd be obliged if you'd ride along with me. I don't reckon I'll stay long…just pick up Samantha and head back to the ranch."

BACK IN COUNCIL Grove, Samantha had been having an extremely difficult time. Her relationship with her father had gotten worse. They fought on a daily basis and she was at her wits' end. She couldn't take it any longer. Her father would absolutely not hear of her leaving with Levi. Samantha truly felt in her heart, though, that he would be relieved once she was gone. He had told her before that she reminded him so much of her mother, and with her living with him it had become a daily reminder.

Samantha wanted to give up on everything. She couldn't focus on her quilts and jewelry or even at the Hays House. She was hurting inside so bad that she couldn't stand it anymore. Not a second went by that she didn't think of Levi. She would wake up late at night longing for his touch. Her heart ached for him so much.

That morning, Samantha was dressing to go to the Hays House when her father walked in the room, face red. "Folks been sayin' that idiot's comin' back for ya. I hear he's been stopping at every whore house in Colorado Territory that he can find. If you have any intentions of leaving this house with him, you better get it out of your head this second! He is trash, that stranger. He's a killer and a woman beater. I forbid you to see or write to him!"

Samantha's blood filled with anger. She had to get the hell out of there soon. She couldn't take his negativity and biased thinking. Why did he even want her here? Oh, if only Levi would rescue her from this hell.

Her father continued. "There are much better men out there for you. He's no good and never will be. He'll drag you down and beat you and sleep with every two-dollar whore in Kansas."

Samantha fought back the tears as long as she could. She cried on a daily basis and her father didn't seem to care one damn bit. It seemed he would intentionally make up lies about Levi just to upset her. She was beginning to see he was an evil and selfish man who showed no true care for his daughter at all.

After listening to her father go on and on about Levi, she stormed out of the cottage and headed to the Hays House in tears like usual. This was just another day, the same as nearly every damn day lately. But nothing was going to get in the way of how Samantha felt about Levi. He was her soulmate, her cowboy, her life.

As she reached the café, she dodged into the alley for a moment and broke down worse than she had for a long time. She covered her face with her hands and cried for several minutes before going inside. She felt like giving up on everything.

A KNOCK SOUNDED, and Bud opened the door. Levi stood there, Colts strapped to his hips, keeping his cane clenched tightly in his hand as he leaned on it. "Mornin', Boss. You look mighty anxious to hit the trail." He moved aside so Levi could enter the room.

"Mornin', Bud." Levi limped in, favoring his right leg and hip. "Reckon it's about time. I'm fixin' to head over and see if I can get my crippled ass in that damn saddle, iffen ya still got a mind to ride with me."

Bud pulled his suspender straps up over his shoulders and put on his vest and boots. He glanced out the window. "Yes sir, Boss, it's gonna be a right purty day for ridin', iffen ya ask me."

"Yes sir, right fine day it is."

Cheyenne came up to the room. "Well, good morning to ya, boys. Where ya off to this early?"

Bud walked over to her and wrapped his arms around her and smiled. He couldn't believe that he was falling so quickly for this woman, but he was sure he wasn't leaving without her. "Cheyenne, the time has come for us to be headin' out. Levi here is getting mighty anxious to go get his girl. I don't reckon he could stay another day." He turned to Levi and grinned.

"Ya damn right," Levi stated. "Get me to my damn horse."

Bud looked into Cheyenne's eyes as he took her by the hand. His heart was filled with excitement. "Well, darlin', you got yourself a horse?"

Cheyenne looked at him curiously. "No, Bud, I don't. Why?"

"Hey, Bud," Levi said. Bud turned to see Levi dig down inside his vest pocket and pull out a couple coins. "Here, you two lovebirds. Take this and see if you can buy this gal a horse and saddle." He tossed the gold pieces to Bud.

Bud couldn't recall ever having a friend quite like Levi. Overwhelmed with gratitude, he walked over to Levi and shook his hand. "Thank ya kindly, Boss. This sure means a great deal to me. I'll pay ya back as soon as I can."

"The hell you will, Bud," Levi snapped. "You go get that girl on a damn horse and let's get on the trail."

Bud wrapped Cheyenne in his arms once more and began kissing her.

Levi cleared his throat.

Bud grinned and blushed. "Sorry, Boss."

"Let's go, you two, I ain't waitin' long."

Bud smiled and they helped Levi down the stairs, which took about half an hour. He could walk better, but he still got around extremely slow. Levi had taken to complaining of feeling like he was an eighty-year-old man. Honestly, Bud thought Levi should wait awhile longer before setting out on the trail. Levi needed to take the time to regain his strength, yet Bud knew that arguing with Levi would be like arguing with a stubborn old nag of a horse.

When they reached the livery, Bud asked which horses were for sale. The man pointed out a white mare.

Cheyenne gasped. "She's beautiful."

Bud looked over the horse. "How much ya askin' for this here mare, mister?" He could tell that the horse was sound and had plenty of spirit and would make a suitable fit for Cheyenne.

The man scratched his black beard. "I reckon a good horse like this oughta be worth thirty dollars."

Bud looked at Levi, who was leaning on his cane. "What ya thinkin', Boss? Think this ol' nag is worth that?"

Levi looked over the horse. "Yes sir, thirty sounds right fair to me."

Bud studied both the man and the mare for several minutes. He really wanted this mare, but he wanted to be sure to get a fair price as well. "You throw in a saddle and you got yourself a deal."

The man shook his head. "No sir, this horse is worth a heap more with a fine saddle. I reckon it will cost ya fifty iffen I throw in a saddle."

Bud reached in his pockets. He only had two silver dollars in addition to the two twenty-dollar coins Levi had given him. Uncertainty gripped him. He looked up to see Cheyenne looking at him intently.

She dug down into her velvet coin purse and pulled out eight silver dollars. "Here, Bud, I've been savin' this up for a bit, and now seems a good time to use it." She handed Bud the money and he smiled as he kissed her hand. He realized at that moment that Cheyenne was indeed destined to be his woman. He felt a bit of embarrassment at first but was too overcome with excitement to let it bother him.

Bud turned to the man. "Well, sir, I reckon fifty dollars it is. You got yourself a deal."

The man saddled the horse as Bud walked over and helped Levi throw his saddle over Star's back. After cinching it up tight, Levi carefully raised his left leg up to the stirrup, keeping his weight on his cane. As he gripped the saddle horn tight, Bud helped him climb into the saddle.

As Levi swung his right leg up over the horse's back, Bud felt Levi tense and suck in his breath. He could see that Levi was struggling but determined to ride out.

Bud saw Levi clench his jaw before he said, "Damn, that feels good. Alright, Bud, let's get the hell out of here and back to Council Grove."

Bud smiled. "Yes sir, Boss." He walked over to Cheyenne and helped her mount her horse. As she placed her foot in the stirrup, Bud grabbed her by the butt and helped her get in the saddle.

"Well, Bud, I do declare!" Cheyenne said with a grin.

Bud saw the man who had sold them the horse get wide-eyed and shake his head as he grinned. He chuckled to himself as he walked over to his horse. He packed his saddlebags with the few belongings that Cheyenne had and then climbed into the saddle. He was excited to start a life with Cheyenne. He was aware of her past occupation, and he was determined to get her as far away as possible from that life and give her the life she truly deserved. Like Levi, Bud had fallen hard at first glance.

Levi rubbed Star on the side of the neck. "By golly, I kinda missed you, girl. You ready for a ride?" The mare shook her head, and Levi pulled on the reins and she left the stable.

As the mare reached the street, Levi stopped her and looked back toward the hotel, then up the street ahead of them. Bud and Cheyenne both rode out of the stable and alongside Levi.

Bud pulled off his hat and scratched his head. "Well, Boss, you ready for this?"

"Ya damn right I'm ready, Bud. I was born ready." There was a smile on Levi's face.

The three kicked their horses and set out.

As they rode along the dusty trail, Bud and Levi's spurs jingled along in a relaxing rhythm. Meadowlarks splashed in puddles, bathing themselves and searching for their morning breakfast. The sun was shining bright, and a few fluffy clouds were scattered across the blue sky. Off in the distance, Bud could hear a herd of longhorns being driven north. The cowboys were whistling and hollering to the cattle as they pushed on for town. One of the cowboys waved to them as they rode by.

Later that day, the three came to a small creek crossing and decided to hold up and rest the horses and get a bite to eat. Cheyenne gathered some wild berries from along the creek. Bud dug into his saddlebags and handed Levi and Cheyenne some buffalo jerky he had picked up in town.

"Damn, that's right tasty," said Levi as he stretched his body out on the ground. "Figured to make twenty-five miles today, iffen you and Cheyenne are up to it."

Bud looked at Levi. "Boss, you sure you're up for ridin' that far in one day? I mean—"

"Why, hell yes I'm up for it!" Levi smacked the ground with his hand. "Council Grove ain't comin' to me so I've gotta ride as far as I can."

Bud shook his head. "It's your call, Boss." He was afraid that Levi was going to overdo it.

Cheyenne passed the berries around again, then headed to the creek. Bud watched as she sat down, unlaced her boots, and pulled them off. He felt overcome with a feeling of contentment as he studied her. Something about her made him feel he had a purpose in this world. His ma had once told him before she died that everything happened for a reason. Bud now understood those words and was beginning to believe them himself.

After about an hour, Levi sat up. "Well, damn, the longer I lie here, the more I start to ache. Reckon it's time to be going. Got quite a distance between us and Council Grove. I wonder what Samantha is doin' right now."

He gazed across the vast open Kansas prairie. Bud guessed he was daydreaming of his gal.

A couple moments later, Levi began to try to get up but couldn't seem to get to his feet. Bud and Cheyenne walked over to Levi, carefully grabbed him by the arms, and helped him up. Levi stretched his body and limped his way over to Star. He reached under the horse's belly and gave her a pat as he tightened the cinch. Bud helped him into the saddle and then walked over to Cheyenne and helped her as well.

Later that evening, Bud saw one of the most magnificent sunsets he had ever seen. Bud looked at his friend, and he could see a tear gently fall down Levi's weathered cheek.

Levi cleared his throat. "This view reminds me of a special evenin' me and Samantha shared together. I can't bear all the miles between us. Ya know, Bud, there's somethin' I need to tell ya. In all my years of driftin' I met many a different caliber of folks. Some good, some not so good. Ladies, they came and went. Friends? Well, I never recall havin' many that I'd truly call my friend. More like acquaintances. A fella livin' the life I lived, you kinda get to know who ya can and can't trust. Most folks, you can trust only as far as ya can spit. They'll be quick to turn their back on ya for a buck or two. I reckon that's why I never had what I would call a true down-to-earth friend. When I first met ya there on the trail, I could tell right off you were in a hurry to get the hell away from something or somebody or both. Somethin' about you reminds me of myself. What you have done for me, pardner, has proven more to me than anyone ever has. I'll be in debt to ya for quite some time. Most folks I've known in my day woulda left me lyin' in that bed and took off with anything they could get outta me. Instead, you took over things and handled them like a true cowboy and an honest man woulda done. You came to find me…" Levi began to get choked up.

Bud lowered his head. "It's alright, Boss, I just did what I figured you would."

Levi turned his head to Bud. "Raise your head, cowboy. I just wanted to tell ya I'm honored to call you my friend."

Bud had never had a true friend quite like Levi either. They had both lived rough and devastating lives, especially since the War had broken out back in '61. He raised his head and smiled and leaned over to shake Levi's hand. "Thank ya, Boss. That's a mighty kind thing to say. I'm honored as well."

Levi sighed, pulling his reins back so Star would stop. "I reckon this will be a good enough spot as any to set up camp until first light."

The three unsaddled their horses and began to gather buffalo chips. Once the fire was set and burning hot, the three ate some jerky that Bud passed around. A couple of hours had gone by when the horses began to get rather skittish. Their ears perked forward, and their heads went up and they began to stop their feet.

Levi looked at Bud. "Quiet now, somethin's out there."

Bud looked out into the darkness. "Probably a coyote or a deer."

"No sir." Levi gazed beyond the fire. "No sir, I don't reckon it is. Better get your rifle, Bud."

Bud looked at Levi and could see that something was not right. He swallowed hard, then took his rifle out from the scabbard on his saddle and jacked a shell into the chamber.

"Easy, Bud," Levi said, listening closely. "You hear that?"

Bud could hear a man's spurs jingling as he walked closer to the camp. Levi and Bud looked at each other for a second, and Levi slid down the tie downs on his Colts.

"Hello the camp!" a voice shouted from the darkness. "Mind if I come in?"

"Howdy, come on in," Bud replied as his hand tightened around the stock of his rifle. A feeling of uneasiness came over Bud as the man came up and squatted next to the fire.

"Howdy, folks," the man said, pausing as he saw Bud holding his Winchester.

Bud studied the man carefully. Something was just not right. "Lose your horse there, stranger?" Bud asked, still not taking his hands off his rifle.

"Mind if I steal a cup of that coffee?" The man pointed to the coffee, and Bud handed him a cup. "Damn horse played out on me about twenty miles back. Had to shoot her." The man looked at Cheyenne and a strange look came over his face. "Say, ma'am, don't I know you from somewheres?"

Bud watched Cheyenne look straight at the man for a second, and he knew she was trying to recall where she had seen him before. A woman in her profession had seen many a different man in her time. Men of all different characters, some good, some not as good. Cheyenne had told Bud that she had worked in various saloons since she was fifteen years old. She had left her home back in Springfield and traveled west when she was very young.

"I know I've seen you somewheres, ma'am," the man went on.

Bud was becoming rather irritated with the man. He could also see

Cheyenne was becoming very uncomfortable. He noticed Levi was watching all three of them.

The man sipped his coffee, and Bud asked, "Where ya headed, stranger?"

The man looked at Bud and then over at Levi. As he looked back to Bud, Bud saw Levi ease his hand over and slide one of the Colts out of the holster, placing it next to his leg, out of sight.

The man looked back at Cheyenne as she got up. He looked her up and down as she walked in front of him and over to Bud, who pulled her down close to him and wrapped his arm around her. He could tell how uneasy Cheyenne was feeling, and he didn't like it one bit.

The man smiled. "Well, well, well. I know who you are."

Cheyenne looked straight at the man and then looked at Bud and lowered her head in shame. He could feel her shrink into his side.

The man chuckled. "Hays City, that's it. Hays City, I recall."

Bud looked at Levi, ready to lose his temper.

The man sipped the rest of his coffee then dropped the cup on the ground. "The Crooked Horn Saloon. Oh, I'd say about four or five years back. You treated me and some of the boys to a right fine time, ma'am."

Bud's blood filled with anger and Levi slowly cocked the hammer on his Colt. Cheyenne grabbed Bud's hand. He pulled his hand away from her, needing to be ready to defend her, even though he ached to comfort her. He stared the man down. "Pardner," he said through clenched teeth, "that'll be just about enough of that talk."

The man laughed. "Shoot, mister. Must be right nice traveling across the prairie here with a whore."

"Pardner," Bud yelled, "I'll ask you once last time to hold your tongue. Cheyenne and I are fixin' to get hitched here sometime soon and I won't have you talkin' to her that way."

The man laughed hysterically. "That's the funniest damn thing I reckon I've heard in all my days. Marrying a whore, don't that beat all."

LEVI TIGHTLY GRIPPED his Colts and waited for Bud's response. He knew all hell was about to break loose. Before the man could notice, Bud jumped over the fire and tackled the man, wrestling him to the ground. The man pulled his knife and tried to stick it in Bud's belly, but Bud was stronger and pried the man's hand away, knocking the knife free from it. Cheyenne ran over and grabbed the knife.

"Get back!" Bud yelled as he punched the man in the face, surely breaking his nose.

Cheyenne ran over to Levi as he struggled to his feet and let Bud handle the man himself. "Mr. Cord, please help him!"

"Stay back, ma'am. Bud's got it under control." Levi was a bit hesitant to jump in due to his pain, but he was more than ready to pull his Colts if Bud needed further assistance. He was in no shape to fight, but he was in perfect shape to pull a trigger.

The man flipped Bud over and grabbed him by the throat.

"Please, Mr. Cord, stop them!" Cheyenne yelled. "He can't breathe!" Cheyenne screamed and ran over, trying to pull the man off Bud.

"Get the hell back," yelled Levi. "Now!"

Before she could move, the man punched Cheyenne in the face, knocking her back and almost into the fire. Bud swung his leg up and over the man's head and sank his spur into his cheek, tearing the flesh from his face. As the man screamed and reached for his face, Bud slid out from under him. "Mister, you get the hell out of here now."

The man touched his face where his cheek once was. "You son of a bitch! Tore my damn face off!" The man twisted in the dirt as Bud rushed over to Cheyenne.

"Are you alright, love?" Bud asked, pushing the hair out of her face. As he turned his back to the man and put his arms around Cheyenne, the man reached down. Levi watched the man carefully, waiting for him to draw, so he could send him straight to hell where he belonged. The man drew his gun from his holster and pointed it right at Bud's back. As he cocked it, the sound echoed across the dark prairie, and Bud quickly threw Cheyenne out of the way and spun around and drew his Colt from his hip, firing a slug right into the man's gut. At that exact same moment, Levi fired his gun from his hip, and drilled the man right above his left eye. The man was dead before he dropped to the ground.

Cheyenne began shaking and crying as Bud held her in his embrace, "It's alright, love. It's alright...hush now."

Levi opened the gate on his Colt and ejected the empty cartridge. He slid out a loaded cartridge from his belt and replaced it, then took his knife and carved notch fifty-one in his belt.

EARLY THE NEXT morning, Levi awoke and tried to get to his feet. The cold damp ground had taken a toll on his body. His muscles had stiffened so much he could hardly move. As he looked over at Bud, he could see him fast asleep, Cheyenne snuggled deep in his arms. Levi smiled, then rolled to his side and reached for his cane.

"Why, good mornin', Mr. Cord," said Cheyenne as she pushed off the wool blanket she and Bud were sharing. "Could you use some help?" She got off the ground and helped him to his feet.

The two looked over at the dead man's body.

"Shall we bury him, Mr. Cord?"

Levi studied the man. "Ma'am, I don't reckon that feller deserves a proper burial."

Bud woke up. "Mornin'," he said as he wiped the sleep from his eyes. "Quite a night last night, weren't it? My apologies to the both of you."

Levi put on his hat and guns. "Nonsense. That feller there, he needed killin'. Man ought not talk to a woman like that. I won't tolerate it none myself."

After heating a pot of coffee over a small fire, they saddled their horses. Bud walked over and took off the man's gun belt and put it in his saddlebags. He kicked some dirt on the lifeless body. "Ashes to ashes, and dust to dust, you disrespectful bastard."

As Levi went to mount up, he couldn't find the strength to swing his leg over.

"Need some help there, Boss?" Bud asked.

Levi looked at Bud. He felt shame and disappointment that he had not been able to mount his own horse yet. He had the reputation of being strong and determined, yet he could not seem to get on his own horse. "Iffen ya don't mind, I'd be obliged. Danged old bones are a mite stiff this mornin'."

Cheyenne and Bud both helped Levi get into the saddle before mounting themselves. As they turned their horses south, no one looked back.

By afternoon, Levi wasn't doing too well. His face was pale, and he was drenched in sweat. He had grown much weaker throughout the day. He hung over the saddle with his head bobbing. Every so often he would look up and gaze across the prairie, then lower his head back down.

"Boss, you alright there?" Bud asked. "You don't look so good."

Levi raised his head and looked at Bud. He was in great pain, but there was no stopping him from pressing forward. He didn't bother to say anything, as he was too exhausted to speak.

They pushed on for another hour or so. Levi and Star began to lag behind. Bud and Cheyenne came riding back to Levi.

"Alright, Boss," Bud said as he got off his horse. "You can't possibly go another mile. We're making camp right here and now."

Levi fought to raise his head and open his eyes briefly, just long enough to nod to Bud. He had to admit he was too weak and desperately needed rest.

Bud helped him out of the saddle and Cheyenne laid his bedroll out on the ground for him. Levi wondered if he would ever recover fully and be the man that Samantha deserved. He wanted to keep pushing on, but he realized that the only way he would make it was to stop and rest a spell. Just before he drifted off to sleep, he heard Bud say, "Don't worry…he's a mighty strong man. He's been to hell and back more than once, and he'll be just fine. The power of true love has kept this cowboy alive for this long, and I reckon it will for a long time."

Levi startled as the sound of coyotes howling across the prairie woke him up. He drew one of his Colts.

"Easy, Boss," Bud said. "It's alright…it's just us."

Levi looked around the camp in the firelight and saw Bud and Cheyenne, their horses nearby.

"How long have I been out?" Levi said as he sat up. The pain was still there but he felt much more rested.

"Quite some time," said Bud. "I was startin' to think I might have to get a heap worried there. How ya holdin' up?"

Levi reached for his cup, and Cheyenne poured him some coffee. "Pardner, I feel like I've been dropped off a cliff." Levi chuckled, and all three of them shared a laugh.

Crickets serenaded each other and the fire popped and cracked as a barred owl called from the distance. Shortly after, another owl answered his call. The black sky was filled with flickering stars and the moon was shining bright.

Cheyenne pointed to the sky. "Look, a falling star! It's beautiful!"

A few moments later, Bud, gazing at the stars, cleared his throat. "Some time back, I was married to a lovely gal up in Wamego. I met her one day as I was comin' out of the Gold Dollar Saloon. She was comin' down the street and looked like something out of heaven. Easy to say, I fell head over bootheel for that gal."

Levi saw Cheyenne look at Bud as he continued. "We got to courtin', and 'fore you know it, we was hitched. We got us a tiny blue cottage in Manhattan. I went off to drive a herd to Dodge City and was away from her for a damn month, which seemed like forever. I couldn't bear to be away from her another lonely night, much like Levi here with Miss Samantha. I spurred my ol' buckskin and lit out of Dodge as fast as that ol' stud could take me back to Manhattan. When I rode into town, I was going crazy to see my Olivia. When I walked in the door, she was nowhere to be found. I didn't think about it too much at the time...I figured she was visitin' her folks down the street, so I weren't worried none. When I got to her folks' place, they told me she hadn't been there at all. That's when everything turned around and went straight to hell."

Bud paused for a moment. Levi could tell it was painful for him, but he was anxious to hear the rest of the story. Cheyenne looked interested, too.

"I headed over to the marshal's office to see if he had heard anything as to her whereabouts. When I walked in the door..." Bud gazed into the fire. "The marshal wasn't at his desk like usual. I heard laughing around the corner in the back cell. I saw the marshal with his shirt off and his pants around his ankles. His back was turned toward me, and I could see a woman's legs on his shoulders. He had the woman on the cot and was..." He stopped for a moment, his eyes never straying from the fire. "I could tell it wasn't the best time, so I decided to come back later. As I turned to leave without botherin' them, the marshal looked back and said, 'Bud?'...I turned around and the woman peeked her head around the marshal and screamed, 'Oh, Lord, Bud!' My heart sank in my chest something awful. It was Olivia. I turned to leave, and she yelled, 'Bud, please, wait! I don't love him, I love you!' I ran out the door and saddled my horse and tore out of town like a cyclone bound for hell. She ran in the street and begged and screamed for me to stop but I couldn't. I couldn't go home, knowing what she had more than likely done in our bed while I was away. I rode out of town a few miles and camped on the old Kansas River. I never in my life felt so hurt like I did that night. I pulled a bottle of bug juice out of my saddlebags and drank myself crazy. The next mornin', I was still drunk, and I rode back to town and hitched my stud outside the jail. I kicked in the door and the marshal jumped up out of his damn chair. I pulled my pistol and beat the hell out of him. He didn't even know it was comin'. There was blood comin' out of his ears and nose and I split his lip damn near off his worthless face. When he fell to the floor, I took his Colt from his holster and shot his privates right off his sorry carcass. After I shot his manhood off, I fled out the door, mounted up, and took out of town, never to return. I hear tell they buried the marshal that week. I didn't wait around to find out."

There was a huge hush over the Kansas prairie around the campfire after Bud finished his tragic story. Cheyenne took him by the hand and held him close, and his eyes still didn't stray from the fire. Levi looked into Bud's saddened eyes and knew he had struck up a friendship with a decent man. A friendship that he would cherish for the rest of his life. He felt sorrow inside for Bud and once again was reminded of himself.

Chapter 14

As the morning sun rose over the Kansas plains, the breeze blew strong, blowing the buffalo grass and causing it to look like waves on the ocean. A rooster pheasant crowed as he awoke for the day, and a bull buffalo grunted as he chased his cows around in a circle.

"Boss, you look a heap better than yesterday," Bud said as the three saddled up.

Levi turned to him and smiled. "You betcha, Bud. Let's go get her." He spurred Star and galloped across the Kansas plains. He was feeling better than he had yesterday, but his body was stiff and ached something awful.

A few hours had passed when they came to a creek crossing. Levi pointed at the ground. "Ya see that? Look at them tracks."

"Buffalo," said Bud.

"Yes sir," Levi said with a grin. "I'm 'bout damn tired of jerky. What do y'all say we shoot one for a steak for supper?"

Cheyenne smiled, and her body sagged with relief. "That would be marvelous."

After about an hour of tracking, they came to a small bluff.

"The herd ain't too far ahead of us now," Levi said.

They dismounted and hunkered down and snuck to the top of the bluff. As they slowly peeked over the bluff, they spotted a herd of about fifteen buffalo grazing a few hundred yards out.

"There they are." Levi studied the herd. "Bud, go grab the rifle off my horse."

Bud snuck back to the horses. When he returned, he had the gun and a handful of cartridges. He handed them to Levi. Levi jacked open the rifle and slid a cartridge into the chamber and then quietly closed the action. He raised the sight and looked over the herd, trying to decide which one to take.

"There's a big bull over to the right there, Boss."

Levi looked to where Bud pointed, and noticed the big bull chasing off a smaller bull. "Yes sir, he's a dandy." He pulled the hammer back and took off his hat and laid it underneath the barrel to rest it on. As he licked his finger and held it up to check the wind, the buffalo threw their heads up. Levi noticed the wind had swirled and was now blowing right at the herd. Quickly lining down the big bore rifle, Levi pulled the back trigger to set the front one. Taking a deep breath, he gently squeezed the trigger as he exhaled. A couple of seconds after the rifle rang out and echoed across the prairie, the bull turned to walk away, then collapsed.

"Nice shot there, Boss!" Bud yelled.

"Much obliged, Bud."

Cheyenne pointed to the herd as they stopped running about four hundred yards out. "Look, boys, they stopped! Think ya can get another one, Mr. Cord?"

Levi placed the gun back on his saddle. "Well, ma'am, we got much more meat than we can eat ourselves here, and there's no need of wastin' such fine meat. Them poor shaggies will all be long gone here soon. It's a damn shame."

Cheyenne looked at the small herd as they looked at the fallen bull. "That is a shame."

They rode down to the bull, then began to skin and field dress it. After they skinned the hide around the neck, they cut a hole in the hide and tied a rope to it. They took the other end of the rope and tied it to Cheyenne's saddle horn. As Bud and Levi cut the skin from the hide, Cheyenne led her horse slowly to pull the hide off the carcass. After they skinned the bull, they cut off as much meat as they could load on their horses.

Bud rolled the hide up and tied it on the back of his horse and Levi washed his hands with water from his canteen. He cleaned his knife and then they prepared to continue south.

Later that afternoon, they stopped to make camp and cook a few of the fresh steaks. Cheyenne set out to gather some berries she had spotted.

"Might be fixin' to cut loose soon," Levi said as he pointed to the sky off to the north. It was clouding up and looked as if a storm was brewing.

"Just might at that," Bud replied.

Lightning cracked across the sky and made a beautiful picture as they sat around the campfire.

THE NEXT MORNING, the three awoke to notice the storm had just passed them by. After eating some steak with some eggs Cheyenne had found in a pheasant nest, Cheyenne went to wash the plates in the nearby creek. Bud and Levi had already saddled their horses and were itching to go. They watched as she reached down in the weeds. Suddenly, she let out a horrifying scream. "Bud! Help! A snake!"

Bud took off as fast as he could. Levi jumped up as quickly as he could in his condition, but he fell to the ground. "Damn it."

Levi struggled to his feet as he watched Bud draw his Colt and empty all six shots toward something on the ground, then run over to Cheyenne.

"Levi!" Bud shouted. "Levi, come quick! Rattler got her!"

Bud threw Cheyenne in his arms and ran to Levi. "Boss, she's been bit. Rattler got her hand."

Cheyenne was crying hysterically and gasping for air. Levi grabbed her by the hand and studied the bite. "Take some chewin' tobacco and spit it on the bite after I cut it open, Bud." Reaching for his knife, he cut the skin where the snake had bit her, put his lips to the bite, and sucked out all the venom he could before Bud spit the tobacco juice on it. Bud took off his wild rag and wrapped some tobacco on the bite and tied it tight.

Within minutes, her whole hand was starting to turn colors and swell up. She began to lose consciousness. Her face was extremely pale, and Levi feared the worst.

Bud looked at him with fear in his eyes. "Boss, what the hell do we do? She can't ride."

"Throw her on her horse and head for Lyons. It's a fair piece down the trail, but it's the closest settlement. I'll be right behind ya."

Bud threw Cheyenne into the saddle and then mounted up himself. He turned the horse and spurred him like he had never done before. Levi followed, though a little slower, guiding Cheyenne's horse. The dust from Bud's horse was the only thing that could be seen of the pair until that too was gone.

Shortly later, Levi rode up and saw Bud sitting on the ground holding Cheyenne's lifeless body in his arms. Before he was upon them, he could already see Shiner lying dead and feared the worst. "Aw, hell," he whispered.

As he rode up to him and got off his horse, Bud cried, "She's gone, Boss, she's gone." His whole body was shaking, and his words were hysterical. "Her arm was swelling and turning colors, spreading faster than fire across the prairie. I could feel the horse getting tired, but, God, I couldn't let her die Boss, I couldn't!"

Levi's eyes closed in pain for his friend, picturing the pair racing against a clock that had already run out. It was as if his friend wasn't talking to him, though, but rather reliving the horror of what had just happened.

"My thoughts were on Cheyenne, we just had to make it just a little further. I didn't see the prairie dog town. Just heard that crack and felt Shiner fall, and knew it was a death sentence. I couldn't bear to see him suffer so I ended his misery. I tried to calm him as I cocked the hammer and pulled the trigger. I killed my best friend, Boss."

"I'm so sorry, Bud," Levi said, placing a hand on his shoulder.

"There weren't nothing I could do neither. She was thrown from the horse when we fell. I rushed to her and picked her up in my arms. I would have carried her all the way to town if I would have been given the time. I prayed to the Lord above not to take her. Why didn't he listen, Boss? Why the hell didn't he listen?"

"I'm so sorry, Bud," Levi said, his voice low and soft. "Lord, I'm so sorry. You did the best you could do, pardner."

Bud shook his head and began weeping hysterically.

Sometime later, after Bud got ahold of himself, Levi said, "I reckon we best get to diggin', pardner."

Bud wiped the tears from his eyes as Levi began to dig a grave with a tin plate. Bud disappeared while Levi dug into the hard soil. Part of him thought about going after him, but he knew his friend needed time to mourn.

Once he had dug the grave, he carefully placed Cheyenne's body inside covered the grave with dirt. Bud returned with some flowers he had picked. He laid them on top of the grave and his eyes filled with tears once again.

A chill came over Levi, and his own eyes filled with tears as he thought about Samantha. He couldn't bear to think of ever losing her. "Shall we say a few words, pardner?" Levi asked as he dusted off his pants. Bud looked him in the eye and nodded but didn't say a single word. The two men took off their hats.

"Lord," Levi began, his throat tight. "This gal was taken from this world too darned early. She had a whole life ahead to live, and that was all just taken away. She was a fine woman and a beautiful one at that. She had a smile that will never be forgotten and a heart that was so sweet and tender. She always woke with a smile and always thought of others before she thought of herself. This ol' world ain't gonna be quite the same without the company of the lovely Cheyenne. Lord, we ask that you look over this fine gal's soul when she reaches heaven's door. Amen."

WITHOUT SAYING A word, Bud mounted Cheyenne's horse and set off. Cheyenne's tragic death had destroyed his happiness and all his hopes and dreams. He reached back and pulled a bottle of whiskey from his saddlebags and pressed it to his dry, weathered lips. His heart was shattered, worse than it had ever been before. It felt like he had a slug lodged deep inside.

Levi rode up alongside him, but Bud's tear-filled eyes never strayed from the trail ahead. Once again, he was a lost soul. Cheyenne had started to make his world make sense and fall into place…and now it was destroyed.

A FEW MILES up the trail, Levi saw big thunderhead clouds off to the north. Thunder crashed faintly and lightning cracked across the sky. Levi could see the rain falling from the clouds as the storm pushed its way east. He looked up. The sun was shining bright and there were no clouds where they were at. In the distance, there was a rainbow that looked like it touched down right in the middle of the town of Lyons.

Once they reached the outskirts of town, Bud turned to Levi with a lonesome look in his eyes. "Boss…would you mind iffen we just press on?"

Levi felt his pain. He recalled being in his boots. "Sure thing, pard. Next stop should be Abilene. They got a nice hotel up there. I'd say it's 'bout twenty miles or so. We'll set up camp further up the trail and set out for Abilene in the morning."

They continued along the trail a fair distance before setting up camp for the night. Levi was hurting all over and had been wanting to get out of the saddle for quite some time, but he didn't want to burden Bud. All throughout the night, Levi watched Bud as he tossed and turned in his bedroll. There was one time he thought he heard Bud crying in his sleep.

The men awoke just after sunrise and saddled up after coffee. Levi was in a hurry to return to Council Grove, but he desperately needed a night in a soft bed to regain some strength. They finally reached the outskirts of Abilene. They could hear cattle bawling across town in the stockyards.

Bud gazed toward town but spoke not a word. As they rode into town there were mud puddles standing in the street and the smell of fresh rain filled the air. Bud studied the town but never said a word or even shook his head. Levi understood exactly how he felt.

Bud rode his horse up to the hitching post outside the saloon and got down from the saddle.

Levi rode up behind him. "Pardner, I'll take the horses here to the livery then get us a room over at the hotel."

Bud turned around and nodded, finally making eye contact. As Bud walked into the saloon, Levi led the horses to the livery stable. He had a rather rough time climbing out of the saddle. His hip had been bothering him something fierce, and sharp pain shot throughout his body. After tending to the horses, Levi grabbed his cane and began to make his way across the street. The townsfolk studied him as he limped his way into the hotel. He took off his hat as he walked inside. The man behind the desk was wearing spectacles and was bald, with sideburns much like Levi's. He wore a checkered vest, along with black garters on his arms.

"Room for two," said Levi.

"That'll be two dollars," said the man.

Levi pulled two silver dollars from his vest pocket and handed it to the man.

He limped his way up the stairs. It took almost twenty minutes. His hip popped every time he walked up another step. He felt like he'd been riding for months. As he walked in the room, he looked around and noticed the room was rather nice. The walls had red wallpaper, and the bed was a beautiful shiny brass. On the floor was a Peruvian rug, and there was a wooden rocker that reminded him of sitting on the porch watching his grandfather smoke his pipe in the hills of Missouri.

After Levi had settled, he decided to head over to the mercantile to get some hardtack and coffee and beans. He also needed a new tin plate since he had broken his while digging Cheyenne's grave. Once Levi walked inside the mercantile and began to look around, he noticed a glass case that held several of the most alluring diamond rings. He walked over and began to browse through the exquisite rings, and one in particular caught his eye. It was a rose gold, single solitaire, diamond cluster ring. It was simply gorgeous. He could imagine just what it would look like on Samantha's finger…her expression when he gave it to her. She would smile and cry at the same time. She would hold him so tight, the way she did at Elm Creek, if not tighter.

As he looked through the glass case at the ring, the store clerk's wife walked over to him. "They're all very lovely, and of the finest quality."

Levi looked up at the woman, then pointed at the ring. "Mind iffen I take a look at that one there, ma'am?"

The woman opened the case and pulled out the ring, handing it to him. "Why, sir, this just happens to be my favorite. I've been after Bob here to buy it for me for quite some time."

Levi smiled at the woman as a man stocking shelves yelled across the room, "Damn it, woman, how many times do I gotta tell ya? We can't afford a damn ring like that."

"Hush up, you old crippled up son of a mule's ass!"

Levi chuckled to himself as he looked at the ring. He placed it on his pinkie, trying to see what it would look like on Samantha's hand.

The woman smiled. "That ring is genuine gold, 18-karat to be exact. It has a remarkable 1-karat diamond, and…"

As the woman went on, Levi found himself daydreaming of the moment he would place the ring on Samantha's finger. He smiled, and he asked the lady how much the ring cost.

The woman took the ring back from Levi. "Forty-five dollars, stranger. I'm sure your missus would be right proud to attend Sunday service with a ring like that."

Levi leaned on his cane and looked up at the woman. "Well, ma'am, I ain't rightly asked her yet. Fixin' to head down to Council Grove, and I reckon to try to ask her hand in marriage iffen she'll still have me. Been quite a spell since I saw her last. Hell, ma'am I'm hopin' she'll still remember me."

The woman studied Levi, looking at his cane, then the ring, then the Colts.

"By Lord, you're him, ain't ya?"

"Ma'am?"

"Bob, it's him! He's that stranger fella that everyone's been talkin' 'bout. He's that cowboy on the trail for Council Grove headed for that Miss Samantha lady. Is it true, mister? Did you really fall in love at first sight?"

Levi looked at the floor, then back up to the woman. "Why, yes, ma'am, I reckon I did. I'd never met a gal like her in all my twenty-nine years. That gal stole my heart the first time her blue eyes ever met mine. My heart liked to jump right out of my own chest and into her arms."

A tear fell down the woman's cheek, and she dabbed it with her apron as Levi looked at the ring again. "Forty-five dollars, huh? Right purty ring iffen I do say so myself, ma'am. Ya think Miss Samantha might like it?"

"She'd love it, mister."

Levi looked around the mercantile. "Ma'am, I reckon I need me a pound of hardtack, about four pounds of beans, two pounds of coffee, one tin plate, and that there lovely ring."

The woman smiled. "Certainly, mister."

"Cord. Levi Cord." After he paid, he tipped his hat to her. "Thank ya kindly, ma'am."

She smiled. "Go get her, cowboy."

Levi smiled in return. "Good day to you both."

As Levi limped his way out the door, he heard the man say, "Damn saddle trash."

"Bob!" yelled the woman. "He's quite a gentleman, and a right handsome one at that."

Levi was offended at the man's insult, but he was used to it by now. He pocketed the ring. He had better things to think about.

BUD HAD BEEN drowning his sorrows in whiskey. His heart was shattered into a million pieces, and each bottle he drank, the angrier he got. He seldom drank, but when he did, he tended to get rather hostile and aggressive.

A couple of cowboys came strutting through the saloon's swinging doors. They walked right up to the bar and yelled, "Barkeep! Whiskey!"

"Hey, you," one of the men yelled, causing Bud to glance up. The men were starting at a saloon girl sitting at the end of the bar. "You whore! Come over here and buy me a drink." The girl ignored him. "Bitch, I'm talkin' to you!"

Bud staggered his way over to the men. "Alright, you boys…hold your damn tongues or I'll cut 'em off and shove 'em up your disrespectful asses. You understan' me?"

The two men looked at each other, then back at Bud, and smiled. "I reckon you need yourself a drink there, stranger."

Bud looked at the bar. He was much too drunk. He could hardly stand up, and his head was spinning something horrible.

One of the men slapped him on the back and slammed a bottle down on the bar in front of him. "Drink! Then go buy yourself a two-dollar whore. You need to relax, pardner. Now drink up!"

Bud reached for the bottle on the bar and then swung it as hard as he could over the man's head, dropping him to the floor. The second man reached for his Colt, and Bud kicked it out of his hand and then tackled the man to the floor. As he pinned the man to the floor, the first man jumped up and onto his back. He flipped the man over and bit him on the ear, just about tearing it clear off his head. As the man screamed, the other man picked up a chair and went to shatter it over Bud's head. Bud rolled to the floor, and the chair crashed over the other man's back. As Bud got to his feet, he picked up a chair and flung it across the bar and it crashed through a window. By that time everyone was fighting and busting up the whole saloon.

After several minutes of fighting, biting, kicking, gouging, and the worst all-out brawl that Abilene had ever seen, one of the men cracked a billiard stick over Bud's back, knocking him out cold.

SAMANTHA SADDLED LIGHTNING and set out for Elm Creek with her cane pole and a tin coffee can full of worms she had dug out of her flower bed. She brought along a basket to carry any fish she would catch. It was a gorgeous day and the sun was shining bright, not a single cloud in the sky. It had been raining in Council Grove the past few days and now it had warmed up and the prairie was covered in fresh green grass and wildflowers.

Once she arrived at Elm Creek, she walked along the bank, looking for a nice hole of water where she could try her hand at some fishing. There was some bass in in the creek, and she was hankering a right nice meal of fresh bass filets. She spotted a pair of whitetail deer antlers in the weeds ahead of her and wished that Levi was there to see them.

She spotted a hole in the water that was full of bass. She sat down and baited her hook. As she looked up, she noticed a pair of bass swim by, following a school of minnows. She tossed her line into the water under an overhanging willow. Moments later, the pair of bass came swimming back by. They circled the line for a minute before she twitched it and one of the bass couldn't resist anymore. He swallowed the worm and she set the hook. The bass put up quite a fight before she landed him.

Dally splashed in the water, trying to catch crawdads as they came out from under the rocks. One big crawdad with shiny blue pinchers latched onto Dally's lip, and she yelped and whimpered and came running out of the water and dang near ran Samantha over. Samantha just laughed and placed the bass in the basket.

After about an hour of fishing, she had caught a good mess of bass and perch. As she lay on her blanket, she got lost in Levi's letter while she twirled her hair in her fingers. How she enjoyed these visits to the creek. After she had finished reading his letter for at least the tenth time that day, she tucked it back in the safety of her bosom and walked along the creek searching for arrowheads.

Later that afternoon, as she picked wildflowers, she noticed the sky beginning to cloud up and turn dark. Thunder bellowed to the west. The breeze stopped, and somewhere to the southwest a turkey gobbled as lightning crashed across the prairie sky. Samantha gathered everything, saddled Lightning, and looked for Dally. "Come on, little girl. It's time to be headin' home for today."

Dally came running up, her face covered in mud, and Samantha giggled.

By the time she arrived in town, the wind had picked up something fierce. She quickly took her horse to the stable and then hurried to the cottage. She cleaned the fish, then went inside to prepare it. After they had eaten and the dishes were done, she went to her room and let her hair down and began to brush it. Then she washed Dally down, undressed, and crawled into bed. The sound of raindrops pitter-pattering on the roof gave a relaxing lullaby as she drifted off to sleep.

Chapter 15

The next morning, Levi awoke to find that Bud had never come in from the saloon. As he sat up, he reached for his watch and opened it to look at Samantha's picture. He smiled as he gazed into her eyes. "Darlin', I'm on my way. I'll see you in a day or two." He closed the watch and got himself dressed and headed out the door to find Bud.

As he reached the lobby, he said to the hotel clerk, "Top of the mornin' to ya, sir."

"Mornin' to yourself," the clerk replied.

Levi tipped his hat. "Did a young man come in for me last night? I was expecting my pardner, but he never come in."

"I'm sorry, sir, but no feller came in here for ya last night."

Levi tipped his hat again. "Much obliged to ya. Reckon he musta stayed at the saloon. Good day to ya, sir."

He walked out the door and stood on the boardwalk, leaning on his cane. The sun was shining bright and Levi squinted his eyes as he looked up the street, which was filled with folks passing by.

Levi limped his way over to the saloon. Inside, he saw the barkeep picking up broken glass. There were busted tables and chairs everywhere.

"Woowhee," Levi said as he looked around. "Musta been quite a party."

The barkeep turned to him. "Some damn cowboy come in here yesterday and filled himself full of whiskey. He was quiet until some fellers started insultin' one of the girls."

"This feller stick around town?"

The barkeep swept up a pile of glass. "Well, after he busted the place up, the marshal took his ass over yonder to the jail."

Levi looked out the saloon doors toward the jail across the street. He tipped his hat to the man. "Much obliged to ya." He limped his way out the door and over to the jail.

Once he reached the jail, he paused for a moment, looking at the bars on the windows. A shiver went down his spine as he cautiously walked inside.

The marshal was a fat man with a white mustache that he had curled perfectly.

"Howdy, marshal," Levi said as he looked at the cells.

"Howdy, stranger," the marshal replied as he studied Levi's twin Colts. "What in the hell do you want?"

Levi gritted his teeth. "Come here lookin' for one of my cowhands."

Bud jumped up from a cot. "Boss! Am I glad to see you! I'm ready to be out of this godforsaken cell."

Levi didn't want to stir up any sort of trouble. He merely just wanted to be on their way. He tipped his hat to Bud but didn't say a word.

"Marshal," Levi said. "I hear tell Bud there busted up the saloon over yonder. I'd like to pay for the damages and clear his bail. I need him now, so you just tell me the damages."

The marshal glared at Levi and then smiled. "This town will be a hell of a lot better off without trash like you two around. Them boys should have killed your man there before he busted up the place. Son of a bitch spent the whole night crying like an ol' bitch. Had half a mind to beat him myself."

Levi looked the fat man in the eyes, then raised his cane and poked him in the shoulder. The marshal's eyes got a scared look and his smile turned to a frown. If looks could kill, the marshal would have been dead in his boots. Levi stared right through him. "You woulda touched him and it woulda been the biggest mistake you ever made, you fat, worthless bastard."

The marshal stood there for a moment, then said, "Alright, that'll be a hundred dollars and he's yours."

Levi reached in his jacket pocket for a hundred dollars as the marshal reached for the keys and opened the cell door. Levi handed him the money as Bud came walking out of the cell. His eye was black and swollen shut and he had a cut over his eyebrow that looked like it had been bleeding all night. He glared at the marshal as he walked out of the cell.

As they left the jail, the two men shook hands while the marshal slammed the door shut and cussed behind them.

Levi looked at Bud's wounds. "Pardner, we better get you to see a doctor."

"Nah, Boss, I'll be fine."

"The hell you will. That eye needs tendin' to before you get yourself an infection."

Bud shook his head. "Iffen you insist."

After getting Bud stitched up, Levi said, "Time for a shave and a hot bath."

"Reckon that'll be right nice, Boss."

As they soaked in the tubs, Levi handed Bud a cigar and lit one for himself.

"Thank ya, Boss," Bud said as he lit his cigar.

Levi turned to Bud. "I know exactly what you're feelin', pardner. It seems like a long time ago when I lost my first true love. She was so…" Levi paused to fight back the tears. "She was the best thing that ever happened to me, Bud. Until I met Samantha, of course. Once that no-good, worthless son of a bitch took her from me forever, I tell ya, pardner, I'd never felt so down in all my years. When she left this world, I cussed God for takin' her instead of me. I felt my whole world had been taken from me. I took to drinkin', and that led to killin' and driftin'. I don't want you headed down that road. It ain't worth it."

Bud's eyes filled with tears as Levi went on. "I've seen and done things that I will regret for the rest of my life. I don't want you to turn that way. I care a great deal for you, pard. I don't want you turnin' out the way I done did."

The two sat there soaking in the tubs for a spell. After they finished bathing, they got dressed and headed to the livery. As they walked across the street, Bud said, "Boss, ya thought any about gettin' ya some new duds before you go get Miss Samantha? I mean, no offense, Boss, but those duds are barely holding the breeze out and you in."

Levi grinned. "Well, pardner, never gave it too much thought. But I reckon you're right." They headed over to the mercantile and he bought a new pair of pinstriped trousers, a black starched shirt with white pinstripes, and a black tailored vest.

"Woowhee," Bud said. "You look just like a riverboat gambler, Boss."

Levi smiled. He thought he looked rather stunning himself.

"Let's go get your girl, Boss."

"You bet your white ass."

SAMANTHA HAD BEEN in search of a small flock of turkeys she had been seeing for the last week or so. There weren't many trees out west except along Elm Creek, and the flock liked to hang out and strut along the creek bottom. As she walked along the creek, she came to a large cottonwood tree. Under the tree was a bunch of turkey scat, evidence that the turkeys were roosting in the tree. She figured they would venture back toward the roost later that afternoon, so she gathered a bunch of brush and patiently sat with her rifle. She had a strong passion for hunting turkeys. She wished Levi was there to hunt with her. She wondered where he was and how he was feeling.

As she sat there waiting, she watched a pair of red squirrels chase each other through the leaves, then up and down a sycamore tree. A third squirrel joined in and then a black squirrel came out from his nest and began barking at the others. Samantha smiled as she watched them play. Several hours later, a whitetail doe came walking up to the creek with a pair of twin fawns. The doe began to drink from the creek as the fawns chased each other and splashed in the cool clear water. Samantha's heart beat wildly as the fawns walked within feet of her. They stared at the brush that she had gathered to hide behind and stomped their feet as they snorted and bobbed their heads. The doe raised her head and stomped her foot and gave out a snort to the fawns. The twins bounced their way back through the water and over to the doe. A short time later, the three ventured down the creek.

Not long after the deer walked out of sight, Samantha thought she heard a hen turkey yelp to the west. Holding her breath to listen, she gazed to the west looking up the creek and didn't spot anything but a pair of blue jays on a small cedar tree. Moments later, she heard a splash in the creek behind her and turned her head to see what it was. As she did, she heard a hen yelp to the west. She grabbed her rifle and prepared for a shot so she would be ready if they came close. She didn't want to chance spooking the birds by moving when they came closer. A couple of minutes went by before she heard the hen yelp again. This time a second hen answered, and a tom gobbled behind them. Samantha's heart raced. Boy, she loved turkey hunting.

The tom gobbled again, and she knew they were getting closer. She began to breathe heavily as she waited, her eyes fixed on the place she had heard them call from. She listened to the turkeys call back and forth to each other. About twenty minutes went by before Samantha heard a familiar sound that got her blood pumping faster. It was a tom turkey spitting and drumming. She could tell the turkeys were getting closer. A few minutes later, she spotted a couple of hens working their way toward her, scratching in the grass. Then she spotted the tail fan of a long-bearded gobbler behind the hens. He was in full strut, and his head was the most beautiful red, white, and blue. She got ready and slowly got up to her knees. For several minutes, the gobbler strutted circles around the hens, putting on a beautiful and exciting show.

After what seemed like an eternity, the gobbler strutted his way into range of Samantha's rifle. The hens led him right along the edge of the creek in front of her, about ten yards away. She carefully raised her rifle and picked a small window she could shoot through. As the first hen went by, it raised its head and looked right at her. She froze, her heart racing so fast she was sure the hen would hear it and fly off, taking the gobbler with her. He gobbled twice, and the hen looked back at him, then put her head down and continued along the creek. The second hen walked by and never raised her head.

Samantha was waiting for the gobbler to work his way out from behind the big cottonwood tree. She could hear him spitting and drumming just behind the tree, not eight yards in front of her. Suddenly, he gobbled so loud that Samantha about jumped out of her skin. He stepped out from behind the tree and she patiently waited for the right opportunity to take a shot. The gobbler strutted by her. His head was hidden behind his tail fan, so she could carefully take aim. As he turned back around and gobbled, she carefully squeezed the trigger, sending lead right into the bird's chest. He flopped around for several minutes before she sent another shot into the bird, finishing him off. Quickly, she jumped up and ran over. After looking over the bird, she flung it over her shoulder and carried it back. Tying it to her saddle, she headed back to the cottage. She couldn't wait till Levi returned so she could tell him about her exciting hunt and her tremendous trophy.

Once she arrived back at the cottage, she began to pluck the gobbler. Mr. McCoy from the telegraph office walked by. "That's a right nice bird there, Miss Samantha. You shoot it yourself?"

"Why, yes sir, Mr. McCoy, I did."

"Hope you shot him in the head, so you don't have to spit out the buckshot."

Samantha smiled. "No sir, Mr. McCoy, I shot him with my rifle."

Mr. McCoy looked at her with amusement. "Well, land sakes, child, you're one of a kind, ain't ya?"

Samantha smiled as she continued plucking. "I reckon."

After she had finished cleaning the turkey, she took it inside and began to prepare it for supper. She was mighty proud of herself, too.

MEANWHILE, BACK ON the trail, Levi was more than anxious to get back to Miss Samantha. What would she say when he asked her to marry him? How would she react when she first saw him? Would she like the ring? At last he would get to hold her in his embrace and get lost in her soft blue eyes the way he did when their eyes first met on the boardwalk in front of the Last Chance Store.

Levi's hip had been bothering him something terrible the last few days, but it wasn't about to slow him down. It was a gorgeous spring day and a beautiful day for riding. There was a smile on Levi's face that was not about to come off any time soon. He was more than ready to get to Samantha. He had been through a living hell since he and Samantha had parted ways. He prayed she wouldn't look at him differently for being crippled up.

Up the trail a fair piece, Bud pointed out some horse tracks in the creek crossing. They weren't shod, which meant they were Indian ponies. As they rode on up the trail, the tracks seemed to just disappear.

"Keep a close eye there, Bud," Levi said as he studied the trail. "Looks like we might be having some company here shortly."

"How many ya figure on, Boss?"

"I don't know, looks like five or six. Hard to tell. Best be ready in case they're itchin' for a fight."

As they rode on, Levi heard a branch break to the left. Three Indians came rushing out of the brush on painted ponies. Out of nowhere, three more rode up behind them, surrounding them and leaving them with no possible escape. Each brave wore war paint on their faces and their horses were painted up as well. They all had lances and bows, but, luckily, no rifles. However, Levi and Bud were still in serious trouble. One of the Indians out front was waving his lance and shouting at them. Levi knew they were in a tight spot, however, he figured they were only about ten miles from Council Grove, and nothing was going to get in the way of his return now.

Levi slowly slipped the tie downs off his Colts and told Bud quietly, "As soon as I start shootin' the ones on the right, you drill the ones on the left and then haul ass for that gully up yonder. Watch behind us, and once you hit the gully, grab your rifle and make every shot count. You understand?"

Bud studied the Indians. "Hell, Boss, there's way too damn many. It's suicide."

"Bud, I said, do you understand?"

Bud swallowed hard. "Yes sir, Boss, I understand."

The lead Indian came charging at them, and Levi drew his twin Colts as fast as he could and began throwing slugs at the Indians from every possible angle. Bud drew his gun and sent two braves flying off the backs of their ponies. By that time, Levi had sent a slug right through the last Indian out front. Swinging his second Colt behind him, Bud took off hell-bent for leather, trying to make the gully. Levi reared the mare up and swung around and killed all three braves before any of them could hit him or Bud. Once Bud reached the gully, he looked back with his Winchester, cocked and aimed, ready for the rest of the Indians. Levi came riding without a single Indian following behind him.

"What in the Sam Hill?" Bud said. "By God, Boss, what in the hell was that? You got all four of them yourself?"

Levi pulled his Colts from their holsters and reloaded them both. "You got yourself two of them, pardner."

"That's some of the damnedest shootin' I ever saw."

The two men looked over the dead Pawnee Indians and Levi said, "We better get outta here 'fore some more come lookin' for their friends."

SAMANTHA DECIDED TO open the windows to let the fresh spring morning air in. As she dressed, she decided that since it was such a lovely day, she wanted to bake a fresh apple pie. She headed to the Conn Store to buy some fresh apples.

As she walked up the boardwalk, she ran into Mr. Schmidt. "I hear tell you got yourself a mighty fine turkey yesterday."

Samantha smiled and told him the exciting story of the hunt. He congratulated her for her success and then said, "Well, Miss Samantha, Sue has me runnin' all over today. Gotta hit the post office, then the bank, and then over yonder to the doc's. Busy, busy today. You have yourself a wonderful and blessed day, ma'am."

After she picked up some flour and apples from the store, she headed back to the cottage to find her father on one of his daily rampages. However, this one was much worse. She tried to ignore him and go about her business, but as she was setting the flour and apples on the table, her father walked over and smacked her across the face.

"This is for leavin' the damn windows open and letting the damn leaves blow all over the house, you ungrateful brat!"

Samantha stood there for a moment in shock. "I'm sorry, Father, I'll clean it up." She bit her tongue and fought back the tears as she went to grab the broom. She thought about Levi and desperately wished he would come rescue her and Dally from her evil father. She had never wanted anything so badly in her life.

As she swept up the leaves, her father started in once more. "That saddle tramp has corrupted your senses!"

"I beg to differ, Father," Samantha argued, her hand going to her hip. "Levi and I care deeply for each other, but you don't seem to understand." She watched disgust spread across his face.

"That's a damn lie, and you're nothing but a snot-nosed kid. What in the hell do you know about love?"

Anger and hurt ran hot through Samantha's blood as her fist clenched at her side. Her voice was soft and sharp as she glared at Father. "He's returning for me, and I'll be damned if you are going to stop me."

"You leave with him and you sure as hell aren't a daughter of mine." The threat hit her hard as he grabbed his hat and stormed out the door.

She went back to sweeping up the leaves, but her heart was aching and her chest felt tight and unsettled. She decided she would bake her apple pie to get her mind off of her father. After she had finished the pie and placed it in the window to cool, she decided to take a nap. After several minutes of crying, she finally drifted off to sleep.

A FEW DUSTY miles outside of Council Grove, Levi turned to Bud and said, "I'm much obliged that you come find me the way you done."

Bud looked him in the eyes. "Boss, I just had a feelin' that somethin' weren't right. It was quite an adventure trying to find you. Met the lovely Miss Cheyenne…she was the best thing to ever happen to me." Bud's eyes began to fill with tears.

Levi firmly shook his hand. "Pardner, I'm right proud to call ya my friend."

Bud smiled. "Smell that, Boss?" The wind was blowing strong out of the south, blowing the smell of the cattle pens in Council Grove right at them.

Levi grinned. "Ya damn right I do. Hot damn, we're just about there." He was dying to see Cheyenne's sweet face and kiss her soft and tender lips.

As they rode on, a jackrabbit ran across the trail and startled Star. She began to buck and rear up, and Levi hung on with all that he had. "Easy, girl, easy!"

After she finally calmed down and stopped bucking, Bud laughed. "Damn, cowboy, that was quite a ride there."

Levi glared at him for a second then smiled. "Damn cotton-pickin' rabbit." The two laughed.

Levi spotted a long-awaited sight up ahead. "By God, Bud, there she is. Ya think she knows we're comin'?" They stopped their horses and looked over the booming town.

"Boss, that gal is in for a real surprise today. I just hope you ain't in for one yourself."

Levi looked at Bud. His eye was still black from his fight in the saloon back in Abilene. He still had stitches over his eyebrow and looked like he had seen better days. "What do ya mean by that?"

"Well, Boss, I just hope we don't ride in and find her lovin' on some young cowpoke. I'm 'bout plumb tired of all this damn shootin'." Bud grinned.

"Pardner, one more remark like that and you'll get more shootin' than you can handle."

As they reached town, Levi's heart raced as he looked for Samantha on the streets. He saw the barkeep run out onto the street and to the Hays House, casting a few looks at them on his way. They rode up the street and hitched their horses out front of the blacksmith shop. Star had had a shoe come loose.

Bud stayed behind at the livery to tend to the horses. Levi grabbed his cane and started limping his way down the street in search of Miss Samantha. He was dying to see her and couldn't wait any longer. He had waited long enough, too damn long.

SAMANTHA HAD AWOKEN from her nap and was now at the Last Chance Store, having decided to shop for some fabric to make her a new dress for the warmer weather. As she browsed through various buttons and lace, she stalled for as much time as possible, trying to stay away from her father. As she sorted through several different fabrics, she found herself daydreaming of wedding dresses and if Levi would ever actually propose to her and make her his wife. She found herself wondering if he would ever really return for her. It seemed like forever since he had left. Hell, it seemed like forever since he had last written to her. Had he changed his mind about her? A sad and lonesome feeling came over her at that horrifying thought. She couldn't give up hope, though. It was all she had.

Deciding on the buttons that best matched the fabric she admired, she wandered across the store and picked up a book to browse. It was a dime novel about a rambling cowboy, and she thought about Levi and his nickel-plated twin Colts. Would he hang them up if he ever returned for her?

She put down the book and walked over to the counter and made her purchase. As she walked out the door to head to the cottage, the barkeep came running up to her. "Miss Samantha! The stranger! He's here!" The man pointed up the street, and Samantha's heart seemed to stop beating. As she turned her head to look up the street, the sun shone in her eyes, causing her to squint. The wind blew dust across the street, and she saw the silhouette of a man limping her direction. As the dust settled, she saw the sun reflect off the grips on the man's guns. Tears filled her eyes, and she dropped her fabric on the boardwalk.

As she watched the man limp down the street, she felt herself wanting to run to him, but instead she just stood there. Her heart ached for him with every step that he took. She could tell he was in great pain. She couldn't believe her eyes. He looked so stunning in his vest and tailored shirt. She thought she was surely dreaming. Was it really him? Could it be?

Levi was here.

AS LEVI REACHED the boardwalk where Samantha was standing, he noticed damn near every citizen was standing outside watching. As he limped onto the boardwalk, he looked deep into her soft blue eyes for a moment, and it seemed as if the whole world had just stopped turning. All the hell and hard, lonely times he had been through finally seemed worth it. He couldn't believe she was standing there in front of him.

"Samantha, darlin'," he said as he leaned on his cane. "Why, you're as purty as ever. I told you I'd be coming back for ya. I'm right sorry it took this long, but, darlin', here I am."

Tears were flowing off Samantha's cheeks and her whole body was shaking uncontrollably. She didn't say a word but stared back into his eyes.

"Darlin', not a second went by since we parted that you weren't heavy on my mind. Truth is, lovin' you kept me alive. There were several times out there I figured I'd never lay eyes on you ever again. It was the most horrible feelin' in all my life."

Samantha took Levi by the hand, then wrapped her arms around him tightly. He had never felt so loved in all his life. It was the perfect feeling. She wrapped her arms around his neck and kissed him. This gal was a godsend. A blue-eyed Kansas angel that was turning his whole life around and for the better. The two stood there for several minutes, just staring into each other's eyes.

Levi kissed her hand softly. "Would you care to take a ride with me?"

Samantha smiled. "Levi, I'd ride anywhere with you."

Arm in arm, the couple slowly strolled toward the livery. The blacksmith was putting a new shoe on Star.

Bud turned to Levi and Samantha. "By golly, Boss. You weren't foolin', was ya? She's the purtiest thing west of the Mississippi." He took off his hat and walked over and shook Samantha's hand as she blushed.

Levi's heart was filled with joy. "Darlin', this here is Bud Christopher. He's my top hand and dear friend of mine."

She smiled. "It's a pleasure to meet you, Mr. Christopher."

The blacksmith straightened up and brushed his hands together. "Well, that oughta do'er."

"Much obliged to ya, sir." After settling up with the man, Levi saddled Lightning for Samantha.

"Where we headed?" Samantha asked, excitement in her voice.

"Well, darlin', I'd like to see somethin' before we leave this territory."

Bud rolled his eyes and grinned. "Boss, I'm gonna head over yonder to that Hays House you told me so much about."

"Alright, pardner, we'll find you when we return to head on out."

Bud headed across the street, and Levi and Samantha saddled up and headed south of town. As they rode up a bluff, they stopped for a second, and down below was the little spot where they had met on Elm Creek.

"Remember that spot down there, darlin'?" Levi asked as he pointed down the bluff.

"I'll never forget that spot as long as I live. I go there often and dream of you."

Levi looked at her. "Ya know somethin', darlin'?"

"What's that?" she asked.

"You're an amazing woman."

Samantha smiled, and the pair headed down the bluff to Elm Creek. Once they reached the spot where they had made the sweetest love they had ever made, Levi took her by the hand and softly kissed it. "Samantha, I never knew quite just what I wanted out of like 'fore I met you. Now I know exactly what I want. Darlin', I've done a lot of things in my life, most of which I'm not proud of. Lots of folks don't care too much for me, but I want you to know that I'm hangin' up my guns and startin' a new life. I'd be much obliged iffen you'd be part of it. You are by far the most handsome woman I've ever laid eyes on. I aim to spend the rest of my life falling in love with you, over and over again, every time I get lost in your intoxicating blue eyes."

Levi clenched his teeth, and it took all that he had to kneel on one knee, ignoring the pain. Samantha's whole body began to shake, and tears rolled down her cheeks as Levi reached down into his jacket pocket and pulled out a little box. He opened it, revealing the ring he had bought in Abilene. He took her by the hand. "Samantha, darlin', I love you more than any other woman I have loved before. I promise you now that I will love you unconditionally, for the rest of your life. Darlin'…will you marry me?"

Samantha gasped as tears rolled down her face. "Oh, Levi! I love you more than words could ever say. I've missed you so much it killed me inside. I thought you had changed your mind about me." She wiped the tears from her soft blue eyes. "Yes, Levi, I will marry you."

Levi's heart raced as wildly as it did that day he had first run into her on the boardwalk. He gently slid the ring on her delicate finger, then pulled himself up on his cane as she wrapped her arms around him and helped him up. He wrapped his arm around her and softly brushed her hair back from her cheek and behind her ear. "Oh, how I love you, Samantha."

"And I love you, Levi." She clung tightly and kissed him for several minutes.

He smiled and looked deep into her eyes. "Darlin', I fully intend to spend the rest of my life makin' you as happy as you can be. I've got quite a surprise waitin' for you back on Soldier Creek."

"Surprise? What kind of surprise?"

"Well now, darlin', it wouldn't be much of a surprise iffen I told ya now, would it?" The two laughed. "Shall we be fixin' to head out soon?"

She looked back toward town. "I must go to the cottage and pack my things and grab Dally. I pray Father's not there." She shuddered.

SAMANTHA'S HANDS TREMBLED with excitement as they galloped back toward town. As they passed the Hays House, a woman stepped out on the street and motioned for them to stop.

"Miss Nancy," Samantha said, smiling.

"Well, child, I reckon you won't be comin' in to work tomorrow now, will ya?" She smiled and took Samantha by the hand. "Child, I'm so happy for you." She nodded at Levi. "Mr. Cord, sir."

"Yes, ma'am?" Levi said, taking his hat in his hand.

"Mr. Cord, you take care of this little gal, ya hear me? She's like a daughter to me."

Levi looked the woman dead in the eye. "Ma'am, you don't have anything to worry about now. I intend to give Miss Samantha here the best life I can possibly give her. I love her dearly."

Samantha squeezed Miss Nancy's hand tightly. "I wanna thank you for everything you have done for me, Miss Nancy. I'm sorry to be leavin' you shorthanded."

"Nonsense, child. If you don't quit right this instant and go marry that boy, well, then you're fired."

All three of them smiled at each other and shared a laugh.

Miss Nancy patted at her eye. "I'll miss you dearly, child."

"And I'll miss you, Miss Nancy."

"Indeed, child. You best be goin' so y'all can get a fresh start out of Council Grove before sundown." The three said their goodbyes and parted ways.

Once they arrived at the cottage, Samantha was relieved to see Father was not home.

"We must hurry, Levi." She quickly packed her few things from her trunk into a carpetbag. "I wanna leave before Father comes home."

After she packed everything she needed, they turned to walk out the door and she yelled, "Come on, Dally!" Dally came running, and Levi patted her on the head. Samantha smiled at Levi, and they headed down the street toward the livery.

As they passed through the peaceful community, Samantha looked back over her shoulder at the cottage and the storefronts. A sad feeling came over her, but her heart was filled with joy at the same time. She would miss the citizens of Council Grove, but she had waited for this day for what seemed like forever. Her cowboy had finally returned.

Chapter 16

As they set out on the trail, they came to a hill that overlooked Council Grove. Samantha stopped her horse and took one last look back. She would miss Miss Nancy's smile every morning as she went to work at the Hays House. She was a dear friend, and she knew in her heart that she might never get to see her again.

"Come on, Dally," she hollered as she galloped to catch up with Levi and Bud. It had been a long time since Samantha had been out of Council Grove. She was so excited for their new adventure. She didn't know what the future might hold and what God had in store for them, but she was ready for anything.

She caught up with Levi and Bud. Levi turned to her and smiled. "You sure 'bout this, darlin'?"

"I've been waitin' for this my whole life. If you hadn't of took your sweet time comin' back for me…"

Levi turned to her and his jaw dropped open. Bud's face was priceless. Samantha tried to keep a straight face but couldn't resist. She began laughing, then they joined in. It felt great to laugh. Dally looked up at them like they were all crazy.

As they rode across the prairie, the sky was full of big white puffy clouds. Yellow sunflowers and purple thistles grew all over the rolling hills, painting a perfect Kansas picture. A covey of bobwhite quail flushed up ahead of them and scattered in several directions. The quail called to each other, trying to regroup.

They had made it several miles up the trail before Levi spoke. "Damn, my bones are achin' somethin' fierce. Mind if we rest a spell?"

Samantha knew he was hurting by the way he was constantly shifting weight in the saddle. She could tell he wouldn't be able to tolerate much more.

As they dismounted, Levi said, "Iffen y'all don't object, I think this will make as good a place as any to hold up for the night."

Samantha watched Bud look up at the sky toward the sun, and she found her gaze doing the same. They could still ride for at least another three or four hours before the sun would set on the open prairie. They both looked at Levi as he laid his blanket and saddle on the prairie floor. "Whew," he said as he fell to the blanket. "Feels mighty good to stretch these ol' legs out."

He was a prideful man, so she didn't let on that she knew he was in pain. She and Bud laid their saddles and blankets down next to Levi to make camp for the night.

"I reckon I'd best be gettin' to gathering some buffalo chips to make a fire before sundown." Bud rose to his feet.

As he set out over the hill, Samantha walked over and pulled her blanket close to Levi. She laid down and put her head on his chest and looked deep in his eyes as if she was staring right into his very soul. Not a word was spoken for several minutes. They just lay there lost in each other's eyes while their hearts beat wildly. Levi leaned up and softly kissed her on the forehead, then began running his fingers through her soft blonde hair. "By God, darlin'," he whispered. "You are so amazing."

She felt her face grow warm. "Shoot, not hardly."

He looked her in the eyes. "Samantha, in all the cow towns I've been through all the way from Abilene to Dodge City and Denver to Santa Fe, I've never laid eyes on another gal that was near as amazing and beautiful as you."

Samantha's heart fluttered, and she leaned down and kissed his lips for several minutes. He wrapped his arms around her and held her tight. There was much more here than lust in her heart, and she figured it was safe to assume it was the same for him.

"You know, darlin', I've never felt anything more meaningful and real in my whole twenty-nine years of livin'." Levi spoke the words aloud, but his eyes were on the sun as it slowly made its descent. "This love I have for you goes beyond what I have ever felt...like I belong with you and finally have my purpose in this here world. I think the good Lord put me here to love, cherish, and honor the most beautiful blue-eyed angel that he's ever created, and I plan to do just that."

Her heart was as light as ever, and the happiness she felt seemed as if it would cause her to burst.

About that time, Dally looked over at them and came crawling up, wedging herself between them. "Jealous old dog," Samantha said with a grin. Dally looked over at Levi, then licked him on the cheek. "Well, thank ya, ma'am," Levi said as Samantha giggled. She had never felt so perfect and comfortable in all her life.

Dally threw her head up and began barking. She took off across the prairie as Bud returned and began to prepare a fire. As they looked to see what all the fuss was about, they spotted a jackrabbit trying to lose Dally behind a patch of brush.

"Hungry, Boss?" Bud said as he reached for his Winchester.

"Pardner, I could eat a horse head to hoof right now."

Bud jacked a cartridge into his Winchester, then cautiously stalked the hiding rabbit. Levi and Samantha watched carefully as he approached the brush. Dally circled the spot where she had last seen the rabbit, and Bud studied the spot carefully, waiting for it to bust out running so he could take a shot.

After a couple of minutes, Bud kicked the brush. No rabbit emerged from the brush, though, and Samantha could hear Bud cursing to himself and Dally. "What the hell…where in tarnation did he go, dog?"

She watched as Dally looked at the brush, then up at Bud, and tilted her head as if to say, "Damned if I know." Bud laid his Winchester down on the ground and knelt to pet Dally on the head. Just then, the rabbit darted out of the brush and Dally took off between Bud's legs, yelping and barking up a storm. Bud fell down, and Levi and Samantha sat there laughing as Bud spun around and jumped to his knees, pulling his Navy Colt from its holster and fanning three shots at the rabbit. The first shot flew just over the rabbit's ears. Unfortunately for that poor critter, the second slug caught him right in the neck, followed instantly by the third, which struck him just below the ear. The rabbit crumpled and rolled about twenty feet.

Dally ran up and grabbed it by the leg and took off across the prairie. Bud quickly reached down and picked up his rifle, then took off yelling after Dally. "Drop it," he yelled as Levi and Samantha sat there laughing. For probably close to twenty minutes, Bud chased the dog around in circles.

Suddenly, Samantha yelled loudly, "Dally! Drop it!" Dally dropped the rabbit and came running over to her and Levi with her tail between her legs. Bud looked back at them and just shook his head as he walked up and grabbed the rabbit. He picked it up and carried it back over to the fire, then began skinning and gutting it.

When he finished, he looked across the prairie and said, "Boss."

Levi looked in the direction Bud was gazing. "What's on your mind, Bud?"

"Boss, I'm fixin' to cook you and Miss Samantha one of the best daggum meals you ever had."

Samantha was surprised. "Oh, really now? A cowhand that can cook?"

Levi and Bud smiled at each other as Bud got to his feet. "I'm going to see if I can find us something special to eat tonight off this here trail," he said before wandering off.

A LITTLE WHILE later, Bud returned. Levi peered curiously at the hat Bud now carried in his hands instead of on his head. He could see the green tops of wild onions. Bud went to the fire and began to boil some water along with some sassafras roots he must have found.

Levi's mouth watered. Sassafras roots didn't often grow this far west of the Missouri hills, but when boiled they made some of the finest tea a fellow had ever tasted. Bud reached into his saddlebags and pulled out a small Dutch oven and a skillet, along with some salt and pepper and a little flour. Taking the rabbit, he battered it in the salt, pepper, and flour. Then he placed it in the skillet over the fire. He dug down into his saddlebags again and this time dug out a can of beans. After he opened it, he poured it into the Dutch oven and chopped up the onions and greens he had found. The last thing he did was chop up some bacon and add it in.

After what seemed like forever, Bud smiled. "Well, y'all, I'd say she's about ready." He passed a plateful of his prairie gourmet to Levi and Samantha, then made a plate for Dally. "Here ya go, you ornery cuss. You had me running all over the dang territory chasing your tail."

Levi and Samantha smiled as they waited for him to make his own plate and sit down.

As he sat down, he looked at them. "What's wrong? Ya think I poisoned it or somethin'?"

Levi looked at Samantha and gave her a little wink. She took a bite slowly and closed her eyes. "Boy, now that's just…amazing."

Bud waited for Levi to take his. As he did, his eyes widened. "Damn, Bud, that's tasty." He took a second bite and smiled. As they began to eat, Bud grabbed their tin cups and poured each one of them some of the sassafras.

"What's that stuff?" asked Samantha.

Bud grinned. "Just take ya a sip and enjoy."

Levi took a sip. "Hot dang, Bud! I ain't had a sip of that since I was no bigger than a corn nubbin. My grandpa Lee down in Missouri always made me some. Tastin' this fine stuff right here brings back a heap of good memories. Grandpa Lee would take me down there on the ol' James River and down on Turnback Creek. We had ourselves a ball out there. Damned fine memories."

Samantha took a sip. "Hmm, that's different. Good, but different." She scooted closer to Levi, smiling as she watched him enjoy his supper.

After they had finished, Levi said, "Well, pardner, that was quite a feast there. Much obliged to ya."

"Agreed," said Samantha.

Bud smiled as he gathered the dishes. "Aw, shucks…it weren't nothing. There's a stream over yonder. I think I'll take these over there and wash them."

"Could you use some help there, pardner?" Levi asked.

"Nonsense, Boss," Bud replied. "You and Miss Samantha got quite a heap of catching up to do." Bud headed for the stream and Dally followed along.

Samantha leaned down over Levi and he lay down and stretched out. Staring into his eyes, she ran her fingers through his hair and along his ear and cheek. He wrapped his arms around her and pulled her on top of him. He placed his hand behind her head and softly kissed her forehead and then her cheek. "You're amazing, darlin'," he whispered in her ear. He gently slid his hand in her dress and rubbed her soft tender breast as they kissed. This time when she placed her lips to his, a feeling came over him that he had never felt with any gal. Lord knows he had had more than his share of them, but there was something much different when he kissed her. He couldn't explain it but it sure was sure an amazing feeling.

They laid there for quite a spell and held each other as they touched and kissed so patiently.

Levi looked deep in her eyes and whispered, "I'm going to kiss you a million times 'fore I'm through, darlin'."

Seducing him with her eyes, she said, "Cowboy, I aim to hold you to it."

After a bit, they heard Bud talking to Dally as he headed back to camp.

"Reckon we oughta behave now, darlin'," Levi said as he looked to Samantha.

She shrugged her shoulders. "Well, that's no fun."

Bud put the dishes back into his saddlebags before kicking off his boots and shaking all the trail dust out of them. Setting them beside his blanket, he lay down. "Boy, I'm sure tuckered out. How far ya reckon we'll make it tomorrow, Boss?"

"Well, pard, I figure we'll set out just after sunup. Figured we only made about twelve to fifteen miles. We should make it there, if not tomorrow evening, the next morning. I don't figure we're in too big of a rush, do you?"

Samantha looked at Levi. "Where we headed?"

Bud winked at her as Levi grinned and said, "You'll see soon enough, darlin'."

She shook her head and then laid her head on her saddle for a pillow.

Levi curled up next to her and wrapped his arm around her and held her tightly, close to him. This was the first night in several years that Levi fell asleep with a smile on his face.

BRIGHT AND EARLY the next morning, Levi awoke with a smile on his face. Samantha was snuggled up close to him and he had his arm wrapped around her. The sun was just clearing the prairie horizon off to the east and they had quite a ride ahead of them, but Levi couldn't bear to wake her up. He leaned over and kissed her on the forehead, then cuddled up to her and went back to sleep.

An hour or so later, Dally came running up and jumped on Levi, waking him up. He eased his way up, trying not to disturb Samantha. He got up and stretched his body, then looked up at the sky. Over to the west, the sky was dark with big thunderclouds stretching across the horizon. Thunder rumbled in the distance, back over Council Grove. The small storm was slowly headed northeast, as they were, so Levi hoped it would miss them. He didn't cotton too much to the thought of getting soaked.

From its perch atop a blooming thistle, a red-winged blackbird called to its mate. Shortly after, his mate answered back and the pair of them flew across the prairie. Levi walked over to Star, running his hand along her neck before beginning to saddle.

Bud awoke and saw Levi standing by the horses. He jumped and reached for his gun and pulled back the hammer. "Lordy, Boss!" he said as he uncocked the hammer on his Colt. "You sure gave me a fright! I figured you was a damn thief after the horses." He got up and slid his feet into his boots, then put his hat on his head.

"Mornin'." Levi heard a soft voice and turned to see Samantha wiping the sleep from her eyes.

"Mornin', darlin', how did ya sleep?"

"Like a baby." She got up and began to saddle Lightning.

Levi walked over to her and put his arms around her. He kissed her on the neck and whispered, "Darlin'..."

"Yes?"

"Darlin', you're as purty as the morning sun."

Samantha turned and hugged him, squeezing him tight and kissing him.

Bud chuckled. "You two lovebirds make me sick."

They all laughed and prepared to start their journey for the day.

A few miles up the trail, Bud's horse started to act up. "Easy, girl, easy," he said, trying to calm her down as she shook her head and stomped her feet. "What on earth has got into you?"

A shot rang out across the prairie to the north. Seconds later, another shot rang out and then a third. A whole mess of whooping and hollering could be heard before a man could be seen racing across the hillside on a buckskin stud. He was running so fast, by the time the dust would kick up he would be another twenty yards ahead. Another shot rang out behind the man.

He was in such a hurry to get away from not one, not two, but eight painted Pawnee braves all armed and madder than a nest of hornets. They were firing at the man, and he wasn't slowing down for nothing.

Levi studied them for a minute. "That poor fella needs a hand."

Bud looked at Levi. "That's suicide, Boss. There's too damn many."

Levi pulled his rifle out of the scabbard. "Well, Bud, that means you better not miss."

Bud went pale and got a look of fright on his face. "Aw, hell," he said as he grabbed his Winchester.

Samantha pulled her Winchester out of its scabbard and jacked a live cartridge into the chamber.

Bud and Levi turned to her and Bud said, "By God, ma'am, what in the hell are you aimin' to do?"

Samantha kept her eyes on the Indians. "I reckon we'll find out now, won't we?"

Bud shook his head. "Aw, hell."

The man on the buckskin and the Indians all disappeared over the hill.

"Well, hell," Levi said as he looked at Bud. "Reckon they're gone now."

He turned to look at Samantha just as she yelled, "Oh, the hell they are!"

Levi turned, his heart sinking in his chest. The Indians were all on a dead run, headed straight back toward them now. "Head for that gully!" he yelled as he turned his horse around.

Bud shook his head. "Damn it!"

The Indians were about one hundred yards away and getting closer by the second. They spurred their horses for the nearby gully, preparing for the worst. Once they reached the gully, they jumped off their horses.

"Don't miss!" yelled Levi as he aimed his rifle at the Indian in front.

"Shit," Bud said. "Why in the hell did they decide to come back for us? What happened to the other fella?"

At that moment, they heard a voice screaming and cussing up a storm. They looked at each other and then back at the Indians.

"What in the Sam Hill is that?" asked Levi.

"There!" Samantha pointed. Right behind the Indians was the man with the buckskin horse, now charging after them instead of away from them.

"What in the hell is he doing?" yelled Bud. "He's plumb crazy."

Levi carefully took aim. "Let's give him a hand." As the Indians got closer, Levi squeezed the trigger and the slug tore through the shoulder of the brave in front, sending him flying backwards off his painted pony.

"Nice shot, Boss!" yelled Bud. He aimed at one of the braves and fired. The bullet whizzed past his head, not inches from his ear.

Levi quickly loaded another cartridge and took aim again. Shots echoed across the prairie, sending gunpowder to fill the sky. As Levi pulled the trigger, the brave did a backflip over his horse and hit the ground and one of the other braves ran over him with his horse.

Bud took aim once again. "Son of a bitch! My damn gun's jammed!"

The Indians were closing in fast now, and Levi knew all his friend would have left now was his sidearm.

"Look out, Bud!" Samantha screamed. She was pointing to one of the braves who was taking aim. Bud drew his Colt and fired twice but failed to hit the brave. Samantha swung her rifle up and shot the brave in the left cheek. By this time, the Indians had reached the gully and lead was flying from every direction.

Bud's eyes were as big as shiny silver dollars. "Damnation, ma'am!"

"Shut up and get to shootin'," she yelled back.

Behind the Indians, the man on the buckskin came riding hard with a Hawken rifle in his hands and the reins in his teeth. Suddenly, one of the braves turned around and shot at the man's horse. His arrow lodged deep in the buckskin's chest, but the horse somehow kept running hard. A second arrow came flying out of nowhere and stuck the horse in the neck. The stud snorted and shook his head from the pain and seemed to become weaker and weaker.

Levi took aim and shot one of the braves in the gut, sending him to the ground gasping for air. Two braves jumped off their ponies and came right at them. Levi was shaking as he tried to load a new cartridge into his rifle. Bud took aim at another brave. "Look out!" Levi yelled.

Samantha spun around and shot both the braves dead in their tracks. Just as Bud pulled his hammer back on his Colt to take aim on the brave coming up on him, Samantha turned and shot that one as well.

Bud was shaking as he tried to catch his breath. "By God, woman!"

Through all the dust and gun smoke, Levi looked carefully to see how many braves were left. Through the dust, he saw the man on the buckskin chasing two last braves.

"You sons of bitches shot my horse!" the man yelled. "I'm fixin' to scalp you while you're still suckin' air."

One of the braves shot his bow at the buckskin, sending another arrow deep into his chest. This time the horse gasped for air and slowed up. "Come on, boy, don't give up on me now, damn ya!" The man spurred the horse hard and the horse took a few more steps and fell to the prairie floor. The man hit the ground and reached for his bowie knife. "You red-skinned bastards!"

The braves stopped their ponies, and one of them turned around and rode straight for the man. Levi took aim at the brave, but just before he squeezed the trigger, the man jumped up and grabbed the brave by his shiny dark black hair and ripped him off his pony and punched him in the face. The brave grabbed him by the neck, and the man took his knife and skinned his scalp right off his head while he was still alive. The brave let out one of the most agonizing screams that could be heard. Levi, Bud, and Samantha stood there with their eyes wide and their mouths open, speechless.

"My God," Levi said.

The last Indian brave stopped his horse and stared at his fallen brother. The man swung his knife up in the air and started screaming like a Comanche.

He took off running on foot toward the brave, and the Indian took off in the opposite direction.

As the dust and smoke cleared, the three watched the man walk over to his fallen horse. He studied the arrows in the horse and shook his head. He knelt and patted the horse on the neck. The man slowly took his bowie knife and wiped the Indian's blood off onto his buckskin pant leg. He took his bowie knife and cut his palm.

"What's he doing?" whispered Samantha. Levi shook his head.

The man then placed the knife to the horse's throat. He then slit the horse's throat and placed his bleeding palm to it. Bud looked at Levi and then back at the man with a look of curiosity in his eyes.

After several minutes, the man got up and picked up his rifle, then walked over to the gully. "Howdy," he called to them.

"Howdy," Levi replied.

The man wore a buckskin shirt and buckskin pants with a beautiful white-and-blue beaded belt that he carried his bowie knife in. He had a bear claw necklace and a coyote skin hat, and Samantha visibly shivered at the sight. You could hardly see his face through his thick reddish-brown beard. He wore buckskin moccasins.

As he walked up to them, he kept his eyes fixed on Levi and his twin Colts. Bud studied the man with a strange look on his face. "Where ya hail from, stranger?" Levi asked.

The man pointed toward the west. "Rocky Mountains." The man looked at Bud, who was still staring. "Where you from?"

Bud pointed to the east. "Up the trail here, a day or two's ride."

The man got a strange look on his face and looked Bud in the eyes. Levi watched the two men study each other. The man asked Bud, "What's your handle, fella?"

"Bud."

"Bud? What's your Christian name?"

"Christopher."

The man took off his cap and through it in the air. "Well, hot damn! Iffen it ain't my own daggum brother!"

Bud's face lit up. "By God! Mike! Is that really you?" The two men shook hands and hugged each other as Levi and Samantha stood there in shock.

The Return to Council Grove

"YOU HAVE A brother, Bud?" Levi asked with a grin.

Bud looked at the man. "Y'all, this here is my brother Mike. I ain't seen hide nor hair of him since, what, twelve, fifteen years, ain't it been, brother?"

Mike shook his head. "Goin' on fourteen years, I believe."

Bud shook his brother's hand again. "Damn, good to see you again, brother."

"You too, brother."

Bud looked at Levi. "Mike here decided when we was youngsters that he wanted to be a mountain man. He wore a coonskin cap that Daddy skinned from a coon we treed up an ol' hollow sycamore down on the Marais Des Cygnes River back in '41. This boy could trap anything with fur. He could outrun a whitetail buck and outfight any fella west of the Missouri."

Under all his whiskers, Mike smiled. "Yes sir, I set out when I was a bit shy of seventeen and headed west out of the Missouri hills for the Rockies. I heard tell of Jim Bridger and Kit Carson and wanted to try my hand at trappin'. Caught a great deal of beaver in Kansas Territory, then went on to Colorado Territory and then up through the mountains. I'd got word from back home that Bud here had runned off and got himself hitched. So I figured I'd ride on up to Manhattan where I heard he was staying and give him my best. When I rode into town there, I hadn't the slightest notion on where he lived, so I figured I'd ask the marshal. Come to find out, just before I'd arrived in town there, some feller filled the marshal full of lead and ol' Bud here was nowhere to be found. I didn't know his wife's name, so I never did catch up with her."

Bud looked at his brother, then out across the prairie.

"So, brother, where's that gal of yours?"

Bud stared at the ground, pain weighing heavy on his heart. He couldn't say a word.

It was as if his brother knew he couldn't bear to talk about it, though, because he quickly changed the subject. "Much obliged for helping me with them damn redskins. They were fixin' to have my scalp when I got tired of them chasing me across half of the daggum Kansas territory. I got bored of runnin' after a spell and turned that ol' horse around and took off right back at them. Y'all shoulda seen the looks on their faces when I did. They turned their ol' ponies on a dime and took off like they'd seen the damn devil himself."

Levi snorted. "Hell, yes, you did. You drove them right at us."

Mike looked at the fallen braves scattered across the prairie floor. "I do apologize for that, sir."

"Yeah," Levi said sharply.

Bud gestured to the lifeless bodies. "Don't look like y'all even had to break a sweat here. I'd say you and Brother Bud here handled yourselves quite well."

Bud grinned at his brother, then at Samantha while she reloaded cartridges into her Winchester.

Levi and Bud looked at each other and Levi grinned. Bud swallowed hard as he recalled his rifle jamming and Samantha saving his hide. He was quite a shot and could handle himself quite well in a shooting scrape, but hell, everyone had their days. If it hadn't had been for Miss Samantha, that would have been Bud's last one.

Mike turned around and stared at his fallen horse for a minute, then said quietly, "Damn shame. That ol' horse and I shared many lonesome miles together over the years."

They all turned and studied the fallen horse as it lay lifeless on the prairie floor. Bud patted his brother on the shoulder. "It's sure good to see you again, brother."

Mike turned around and looked at Bud. "You too, Bud. Where y'all headed?"

Levi looked at Bud. "Wilmington area." Bud grinned. Samantha had no idea about the ranch.

Mike scratched his beard. "Wilmington, eh? Don't recall ever hearing of it."

Bud pointed to the east. "'Bout twenty miles, then a gallop north a piece."

Mike continued scratching his beard as he looked that direction. "How's the game up in them there parts?"

Levi looked at the man. "Pardner, Soldier Creek is plentiful. Badger like you've never seen and beaver…boy, let me tell ya."

Mike's eyes lit up. Levi turned to Bud and winked, then said, "We could sure use a hand at trapping them damn ol' beavers that have the creek all dammed up, couldn't we?"

Mike looked at Levi and grinned. Bud said, "Yes sir, Boss, them damn ol' beavers got that creek dammed up from the ranch all the way to Burlingame."

Levi looked at him sharply, and Bud knew exactly what he had done.

Samantha looked questioningly at him. "Ranch? Whose ranch?"

Bud had put his whole daggum foot in his mouth once again. "Uh…"

Samantha looked at Levi with a confused look on her face as Bud continued. "Oh, there's a ranch back east I passed on the trail when I went to find Levi."

Samantha nodded her head. Levi shook his head.

Mike smiled. "I'd say it's time for a change of scenery anyways. Damn beaver is getting scarce Colorado way these days. I'd sure give ya a hand with the trappin' iffen ya had a mind for some company."

"Got yourself a deal there, pardner," Levi said. "That is, iffen you're done running the damn Pawnee right at us."

AFTER VISITING FOR a bit, it was time to set out on the trail.

Mike looked at his fallen horse. "Goin' to be quite interestin' totin' this dang saddle and traps across the prairie afoot."

Levi looked at Samantha. "Darlin', why don't you hop on Star here with me and Mike there could ride your horse a spell."

Samantha nodded, but Mike said, "No, ma'am, I'd hate to take your horse."

She looked at him. "Which would you hate more, takin' my horse or totin' that saddle and traps across the damn prairie?"

Mike grinned. "Well, ma'am, I reckon you're right." He walked over and unsaddled his horse, then took the saddle and tightly tied it to the back of Lightning with a rope. After he got his traps loaded, he reached down for his Hawken rifle.

"By God, pardner," Levi said. "You took on that whole huntin' party with one shot, huh? How the hell did you reload that cannon on your horse?"

Mike took his rifle and pulled the hammer back. He pointed the gun across the prairie and pulled the trigger. Only a click sounded.

"Empty?" Bud asked, shaking his head.

Levi's jaw dropped. "You mean to tell me you took off right at them Indians with an empty gun?"

Mike grinned. "Well, I didn't rightly have the time to reload it. After I had fired the first shot, they rode up on me so damn fast all I could do was run. I'd run that ol' horse across every ditch and gully across the Kansas territory it seemed, so I figured since I was gettin' bored I'd just turn that ol' horse around and give them redskins a run for their money."

Samantha looked back at Bud in total surprise. Levi shook his head. "You took on that whole party without a single bullet?"

Mike grinned. "It seemed like the right thing to do at the time. Them redskins saw me turn that ol' horse around and wave that gun in the air and they turned their ol' ponies around right there in their tracks. I reckon they didn't know my ol' gun weren't loaded, huh?"

The three shook their heads and Mike mounted up.

"Come on, Dally," Samantha called. Dally had taken cover under a nearby clump of brush. She slowly peeked her head out and looked around to make sure it was safe.

Levi crawled in the saddle and Samantha climbed on behind him. "Alright," he said as Samantha wrapped her arms around him tightly. She felt the taut muscles beneath her fingers and the warmth of his body on hers and it felt comforting to her. "Let's do it."

They spurred their horses and set out. As they rode along, the storm that was behind them grew closer and closer. Thunder rumbled to the west, and when they looked back, they could see lightning as it zigzagged across the sky. A few minutes later, a big thunderhead cloud passed over them and raindrops began to fall, bouncing off the brim of Levi's hat. A couple minutes later, the raindrops became bigger and bigger.

Soon a good shower broke out, and Levi untied his duster from his saddle and gave it to Samantha. He turned to see her trying to cover her head with it, so he took his hat off and handed it to her. "Here, darlin', wear this. It will keep your head dry." She smiled and placed it on her head and snuggled up in the duster. It smelled of a mixture between a wet, sweaty horse and Levi. Samantha smiled and wrapped her arms tighter around Levi.

About twenty minutes after the shower had started, the sun came out and the clouds moved northeast, taking the rain with them.

"Well, that's nice," said Levi as he shook the rain from his hair.

Samantha smiled. "What's the matter there, cowboy? Get a little wet there, did ya?"

Levi turned around. "Nah, maybe a little." He grinned at her and she took his hat off and shook her head and placed the hat on Levi's head. "Thank ya, darlin'," he said as he leaned around and kissed her.

She giggled. "Thank you, my handsome cowboy."

As they rode along, the prairie came to life with wildlife. Meadowlarks were thick as flies, hunting for worms. They splashed around puddles and were quite content as they fed along. On the far horizon, a pair of buffalo cows grazed as a calf ran circles around them. Flying high above, a red-tailed hawk let out a shrieking call that echoed across the plains.

A couple hours had passed by, and Samantha's backside was getting rather sore from riding on the back of the palomino.

"How ya holdin' up back there?" asked Levi.

Samantha adjusted herself. "I'll manage." She was dying to get off the mare and stretch her legs.

Up ahead on the trail they spotted Elm Creek, snaking its way through the prairie. The water was up and rolling quickly due to the storm that had just passed by, which would make crossing mighty dangerous.

"Well, this oughta be interesting," Levi said. The four studied the creek, trying to decide the safest route of crossing.

"Water's movin' awful quick," said Bud.

Levi nodded. "Rain was comin' down mighty steady, musta came down heavier here."

Samantha looked at Levi. "How on earth are we going to cross?"

"BOSS," BUD SAID. "I can't swim a lick!"

Levi studied the water, then untied the rope from his saddle, sliding the loop around the saddle horn and cinching it tight. He then passed the free end of the rope to Bud. "Tie this to your saddle horn like I did mine." Levi waited for Bud to dally it around his saddle horn. "Now, take your rope and do the same to Mike's." Once again, he waited for the men to secure the rope to their saddles. He wasn't about to let anyone be swept away.

Mike studied the creek, then looked at him. "What's your plan, Levi?"

Levi pointed across the creek to a low spot in the bank. "I'll take the lead, and you all follow behind me, single file. Whatever you do, don't stop kickin'. If one of ya gets swept away, we all go together. I don't cotton much to the thought of leavin' any of ya behind. Just remember, the current is gonna be mighty strong, but whatever you do, just keep kickin' till you reach the other side."

Bud sighed. "Aw, hell."

Samantha squeezed Levi tight. "Are you sure about this?"

Levi looked across the creek, then into Samantha's eyes. "Not hardly."

Samantha bit her lip. "Aw, hell."

Bud shook his head, his face pale. "Amen to that."

Mike chuckled. "Give her hell, boys."

"Aw, hell." Levi shook his head and clenched his teeth, then spurred Star.

Star snorted and pawed her feet at the edge of the water. As Levi gave her a kick, she shook her head and refused to cross. "Easy now, girl, easy," Levi said softly. "Just gotta get to the other side is all. We been through worse than this down on the Rio." He gave her one last good kick and proceeded to make a daring cross. A few feet into the water, the horse struggled to keep its footing as the water got deeper and rushed quicker. For a moment he felt as if his heart had dropped into his stomach, and he worried Star wouldn't make it.

Bud began to kick his horse and follow closely behind Levi. About halfway across the creek, Mike's horse began to spook.

"Careful there, Mike, I can feel your horse pulling on the saddle," Bud hollered, his voice sounding anxious.

Mike yelled out, "Easy now! Come on!" He kept kicking the horse as Levi and Bud pushed on. Finally, Mike's horse leapt forward and followed.

After what seemed like an eternity, the palomino finally reached the bank on the other side. Shortly after, Bud and Mike arrived safely as well.

"'Bout time you girls showed up," Levi said with a grin.

Bud crawled off his horse. "I need to go check my longhandles after that." They all shared a laugh as Bud headed for a nearby stand of trees.

After Bud returned, he saddled up and the four pressed on. Just ahead on the trail, they spotted a farm with a white fence and three big red barns. There was a big two-story farmhouse with a white wrap-around porch. On the porch there was a white swing and an old wooden rocking chair. Next to the chair was a big brass spittoon.

As they rode closer to the farm all sorts of critters came into view. There were chickens, ducks, guineas, donkeys, goats, pigs, and even turkeys. A big white dog came running up to meet them, and not far behind was a tall woman with a worn and weathered brown hat that looked to be just a bit too big for her head.

"Howdy," she called to them as they rode up. "Beautiful day, ain't it? Darn rain just missed us again."

Levi tipped his hat. "Howdy, ma'am. Right nice place ya got here."

Samantha looked at the house. "Beautiful place."

The woman smiled. "Well, thank ya kindly, folks. My husband and I moved out here about four years ago and I just love it."

Mike looked around the farmyard. "Good lookin' stock ya got there, ma'am," he said as he pointed to the corral.

"Why, thank ya," she replied.

Mike smiled. "You wouldn't happen to have an extra one you would sell for a good price, would ya, ma'am?"

"Well, sir, come on over to the corral and let's take a look."

They dismounted and walked over to the corral and carefully studied the horses. There were two bay geldings and a little strawberry roan mare. The woman pointed to the barn. "There's another bay in the barn, but he turned up lame a few days back."

"Mind iffen I take a look?" Levi asked.

"Certainly," the woman replied. She led him over to the barn where a beautiful bay gelding stood. She placed a hand on the gelding's forehead. "How are ya, Buddy?"

Buddy stood there favoring his right hoof.

"Howdy, pardner," Levi softly said as he reached out his hand to let the horse smell him. After a couple of minutes, he knelt and studied the horse's hoof. The hoof had blown out and there was a hole through the hoof wall. The wound had become infected and needed to be drained and cleaned before it spread and got much worse. "Bud!" he hollered.

"Yes sir, Boss," Bud answered from the corral.

"Bud, bring me a knife and some tobacco from my saddlebags, would ya?"

A few moments passed, and then Bud came over. "Here ya go, Boss," he said as he handed the things to Levi.

Levi carefully picked up Buddy's foot and scraped away all the mud that he could from his hoof. "Ma'am, would you happen to have a pail of water and a rag handy?"

"Certainly," she replied as she went to fetch one.

"Oh, and ma'am? Some old clothes iffen ya have some to spare."

She nodded and disappeared for a few minutes. When she returned, Levi took the cloth she handed him and cut it into big strips. He then took his knife and carefully made a small incision in the infected area of the hoof wall. Yellow pus came draining out. "There we go," Levi said as he took the chewing tobacco and placed it in his mouth for a minute. Once the tobacco was nice and juicy, he spit it into the horse's wound and then took the cloth and wrapped it up good and snug. Levi felt the woman watching him closely.

"Why on earth did you spit tobacco on him?" she asked.

Levi cleaned his knife off on his pant leg. "Well, ma'am, the tobaccy will draw out the infection."

"I see."

As Levi stood and stretched, the lady said, "I'm much obliged to ya, sir. What do ya figure I owe ya?"

"We could sure use some water, iffen you could spare a bit."

"Sure thing."

They headed toward the corral. Mike was looking over the horses. "Which one ya figure on partin' with, ma'am?"

"I aim to keep that short bay, but the others are all for sale."

Mike nodded, then went over to check the little strawberry roan's feet. "How much for this little roan?"

The woman studied over the horse for a minute. "She's got spirit, that one. I'd take thirty for her."

Mike continued to look the horse over. He dug down into his poke and pulled out all the money he had. "Twenty-two sixty-seven. Afraid I'm a bit short there, ma'am. Reckon she'll have to make someone else a fine horse."

The woman looked over the roan. "Well, sir, seein's how this gentleman tended to Buddy's hoof here, I reckon I'll let ya have her for that."

Mike smiled and Samantha let out a sigh of relief. Levi was sure she must not have been very comfortable having to ride behind the saddle for that many miles.

Mike walked over and paid the woman. "I'm much obliged to ya, ma'am." He walked over and grabbed his saddle off Lightning and went over to saddle the strawberry roan.

"Where y'all headed?" asked the woman.

"Fixin' to head north, up Wilmington area from here," Levi answered. "Been a long while since I was there. Had a few unexpected encounters that slowed our return. Figure we'll make it sometime tomorrow afternoon."

The woman smiled. "Would y'all care to stay for supper? We also have a couple spare rooms iffen ya want to hold up here for tonight and set out fresh in the mornin'."

Levi smiled. "I appreciate that, ma'am, but we'd hate to put you out for the night. Besides, I don't think your husband would cotton too much to the idea of strangers bunkin' with y'all."

The woman looked at them. "Hang on, then. I want to send some stuff with ya." She ran into her house and came out with a basket. "Hopefully this bread, apples, and eggs will get you by for the time bein'. I just baked the pie this mornin' and figured the word of the Lord might help keep ya safe on your travels."

Levi helped Samantha to her horse, and everyone mounted up and prepared to head north.

"Here." The woman handed Samantha the basket.

Samantha gasped. "We can't take this from ya, ma'am. It's beautiful."

"Nonsense, child," the woman replied. "Iffen you're ever in this neck of the prairie again you can drop by and say hello. It would do right nice to have company again. Don't see too many folks around here often."

Samantha smiled. "Well, thank ya kindly, ma'am. We're in debt to ya."

"God bless y'all," the woman said as they said their goodbyes. "Hope to see y'all again. Have safe travels, and may God be with ya."

As they set out on the trail once again, the Kansas breeze blew through Samantha's golden hair and Levi looked over at her and smiled. "By God, girl you sure are purty." She looked at him with a smile, then began to blush.

A few miles up the trail, the four spotted a group of riders on horseback. They were headed straight toward them. Levi carefully studied the men. There were six of them. As they rode closer, Levi slid the tie downs off his guns, and out of the corner of his eye saw Bud slid his jacket away from his holster, exposing the grip of the Colt.

The six riders appeared to be in quite a hurry to get away from something. Their horses were plumb tuckered out, and each rider could have used a serious bath.

"Howdy!" Levi hollered out, not moving his hands far away from Colts.

Each rider wore a six-gun and had Winchesters at their sides. One of the rough men had a double-barrel coach gun clutched in his hand. Levi could tell that these men were of the roughest and most dangerous sort.

The leader of the bunch stopped his horse. "Got any whiskey?"

Levi looked the man in the eyes. "No sir, I'm afraid I'm fresh out. Sorry."

The leader looked at Bud. "'Bout you? What ya got in that there poke?"

Bud gave him a glare that could kill. "No sir."

The other riders kept looking behind them, as if they were expecting someone or something.

Levi carefully studied each man and then noticed a pair of sacks draped over one of the men's saddle horn. They appeared to be full, and Levi was sure he knew just what it was they were full of.

The leader was a young man about nineteen or twenty and clean-shaven. He wore a slouch hat and blue wild rag with white polka dots. He had a brown vest with a dirty brown jacket with a hole in the elbow. The kid seemed really nervous and twitchy, yet fearless and smart. He looked them over. "You mean to tell me you travel across the prairie without any rotgut? What, are y'all stupid or something?" The leader shook his head and turned back toward the rest of the gang. "These damn carpetbaggers say they're traveling with no whiskey!" He looked back at Bud and stared him right in the eyes as if he was staring right into his very soul. "I reckon I'd say they was lyin' through their teeth, boys! What do y'all say?"

The man with the double-barrel coach gun cocked the hammers back and laughed. "Hell, Johnny...I should fill 'em with buckshot this instant and take them horses."

Mike cocked the hammer back on his Hawken. The sound was amplified and seemed to echo across the Kansas prairie. Everyone froze, staring at the hands of each other, waiting for someone to draw first.

Johnny looked at Levi, his eyes on the twin Colts, and Levi was sure he would notice he had slid off the tie downs. His eyes held the look of challenge. "You fast, mister? Or ya just wear them guns for show?"

The gang all started laughing, and Levi said, "Would ya be obliged to find out?"

The kid grinned. "I admire your sand there, stranger. Most men that have spoken to me previously in that tone have been executed in the worst way. Say, where do I know you from, mister? I swear I've seen you somewhere before."

Levi didn't recall ever laying eyes on this kid before.

"Ever been to Pueblo?" he asked Levi.

"Not for quite a spell," Levi replied. He stared into the kid's ruthless eyes, daring him to draw without even speaking a word.

The kid's smile seemed to fade away when he took another look at those Colts. "No sir. I heard tell of a feller with a pair of ivory-handled Colts. They say he's quite handy with 'em, too...knows how to use 'em."

Levi, looking the kid dead in the eyes, gave him a little grin and a wink. "Sounds like ol' Bill Hickok, but he carries twin .36 Navy Colts." Levi tapped his finger on his own Colts, daring him to find out just how quick he really was. "These are .45s, son."

"No, stranger, not Hickok."

Levi nodded. "Billy Bonney, maybe?"

The kid seemed to pause in thought for a moment. "No, stranger. Bonney don't leave New Mexico, and you look a heap too old."

Levi grinned. "Is that a fact?"

The kid scratched his neck. "This feller is a tough sum bitch. They say he took out a whole gang single-handedly up Monarch Pass way. They say he's a cold-blooded bounty-huntin' Yankee."

Levi sat up tall in the saddle and said through gritted teeth, "Is that a fact?"

The kid grinned. "Yes sir, stranger. That's what they say."

Levi's blood was boiling. He stared at Johnny. "What's this feller's name, kid?"

Johnny became visibly angry. "I ain't your damn kid, you stupid carpetbaggin' bastard."

"You damn right, you ain't! Otherwise I'd whip you right off that mangy excuse you call for a horse and teach you a little thing I call manners!"

Johnny's mouth dropped open in shock. Levi assumed not many folks spoke to him like that, at least not that got away with it. The tension was so thick you could cut it with a knife. Levi saw a look come over the kid's face that he had seen on several men just before he sent them to their maker. It was a dangerous look. When a man got that certain look in his eyes, you'd better be ready, because he was fixing to clear leather really quick. Levi grinned. "Sure in a hurry to die, ain't ya…kid?"

The kid's fingers were twitching at his walnut grip on his .44. "How's that?"

"I said, you're sure in a hurry to die, ain't ya…kid?"

At that very moment, the kid's hand moved like a bolt of lightning. As he grabbed his Colt, Levi gave him a crooked little half grin and yelled, "Come on, kid! I dare ya! Pull that hogleg and I'll send ya to hell directly!" Just before the kid jerked his Colt from its worn-out leather holster, it seemed something came over him. He looked at Samantha and then back at Levi's twin Colts. Had this kid heard of Levi before? After all, he and his Colts had been the talk of the trail for quite some time now.

Seconds went by for what seemed an eternity. The kid and Levi stared into each other's eyes and not a sound was heard. The kid's hand was gripped tightly around his Colt, ready to draw. Moments later, one of the men got an itchy trigger finger and quickly drew his Colt and aimed at Levi. However, Levi managed to clear leather quicker than many a man was capable of. Without looking to aim, he shot two slugs from the hip into the man before he could even cock his gun. One slug shot the man's hat right off his head, and the other shot right through his ear. Levi twirled his Colts quickly and beautifully and placed them both back into their holsters. Not a single soul drew their guns. Their eyes were all widened as they stood there, disbelief clear on their faces.

The man Levi had shot let out an awful scream and reached for his ear.

Johnny looked at Levi. "If I draw on you, it'll be suicide, Mr. Cord." When the kid spoke his name, he knew for certain he had heard the tales.

Levi tipped his hat back. "There's that possibility, kid."

They locked eyes for a minute and then the kid took up his reins and hollered, "Come on, boys! Let's leave these folks in peace." He spurred his horse and took off on a run, and the rest of the gang followed him.

"Woowhee," said Bud as he sighed in relief. "I think I need to go check my trousers again."

Samantha shook her head. "I thought I was gonna have to show you boys how to shoot again there for a second, Bud."

Bud lowered his head in shame and Levi chuckled. He turned back and watched as the gang disappeared out of sight.

"Rough bunch," Mike said as he uncocked his rifle.

Levi nodded. "Mouthy cuss, wasn't he?"

Chapter 17

The sun was shining bright as it peeked through the white puffy clouds that hung in the Kansas sky. A few miles ahead they spotted a cloud of black smoke stretching up to the sky.

"Indians?" asked Samantha.

"I don't reckon it is," replied Levi.

"Wildfire?" asked Bud.

Levi studied the smoke. "Smoke's too black for a prairie fire. Looks like trouble." He kicked his horse and set off at a run toward the smoke. The rest of them followed.

Just as they reached the top of a hill, Levi looked down below and spotted a red stagecoach, smoldering and in flames. The team of horses had been shot dead and the driver was hunkered over in the front seat.

Samantha gasped. "Oh, my Lord."

"Hyah!" Levi yelled, spurring Star and taking off at full speed. He could feel the heat of the fire burning his face and eyes. He shielded his face with his arm and tried to open the coach door, but the flames were too big and hot. "Damn it," he cussed as he ran to the other side of the coach, trying to see if there were any passengers. There didn't appear to be anyone inside. Levi remembered seeing the sacks on the outlaws' horses earlier. Could they have been the ones who caused this destruction?

When he reached the driver, he could see the bullet hole in his temple, and he knew he was dead for sure. He swung the man up over his shoulder and jumped down off of the burning coach. He laid the man's lifeless body on the ground away from the coach. His jacket and vest were ripped to shreds where he had been shot at close range with a scattergun. He was now sure of who had killed him as he recalled the outlaw with the scattergun. "Miserable bastards," he whispered to himself.

All of a sudden, a shot rang out from behind a nearby thicket. Levi saw Bud's horse spook and rear up high on its back legs, throwing Bud to the ground. His grabbed for his gun just as Mike grabbed for his. Another shot rang out, and the bullet smacked the ground beside Star, causing her to buck. Mike swung his rifle in the direction of the thicket where the shots had been fired and sent a lead ball directly at it.

Another shot rang out, and Levi saw Mike's horse buck, sending Mike in a dive for the ground. "The hell with this!" Mike cursed. "That bullet about hit me between the eyes!"

Levi could hear the bullet whizz out across the prairie as another shot rang out. He ran over to Star, trying to calm her down, but she continued bucking. He saw Bud watching the thicket. His friend fired two shots at it.

"I'm hit, Christine!" a man's voice screamed out.

Bud, Mike, and Samantha all looked at Levi, and he read shock clear on their faces, mirroring his own. Christine? A woman?

"I'm hit!" the voice yelled out again.

Levi studied the thicket and could see movement but couldn't make out what it was exactly.

Bud fired another shot, and the man's voice yelled, "Hold your fire!" Bud took another shot and a woman yelled out, "Please! My husband's been hit! Hold your fire!"

Levi nodded for Bud to hold his fire. "Who the hell are ya, and what do you want?"

The man stood, holding his arm, which had been shot. "Please don't kill us! We're just headed to Dodge for our honeymoon."

"Throw that damn Colt in the dirt! Now!" Levi watched as the woman stood up beside him.

The man didn't hesitate, tossing the gun on the ground.

The woman gave her husband a look of disgust as she whispered, "Are you stupid or somethin'? You just dropped our only way out of here!"

Levi looked the two over as they bickered. They didn't look like they had been living too terribly rough, as they were both on the fleshier side. Their clothes were dirty, though, suggesting they had been out on the trail for at least a little while. Both had brown hair; the man's cut short to his scalp and the woman's a mess atop her head.

The man grabbed her by the arm. "Damn it, Christine! Shut the hell up and let me handle this."

She looked him in the eye. "Let you handle this? The last time you said that I ended up outside Ottawa livin' in a dadburn teepee with a man they called Eagle Shit or Feather, or somethin' like that! Smokin' some sort of prairie weed that gave me a rash on my cunny that you wound up somehow miraculously gettin' all over your dog-ugly face. Then you told your ma that you got the measles!"

Bud turned to Levi. "What in the hell is that woman talkin' about?"

Levi shook his head as the crazy woman went on. "I told you you didn't have the damn measles!"

The man suddenly seemed irritated and a look of embarrassment came over his face. "Well, if it wasn't the measles, then how the hell did my brother Allen get it too? Not to mention Cousin Kevin and Uncle Eddie. Damn it, woman, after you got hold of it, half my family did too!"

Everyone's mouth dropped, including Christine's. "Dadburn it, Cody! I told you it was that damn prairie weed we was all smoking!"

Cody shook her by the arm. "Damn it, Christine! You told me it was somethin' in that damn well water on neighbor Linsey's farm!"

As the two were fighting about God only knows what, a rabbit took out from under a clump of brush headed straight for the unusual couple. Dally sprang to her feet and took off after the rabbit, barking and carrying on like a wild Comanche. Christine turned and saw the dog barreling their way and set into a panic. Screaming at the top of her lungs, "A wolf!", she shoved her husband between her and the dog as Dally came crashing into Cody's legs, causing him to fall and take Christine with him.

"Damn it, Christine, that ain't no wolf!" Cody said. "If that dog bit you, he'd never eat meat again."

Levi hollered out, "Dally! Get your ass over here!"

Dally cowered down, fearing she was in trouble as she crept back over to Levi. For a moment there wasn't any movement from the unusual couple and Levi demanded, "Get on your feet! Who the hell are you, and why the hell are you shootin' at us?"

Cody attempted to get to his feet, but his wife had fallen on top of him and was refusing to attempt to get up on her own. "Damn it, Christine, you're on my arm!"

"Then help me up, damn it!" she yelled as she made very little effort to rise on her own.

"I've been shot, woman! I can't lift your fat ass off that godforsaken ground."

Christine's posture wound itself tight, Cody's comment obviously hitting a nerve. "I don't recall you complainin' 'bout liftin' your cousin Jenny Lee up to your grandpappy's loft in his barn last Christmas when Aunt Marie caught you two up there—"

Cody's face got beet red as he shoved her off and got to his feet. "Shut up, woman! Now you're just makin' shit up. I told you we were just up there talkin'." He walked closer to the group. "My name's Cody Sage, and this mouthy cuss is my wife Christine. We're from a piece of a town called Ottawa back east of here a spell. We was headed west to Dodge for our honeymoon when some outlaws held up the stage and killed the driver. Christine jumped out of the stage and commenced to cussin' and demandin' the men to leave us be and let us go on our way. They threatened to kill her as I sat in the stage, and I figured they were going to do just that when she started runnin' her dadburn mouth. They killed the team, and as Christine was runnin' her mouth, I snuck out the stage and hid in the ditch. As I looked back, I noticed the stage on fire and thought for sure they'd killed her. Unfortunately, after I saw the men ride off, she was headed my way cussin' her fool head off. When we saw y'all ridin' our way, I thought y'all was them comin' back for us, so I started shootin'."

Christine finally attempted to get to her feet on her own but struggled as she rolled down the bank.

"You cotton-pickin' bastard!" Mike said, thrusting a finger at the man in frustration. "Damn near shot my head off!"

Cody lowered his head. "My apologies, sir."

Mike shook his head as Levi said, "Well, I'll be god-damned and go to hell." He laughed, and everyone looked at him as if he had lost his mind.

Samantha stared wide-eyed. "You know, I've met many sorts of people comin' in off the Santa Fe in Council Grove, but none as interesting as these two," she whispered, her voice low so only Levi would hear.

Levi could tell they posed no serious threat, so he looked to Bud. "I reckon we oughta dig that slug out of him before he bleeds to death." They walked over to Cody. "Take off your coat and pull your sleeve up, and, for the love of God, keep that damn woman of yours quiet." Levi studied the wound, and then Bud proceeded to remove the bullet with his knife.

Cody began to squirm something awful and Christine began screaming. "You're killin' my husband!"

Bud turned to her. "Doggone it, woman, if you don't shut your square-headed mouth, you're next!"

Christine shut her mouth and moped. Bud was struggling to remove the bullet and hollered for Samantha to fetch him some whiskey from the saddlebags. She brought him the bottle and he handed it to Cody. "Here, pardner, take a shot of this. It's fixin' to hurt like hell."

Cody took a swallow and then Bud reached for the bottle. With a hesitant hand, Cody went to hand the bottle over, but his demons must have gotten the best of him because he dropped his head back and finished the entire bottle at once. Bud's mouth dropped, and Levi chuckled as Cody handed him the now empty bottle.

"Well, alrighty then," Bud said as he finished carving out the bullet.

While they were working on Cody, Mike had gone and caught up his and Levi's horses and made his way back to the group. After they had wrapped Cody's wound, Levi said, "Well, y'all, I reckon it's time we ought to be hittin' the trail for the last stretch."

Christine looked at Cody. "What are we going to do now? Are they just going to leave us here? We'll die out here. What will we eat?"

Cody looked at her and then across the prairie. "I reckon we'll walk now."

Shock showed on her face. "To where? Dodge City?"

Cody pointed back east. "I reckon our honeymoon will have to wait. Looks like we are going back to Ottawa."

Christine shook her head. "Oh, please, no. I don't want to ever go back. We have nothing left for us there." Cody looked to be in deep thought as she went on. "We have no home. We have no money. We have nothing but the clothes on our backs and that damn Colt you threw in the dirt."

Cody's eyes brightened. "We can live on the land. You're part Cherokee, ain't ya?"

Christine's face paled, and Levi assumed it was because she was thinking of how hard it would be to live off the land with the cold prairie nights, snakes, and wolves. Not to mention the meals would not come as easy as she appeared to be used to. "I told you that was on my mother's side. And what happened the last time we lived in a teepee?"

Levi cleared his throat. "I'm sorry to interrupt, but we gotta ride. We still got a fair piece to go and it's getting late. First chance you get, might not hurt to get yourself to a doctor to take a look at that arm." He shook Cody's hand and tipped his hat to Christine and then mounted Star.

Everyone else settled into their saddles, readying themselves for the last stretch of their journey.

Christine looked at Cody, looking close to a panic. "What are we going to do?"

Cody shook his head. "I don't know, Christine. I don't know."

Samantha was watching them, and Levi could tell it was pulling on her soft heartstrings to leave them behind like a pair of lost pups. Mike and Bud had already turned their horses north with Levi, and Samantha was following along more slowly. Her face was pulled tight in thought and Levi could only assume she was thinking about Cody and Christine. Levi had one thing on his mind, and that was getting back to the ranch safely at last with his love, not picking up more travel companions.

A couple hundred yards up the trail, Lightning stopped. Levi pulled Star up and looked back, noticing Samantha was gazing once more at the couple. She looked back at Levi, and a feeling of guilt tugged at his heart. He shook his head, knowing exactly what she was thinking. Levi looked back at Bud and Mike and saw they had pulled to a stop as well. By the looks on their faces, they also knew what was about to happen.

Mike shook his head and rolled his eyes. "Well, shit a brick."

"Aw, hell," Bud muttered.

With a sigh, Levi looked at Samantha. "Well, go on then. Go get 'em, if you insist."

Samantha smiled. She turned and spurred her horse into a jog as she headed back to Cody and Christine.

Levi shook his head. She had no idea what she could be getting herself into. He watched Samantha ride up to the couple. They had not taken a single step in any direction.

Levi pulled an apple from his saddlebag and began to enjoy an afternoon snack.

Bud turned to Levi. "Boss, what do you intend to do with these two tender ninnies?"

Levi shrugged. "I haven't the slightest damn clue."

"Hell." Bud shook his head. "Ya know, Boss, I reckon you just didn't wanna tell your gal no." He chuckled. "Did ya?"

Levi looked at Bud. "I beg your damn pardon?"

Bud smiled. "I don't know, Boss, iffen you was to ask me, I'd say those blue eyes went and made you…what's the word for it? Soft?"

Levi chucked the apple core at Bud, hitting his belly with a thud.

"Shit!" Bud hollered out in surprise as Mike and Levi laughed.

SAMANTHA'S HEART FELT lighter as she drew closer to Cody and Christine. Although they were strange, she couldn't imagine leaving someone behind to fend for themselves…not having a place to go and being out on their own.

"Did you forget something?" Cody asked as she reached them.

"Well, we got to talkin' and figured y'all just as well come with us. We can get ya somewhere safe until ya decide where you're headed next. It'd be much safer travelin' together," Samantha said with a soft smile.

A grin split Christine's face from ear to ear and Samantha noticed the tobacco stains on her teeth. She felt her stomach turn, but she offered the woman a smile in return. There was something different about this couple, but she could tell they had honest intentions.

"Where we headed, sis?" Christine asked.

"I'm not rightly sure, but Levi said it ain't much further from here. Wherever it is we're headed, I can assure you it'll be much safer with them than it will be out here alone with those outlaws in the area. Not to mention, the wolves." Samantha giggled, remembering the woman's encounter with Dally. She turned her horse back toward Levi and the boys. "Well, ya comin'? Or ain't ya?" Her horse walked at a relaxed pace, and after a few strides she noticed the two were slowly following behind her. They shuffled along, taking four steps each for every one that her horse took. She realized that she may have just bit off more than she could chew, but she wasn't about to leave the two behind.

Once they reached the boys, the group finally set back out. Progress was going to be much slower now that they had two tagging along on foot. The sun was making its way toward the horizon quickly. Samantha knew Levi was anxious to reach their destination.

Bud looked toward the west. "Gonna be 'bout time to set up camp for the night, 'fore too long. Don't you think, Boss?"

Christine and Cody looked at the sun and Christine said, "You mean to tell me we're gonna be sleeping out here on the ground?"

Samantha saw Mike look at Bud with a grin and shake his head.

Levi nodded. "Yes, ma'am. One more night and we'll be home at last. I figure we should arrive sometime midday tomorrow."

Butterflies fluttered in her stomach at the word 'home'. It hadn't really hit her until now…they would be living together in a place of their own. She was his and he was hers, and they would be creating their own little place in the world. Maybe even a place to start a family? A smile tugged at the corners of her mouth and she felt a warmth in her gut at the thought. Could she really turn this hardened cowboy into a family man?

NOT TOO FAR up the trail they decided to set up camp near a small spring-fed stream. Levi began to make camp and they all laid their bedrolls out. Bud commenced to preparing a tasty meal of beans, venison, and some bread from the basket they were given. After they finished their supper, they each enjoyed a piece of the fresh peach pie.

"That is damn right tasty," Levi said around a forkful of delicious pie. He turned his head and noticed that the plates of the newcomers were both licked clean before he had even taken a second bite. The pair must not have had a full meal in quite a spell.

Once everyone had finished their dessert, Samantha gathered the dishes and headed to the stream to wash them. Bud stretched his arms and kicked back on his bedroll, laying his head on his saddle. "Any of y'all believe in ghosts?" he asked.

Mike chuckled and shook his head. "Oh, Lord, here we go."

"Shut your mouth, brother," Bud replied. "I'm serious." Everyone looked at him with wondering eyes and kind of shrugged their shoulders as he went on. "I can talk to them, the spirits of our ancestors." He took a dramatic pause as he peered at those around the campfire.

Christine's eyes widened and her face grew a little pale. Cody slid a little closer to Christine, as if they were not wanting to be sitting alone in the darkness, especially when they were talking about ghosts. Samantha had returned with the stack of cleaned dishes and cuddled close to Levi.

They were all captivated as Bud rose from his bedroll and began to dance around the fire like a Cherokee. His arms were raised to the sky and he chanted in what was assumed to be Indian talk. Suddenly he stopped, and everything was dead silent. Bud's hand raised to his ear as his eyes widened. "Wait...I hear them. The spirits are here! They are all around us!"

"I hear them! I hear them too!" Christine hollered out and Cody pinched her arm as if that would quiet her.

"Our ancestors often speak to us through the animals of the prairie," Bud went on. "Speak to me, ancestors! Let us know you are here!"

A coyote howled, long and lonesome and too close for comfort. Everyone jumped, their faces full of disbelief. Even Bud's face had gone white.

"That'll be enough of that! Quit it, Bud!" Levi could hear the fear in Cody's voice.

Christine held Cody's hand tight as she spoke. "Don't worry, Cody. Remember, I am part Cherokee. They will not harm you or me and that's why I could hear them like Bud could!"

Levi saw a look of mischief dance in Bud's eyes. Samantha squeezed his hand, and he squeezed back, a silent conversation as he let her know there wasn't anything to be afraid of. Bud crossed back around the fire and flopped down onto his bedroll with a thud, dust rising in a cloud around the fire.

A few moments of silence went by, a gentle breeze the only thing stirring in the area. Suddenly, there was a faint rustle out in the darkness and Bud's head snapped around to look at Christine. "The ancestors are angry with you, Christine! They do not like white folk speaking of false heritage. They are coming for you! Ancestors! Please let us know you are here with us!" Bud's voice was loud as he called upon the spirits again.

This time an owl called out from the darkness, and that was all it took to shake Christine to the core. She jumped to her feet, her eyes wide with fear as she tugged at Cody. "I...I have to go to the privy," she said, and Cody stood up beside her, the two huddled together like a covey of scared bobwhite.

Levi chuckled. "Ain't no privy here. Best pick yourself the nearest bush."

She looked at him with disbelief but once she realized he was serious she looked to Cody. "You need to come with me. I refuse to go out there alone!"

"I'm not going out into the dark!"

The look she gave him shut him up quickly. He grabbed the lantern and lit it, holding it out in front of him and turning slowly to see that there wasn't anything waiting for them at the edge of the camp. Slowly the two disappeared into the darkness, leaving the others to share a laugh around the fire.

The peace and quiet was short lived, though, as a bloodcurdling scream broke out from a short way away. They could hear something crashing through the grass and little bit of brush the prairie held, heading straight toward them. Hands were flying to guns as the group prepared for whatever was coming their way, man or beast. Christine and Cody came rushing into the camp, sending bedrolls and clean dishes everywhere.

"What in the Sam Hill is goin' on?" Levi yelled as the two came to a stop.

They were so out of breath it took a moment before they were able to gather themselves enough to talk. "The ancestors! They're out there!" Christine's words were frantic and breathless as she spoke loudly. "I was taking a piss and I turned and there were eyes staring at me and I heard a growl! I leaned down to pull up my bloomers and it about had me!"

Everyone relaxed as they lay their guns down. They all seemed to sigh.

Levi let out a chuckle. "Well, damn, if it had taken ya, that would have made more food for us!"

Mike and Bud laughed at the joke, but Samantha elbowed him lightly in the ribs and smiled at Christine. "We will keep a close eye out tonight, Christine. I'm mighty glad you were able to make it back to camp in one piece."

They all bedded down. Levi noticed Christine kept a close eye out, and Cody's head kept turning back to make sure nothing was coming up behind him. Levi looked at Bud and Mike and shook his head and chuckled.

Samantha snuggled up close to Levi and he held her tight in his warm embrace. The stars danced across the sky and painted a breathtaking picture. Off in the distance a whippoorwill called softly from a stand of locust trees and a second one answered his call. To the north, a pack of coyotes howled to each other as they prepared for their nightly hunt. Crickets serenaded the group as they slowly drifted off to sleep.

The next morning, the group would saddle up and head out once more before finally reaching their destination. He had gone through pure hell to get back to Council Grove to be with her. Nothing would ever come between them.

JUST AFTER SUNUP the next morning, Levi awoke with a stiff and aching body. He had spent most his life sleeping nights on the hard prairie floor, but the older he got, the more the arthritis began to set in. He could feel he had been extremely hard on his body throughout the years.

Samantha was fast asleep as he stretched and got to his feet. As he looked around the camp, he leaned down and saw the only other member of the group awake. It was Dally, sitting at his feet, waiting for him to lean down and scratch her ears. As he did, she wagged her tail and jumped up and wrapped her paws around his waist. "Mornin', ol' girl," he said as he patted her head.

He dug down into his saddlebags and pulled out a plug of tobacco and shoved it down in the lip, then spit into the prairie dust. He placed his fingers on his wounds, which were healing quite nicely in their own sweet time. He looked down at Samantha and his mind drifted back to all the hell he had gone through in his life. Could he give Samantha all she dreamed of and deserved? What would she think of the ranch?

A few minutes later, Mike rolled over and quietly said, "Mornin' Levi."

"Mornin', Mike." Levi reached for the coffee pot and proceeded to fetch some water to brew them a cup for breakfast. "Care for some coffee?"

"Don't mind iffen I do." Mike got up and rolled his bedroll up.

As the others lay sleeping, Levi started a fire and heated some water. Mike leaned over the fire to warm the chill from his hands. "How much further ya reckon we got, Levi?"

Levi gazed up the trail. "We should be there today. Though not as quick as I'd like now that we have unfortunate company."

Mike looked down at Cody and Christine. "What do ya plan on doin' with these folks?"

Levi shrugged. "You know, I don't rightly know. Samantha couldn't bear to leave them behind, and, let's be honest, pard, we both know they couldn't survive out here alone."

Mike grinned. "But remember, Levi, she's Indian."

The two shared a chuckled and enjoyed their hot coffee.

"What're you boys snickerin' 'bout over there?" Samantha asked as she woke up. "You sound like a pair of schoolgirls."

Levi turned to her. "We were just discussin' your new friends here and what we aim to do with 'em now."

Samantha grinned. "They seem friendly enough, and quite harmless. I figured they could travel along with us till we get to a town somewheres."

Levi shook his head. "They just as well, I reckon."

Mike nodded. "I reckon."

Levi looked over at Bud, still asleep. "Tell me, Mike, how is it that ol' Bud there learned to handle himself in a shootin' scrape like he can?"

Mike pressed his tin cup to his lip. "Coffee sure is good. Ol' Bud there grew up with me back on the family farm outside what is now Rolla, Missouri. Uncle Norm was a preachin' man. He taught us how to live on the land when we were youngsters, just after we learned to walk. He took us mushroom huntin' and we picked wild greens along the river. One time when we was headin' down the river in a small boat, we hit a shallow gravel bar and Uncle Norm told Bud to get out and pull us through the shallows. Uncle Norm hollered 'snake' just to scare ol' Bud there outta his longhandles. Bud had one leg in the boat and one leg in the water and was hung up by his privates and liked to turn the whole boat over. It was the damnedest thing I ever saw." Mike grinned. "Bud was picked on by the other fellas quite often when we was young. I taught him to stand up for himself and how to handle himself when he got into a scrape. He always had a way with guns, though. Never a time did ya see him without a rifle in his hand headed out to hunt somethin'. He was quite a hand at fillin' the family supper table."

"I ain't known him all that long myself, but I knew right off he was a decent fella just strugglin' to find his place in this world, same as you and me. He reminds me a lot of myself. I'm right glad I met him. He's a top hand. You boys are alright." Levi reached out and shook Mike's hand.

Mike walked over and kicked Bud in the butt. "Hey, sunshine, wake your ass up. I know Momma raised you better than that. Momma woulda tanned your hide had she known you was sleepin' past sunup."

Levi chuckled as Bud woke up and got to his feet. "Mornin', y'all."

Samantha looked at Cody and Christine. "Do y'all reckon we should wake them up?"

They all looked at them sprawled out on the ground and then looked at each other and shook their heads and shared a chuckled.

"I reckon if they're comin' with us they better get to it," Levi said.

Samantha walked over and shook Christine. "Ma'am? Time to wake up. We'll be movin' out here shortly." Christine shook Cody and he tossed and turned and moaned and went right back to sleep.

Levi watched as Christine rolled over and snuggled up closer to Cody. "Well, I reckon if they ain't comin' with us, we can get saddled and head out directly."

Neither Cody nor Christine responded.

Levi began to saddle his horse, and Bud, Mike, and Samantha followed suit. "If they don't wanna get their asses up, they'll be left behind. I'm sure they will find their way to town."

Samantha looked at Levi with a glare. "Nonsense."

Bud said, "Boss, you know those two couldn't find the ground with their hat if they threw it down in three tries."

Levi shook his head because he knew Bud was indeed correct on that matter. "Well, I ain't waitin' all cotton-pickin' day." He crawled up into the saddle. "I reckon they'll be alright, seein' how that Cody fella has that Colt. This here is Sac and Fox country, but they ain't got to worry none 'bout Indians, cuz she's an Indian herself."

Christine opened her eyes wide, but Cody didn't move an inch.

"No sir," Levi went on. "They ain't got to worry none 'bout Indians. I'd be more worried about griz in these parts." He stopped for a second. "Or wolves…"

Christine jumped up quicker than if she had eaten a batch of sour green apples and had to make a dash to the privy. "Cody!" she whispered loudly. "Cody, get your ass up this instant!" Cody rolled over on his side and she grabbed him by the ear and yanked him up. "I told you to get your dog-ugly ass up now! They's fixin' to leave and I'll be damned iffen I'm stayin' out here alone. Get your carcass up from there now!"

Cody slowly got to his feet, wiping the sleep from his eyes.

"If you're comin' with us, pardner, we're fixin' to make tracks," Bud said as he climbed into the saddle.

Cody dusted off his clothes. "What's for breakfast?"

Levi looked at them and dug into his pocket and pulled a piece of antelope jerky out and tossed it to them. "Had some fine coffee, but folks 'round here that sleep in past the sunrise miss out on that chance."

Samantha gave him the look she gave him before and he knew he had to try to be a bit more polite, even though he dreaded the thought.

Shortly after everyone was settled, the group was back on the trail. They had to slow down their pace quite a bit now since Cody and Christine were on foot. In addition, Christine had some sort of birth defect that made it difficult for her to walk normal like other folks. She could walk fine, just seemed to struggle a bit more than others. This made the remainder of the trip rather agitating. Levi was more than anxious to be making more ground than they were, so he was unintentionally getting a bit short with everyone.

"You think we could double up and make this trip a bit faster, Boss?" asked Bud.

Levi's eyes widened and he gave Bud a crooked grin. "Well, pardner, that's entirely up to you there. I mean, which one of you boys is gonna let that crazy woman on the back of his horse and let her wrap her arms around him?"

Mike turned around and gave a visible shiver. "Not a chance in hell," he said as he kicked his horse a bit to speed up the pace.

Bud kind of grinned. "Yeah...I reckon you're right at that. Besides, what's the rush anyways? I don't object to takin' our time a'tall."

Levi chuckled and they continued the extremely slow pace, stopping every fifty to sixty yards to wait for Cody and Christine to catch up.

A few miles later, they came to a small stream that Levi assumed to be about waist deep, as the rocks could be seen on the bottom and appeared to be about three horse lengths wide. He wasn't concerned at all. It was small enough to cross easily and there was a shallow spot where Cody and Christine would be able to cross on foot just fine.

Levi led the way and Bud and Mike followed. Samantha followed Cody and Christine. About halfway across, Christine began to sink in the mud, and she reached out for help. Cody was struggling to get across on his own.

Christine started screaming at the top of her lungs, "Help! Help! I'm stuck."

"Damn it, Christine," Cody hollered back. "It's not that bad. Just walk!"

Christine tried to walk but got stuck and somehow wound up waist-deep in the flowing water.

Levi shook his head. "Oh, my Lord, what the hell have we got ourselves into?" He jumped off Star and tried to pull Christine out of the water. Her boots were stuck in the mud, and she showed no effort to try to walk on her own. She acted as if she was a mere child wanting to be picked up and carried across the rest of the way.

"Pull yourself out, ma'am." Levi said. "Don't give up...ya gotta try a little harder than that."

Cody finally came over and grabbed her by the arm and Levi took her by the other arm and together they tried to help her across. Not a foot from the bank, Christine began to slip, so she shoved Cody out of the way in order to balance herself. Cody fell straight back in the creek and came up sputtering with a look on his face that said he was ready to kill her right then and there.

As Levi pulled her by the arm, she began to shove him, and he went down face first in the opposite direction in the stream. He was livid, but he fought to contain himself and get her across the stream and back on the trail whether he liked it or not. Things were already bad enough without his words causing a full-on argument. When they finally reached the other side, all three were soaked all the way through.

Samantha crossed the stream. "Well, now, let's try this again, shall we?" Levi looked at her with the same look she had given him before.

They continued on once again, but much slower than before. The sun was shining bright, and there were big white puffy clouds scattered across the sky. It was a bit chillier than the day before, but still made for a nice day. That is, if you were dry.

Off to the east they spotted a herd of buffalo grazing across the plains. There was about twenty cows and one big bull. As the group passed by some two hundred yards out, the herd raised their heads and snorted, then watched them as they rode past. The bull pawed the ground and stomped his hooves, kicking up dust over his back, showing his dominance.

Dead ahead on the trail, a badger foraged in the prairie grass, looking for something to eat. Dally spotted him and took off quicker than ever, headed straight for him. The badger looked up and took off running as quickly as it could. A rooster pheasant cackled and kicked up and flew across the prairie. Once Dally reached the den the badger had hurried into, she barked hysterically and began digging through the soil.

As the group arrived, Levi called out to Dally, "Come on, ol' girl. You don't wanna mess with that ol' critter. He's a heap more devilish than a rabbit."

Dally continued barking and carrying on and the group rode right on past.

"She'll catch up when she has a mind to," Levi said as they rode on.

Chapter 18

After several miles, Christine began to complain. "My feet are killin' me something fierce. These damn old boots are 'bout to fall apart. How much further do we got?"

Levi studied the trail. "I reckon about seven or eight miles or so. Figured to be there 'bout now but we ain't makin' good tracks."

"Sure wish we had a couple horses now, Cody," Christine said. "My damn feet are hurtin' somethin' awful." No sooner did she finish her sentence, her legs buckled and down she went, looking up at everybody like she was demanding help.

"Come on, Christine, we gotta keep goin'," Cody said, helping her up.

"Not much further, I reckon," Bud said as he stretched his back.

As they traveled along the dusty trail, Star began to favor her left front leg.

"What's the matter, ol' girl?" Levi continued on for a short distance with no sign of the mare stopping. "Whoa." He pulled her to a stop and dismounted. He walked around and lifted her leg and inspected her hoof. "Picked up some flint," he said as he took his knife out and carefully removed the rock from the mare's hoof. Star patiently watched him and nickered as he patted her on the neck. "There ya go, ol' girl, as good as new." As he walked around inspecting Star's other hooves, he looked down and noticed horse tracks. Unshod horse tracks…three sets of them. Didn't appear to be more than an hour old. "Not to alarm any of y'all, but ya might wanna keep a close eye out."

Cody looked at Levi. "Why's that?"

Bud and Mike and Samantha noticed the tracks and shook their heads, and all checked their guns to ensure they were loaded.

Levi climbed back in the saddle and studied the prairie, looking for any other signs. Nothing out of the ordinary struck his eye. Still, it was better to be aware and ready than to be attacked or ambushed with no idea.

"What is it, Levi?" Cody asked.

"Indians, appears to be Shawnee."

Christine's eyes showed fright as she clenched Cody's hand.

Cody squeezed her hand. "It's alright, Christine, they'll know you're Cherokee and we'll be just fine."

Levi turned around and screwed up his face with bitterness. "The Shawnee hate the Cherokee. Iffen they see your wife there and get the notion she's Cherokee, they'll take her scalp and yours too, just outta plain hate!"

Christine fell to the ground and began to have a fit. She appeared to be having some sort of convulsion or seizure.

Samantha jumped down from her horse and rushed over and cradled her in her arms. "Oh, you poor woman," she cried out. "She needs help, Levi."

Levi looked at the woman as her husband stood beside her, looking across the prairie for Indians. "What's wrong with her?"

Cody waved his arm. "Oh, she's probably havin' one of her spells again."

"Spells?" Bud asked.

"Yeah, she has 'em on occasion. She'll snap out of it 'fore long. Does it for attention most the time, iffen ya ask me."

Christine miraculously snapped out of her fit and slugged Cody in the leg, and then she went back to having her episode. Samantha looked at Levi with curious eyes. This woman was flat crazy.

Mike looked at the tracks again. "Levi, I reckon we'd better get outta here and put a hitch in our giddy up this time. The more distance we make now between them and us the better we'll be."

Levi nodded in agreement. He turned to Cody. "Pardner, if they try to take us in this open country now, we'll be in a tight spot. The odds ain't in our favor one bit. Get that woman up and let's ride."

Christine continued her fit. Levi was no longer able to hold his temper. "Alright, I've had about enough of this hogwash. Get that woman on her feet and let's go!"

Christine opened her eyes and glared at Levi. Levi turned around just in time to see. "Woman, I swear to the good Lord above that iffen you ever glare at me like that again, I'll leave your crazy ass out here. Don't you ever look at me like that again, do I make myself clear?"

Christine looked at Cody. "Are you gonna let him talk to me like that?"

Cody shook his head. "Damn it, Christine, knock off your shit and let's go! All he's tryin' to do is help us. You should be thankful for that. Stop your little games and come on. If you don't, I'm with him. I'll leave your ass out here."

Christine got a look of terror on her face, and she got to her feet. "Well, alright then," she huffed, brushing the grass from her skirt.

Levi looked at her. "Ma'am, I ain't tryin to be rude a'tall. It's just that if we don't get out of here, we could find ourselves in a shootin' scrape. Let me tell you, I've had about all of those that I can muster lately."

The group pressed on, not seeing any more sign of Indians. After a few miles, they stopped for a quick bite to eat. They prepared a very small fire from buffalo chips and some prairie grass, just enough to heat some beans and bacon. They didn't want to risk having Indians spot their smoke from the distance and catch them off guard.

"Some biscuits would be right nice with them beans," Cody said.

"Yes sir, they would at that," answered Mike. "But we ain't riskin' getting scalped for no damn biscuits."

Just as Bud had the bacon and beans warmed up and ready to serve, Christine let out a shriek. Everyone jumped, and Bud spilled the beans all over the coals.

"What in the hell was that all about?" Levi hollered.

Christine took off running. Levi tried to see what on earth was the matter, but he could see nothing. Just open prairie and rolling hills of grass. "That damn woman is flat crazy."

Cody stood there for a moment, then took off after her.

Mike and Bud looked at each other and Mike said, "Boss, that woman is gonna get someone kilt, if not herself."

Samantha, watching the couple run across the prairie, muttered, "What is wrong with these people? Has she always been this crazy, or was she born a little touched in the head? Cody seems a few cards short of a dealer's deck, but she's a whole other story!"

Levi couldn't help but smirk.

Once Cody caught up to his wife, he grabbed her by the arm.

"Indians!" she screamed.

Cody looked around, then appeared to be trying to assure her. Bud leaned toward Samantha. "She doesn't seem to be the brightest of women…he must love her dearly." She chuckled.

Everyone kept looking in the distance for what might have scared this crazy woman.

"I don't see a damn thing, Boss," Bud said.

Mike groaned. "That damn woman...she's somethin' else, alright. Scoop me up some of the beans there, Brother Bud."

Bud scooped the beans up as best he could and served them to Mike.

Cody led Christine back to the fire and Samantha asked, "Ma'am, are you alright? What in tarnation had you so riled up?"

Christine looked back across the prairie and pointed. "Indians...they're comin' to revenge..."

The others all looked, but there was nothing there besides buffalo grass and a few scattered limestone rocks.

"Alright, ma'am, hush now and try to eat you some of this bacon." Bud handed her a piece of bacon and she ate it, never taking her eyes off the trail they had come from.

Moments later, Cody looked up. "You hear that? That sound. What is that?"

The others all looked around, but no one seemed to hear anything. Levi still couldn't see anything, but he was beginning to get mighty paranoid, and was sure the others were too.

"Alright, y'all!" said Mike. "Y'all are beginning to give me the willies with your crazy talk."

A few minutes later, Cody looked up again. "There! Did you hear that?"

Samantha turned her head to Levi. "I ain't certain, but I thought I heard something strange myself just now."

Christine let out another scream.

"Hush up, woman," Bud hollered out.

"Keep your wife quiet, Cody." Levi got to his feet and gazed across the prairie. "All I see is grass and rocks...They're beginning to get to you, ain't they?"

Cody pointed to the trail ahead of them. "There, what is that?"

They all looked ahead and saw a faint cloud of rising white smoke.

"Smoke?" asked Samantha.

Bud stood. "What do ya think it is, Boss?"

Levi studied the smoke. "I don't rightly know."

"Looks like someone else might be havin' themselves some dinner as well," Mike said.

A moment later, they spotted another cloud of white smoke on the trail behind them. They could hear crackling as it began to spread across the prairie. They noticed yet another cloud of smoke to the side of them and another to their other side. They were boxed in. Trapped.

"Look, there, in the smoke! Looks like a Sac and Fox brave on a painted pony with a burning branch!" Mike continued to scan the area. "There's other braves lighting the buffalo grass on fire around us!"

Christine went into a complete panic, grabbing for Cody's arm.

"Quick!" Levi hollered out over Christine's screams. "Everyone take off your bedrolls from your saddles!"

The fire had begun to grow and create its own wind. It was now burning a complete circle around them.

Bud and Mike covered their faces with their wild rags.

"What do we do?" yelled Cody.

"Stay calm and fight the fire with your jacket! Everyone else, use your bedroll!" Levi handed Samantha his wild rag. "Here, darlin', take this and cover your face."

She tied it over her face and reached for her blanket.

Everyone was stomping on flames and beating them with their blankets as quickly as they could, trying to stop the fire from burning them alive. Things were not looking in their favor at all. As fast as they would put the flames out on one side, the other side was closing in even quicker.

"Look out!" Bud yelled as one of the braves rode in with his lance raised. Cody drew his Colt and fired rapidly, nearly shooting his own foot off with the first shot. The second bullet hit the Indian's pony in the neck, causing him to buck something fierce. The brave was thrown over his head, and Cody screamed and ran over and emptied his Colt into the brave's chest.

"Son of a bitch!" yelled Mike. "He might be worth a dime after all!"

"We gotta get the hell outta here!" Levi yelled. "The fire is closin' in all around us. We gotta bust through the flames and get to where the grass is already burnt. That's our only way out!"

Cody looked at the flames. "How the hell do we get through?!"

Mike and Bud ran for their horses, and Samantha jumped onto hers.

Levi ran over and grabbed Christine and threw her onto Star, shouting, "Get on, Cody, now! Give her a kick and follow us!"

Samantha slid to the back of her horse and Levi jumped into the saddle. "Hang on, darlin'! Hyah!" He kicked Lightning in the ribs and spurred him with all he had.

The others followed as quickly as possible, shielding their faces from the heat of the flames.

"The flames are too high!" Bud yelled.

They circled each other for a brief second, then Levi yelled, "Come on! We gotta make a run for it! Don't slow up! Give your horses the reins and kick 'em with all ya got!"

Bud looked ahead as Levi gave him one last nod. "Aw, hell!"

They took off at a run as fast as their horses would take them, straight for the flames.

"Hang on!" Levi yelled to Samantha. He felt her arms tighten around him.

As they reached the flames, each horse took one terrifying leap and burst through the flames to safety on the other side.

Cody pulled back Star. "We made it!"

Levi smacked Star on the ass as he rushed past them. "Hyah! Not yet, we ain't! Keep that horse a-runnin' till we get the hell outta this open prairie."

The others all followed closely behind. Once they had put a safe distance between them and whatever Indians were left out there, they slowed up and eased their horses to a gallop.

"We gotta keep goin' forward," Levi demanded. "We ain't stoppin' now."

They pushed on, then looked back to notice that the smoke had descended.

"How in the hell did that damn fire go out?" asked Mike.

Levi shook his head. "I ain't goin' back to ask 'em. They were tryin' to prove a point, and they made it."

Bud sighed. "I'm gettin' a heap too old for this shit."

"You and me both, Bud," Levi sighed, brushing the back of his hand across his brow.

Mike grinned. "Is travelin' with you always this exciting, Levi?"

As they pressed on, they could see the tops of buildings in the distance. The sun had disappeared now behind the clouds, and a storm was brewing.

Levi pointed toward the settlement. "By God, Bud. Lookie there...ol' Wilmington."

Bud smiled. "You know what that means? We're almost there! Yee-haw!"

The ranch was just a couple more miles or so up ahead on the creek. As they rode on toward town, Levi turned to Cody. "Well, pardner, we'll take ya into town and show ya to the hotel and you can make arrangements there."

Christine looked at Cody with worried eyes and neither said a word.

Once they arrived in town, folks watched from the boardwalks as their spurs jingled along. Star let out a knicker.

Levi pointed across the street. "Well, there's the hotel. Y'all take care, and good luck to ya."

Cody nodded and turned Star toward the hotel and Levi hollered out, "One second, are y'all forgettin' a li'l something?"

Cody pulled the reins back and Star come to a stop.

"I'll take my horse back now," Levi said.

"We'll buy her from ya," Christine said.

Levi's jaw dropped. "I beg your damn pardon?"

Cody turned to Christine. "Damn it, woman, just how do you plan on payin' for this here horse? We ain't got a damn cent to our name, after payin' that damn stage."

Christine looked at Cody and then turned to Levi. "We'll make payments."

Levi laughed. "That horse ain't for sale." He pointed over to the livery stable. "I reckon iffen ya go get settled in over yonder at the hotel, then head over there to the livery, that feller might have a horse for ya at a good price."

Christine and Cody both looked at the livery stable and Christine said, "I wonder if he will take payments."

Levi shook his head. "I don't reckon so, but never hurts to ask." He stood up in the saddle and stretched his back. "Iffen you boys or you, darlin', need anything at the mercantile, this'd be your chance to stop. If not, it's only a couple miles up the creek."

Mike and Bud decided they would head over to the mercantile for a few things. Samantha decided she would go as well just to see what all they carried in stock.

"I've never been to Wilmington before," Samantha said. "It will be nice to meet some new folks."

Levi shook hands with Cody and then Cody got down from the saddle and helped Christine down. He handed the reins to Levi. "We're much obliged to y'all."

Levi shook hands with the man again and they parted ways. Levi led Star over to the mercantile, then they all got down and stretched and tied their horses up at the hitching post and headed inside the store.

While they were inside, Levi looked out the window and watched Cody and Christine head toward the hotel. Moments later, he saw them come out of the hotel and walk toward the livery stable. He shook his head and began to walk around the store, browsing the merchandise.

When they were ready to leave, they walked out the door. Cody and Christine were standing on the street corner, looking like a pair of lost dogs.

"Boss?" Bud said.

"Yes sir?" Levi replied.

"I kinda feel bad for them folks, ya know? I mean, yeah, that Christine woman is the craziest dagburn woman I've seen across the whole prairie, but doggone, Boss, I just feel bad for 'em."

Levi chuckled. "Crazy, you say? That damn woman could scare the hair off a grizzly's back just with a smile." Levi thought for a second. They were nice folks, just a bit on the odd and unusual side, to say the very least. "Y'all stay here I'll be back."

He walked down the street to Christine and Cody. "Cody, I've been ponderin' this over in my head, and I reckon y'all would have quite a rough time gettin' yourselves a room iffen ya ain't got any money, huh?" Cody lowered his head. "Raise your head, pardner, you ain't got nothin' to be ashamed of."

Cody raised his head, and Levi dug down into his pocket and gave him two shiny silver dollars. Cody squeezed his hand around the coins. "Thank ya kindly, sir. I'm in debt to ya."

Christine looked at Cody and smiled. "Now we can go get us some chaw."

Levi looked her in the eye. "Go get yourself a room first…and wouldn't hurt to run ya a hot bath. Then you can think about tobacco."

Christine smirked at Levi, then leaned down and smelled her armpits and wrinkled her nose.

Levi chuckled, then shook Cody's hand. "Good luck to y'all."

Levi headed back to the others and they all mounted up and headed for the ranch. Levi's heart was racing. He had been waiting for what seemed like forever for this moment. Nothing could have made him happier.

Chapter 19

Shortly after leaving Wilmington, Levi looked at Samantha and smiled. "We're just about home," he said. Star let out a knicker.

Samantha smiled back. "Splendid. I'm excited."

Bud and Mike followed along as the trail slowly came to an end. It seemed like forever since Levi had left the ranch. He had been through hell since he had left the ranch and rode back to Council Grove to return for Samantha. His cold and bitter heart had turned a heap softer than before.

He had begun to appreciate the finer little things in life, like the taste of warm whiskey on a chilly evening, and the way Samantha's soft and tender hand felt in his. The way the sun would glisten off the frost on the grass in the morning, and the way the stars danced on the crystal-clear stream below. The friendship he had acquired with Bud, and how he had won the heart of a beautiful woman. The sounds of children playing in the street, and an old stray dog wagging its tail when he scratched its ears. Levi Cord had changed.

Levi spotted the tops of a few scattered cottonwood trees that stood on the banks of Soldier Creek. Bud spotted the cabin. "Yee-haw! Would ya look at that, y'all! There she is! We made it!"

Levi pulled the reins back and stopped Star and stood there gazing across the yellow prairie grass as the wind blew across the prairie. "By God, we made it." He smiled as a tear gently trickled down his cheek. He turned his head and quickly wiped his face with his sleeve so nobody would see.

Bud spurred his horse and took off at a gallop, hooting and hollering at the top of his lungs. Mike followed at a trot. Levi leaned over the saddle and kissed Samantha. "I hope you will find the happiness that you deserve here on the ranch, darlin'."

She grinned. "I will find happiness wherever you are, my love."

Levi smiled and gave Star a kick and took off at a gallop for the cabin. Samantha followed. Soon the two raced past Bud and Mike and then all four were on a dead run. Dust and grass were flying up from under the horses' hooves as they crashed across the prairie soil. The wind was blowing through

Samantha's hair, and Levi's hat flew off and was caught around his neck by the stampede string.

As they reached the creek, they slowed their horses down and shared a laugh as they tried to catch their breath.

Levi smiled. "Well, I'll be." The cowhands that had stayed behind to tend to the ranch had built an archway at the gate with a big longhorn skull over the top. They had kept themselves mighty busy since Levi had left. There were young calves running everywhere, and the herd looked right fine.

As they rode up, Dally took out after a cow and calf and barked up a storm. A couple of the hands heard the commotion and turned to see what was wrong. The cowboys dropped their branding irons and jumped to their feet. "Boss!" they hollered out.

Levi raised his hand. "Howdy, boys! Did ya miss me?"

The travelers stopped their horses and jumped down and everyone shook hands.

"We were getting mighty worried 'bout ya, Boss," said one of the cowboys.

"Worried about me?" Levi asked. "No need to worry over me, boys…I was just up in Ellsworth takin' myself a li'l nap while you girls were back here doin' all the work." They all shared a chuckle and one of the cowboys took the horses to the barn.

Levi introduced Samantha to everyone and began to show her around the ranch. "It's beautiful," she said as she walked inside the cabin door. There was a rock fireplace with a beautiful oak mantel that had a mountain lion carved on it. There was a pair of wooden rockers around an elk hide rug on the wood floor and two picture windows overlooking the prairie to the north and Soldier Creek to the west. On the walls hung several whitetail and mule deer racks and even a bull elk skull over the fireplace. In the kitchen there stood a long family dinner table with bench-style seats. There was a big cast iron stove with four burners on top for cooking. On one of the burners sat a gray enamel coffee pot with black stains around the edge from the heat of the flames scorching the pot during its many times of use. On one of the walls there hung several cast iron skillets, and in the corner stood a stack of cut hickory for heating the stove.

Levi shrugged. "It ain't much, darlin', but it's ours."

Samantha wrapped her arms around Levi and kissed his lips. "I love you so much. I was scared you would never return for me. I would find myself believing you would never come back to Council Grove. I wanted you to return so badly it hurt. I missed you so much."

Levi ran his weathered fingers through her golden hair and gently brushed her bangs away from her cheek. "I know, darlin'. There were many a night I felt like I would not make it back myself. The fear of lettin' you down and breakin' your heart was more than I could bear. It was your love that kept me alive." He wrapped his arms tightly around her and kissed her for several minutes. He gently took her by the hand and led her up the stairs to the room that would now be theirs. There was a large bed with a wooden frame made from logs that the cowboys had made for them while Levi was gone. At the foot of the bed was a cedar chest with a black-and-white-spotted longhorn calf hide draped over the top.

Levi turned to Samantha. "Do you like it?"

She placed her hand over her mouth as she gasped. "It's perfect. It's simply perfect." She took Levi by the hand and led him over to the bed and pushed him down and crawled on top of him.

OUTSIDE, BUD AND Mike had gathered with the cowhands and were telling them of their journey. Bud told them how he had found Levi up in Ellsworth, then of the ride to Council Grove and all the Indian engagements on the trail. He told them about Cheyenne and how he had fallen in love with her at first sight. He spoke of her death on the trail through gritted teeth and tears in his eyes. He told them of how he met his brother and of the crazy couple that had tagged along. He spoke of all he could recall since he had left the ranch in search of Levi—everything except the twister and the little girl he had to bury. His mind strayed to the horrific scene and he paused his storytelling.

"What else happened, Bud?" a cowboy questioned.

Bud shook his head. He still had nightmares of that little girl's lifeless body lying in the rubble of the crumbled sod house. It felt as if by speaking the story aloud that it would bring him back to that moment, and he would rather just keep it at the back of his mind. They claimed almost all moments of his sleep…he would be damned if he allowed them to claim the time he was awake as well.

"I think that's all we can get for today, Bud," one of the cowboys said, and Bud was thankful for the escape.

LEVI AND SAMANTHA walked outside on the big wrap-around porch and sat down on the swing.

"It's so lovely here, Levi." Samantha said.

Levi looked up at a flock of Canada geese flying overhead. "Darlin', did you know that geese tend to mate for life? They search for their true love and spend eternity devoted to only that one."

Samantha smiled. "Like us, I imagine."

Levi took her hand in his. "Yes, darlin', just like us."

Dally came running up the steps and lay down next to them on the porch, tuckered out after their long journey and exploring her new surroundings. "Crazy ol' dog," Levi said as he patted her on the head.

For the first time in a long time, Levi felt contentment. He felt like he had finally discovered his purpose after searching for so long. Everything was perfect. Nothing would come between him and Samantha.

For the next couple hours, Levi sat with Samantha, watching the cowhands and Mike laugh and joke in the yard. Just before sundown, Samantha stood and headed inside to prepare some supper.

Levi walked out to the barn and gave Star a good brushing. "I'm right thankful to have you in my life, ol' girl," he said softly. "You've saved my scalp more than I can count."

Moments later, Levi heard spurs jingle behind him, and he turned around to see Bud standing in the doorway.

Bud walked in and scratched Star on the neck. "Boss, I'm right glad we made it back. I tell ya, there's a few times I didn't reckon we were gonna be so lucky."

Levi put down the brush and looked at him. "You and me both, pard. It's good to be home. I'm in debt to ya, Bud. Iffen it weren't for you, I reckon I'd be layin' with an arrow or two in my middle. I owe ya my life. You're more than welcome to stay on here at the ranch as long as ya like. Truth is, I couldn't run this place without ya. You're a top hand." Levi reached out his hand and shook Bud's, then looked around. "Aw, hell…come here." He reached his arms out and gave Bud a hug. "Much obliged, pardner, for everything. I'm deeply sorry for what happened to Cheyenne. I truly am. You looked at her the way that I look at Miss Samantha. I know you two hadn't known each other for long a'tall, but neither did Samantha and I. However, I fell head over bootheels for her with that first smile. I know just how ya feel, pard. I was there once myself. The pain will never fully go away, but it will get easier with time."

Bud stared blankly into the sunset and then said, "Boss? There's somethin' I think I should tell ya."

Levi walked Star to the stall for the night. "I'm listenin'. What is it?"

Bud took off his hat. "Well, Boss, you see, when I was a heap younger I kinda left home in Rolla and joined up with a band of men that, well, sir, let's just say they didn't quite follow with the law's way of doin' things."

"Go on, Bud. I'm listenin'."

Bud stared out the barn door. "I was young and lookin' for some excitement in my life at the time and lookin' for an easy dollar, ya might say."

Levi grinned. "Boys will be boys. I was once one myself."

Levi had gotten the impression that Bud was afraid of what he would think of his past, but he could tell he just needed to go ahead and get it off his chest.

"Boss, one night we snuck outta Rolla and held up a stage headed for Springfield. Didn't hurt nobody…just made off with about three thousand dollars. Didn't think much of at first, but then we wound up in St. Louis and held up a bank. We made out with a little over seven thousand dollars. Only difference that time was a shootin' scrape occurred and the teller took a slug in the head and died there on the bank floor. After that we took off and commenced to robbin' banks and trains all over Missouri, Tennessee, Arkansas, and Illinois. The Pinkertons got hot on our trail outside Liberty, so I took off for Kansas. Was layin' low and goin' straight till I arrived in Manhattan and fell in love, and then things turned south, and I caught her with the marshal in his jail. I filled him with holes, and here I am…"

Levi stood there for a couple minutes. He had figured Bud had been running from something. He himself had lived a rather rough and relentless life outside the law for most of his life. Everyone had a past. Some good, some not so good. Levi reached out his hand once again. "Pardner, I don't cotton too much to the idea of judgin' a fella on his past. Most folks take one look at me and turn up their nose and won't give me the time of day, just because of the color of jacket I wore during the War. They'd spit if they only knew the half of what I had done in my life. We live and learn, as they say.

Move on and never look back. You secret is safe with me, pard." The two shook hands. "Now, come on, Samantha is fixin' some supper in the house. 'Bout damn time we had a good and hot home-cooked meal."

Bud smiled. "It's good to be home."

"Ain't it?" Levi punched Bud in the belly and took off running with a limp toward the house.

THAT NIGHT, SAMANTHA shared one of the finest suppers she had had in a very long time. Afterwards, Bud said, "Here, ma'am, I'll tend to the dishes. You and Boss go get ya some rest."

"Are you sure, Bud?" Samantha asked. She felt guilty putting her work off on him, but she was tired.

"Yes, ma'am, go on and I'll tidy up here. Thank ya kindly for a fine supper. Finest I've ever had myself."

Samantha smiled. "Well, thank ya, Bud. I'm right glad you enjoyed it. It's nice to be appreciated once in a while." Samantha set down her washcloth. She thought back to her home in Council Grove and her father. He had never thanked her or given her credit for taking care of the household. It was expected of her, which was the case here as well, but it was always nice to be thanked.

"Good night, ma'am," Bud said.

"Good night, Bud." Samantha walked upstairs and lit a kerosene lamp next to the bed. A few minutes later, Levi came up the stairs and opened the bedroom door and stood there as she slowly began to undress. He walked in the room and unbuckled his gun belt and hung the twin Colts on a hook on the wall. It was the first time Samantha had seen him without his guns on since the night they had first made love on Elm Creek.

Levi walked over to her and gently wrapped his arms around her. "Your skin is as soft as velvet and your hair smells of lilac blossoms," he whispered in her ear. He gently pressed his lips to her neck and then worked his way down her body, kissing and caressing her as he softly rubbed his fingers along her thigh. She arched her back and neck and pulled him closer to him.

"Oh, Levi," she moaned softly. She turned around and sat down on the big feather bed and pulled his boots off and set them next to the bed, and then she began to undress him as she kissed his tender but weathered lips.

They slid into bed and began to make passionate love that neither of them would soon forget. The two shared a night of intimacy in the light of the full moon as it peered through the window. Sometime in the middle of the night, the two drifted off to sleep in each other's arms. The night had brought a slight chill to the cabin, and Samantha crawled underneath the quilt Levi covered her with before wrapping her in his arms. She snuggled up to him, and Levi kissed her on the cheek and drifted back to sleep.

SHORTLY BEFORE SUNRISE, the kerosene lamp began to run out of oil and flickered a few times and then died out. Bud, sitting outside the bunk house, saw it flicker out as a barred owl called from atop the barn as whippoorwills serenaded the Kansas prairie. He had finally made it back safe and was able to unwind, but yet the girl plagued his sleep. He looked to the now dark window and couldn't help but feel a little envious. How nice it would be to just close your eyes and drift to sleep…to not wake up in a sweat with fear thick in your heart. A falling star shot across the sky and soon a second one fell from the dark clear sky. A skunk snuck across the yard and walked over to the bunkhouse and snooped around, scavenging for food, and then went along its way to the creek. Bud watched it for a moment until he was startled by a growling from the window. Dally must have smelled the skunk and was letting the creature know he was not welcome.

"Easy, ol' girl," he whispered as he continued his watch.

AS THE SUN came up over the ranch, Samantha awoke. She rolled over and saw that Levi was still fast asleep. She lay there, staring at him. She assumed his mind and body must be exhausted and desperately needed to catch up on sleep and revive itself. She feared trying to get up and waking him, so she lay there running her fingers through his dark hair.

Just shy of an hour later, Levi awoke. "Good mornin', sleepyhead," she said softly.

"Mornin', darlin'. How long have you been awake?"

"Awhile now. Didn't wanna wake you. You needed the rest."

Levi grinned and kissed her forehead. "Thank you, darlin'. I love you."

"I love you too, cowboy." She got up and walked across the room to fetch her clothes, feeling Levi's eyes as he watched her dress and mess with her hair.

"As purty as the mornin' sun," he said softly.

Samantha blushed. "I'm sure you have told many a gals that very line."

Levi also blushed. "Only you, darlin'." He stretched and slid his legs over the bed and sat up. "It's hell to get old."

Samantha looked at the scars on his naked body as he stood and reached for his clothes. He had scars all over from his rough past, yet none of them had kept him down for too long.

After they both finished dressing, they went downstairs. Levi walked to the door to let Dally out, and as soon as he opened the door she took off with her nose on the ground. Levi yawned and scratched his head as he looked outside and saw Bud and Mike and the rest the boys gathering a bunch of steers to be branded and doctored. Samantha opened the stove and threw a log inside and lit it. She prepared some water for a pot of coffee.

"Darlin'," Levi said. "What ya say you and I take a li'l ride into town after a bit and get you a couple of dresses and whatever else ya might be needin' or wantin'?"

Samantha had left most of her belongings back in Council Grove, so she didn't have much of her own. She smiled. "That would be right nice. I could use another dress or two and a few things." She had been hesitant to ask for them when they went into town the day before. This type of companionship was new to her, and she feared ruining it. She had feared he may be offended by her asking for items that she knew would cost money she didn't have.

After the coffee had been brewed, Samantha and Levi sat on the porch in the swing and enjoyed a cup while watching the cowhands tend to the chores. Samantha leaned her head down on Levi's shoulder and he put his arm around her as they rocked. Dally had gone down to the creek, and a cottontail rabbit came hopping across the yard and over toward the garden the cowhands had grown while Levi was gone.

"Where's that dog when we need her?" Levi whispered. He carefully took his arm out from behind Samantha and quietly got off the swing. Samantha watched closely as he eased his way to the edge of the porch. He slipped the tie down off one of his Colts and watched the rabbit as it fed on the turnip greens that were growing in the garden. "I don't reckon you'll be eatin' any more of that today," Levi said softly as he carefully made his way down the steps. The rabbit continued chewing away as Levi cautiously stalked his way toward him. Just as Levi took another step, a branch cracked underneath his foot and the rabbit looked up and saw him and took off on a dead run. In one motion, Levi drew his Colt and sent a slug into the back of the rabbit's head, right between the ears, sending him rolling across the ground.

Samantha's eyes widened and her jaw dropped. Bud and the boys jumped and drew their guns and spun around to see what was wrong.

"Boss!" Bud yelled out as he took off for the cabin. The others came running behind him as fast as they could. Once they reached the yard, they saw Levi standing there, holding the rabbit by the back legs and grinning.

Levi laughed. "Got you boys a li'l dinner."

Bud shook his head. Mike threw his hat on the ground. "Damn it, Levi, I thought sure as hell you was in trouble."

Levi chuckled. "Shit, boys, Samantha's only been here one night. Give it a week, and then she might go to shootin' at me."

The boys laughed, and Levi turned to Samantha as she cocked her head to the side and said, "Now, Levi Cord, what on earth do ya mean by that remark?"

Levi lowered his head and the boys all took off back across the yard to tend to their chores. Samantha followed Levi over to the woodpile that was stacked nicely against the side of the cabin. He grabbed the rabbit by the hide on the back of the neck and made a small cut with his knife, just enough to break the skin. Then he gripped his fingers around the hide and pulled the skin down over the rabbit and off its back legs. Being a hunter herself and having helped her father clean the game, this was normal to her and the motions were almost comforting; a sense of normalcy in a new and exciting life. After he had the skin off, he took his knife and cut the head off and each one of the feet. He then carefully cut a slit into the stomach and reached inside and pulled the guts out. After he had made sure he hadn't missed anything, he took the rabbit and washed the hair and blood off and then gave it to Samantha to store for dinner.

"That was some right fancy shootin' there, cowboy," Samantha said as she took the rabbit inside. "You gonna teach me how to shoot like that someday?"

Levi looked at her. "No, ma'am."

Samantha looked him in the eye. "Why in the hell not?"

Levi grinned. "Cuz if we ever get to quarrelin' you might outdraw my ass."

They both laughed. After they saddled up the horses, they trotted over to Bud and the boys as they were branding steers.

"Where ya off to this morning, Boss?" Bud asked.

Levi pointed toward Wilmington. "Gonna take Miss Samantha to town and get her a few things to help her get settled in here. Any of you boys need anything from town?"

One of the cowhands looked up and grinned. "A case of mescal and a two-dollar whore."

Samantha blushed. She hadn't been prepared for the blunt request.

"Well," Levi said. "If you go to pokin' a two-dollar whore in these parts, you might get a rash that your family might get, not to mention the neighbor."

The cowboys looked at Levi like they were dazed and confused, but Mike, Bud, and Samantha all chuckled, knowing exactly what he was talking about. She thought back to Cody and Christine and that first impression they had made. Oddly enough, she almost missed them. They were strange and crude, but they kept things entertaining.

Levi picked up the reins. "We'll see ya boys after a while."

One of the boys looked at him. "Now, Boss, you recall what happened the last time you said that?"

Levi shook his head and gave Star a kick and away they took off at a gallop headed up the creek for Wilmington.

It was getting warmer every day now, and the sun was beating down on the Kansas prairie. Off to the south, big thunderhead clouds hung in the sky, which had turned a dark blue, indicating a storm was on its way.

Levi looked toward the clouds. "Might rain this afternoon. We should be back 'fore then, I reckon."

As they crossed Soldier Creek, a crawdad bounced through the clear water and crawled under a rock to hide from them as they passed by. A school of minnows swam upstream, zigzagging back and forth before going up the ripples. A largemouth bass hid along the overhanging bank tucked back in the roots of an oak tree. A whitetail doe jumped up and flagged her tail and snorted her familiar alarm before running off. Behind her followed a yearling buck that appeared to be her fawn from the year before. It was so beautiful here, and Samantha could barely believe that this was her life now.

As they rode along, obvious signs of beaver living along the creek could be seen. There were several dams in the stream and slides down the creek banks where they had been dragging dead trees to the water below.

Samantha found herself giving Lightning a reassuring pat on the neck, although she was the one that needed it. She watched Levi as they arrived in town and saw that he was sitting taller in the saddle than he had previously. It was as if he was prouder and more content than before. People stared at them as if they had never seen a lady with a man wearing two guns. She followed their gaze and noticed each of them was focused on the Colts at his hips. Most folks carried a sidearm, but it wasn't common to carry two. Not in plain sight anyhow. Some folks carried one on their hip and a hideaway in their jacket or boot, however, Levi carried both his on his hips for the world to admire or fear.

"Why is everyone lookin' at us that way, Levi?" Samantha asked curiously.

LEVI LOOKED AT the townspeople's faces. They didn't seem as friendly as they did back in Council Grove. When he had passed through before, he had genuinely enjoyed the town and thought the people were friendly, but now that he had been to Council Grove it seemed nothing could compare.

"I don't know, darlin'," Levi said. 'I don't know." The words were the smallest of white lies, done in hopes to ease her mind. Most women were uncertain of the gunslinging life, so he didn't really cotton to drawing Samantha's attention to the way people looked at him for it.

They rode over and hitched their horses out front of the mercantile, and Levi opened the door for Samantha and watched behind him as she walked inside. Although he had done business here before, he found himself feeling the need to protect Samantha. Folks on the boardwalk were still staring at his Colts and looking at Samantha oddly. Levi made eye contact with one woman on the boardwalk, and the lady shook her head and whispered, "I do declare." He was familiar with being stared at and looked upon as an outsider, so it didn't bother him. However, he hoped to avoid it affecting Samantha.

Levi walked inside the store and followed Samantha as she browsed through various patterns of fabric for dresses. As he looked over toward the counter, he caught the storekeeper and his wife glancing at his Colts. He looked at Samantha and then down at his Colts, and it was then that he knew what he had to do. He wanted to live a normal and peaceful life but wasn't sure just how to go about doing that. He knew that folks looked at him differently when he wore his twin Colts, but not many folks got lucky enough to catch him without them on. Otherwise he wouldn't have lived as long as he had. Nonetheless, he had to give Samantha the life she deserved. It would be a true struggle, but he knew what he had to do.

"What do you think of this?" Samantha said as she picked up a white fabric with blue and yellow flowers on it.

"It's lovely," Levi replied.

Samantha set the fabric back down. "Nah, I don't like it." She kept sorting through the different patterns until she pulled out another one. "How 'bout this one?"

Levi smiled. "That one is nice."

Samantha kept the fabric in her hand and continued looking. "Oh, it's stunning," she said as she picked up a roll of beautiful fabric. It was a soft lilac color with a dainty paisley of dark blue throughout.

Levi winked at her. "Darlin', that would make your eyes stand out for days."

Samantha blushed. "Why, Levi, you're quite a charmer."

As they browsed around the store, Samantha picked up a looking glass and brush.

"Those came all the way from Paris, France," the store clerk's wife said.

Samantha turned to the woman. "Did they now? They're just lovely. How much are they?"

The woman walked out from behind the counter. "They are seven dollars for the pair."

Samantha put them back down quickly, yet carefully. "Oh my…"

Levi could tell how much she admired them. They browsed around the store, and Samantha picked out several buttons and a bunch of needles and thread and enough lace to adorn the collars of two dresses.

As Samantha placed the items on the glass countertop, the store clerk said, "Will this be all for you today, then?"

Levi walked over and picked up the silver looking glass and brush and placed them on the counter. "These too."

"Darlin'," Samantha said, hand to her chest, "these are much too expensive."

"If you don't like the price then you should go elsewhere," the store clerk's wife snapped.

The store clerk grabbed her by the arm. "Hush, Nellie. You ought not talk to customers that way. The woman is right. No one will pay that price, especially in these parts."

Levi reached in his pocket and slammed his money on the counter. "Well, we are today, and then I reckon we'll just go on over to Burlingame to do our business from here on out. I won't tolerate rude behavior in man nor woman."

The store clerk shook his head. "No sir! You ain't gotta do that. Nellie here has just not got enough beauty sleep, I reckon. Nellie, go sweep off the boardwalk like I asked you." As Nellie picked up a broom and walked out the door, he leaned over the counter and whispered to Levi, "It's that time of season, iffen ya know what I mean, sir."

It took a minute for it to sink in, but when it did, he grinned and raised his head. "Ah…well then." Levi reached out his hand and shook the store clerk's hand. "My name is Levi Cord. I got a ranch just east of town now. We'll be needin' supplies on a regular basis, iffen ya can get 'em in."

The store clerk glanced down at Levi's guns. "Cord, huh? I've heard about you. The famous gunslinger that set out for Council Grove to fetch his gal." He looked at Samantha. "And you must be the gal. I'll be damned…"

As the man paused, Levi said, "I beg your pardon?"

The man took off his hat, his eyes still on Samantha. "Ma'am, you are just as purty as the stories we heard."

Levi cleared his throat as he stared at the man, who swallowed hard as he broke his gaze away from Samantha. "Excuse me, Mr. Cord, my apologies." He reached out and shook Levi's hand. "Mr. Cord, sir, I gotta tell ya, folks 'round here might not welcome a gunman as yourself, but I bid you welcome."

Levi nodded. "Well, much obliged to ya, pardner."

As they walked outside, Samantha turned to the store clerk's wife. "Good day to ya, ma'am."

The woman stopped sweeping the boardwalk and stood there for a moment, then nodded.

Samantha nodded back and they unhitched their horses. Levi helped Samantha in her saddle and then walked around to mount up himself. A commotion coming from the blacksmith caught his attention.

Horseshoes came flying out the door, and a man hollered out, "You dumb son of a bitch, get your ass outta here!"

A man came running out the door and tripped over a pail of water, dumping it all over the ground.

"Why, you worthless peddler, get your ass outta here now 'fore I break your scrawny-ass neck!" the voice yelled again.

Levi saw the man get to his feet and look back into the blacksmith shop, then take off down the street as quickly and clumsily as he could. As he ran past, Levi could tell it was Cody.

The blacksmith followed him out to the door. "You're goin' to pay for those two wagon spokes you broke and the forge you melted all to hell!"

"Boy, oh boy, would ya lookie there," Levi said. "Wonder what on earth that was all about?" He shrugged, then kicked Star, and they headed out of town and back toward the ranch. The storm that was brewing to the south had moved its way toward them and was fixing to hit anytime.

As they rode across the prairie, thunder crashed across the dark sky and lightning flashed just south of town.

Levi watched the sky above. "Looks like that ol' storm might hit us a heap sooner than I had figured."

Samantha looked at the clouds, and her face set in a grimace.

Thunder crashed loudly again, this time spooking Star so badly she almost ran right out from under Levi. "Easy girl," he hollered out. "Easy there."

Raindrops splattered against their arms. Thunder crashed again and Levi said, "Looks like we're fixin' to get wet, darlin'."

No sooner did Levi speak than the sky cut loose and began pouring heavy raindrops. The ranch was only a couple miles away, so they spurred their horses and took off at a dead run, laughing and hollering. By the time they reached the ranch, they were soaked all the way through. As they arrived, Dally came out to greet them, wagging her tail.

"Woowhee!" Levi hollered out as they rode into the barn and tried to shake the water off. They laughed and stood there looking at each other for several minutes, then Levi grabbed Samantha and wrapped his arms around her and kissed her. "Darlin', I believe I fall more in love with you every day."

Samantha smiled and held him close. "I love you too, Levi."

They unsaddled their horses and put them in their stalls for the night and then made a mad dash for the cabin, splashing in every single mud puddle that crossed their path. Just as they reached the porch, thunder crashed so loudly that it rattled the whole cabin and Samantha let out a scream. Levi laughed and grabbed her by the hand and led her inside. As they shut the door behind them, they fell to their knees, laughing and trying to catch their breath. Levi knew they were acting as if they were a pair of schoolchildren, young and in love forever, and he was enjoying every second of it. He chased Samantha up the stairs.

After changing into some dry clothes, they went downstairs and sat in the wooden rockers, listening to the pitter-patter of rain on the roof. They watched it run down the side of the house and splatter on the porch railing. Contentment overcame Levi as he smiled to himself and thought about how good it was to be home at last.

Chapter 20

As the morning sun appeared over the foggy Kansas horizon, Levi awoke to the sound of a turtle dove calling from a fence post outside the bedroom window. He opened his eyes and wiped the sleep from them and quietly rolled over. Samantha was still asleep, nestled deep in the blankets. He smiled as he gazed at her beauty. His heart was content at last. He wouldn't trade that feeling for anything in the world.

He quietly tiptoed out of bed and got dressed, careful not to wake Samantha as he slid his boots on. He walked over to the dresser mirror and looked himself in the eyes for a second, then smiled. This was a big change for him. He hadn't thought much of himself in quite a few years. He was rather ashamed of himself and what he had gone through in his life. But now he was proud. He was becoming the man he had so badly wanted to be.

Something was missing, though. He reached over to the bed frame and grabbed his hat and put it on his head. Still something was missing. He looked at his waist in the reflection and then slowly reached for his hips. He looked over at his twin Colts hanging on a hook on the wall and then looked himself in the eyes and shook his head. He thought for several minutes. It wouldn't be easy, but he wanted the very best for Samantha. He took one last look at the Colts and reached down at his hips again, imagining the weight of the guns tugging at his waist. He envisioned the ivory grips and the nickel-plated guns standing out from his black pinstriped trousers and vest. Levi couldn't recall the last time he had gone anywhere without his Colts at arm's reach. This was one of the hardest decisions he'd had to make in a long time. He hadn't been able to risk going unheeled. It had been a matter of survival.

He turned around and looked at Samantha, Dally lying on the floor next to the bed. He quietly eased his way to the door and down the stairs. His jingle bobs on his spurs jingled as he cautiously inched his way downstairs. After warming himself a cup of coffee, he walked outside and to the corral.

Levi studied a few horses they had brought back from Ellsworth. One was a big three-year-old sorrel gelding standing near sixteen hands. Another was a four-year-old bay mare that stood around fifteen and a half hands, and the other was a beauty of a mare. She was a two-year-old blue roan filly with a lot of spunk. Levi had bought the horses with the intent of breaking them and making cow ponies out of them.

A few minutes later, Bud and the boys came riding up to the corral. "Mornin', Boss," Bud said. "We got two sick heifers over south of the creek. We doctored 'em the best we could, but we'll ride back out after dinner and check on 'em again."

Levi shook his head. "We need to check on all the new calves this morning and make sure to doctor any sick ones we find. We can't afford to lose many head right now."

"Yes sir, Boss." Bud nodded. "We just come in to rustle up a new rope…mine played out on me ropin' one of them heifers. You gonna ride with us?"

Levi thought for a second. If there was anything that he loved most, it was working cattle. "I reckon I will."

Bud started toward the barn but stopped as Levi spoke. "Tomorrow I aim to get started on this li'l filly."

Bud looked at the horses in the corral. "The roan?"

Levi nodded. "Yes sir, she's quite a spirited nag, but I reckon she's got the makin's of a right nice cow pony."

Bud looked at the roan and shook his head. "Sure you ain't bitin' off more than ya can chew?"

Levi chuckled. "I reckon we'll have to see. Might take a heap of work, but I reckon we'll make somethin' outta her sooner or later." The blue roan danced around in the corral, snorting and blowing and stomping her feet. It was going to be quite a chore, but Levi believed it could be done.

Levi walked to the barn and caught Star and saddled her up.

"Mornin'," Samantha called out as she walked over to the barn.

"Mornin', darlin'," Levi replied. "How'd you sleep?"

"Splendid. What are you boys settin' out to do?"

Levi tightened the cinch on his saddle. "We're gonna go check calves and doctor any sick ones we come across. Boys said there's a couple sick heifers that need tendin' to so we're gonna see what all we can get done 'fore dinner. Would you like to saddle up and come along?"

Samantha smiled. "I'd be delighted. It sounds like an adventure."

"Well, go catch your horse and we'll get her saddled up."

Once they were all set, Levi crawled in the saddled and everyone stopped and stared at him, shock plastered across their faces. Bud's jaw dropped and his eyes widened. Even Samantha looked like she couldn't believe her eyes.

Bud said, "Boss? Are you sure you're feelin' up to ridin' along?"

"Why in the hell not?" Levi asked.

Bud looked down at Levi's hips. "Well, Boss…your Colts? You ain't heeled?"

Levi grinned and turned to Samantha. "I don't reckon I'll be needin' them today to doctor calves."

Bud shifted in his saddle, a look of unease spreading plain across his face. "Are ya sure, Boss? I mean—"

Levi cut him off. "I'll be fine, pardner. Besides, as long as we're ridin' with you and your hogleg, I reckon we'll be in good company. I've seen you shoot."

"Boss, I don't reckon—" Bud said, his voice nervous.

"Nonsense," Levi said. "Now let's ride. We got cows need doctorin'."

Bud nodded. "Alright, Boss. Iffen you say so."

As they crossed the creek just west of the cabin, Levi pointed at all the signs of beaver. "What do you think, Mike? There's a passel of 'em all the way down the dagburn creek."

"I reckon I may have to set a line of traps over yonder and rustle me up a handful of pelts," Mike said. "Aren't many critters I can't hunt or trap. Lookin' forward to seeing what luck will bring me."

Levi spotted a couple pairs of cow and calves. He studied them as they rode by. "I reckon those are fine. They're eatin' good and the mommas look right fine."

Not far up the creek, he spotted a pair of buzzards circling up in the sky. Something must have died, and the buzzards were about to have their dinner.

"What do ya think they're circlin', Levi?" asked Samantha.

Levi shrugged. "Could be a deer, a fish, or anything."

"I just hope it ain't one of our head," Bud said.

Levi shook his head. "There's that possibility."

A few moments later, the scent of something rank blew in their direction.

"My Lord, what in tarnation is that awful smell?" asked Samantha as she covered her nose and mouth.

Levi looked ahead and saw it was what the buzzards had been circling. It was a first-time momma cow that had died giving birth to her first calf.

"Damn it," Levi cussed. "Just what I was afraid of."

As they rode up to the dead cow, the smell made Bud gag. Levi chuckled. "What's the matter, cowboy? Makin' your ol' stomach churn?"

Bud's face turned green and he started dry heaving.

Levi studied the momma cow. "Poor ol' girl musta struggled and finally played out on us. That's a shame. Well, coyotes gotta eat too, I reckon. Let's keep ridin'."

A little while later, one of the cowhands spotted a group of cows bedded down in a small draw. "Over there, Boss, bedded up in the ditch."

Levi turned Star, and they all rode up to check on them and see if they needed tending to. One of the cows was coughing and moving kind of slow. Her head hung low and her back was all hunkered over.

"Well, boys," Levi said. "That cow is surely needin' doctorin'. Throw a rope on her and we'll tend to her first."

Bud took his rope from his saddle and swung it around his head and, just as pretty as ever, gave it a toss and landed it right over the cow's horns. One of the other cowboys took his rope and caught the cow by the heels. Levi dismounted and walked over to his saddlebags and grabbed his knife, then walked over to the bawling cow and inspected her. Her right back hoof was swollen and infected something awful. "Well, boys, this ol' girl has got a nasty case of hoof rot." It appeared she had been bitten by a snake or had possibly gotten a locust thorn stuck in her leg and now something was causing a nasty infection.

Levi waved for one of the cowboys to come assist him, and together they laid the cow on her side. Bud and the other cowboy kept their ropes tight so she couldn't kick and toss around. Levi took his knife and gently cut open the wound, then carefully began to squeeze the infected area. A yellowish puss began to ooze out and soon started pouring to the ground. It was a mighty nasty job, but the cow would likely have died if the infection wasn't cleaned out.

As soon as all the puss finally stopped coming out, Levi took a needle from his saddlebags and walked behind Star and pulled a single strand of hair from her tail. He walked over to the cow and patted her on the neck. "We're just about done, ol' girl." He used the strand of hair to sew up the wound, then spit some tobacco around the incision to help clean the infection. Once he was finished, the boys took their ropes off the cow and stood back as she laid there for a moment.

She wouldn't attempt to get to her feet on her own, so Levi walked over and started pushing on her butt. "Come on, girl, get on your feet."

The cow continued to just lay there, and Bud came over and pulled up on her head as Levi pushed her back end. She finally stood on her feet and regained her balance.

Levi patted her on the butt. "There ya go, ol' girl. Got ya all patched up."

The cow slowly limped her way over to the other cows. Most of the swelling had gone down already.

Levi saddled up. "We'll need to keep a close eye on her the next few days and make sure that infection clears up and don't come back."

For the next few hours, they rode along checking cows and doctoring anything that needed it. As they were riding the north side of the ranch, they came across a small group of cows that each had a fairly new calf.

"Them calves will be needin' doctored and we'll need to look after their mommas too," Levi said.

One of the momma cows had a large set of horns that spread out over four feet wide. As Levi crawled out of the saddle, the cow started pawing the ground with her hooves and throwing up dust over her back. She was not happy at all about their presence around her new calf. Levi slowly worked his way around the horses and carefully tried to sneak up to the calf, but the momma wasn't having it. She came charging full blast right at him, and he almost broke his neck trying to get out of the way.

"Look out, Boss!" yelled Bud. "That ornery cuss is about to nail your backside."

Levi tried to sneak up on the calf again but with no success. That old cow was blowing and snorting and stomping her feet. Bud crawled down from the saddle to give Levi a hand.

"You boys be careful," Samantha said quietly. "She's liable to take ya both."

The cow watched Levi's every move as he walked to the side of the cow. Meanwhile, Bud slowly inched his way behind her. The calf was standing just behind his momma, trying to suck as Bud eased his way closer. Just when he was almost close enough to get a handle on the calf, old momma cow whipped around, swiping him to the ground with her horns.

"Shit!" Bud yelled. That old cow got him down on the ground with her head and was slamming him to the ground. Dust was flying everywhere, and Levi ran over and tried to distract the cow and free Bud from her massive horns.

"Hyah! Hyah! Get outta here!" Levi yelled loudly as he rushed in front of the cow. The cow raised her head and paused for a brief second and decided to leave Bud and take off for Levi. "Oh shit!" Levi yelled as he took off on a run.

Mike jumped down from his horse and took off around the cow and tried to distract her away from Levi. The other two cowhands rode around trying to cut her off, but she came charging with her horns swinging from side to side and just about crashed right through them.

"Screw this!" one of them yelled as he turned his horse and tried to get out of the way. The other cowboy quickly reached down and grabbed his rope from his saddle and threw it toward the cow. Luckily, he roped her by one of her horns and around her face. The rope didn't reach all the way around her head due to her massive horns.

"I got her, Boss!" he yelled out as he dallied around his saddle horn. "Not the best, but I reckon she'll hold alright." The cowboy tried to keep slack out of his rope as Bud jumped up off the ground and ran over and grabbed the cow by the tail.

"Keep that rope tight now!" Levi hollered as he ran over and grabbed the calf and commenced to doctoring him quickly before all hell broke loose with its momma. She was shaking her head and bawling up a storm as Levi handled the calf. "Easy, girl," he called out to the cow as he checked over the calf. "Looks like we got us a little bull calf, boys. We'll cut him soon with any other bulls we round up."

After Levi finished tending to the calf, he quickly jumped back into the saddle. Bud let go of the cow's tail and jumped back in the saddle after dusting himself off. The cowboy shook his rope free from the cow, and she headed over to her calf to sniff him over and make sure he was unharmed.

"There ya go, girl. See, he's just fine." Levi shook his head.

Bud dusted off his hat. "Boy, Boss, that was mighty entertainin'."

Samantha looked Bud over. "Are you alright? You took quite a beatin'."

Levi turned to Bud and waited for his response.

Bud grinned. "Had me sweatin' bullets there for a minute. I'd of had her by myself iffen y'all hadn't jumped in." Everyone shared a laugh, then Bud went on. "I'm just fine, Miss Samantha, ma'am. Just a li'l bruised up, I reckon, but I'm just fine."

Samantha shook her head, and they kicked their horses and set out in search of more cows.

They worked right on past dinner and up until just before sundown.

"Boy, oh boy, I'm right hungry," Levi said after his stomach growled loud enough that Samantha looked over at him and giggled. He blushed.

"I'll rustle somethin' up when we get back," she said.

Bud rubbed his stomach. "I'm so damn hungry I could eat a whole cow, hooves and horns and all."

Mike chuckled. "I know where ya can find yourself one, too."

Bud turned to him. "What do ya mean?"

Mike grinned. "Back up yonder on the creek."

Bud still looked at Mike, apparently at a loss to what Mike meant. Mike looked at Levi and winked. "You might have to fight the buzzards off it first."

At that, Bud's eyes widened in recognition, and he started gagging.

Levi laughed. "Hell, Bud, you wouldn't even have to cook that one. The sun has likely cooked it enough for ya. Just might have to brush off a maggot or two now and then, but I reckon that'd make ya a fine meal with some onions and greens."

Bud gagged again, and Samantha made a sour face and covered her mouth.

AFTER SUPPER, LEVI walked outside and down to the corral to check on the horses. As he reached the corral, the blue roan filly snorted and stomped her feet and pranced around the corral.

Levi smiled as he watched her study his every move. "Now, ain't you full of piss and vinegar?"

There was a bright new moon out that night, and Levi could faintly hear a lone wolf howl to the east and then a pack of coyotes crying and yipping to the south. A barn owl swooped overhead, lit on top of the barn, and let out a piercing screech. A crisp cool breeze blew from the west and blew Levi's wild rag tails across his shoulders. Levi could hear laughter from the bunkhouse as the cowhands most likely told stories about lewd beautiful women and rank bucking horses.

Levi smiled and gazed up to the moon. "Life is grand," he whispered. He looked back at the cabin, and a light formed across the yard as the front door opened and Samantha walked outside. A few moments later, she walked out to join him as he leaned on the corral's log fence.

"Everything alright?" she asked.

"Why, yes, darlin', everything is just fine. I just come out for some fresh evenin' air."

Samantha wrapped her arms around him. "She's a lovely filly, that roan there. She's got the spirit of a wild Wyomin' mustang mare."

Levi looked at the filly. "Indeed, she does at that. I aim to get to breakin' her at first light."

Samantha watched as the filly bucked and kicked around the corral, shaking her head and blowing. "You might have your hands tied there, cowboy. Are ya sure you're up for it?"

Levi hadn't been healed very long and his body still ached and was stiffer than hell. However, he wasn't about to let that slow him down. "I aim to make her one of the finest cow ponies in all the territory. I may not be in the shape I once was, but I reckon I ain't gettin' no younger neither."

Samantha smiled. "You know, I think you're goin' to make something remarkable of this filly. Although I worry about you hurtin' yourself, it is great knowin' that you are happy doin' what you love."

In the distance, the sound of water rippling over limestone rocks in the creek soothed their souls as stars glistened from the prairie sky above. It was a beautiful evening, and Levi was anxious for morning to come so he could begin his quest of taming and breaking the filly.

Later that night, as Levi and Samantha were headed to bed, Levi undressed and crawled into bed and watched Samantha as she undressed and slid into her nightgown. She sat on the edge of the bed and began to brush her golden hair, and Levi glanced over at the wall and looked at his twin Colts. He had gone a whole day without even taking them down from the hook and strapping them upon his hips. A sigh of relief came over him as he leaned back and placed his head on his pillow. Life was falling into place for him for once.

BRIGHT AND EARLY the next morning, Levi was up with the sun and headed downstairs for his morning cup of coffee before he went out and began his mission. Levi stretched his back, then slid his boots on his feet and grabbed his leather gloves. He enjoyed his cup of coffee, although he made it a bit stronger than usual. He shook his head and forced the last swallow down like a shot of rotgut whiskey as it warmed his blood. As he walked outside, he spotted a pair of whitetail does grazing along the creek, feeding on the acorns from a lone oak tree that stood just west of the cabin about a hundred yards out. As he walked off the steps, the deer threw up their heads and flagged their tails, watching him as he headed toward the barn. Once they realized he was no threat to them, they continued grazing.

When Levi walked into the barn, he heard a commotion coming from the loft. As he looked up, he saw a grayish calico cat looking down at him.

"Well, howdy," Levi called out. "Where on earth did you come from?" The cat looked down at him and meowed, then began purring and rubbing against the ladder. Levi had no idea where on earth a cat would have come from clear out there on the ranch. Any nearby town was miles away, and he didn't know of any other farms the cat may have strayed from.

"Help yourself, friend," he called out to the cat. "Damn mice are a dime a dozen 'round here. I don't mind ya droppin' in for a spell, but ya better earn your keep." Levi chuckled as he grabbed his rigging from the barn and headed to the corral.

As he walked over to the corral, he hung his rigging on the fence and grabbed a rope. He slowly walked out into the corral. "Easy, girl," he called out. "Easy now…I ain't aimin' to hurt ya."

The filly jumped and kicked and snorted up a storm. She ran circles around him and tried to hide herself behind the other fillies. Levi cautiously walked around the corral, trying to sneak up behind the horses and separate them, but no luck at all. The three of them gathered up together and would not slip up whatsoever. He decided to try something a bit different. This time he was going to make a dashing run right into the middle of the horses in hopes that they would split up just long enough for him to make his move. As he dashed right into the middle of them, one of them reared up high, kicking her front hooves and snorting. All hell broke loose, and the three horses took off in every direction. Levi quickly swung his rope over his head and caught the roan. Once he pulled the rope tight, she went to bucking something awful. Snot was flying from her nostrils as she commenced to raising hell all over the corral.

For several minutes, Levi fought the filly as she bucked and kicked around the corral tugging on his rope. Finally, he managed to lead her to the round corral the cowboys had designed from logs they had cut along the creek. In the center of the pen, they had driven a hickory post into the ground that could hold its ground against just about any critter. Levi aimed to test the strength of the post with this raging young filly. He managed to drag her close enough to the post and tie her up. He had begun to walk back to the fence when she jumped up and bit him in the shoulder.

"Son of a bitch!" he cussed as he balled up his fist, wanting to slug her in the mouth. As he turned around, he paused for a second, then gritted his teeth. "Now was that polite a'tall?"

The filly snorted and looked him in the eye curiously as he rubbed his shoulder and walked over and sat down along the fence. She never once took her eye off Levi. For the next hour, Levi sat there, and the filly never once seemed to get the slightest tired of being tied to the post. His shoulder ached where she had bitten him, and it throbbed as he waited. Every so often, she would kick and try to rear up, and Levi would patiently sit there and watch, whittling at a twig with his pocketknife. It was simply a waiting game.

The filly eventually began to slightly calm down. Levi got to his feet, and she threw her ears up and stared him down. He walked halfway to the filly and sat down again. She raised her head high and studied his every move as she blew and shook her head. Levi sat there for about another hour and the filly never once lowered her head. She just stood there, anxiously awaiting his next move. As Levi got off the ground once again and stood up on his feet, he stretched his back and dusted off his trousers and headed for the barn.

When he returned, he walked over to the filly slowly and held out his hand a few feet in front of her. He had a handful of oats to reward her for her patience with him. The filly snorted and perked her ears forward, but fear would not allow her to sniff his hand.

Levi shook his head. "Very well, then. If it's just the same, I'll just leave it here on the ground." He leaned down and placed the handful of oats on the ground. The last time he had been this close and turned his back on her, she had tried to take a hunk out of his shoulder. However, determined to gain her trust, he allowed himself to turn his back on her once again. Looking out of the corner of his eye, he saw the filly lay one of her ears back, keeping the other one perked forward. He slowly walked away and out of the gate, knowing that if he showed her trust, she would gradually show him the same. At least, he prayed so.

As he walked to the cabin, he saw Samantha sitting on the porch swing.

"Howdy, darlin'," he said. "How long have ya been out here?"

"Quite a spell, I reckon," she replied. "All the commotion woke me up, and I've been out here watchin'. How's that shoulder?"

Levi unbuttoned his shirt and pulled it down over his shoulder to inspect where the filly had bit him. "Ah...she aimed to take my whole arm, I reckon. Just wanted to show me she means business. Give her some time and she'll come around."

Samantha inspected Levi's shoulder. "Let me clean that up. That's a mighty nasty lookin' bite."

Levi nodded. "Yes, ma'am, iffen you wish."

As Samantha tended to his wound, Levi watched the filly. She stood staring at the cabin, watching for Levi to return. After about twenty minutes, she looked down at the oats. Levi knew she badly wanted to lean down and take a bite, but pride wouldn't permit her to do so.

After having a bite to eat, Levi walked back to the pen. He noticed the oats still lying on the ground untouched. He scratched his head and untied the filly. "See, ol' girl, that wasn't all that bad now, were it?"

As he began to try to lead her out of the pen, she stood still and wouldn't walk a step. He tugged on the rope a couple times and had to pull her out the gate and over to the corral. Once he turned her loose in the corral, she took off trotting over to the other fillies, which were nickering and prancing around and smelling each other over.

Levi walked out of the corral, noticing her watching him as he went to catch Star. He saddled her up, then headed out to check on the cowhands as they tended to the daily chores.

Not a cloud hung in the blue skies as Levi trotted along looking for the boys. Star's hooves hitting the prairie ground blended with Levi's spurs and made a comforting sound as Levi began to whistle a tune. As they proceeded to cross a small ditch, a large six-foot black rat snake slithered across the rocks, and Star made a sudden stop, almost throwing Levi right over the saddle.

"Whoa, Nellie!" Levi hollered. One of Star's hooves slipped on a rock, and Levi caught himself just in the nick of time. She caught her footing, and Levi readjusted his feet in the stirrups and picked up the reins and turned her away from the snake as it coiled up and began imitating a rattler. A shiver shot down Levi's spine as they rode on.

As he rode to the top of the hill, he pulled back his reins and slowed Star to a stop. He looked around the prairie, trying to spot Bud and the other cowboys. Off to the north he saw something that caught his eye. He stood up in the stirrups. "What in the hell is that?" He kicked Star to a gallop and rode over to investigate. As he got closer, he noticed that what he had seen was an old headstone sticking out of the prairie grass. He could see the top of the stone sticking out, but the rest was all overgrown with weeds. He jumped down from the saddle and walked over to the headstone, then knelt and began pulling weeds away to clear the stone.

He read what was inscribed on it aloud, "Samuel Hunt, Private U.S. Dragoons, September 11, 1835." He took off his hat. "Well, I'll be damned." As he was peering at the stone, he could hear the sound of a buggy creaking along the trail. As they came closer a man's voice called out, "Howdy!"

"Howdy," Levi said as he stood and tipped his hat to the man.

In the buggy was an older man and what appeared to be his granddaughter riding beside him on the seat. "Lovely day, ain't it?" the gentleman said.

"Yes sir, it sure is," Levi replied.

The old man looked down from his buggy at the grave. "I see you've found Mr. Hunt there."

Levi nodded. "Yes sir, just stumbled upon it."

"Ya know, this young man from Company A set out on a military expedition across the plains to the Rocky Mountains. He was gonna try to dissuade the Indians from confrontin' travelers on the trail. His command was returnin' to Fort Leavenworth when he fell deathly ill. Captain Ford called it inflammation of the bowels. We pay our respects to him every time we pass him on our way to town."

The young girl slid down off the seat and placed a handful of wildflowers at the grave. She gave a smile to Levi before quickly climbing back up into the buggy.

Levi thought of how painful it must have been for Samuel Hunt to die in such a way. He must have fallen silent for a moment too long because the man interrupted his thoughts. "Well, sir, we best be gettin' on our way."

"Good day to ya," Levi said, tipping his hat once more and offering them a smile.

The man whipped his horse with his reins and the buggy pulled away, bouncing along the prairie. Levi knelt back down and dusted off the stone and finished clearing all the weeds around the grave as a sign of respect for the fallen dragoon who had passed away before Levi was even born. He noticed the remnants of dead flowers buried in among the weeds and he wondered if anyone would be so kind as to visit him when his time in this world was long gone.

As he turned toward the east, he spotted three riders heading his direction. Each man rode a black Morgan gelding that stood tall and proud. They wore blue wool single-breasted jackets with gold-colored buttons and yellow facings that indicated they were members of the United States Calvary. Their pants were wool sky blue with a yellow stripe down the sides. They each wore beaver skin black hats with a yellow cord, bands, and tassels. Levi noticed they were all dark-skinned. He figured they were Buffalo Soldiers. Their general mission was to subdue hostile Native Americans, outlaws, and Mexican Revolutionaries. Due to their reputation and skills, they consistently received some of the most dangerous and difficult assignments the army had to offer.

Levi had heard stories of Buffalo Soldiers but had never encountered any himself. The Pinkerton Agency had sent out a regiment in search of him and a band of bushwhackers that he had rode with sometime back. Unfortunately for them, Levi had gone by an alias at the time and had disappeared, leaving the outlaws and the territory for a couple years. He had heard tell that they had caught up to several of his comrades and feared they would tell his Christian name.

As the soldiers approached, a mighty uneasy feeling overcame Levi. He reached down to remove the tie downs from his Colts and remembered he no longer carried them. He had even left his derringer back at the cabin in his jacket pocket. He was unarmed and alone. A feeling of fear overcame him, and a trickle of sweat dripped down from his sweatband in his hat and ran down his forehead. One of the soldiers raised his arm in the air, and they all slowed their horses down to a walk just before reaching Levi.

"Whoa," the soldier's voice called out, and the horses came to a standstill. "Howdy, sir. Fine day, ain't it?"

Levi studied each man. They were each wearing a Calvary-issued Navy Colt and carrying a Spencer repeating rifle. "Howdy, boys," Levi replied as he got to his feet casually. He turned his head slightly and looked toward the cabin in the corner of his eye. He was quite a ways out, and there was no possible way of escaping and getting to his Colts. They were all mounted, and he was on the ground with Star standing at least ten feet away. They would gun him down like an egg-sucking dog before he even made it to the saddle. He attempted to take a deep breath and not seem so nervous, although it was an extremely hard chore. "What brings ya boys out this way?"

"We've been sent to patrol the Santa Fe Road. A band of wild Pawnee savages has been raiding homesteads, killin' and rapin' settlers and stealin' their stock. We've been sent to keep an eye on things for a spell."

The soldier seemed quite friendly, but Levi still had an uneasy feeling. One of the other soldiers looked at Levi and carefully studied him and then spit tobacco on the ground near Levi's boot. Levi looked up at the man and for a minute their eyes locked. The soldier seemed a heap rougher than the other two. He stared Levi deep in the eyes. "Say…you ever been to Missouri?"

Levi's heart sank. He was sure to be in trouble now. "No sir, I ain't. Been in these here parts all my life. Never got far from the homestead." Levi was lying through his teeth, and he didn't believe the soldier was buying any of it.

The soldier slightly cocked his head to the side. "So you didn't stand alongside them slave-owning Rebel trash during the War?"

Levi shook his head and said the first thing that came to his mind. "No sir, to tell ya the truth I was downright sick with the measles when the War broke out. My pa and brothers left to stand against the Rebellion, but I was left at home to die in my bed. I reckon the good Lord had other plans for me, though."

The soldier grinned, and Levi could tell he knew he was feeding him a pack of lies.

The commanding soldier pointed toward the cabin. "Is that your place over yonder, sir? We're looking for a place to bed down for the night."

Levi turned his head toward the cabin. "No sir, I was just passin' by and stopped to clean up my uncle's grave here before ridin' into Burlingame." Levi pointed toward Wilmington. "Iffen ya ride due west a couple miles you'll reach Wilmington. Fine little town, iffen ya ask me. I'm sure there's some good rooms over there at the hotel."

The commanding soldier looked toward Wilmington. "Splendid. I reckon we'll carry on a ways further then. I'm obliged for the information, Mr…?"

Levi's mind scrambled for a random name to give, then he boldly said, "Josiah Harvey."

The commanding soldier shook his head. "Well, Mr. Josiah Harvey, I bid you good day, sir." He raised his hand. "Move it out, boys." He tipped his hat to Levi and spurred his horse onward. As the other soldiers kicked their horses, the one glared at Levi and spit at his feet again and then grinned and damned near ran him over with his horse as he trampled over the grave of Private Samuel Hunt. Levi watched them for a second, then walked over and picked up the reins and mounted Star and took out across the prairie at full gallop, trying to find Bud and the boys.

Chapter 21

Morning came sooner than Levi wanted. He'd had quite a restless night dreaming of his troubled past and his encounter with the Buffalo Soldiers the day before. He hadn't had many nightmares in quite a spell, but something had gotten to him when he was approached by the soldiers while unarmed and alone. He had tossed and turned most of the night.

After he dressed and kissed Samantha good morning, he walked out to the barn and fed Star a bucket of oats, then headed to the corral to catch the blue roan filly. Once again, he had a hell of a time. She commenced to bucking and kicking and rearing up like a wild mustang defending her new foal. Levi finally roped her and led her to the pen and proceeded to tie her up as he had the day before. She pulled on the rope and snorted until he finally had her securely tied. He walked to the fence and sat down just as he had before. She paused and watched him cautiously with her ears perked forward. Levi knew she remembered the routine and was still not inclined to give in. She lowered her head to the ground and smelled the small handful of oats that were still where Levi had laid them before. Still, she left them untouched, no matter how appetizing they might have appeared. Levi continued the same routine for several hours before leading the filly back to the corral. For the next several days, the two spent countless hours repeating this very scene.

The next week brought wind and showers that made everything soaked and muddy. Nevertheless, Levi put on his oilcloth duster and continued with the filly. He sat on the ground while the filly stood staring at him. Thunder crashed loudly above, loud enough to cause his ears to ring, and he thought of Samantha. He was sure she would likely rather have him inside out of the elements but was glad she didn't take it upon herself to tell him how to do his job and instead let him be.

After what seemed like two weeks of monsoon weather, everything finally began to dry out. Finally, Levi's luck with the filly began to change. The rain had washed away the oats he had left on the ground, so he decided he would try once again to give the filly a handful of oats. She snorted a couple times and even considered smelling his hand, but still had not worked up enough trust to do so. Once again, he leaned down and put the oats on the ground and walked away, sitting down by the fence. She was a very proud mare, and Levi showed much respect for that. Most cowboys would have tied her up and thrown a saddle on her the first day, riding the buck out of her, but Levi was different this go-round. He saw something in this particular filly that most folks looked past.

After about an hour, he decided to go inside for dinner but found himself watching her from the window. The filly sniffed the air and then looked down at the oats as if tempted to taste them. She seemed to be very smart, a bit on the watchy side but that was desirable in a horse that you planned to take out onto the prairie where danger was always hiding. Finally, the smell of the oats must have been too much for her, though, because she peered around as if to see if anyone was watching her before finally dropping her head to eat. Levi smiled and backed away from the window to join Samantha for dinner.

After dinner Levi went back out. This time he walked just out of reach of the filly and sat down. She watched his every move but seemed a tad calmer. Levi walked to the barn and grabbed another handful of oats and brought them to the filly. When he reached out, she pulled her head back and refused to eat from his hand. He laid the oats on the ground as before, but she refused to touch them. As he walked away, though, she began to eat. She was taking her sweet time, but Levi was more than patient with her. He didn't want to break her spirit, merely just wanted to gain her trust.

One evening after supper, Levi walked out to the corral with Samantha and looked over the horses. "One day soon, darlin', that filly will be right in my hand. I bet my life on it. She's comin' along slow, but she's makin' promisin' progress." Levi wrapped his arms around Samantha and kissed her tender lips. "I'll love you till I die, darlin'. I don't reckon I know what would have become of me iffen I hadn't met you when I did. My life changed drastically when I rode into Council Grove that day."

Blushing, Samantha kissed his lips and wrapped her arms around his neck. "Oh, Levi, life is grand with you in it. That's for sure. I could never imagine life without you now."

They gazed up at the full moon shining brightly over the ranch and danced in the yard as coyotes howled across the prairie. Levi stared in her eyes and knew that everything was just as it should be.

THE NEXT DAY brought a misty foggy morning. Levi figured Mike was itching to do some hunting. Levi enjoyed trapping, although it had been several years since he had run traps. "Mike, I've been seein' lots of beaver signs down there on the creek just west of the cabin. Critters been buildin' a mess of lodges and got themselves a big ol' dam up the creek a piece."

Mike looked at him with excitement in his eyes. "Really now?"

"Yes sir, pard. Iffen ya want, we can ride out yonder and set a trap line this mornin' along the creek."

"Let's do it." Mike smiled. "I'll go fetch my traps and round up my gear."

The men saddled up and rode out along the creek, scouting out different areas where they found all sorts of fresh beaver signs. Levi led Mike to where he had discovered the large dam. There were trees that had been freshly chewed on the night before and fresh slides along the bank where they had been dragging logs to stack on the dam.

"Lookie there, pard." Levi pointed to the ground. "Fresh tracks all over."

Mike got down from his horse and scouted around a bit for the perfect place to set the first trap. He tied his horse up to a small hedge tree and walked along the edge of the creek bank as Levi got down and tied Star up to a nearby cedar tree.

Levi spotted a poplar tree and noticed there were fresh shavings all the way around the base of the tree where a beaver had been gnawing at the trunk. "Mike," he called out. "Over here, pard."

Mike walked over and inspected the shavings. "Looks mighty good right here, don't it? Dagburn beavers been all throughout this bottom here. Ya reckon we could set a few traps 'round this here tree?"

Levi pointed over to the opposite creek bank. "Over there is a nice lookin' slide. I'd set one just under the water there, leavin' just the top stickin' out. That way when that old critter goes slidin' down the bank, he'll likely slide right into it."

Mike walked back to his horse and grabbed one of his steel traps and carefully set it, making sure it was secured to an overhanging root of an oak tree. "That oughta do it, I reckon." He looked over a high spot in the creek where the beavers had destroyed every single small tree and sapling around the general area. "Hot damn! Levi, get a look at this."

Levi walked over. "By golly, I'd get a couple set in this spot."

They searched around for any sign of tracks or slides where the beaver had been traveling to or from the creek to the top of the bank. Not long after they started searching, they came across two separate spots where beavers had been exiting the creek. Mike looked around for the perfect place to set a couple traps, but the only trees or logs they could secure the traps to were nowhere near the slides. They searched around for some sort of bait to use to lure the beaver away from the slide and to the closest log jam they found. The creek had flooded back early in the spring, causing several trees and logs to wash up and jam across the creek, which was the closest thing to secure a trap to.

Levi watched as Mike looked over the location. He could almost see the gears of his mind turning as he thought over how to catch the beavers. Quietly, Mike moved off, looking for something…possibly some sort of bait to lure the beaver over to the edge of the log jam and into the trap.

Levi began gathering an armful of poplar twigs. Knowing beavers love poplars, he thought that maybe if they played their cards right one of them beavers might get curious and come looking for an easy snack. He figured they would set the trap along the edge of the bank along the water next to the log jam and then place the twigs around the trap as bait. When he told Mike of the plan, Mike agreed. "It's worth a shot, I reckon."

For the next few hours, Levi and Mike scouted along Soldier Creek, placing traps anywhere that looked promising. They noticed quite a bit of coon signs as well. Game was plentiful along the creek, and Levi and Mike were both anxious to come run the trap line the following day.

After they had finished setting their line of traps, and were headed back toward the cabin, Mike said, "Levi? I wanna thank ya for takin' Bud in like ya done. He's a damn good man. Folks just got the wrong idea of us when we was younger, and we both went our own ways. I left Missouri and headed west after the War and he stayed behind and fell into…well, let's just say a whole different sorta lifestyle than what we was raised on."

Levi knew what Mike was talking about, but he just let Mike continue.

"He was always quite a momma's boy, if ya will. When she and Pa passed on, ol' Bud kinda, well…just drifted off to another life and in the worst way. He weren't ready to say goodbye a'tall. Ya see, Ma and Pa both died the same year not far apart and Bud had never spent a day without them until then."

Mike turned his head and choked up for a minute. Levi placed his hand on his shoulder. "Easy, pard. Ol' Bud is a top hand. He saved my neck a number of times, and I reckon he'll save it a heap more 'fore we're through. I'm right proud to have you boys on here at the ranch now. I'm honored, to say the least."

Mike shook Levi's hand and nodded. "Much obliged to ya, Levi."

When they got back, Samantha was outside scrubbing their laundry on a washboard with a bar of lye soap over a washtub. Levi pull Star back to a stop and sat there for a moment gazing at Samantha as Mike rode on over to the bunkhouse.

"Ugh…landsakes." She sighed, blowing her bangs away from her eyes, only to have them fall back as she continued scrubbing away. Sweat trickled from her forehead and ran down her cheek. She had rolled the sleeves of her dress up to keep them from getting wet, and he knew her fingers were sore and aching from scrubbing their clothes all morning. After she washed the clothes, she threw them into a grapevine basket and then carried them across the yard to the clothesline where she would hang them to dry.

Levi sat there and watched her and smiled. She had no idea he was back yet. Her long blonde hair flowed down her back and she looked like something right out of an Elizabeth Browning poem. For several minutes, he sat there in the saddle and watched her work as she hummed a peaceful tune to herself. She had one of the most beautiful voices he had ever heard. Levi smiled. It was as though he was hearing angels singing from on high. Her voice was so pure and collected. It spoke right to Levi's soul.

All of a sudden, Star let out a nicker, and Samantha looked up. "Why, Levi, you frightened me! How dare you sneak up on me like that! If I'd of had a gun, I'd likely have shot ya."

Levi chuckled. "My apologies, darlin'. I was just admirin' your soothin' voice. I'da sworn I went to Heaven."

Samantha blushed. "Do I deserve a kiss?"

Levi smiled and got down from Star. He wrapped Samantha in his arms and kissed her soft and tender lips. She giggled, and Levi said, "What's so funny, darlin'?" Just then, she flung a wet rag around and smacked Levi in the mouth with it, then took off laughing across the yard. Levi stood there in shock for a moment and then chased her across the yard, laughing and carrying on. The blue roan filly watched them from the corral as if they had lost their minds.

As they chased each other around the yard like a pair of schoolchildren, Samantha tripped on her dress and fell to her knees. Levi came running over to her and pinned her to the ground. "I got you now, you ornery cuss."

Samantha winked and grinned. "Why, as a matter of fact I do at that." She tickled Levi in the ribs, and as he jumped and threw up his arms, she rolled over and flipped him underneath her and then pinned him down. She laughed. "I told ya…" She leaned down and kissed him and he tried to tickle her off of him but every time he would get close, she would tickle him, and he would laugh and lose his strength.

"Ah, darlin', I love you so much," he said as she finally rolled over and settled beside him in the grass.

"I love you too, my handsome cowboy." She reached over and held his hand. "Promise me somethin', Levi."

Levi looked at her. "Anything, darlin'."

Samantha looked him in the eye. "Promise me that you'll never leave me."

Levi grinned. "Darlin', I'd rather take a bullet in the chest than ever even consider spendin' another single day without you." He rolled over and placed his hand upon her cheek, then brushed her bangs away from her cheek. She placed her lips to his and then lay there in his arms right in the middle of the yard.

AS THE NIGHT drew on, Bud lay there staring into the darkness in his bunk while the others were fast asleep. His mind had been drifting back to Cheyenne and how he prayed he could have saved her life. He held a lot of blame on himself for her passing. Truth is, he held a lot of blame on himself for numerous things that had occurred in his past. He had come a long way from where he had been, but some nights he fought rest and his mind and heart would become exhausted. He couldn't shut off his mind when he put his head on his pillow at night. He would close his eyes and all he would see was Cheyenne's face just before she died in his arms from the rattler bite. A tear gently fell down his face and he rolled over and faced the wall. He pulled his blanket up and bit down hard as the tears came rolling in. He closed his eyes and prayed like hell that he would fall asleep and wake up with his memory magically erased.

LEVI AWOKE AND dressed, then headed downstairs to make the morning coffee before setting out with Mike. As he waited for the coffee to warm up on the stove, he walked over and sat down on his rocker.

Mike quietly opened the cabin door and walked inside, surprising Levi. "Mornin', Levi," he said softly as he walked over to the kitchen table and sat down. "Coffee sure smells good."

Mike was dressed and looked ready to go. By the neatness of his hair and the bags under his eyes, Levi assumed he must have been up for quite some time already. Levi slid his foot in his boot. "Mornin', pard, help yourself. You reckon we had any luck last night with that moon? Critters shoulda been on the move."

Mike poured himself a cup of coffee. "I sure hope we got something. I couldn't sleep worth a piss last night. All I could think of was beaver."

Levi chuckled softly and poured himself a cup of coffee, then walked to the fireplace mantel and took down his trusty Winchester carbine. It had been some time since he had held the rifle, and it felt mighty good in his hands. He brushed his hand along its walnut stock and pointed it toward the bull elk skull on the wall. He contemplated the idea of going upstairs and strapping on his twin Colts but figured if they were to get into any trouble, he would have his rifle and Mike would have his Hawken. Not to mention Mike's Colt strapped to his hip as well. Levi reached into a box of cartridges on the mantel and grabbed a handful of shells and put them into his pocket.

The sun had just started to rise as the two men saddled up and headed out along the creek. A cardinal called out from its perch atop a cedar tree, and just a ways up the creek another one answered. A black-capped chickadee called to its mate from a small thicket as a fox squirrel foraged through the leaves. Star let out a nicker, and the squirrel looked up and spotted them and ran up a nearby cottonwood tree, where it began barking and carrying on. A field mouse chewed on a deer antler that had been shed back in the early spring.

As they arrived at the first trap, Levi's heart began to race with anticipation. They got off their horses and quietly walked up to the trap.

"Damn it, nothing." Mike scratched his head.

Levi looked around, wondering why nothing had used the fresh slide they had found.

They left the trap set and moved on down the creek toward their next trap. As they walked along the creek bank, they spotted several fresh tracks and their steps quickened in their eagerness. But when they came up on the second trap, once again they were left with disappointment.

"Doggone thing is still set again." Mike scratched his beard and looked around. "If that don't beat all. I figured we'd have at least one in this one."

Levi looked at all the tracks on the ground. "By God, pardner, there's daggum tracks everywhere from last night."

"I just can't figure it," Mike said as they continued on toward the next trap.

A mule deer buck that had small velvet antlers growing back jumped up ahead of them and stared them down as they walked along the creek. He bobbed his head a few times, then bounced over the hill. A crow called from atop a locust tree as it watched the men pass by. Up the creek, just around the bend, Levi began to hear a trio of blue jays causing quite a ruckus. They were worked up about something, but he couldn't see what all the commotion was about.

Levi pointed ahead as he saw the jays circling the bend in the creek. "Somethin's sure up there, I reckon. Damn birds are makin' all sorts of racket."

Mike looked ahead. "Yes sir, I reckon so. Wonder what it could be? Another deer or maybe a coyote?"

Levi shrugged his shoulders as they cautiously walked ahead.

As they reached the creek bend, the blue jays took off, flying up the creek. They looked around and didn't see anything out of the ordinary at first, but something caught Levi's eye with a second glance and careful observation. "Well by golly, pardner, look over yonder on the other side of the creek." He pointed across the creek.

"Hell, yes!" Mike hollered out. "'Bout damn time."

Their luck had begun to change for the better. A big old male beaver had made his way down the slide and gotten caught in the trap. Mike turned to Levi and shook his hand and said, "That, my friend, is what it's all about." He walked over and released the beaver from the trap and handed it to Levi, then proceeded to reset the trap to see what luck might bring them come nightfall.

Levi pulled some rope from his saddlebags and tied a slip knot around one of the beaver's back feet and then tied another slip knot at the other end and slid it over the beaver's other back foot. He draped the rope over his saddle horn and Star looked back at the beaver and smelled it.

Levi then watched Mike as he attempted to get back across the creek. As he went to walk up the slick and muddy bank, he slipped and fell with a thud. Levi chuckled. "You alright there, pard?"

Mike got back up on his feet. "Damn ground went and disappeared right out from under my moccasins."

Levi walked over and gave him a hand.

"Much obliged, Levi." Mike walked over and studied the beaver. "Damn fine critter right there. Big old male, too." He looked at Levi. "Ya reckon we caught more?"

Levi grinned. "Very likely, but I ain't 'bout to go gettin' my hopes up neither."

The next couple of traps turned out to be unsuccessful, with one of the traps being unset but with no beaver, and the other one still set. The next three after that were all unset, and each held a good beaver. Two of them were large males and the other was a smaller female. It was ending up quite a successful turnout.

As they headed up the creek to check the last couple of traps, Levi noticed that the next one was unset, but no beaver was in sight. However, the men looked over the trap and noticed there had been a beaver stuck in the trap sometime during the night hours. They could see where the critter had torn up the ground trying to escape the jaws of the trap. Sometime during the struggle, he had chewed off his own foot, which was still stuck in the trap, and escaped to safety.

"Damn shame to see that," Mike said as he reset the trap. "I'd rather him not even got caught, iffen ya know what I mean."

Levi looked around to make sure he couldn't spot the beaver laid up somewhere nearby. "I reckon that ol' beaver will be a heap smarter next time, wouldn't ya say, pard?" He looked up the creek and spotted something peculiar caught in the trap. "Looks like we got somethin' up ahead."

Mike looked up and squinted his eyes. There was movement in the brush, and the critter was splashing in the water along the creek bank, but they couldn't make out just what it was. Levi walked over and grabbed his Winchester from its scabbard on Star and cautiously crept up on the trap. As he got closer, he saw a striped furry tail, which was an obvious sign the animal was definitely not a beaver.

"Ah, hell," Levi said with a grin.

"What is it, Levi?"

The weeds started moving, and the animal tucked itself deeper in the brush. The men crept closer and Levi pointed the barrel of his Winchester toward the critter and pushed the weeds aside.

Mike shook his head. "Well, I'll be gawd-damned and go to hell. A dagburn coon." He turned to Levi. "Well, it sure ain't no beaver, but I reckon it'll do just fine."

Levi slid his hand into the lever action on his Winchester and jacked a cartridge into the chamber. He took careful aim at the coon's neck and fired. Smoked filled the air as the rifle's hammer struck the primer of the cartridge and the powder ignited and sent the slug flying into the coon's hide, killing him instantly.

Mike walked over and released the coon and hung it on his horse. He reset the trap and then walked over to Levi. "Well, now, it's been quite a party, ain't it? I'd say we done a heap of good today."

Levi turned around and looked at the four beavers and the raccoon. "Yes sir, it's been quite a party, but I'll tell ya one thing."

"What's that?"

Levi smiled. "All this trappin' has worked up my appetite."

WHEN THEY ARRIVED back at the barn, Levi went inside and told Samantha all about their morning adventures. She was excited for them and walked outside to watch them. After they had tended to the horses, they each grabbed their knives and commenced to skinning each critter. First, they started at a beaver's ankles and removed the feet. Then, they started a center cut at the base of the tail and carefully cut all the way up to the chin. Next they cut around the tail and began peeling and cutting the hide away from the carcass. After they got the fur skinned, Mike asked Samantha for some salt. When she returned from the cabin with a jar of salt, he carefully poured the salt over each hide to cure them. They stretched each hide into a round shape and then tacked them tightly to the barn wall. After they had finished skinning and preparing the beaver pelts, Mike grabbed the coon and began skinning it as well. When finished, Mike also hung the raccoon hide on the barn wall, and Samantha took one of the beavers inside to clean and prepare it for supper.

That evening, as everyone sat around the kitchen table, they shared one of the most magnificent feasts they'd had. Samantha had prepared a meal of beaver with a side of boiled carrots and taters. For dessert, she blessed them with a hot apple pie. Dally sat on the floor by Levi's feet, waiting and watching everyone's every move, hoping to catch a bite of anything they happened to drop on the floor. Levi watched as Mike slid a bite of food under the table to Dally and then gave her a pat on the head. He was subtle about it and slowly brought his hands back up to the table, as if to keep himself from being caught. If there was one thing Levi did not like, it was a begging dog. He was quite fond of dogs, but he didn't cotton to the idea of them begging and watching him eat his dinner. They had had a great day, though, and Levi didn't want to spoil it with a silly argument.

Levi ate more than he had in ten meals. "Darlin', this is spectacular!" he said as he wiped his mouth with a cloth napkin.

"Yes, ma'am, Miss Samantha, this here supper is right fine," one of the cowboys added.

Samantha smiled. "Thank ya kindly. I'm right glad you boys enjoyed it." She turned to Levi and winked. "And since you boys enjoyed it so well, I reckon y'all won't mind tendin' to the dishes now, will ya?"

Levi grinned, and the cowboys all laughed.

"Yes, ma'am, certainly," Bud answered.

After supper, Levi grabbed some beaver scraps along with some taters and carrots and placed them on a tin plate. He picked up a lantern, lit it, and walked out to the barn with the plate of food. He carefully climbed up to the loft and placed the plate on the ground for the visitor he had seen up there. He wasn't sure if the cat was still around or not, but he left the plate for her just in case she decided to pay them another visit.

As he walked out of the barn, he grabbed a handful of oats and walked out to the corral. The blue roan filly raised her head and snorted once, then watched him as he stood by the fence. She shook her head a couple of times and perked her ears up, and Levi stood there quietly and patiently.

After standing there for several minutes, the filly reached her head out and nodded a couple times. "That's it, girl, you're alright now," Levi said softly. He reached out his hand and showed her the oats. "Come on now, ol' girl. Are ya hungry this evenin'?"

The filly never took her eye off him as he walked into the corral and placed the oats on the ground. He turned around and walked back a few steps, then sat down in the corral with his back facing the filly. He knew that it was not a very smart thing to do especially after being bit previously. Nevertheless, he so badly wanted to win her trust. For quite a spell, he just sat there in the darkness with his lantern on the ground next to him giving him a little light. As Levi sat there hunkered over, he began to get sleepy, so he got up and walked over to the fence and sat down facing the filly. He leaned his back against the log fence and drifted off to sleep.

LEVI SLOWLY OPENED his tired eyes and his view focused on the ground. For a couple of seconds, he fought to wake up. His neck was stiffer than a board and his entire body ached something awful. He looked down to see that he was still outside against the fence, except he had a blanket wrapped around him, and the sun was rising. Confusion clouded his mind for a moment, but as he became more aware, he smiled. Samantha must have come out after he had fallen asleep and wrapped it around him. Warmth filled his heart. How could he have been so lucky to find a woman so understanding? Samantha seemed to know him better than anyone. She understood his dedication to the filly and just how much it meant to him. The ranch was quiet, and Levi knew the others must still be asleep, no doubt enjoying their day of getting to sleep in since he wasn't around to rouse them.

All of a sudden, he felt a warm sensation of hot air hitting him in the face. He listened closely and could hear the sound of breathing above him. He froze for a minute and studied the sound. Slowly, he raised his head and looked out from under his hat brim. Standing over him was that blue roan filly. Levi grinned as she lowered her head and smelled his face and chewed at the brim of his hat. He slowly began to get up off the ground, expecting her to bolt, but was astonished to see her stand in front of him, unafraid. He slowly reached his hand out and let her smell him and then softly rubbed his fingers along her neck.

"Howdy, girl," he said softly as he scratched her neck and rubbed her forehead. "I don't aim to hurt ya as long as you don't aim to hurt me." For several minutes he stood there bonding with the filly, then began to walk toward the gate. She followed him closely. Levi smiled as he turned around and patted her on the neck. "I reckon you'll turn out just fine. It'll take some time, but you're going to make a magnificent horse sooner or later, I just know. And I just love a good challenge."

Chapter 22

Several months had passed, and it was now October. All was well around the ranch. Levi had finally finished breaking the blue roan filly and she had turned out to be just what he had expected. Mike had run traps with success the first couple weeks, and then things had slowed down. Levi believed that once the summer heat gave way to the colder northern temperatures the game would move back up the creek and settle in and they would have much more success.

Bud had changed some over the summer months. He wasn't as chipper as he once was. Levi would often catch him staring off into space. He seemed to be in a state of depression that he couldn't seem to lick. He still smiled and laughed at times, but Levi could tell that something just didn't seem right. Levi prayed that his friend would find happiness and contentment in his life once again.

One lovely evening near the end of the month, Levi and Samantha saddled up and took a ride across the prairie. As the sun began to disappear, the full moon was glowing the brightest red orange. It lit up the prairie and cast an exquisite light in Samantha's blue eyes. Her blonde hair flowed down over her shoulders and her lips glistened in the moonlight. Levi admired her beauty. He admired everything about her. He appreciated Samantha. She was all his and would be till the day he died. He had never recalled feeling so in love and content with life. He couldn't even imagine a life without her.

As they rode across the prairie in the full moonlight, Levi watched Samantha as she straddled that old paint gelding and rode along next to him. Her eyes never strayed when she looked at him, never had since the day they had met back in Council Grove. Dally followed along behind them, nose to the ground, poking into every patch of weeds along the way.

At the top of a bluff that overlooked the Santa Fe Trail, they spread a blanket down and laid there in each other's arms, gazing up at the stars.

Levi leaned over her. "Samantha, darlin', you're my whole world…my everything that makes this ol' life worth livin'. I never wanna spend a single second without you. Not ever. You truly saved me." He leaned down and brushed her hair away from her face and gently pressed his tender lips to hers as he rested his hand behind her ear along her cheek. He softly caressed her bosom as he kissed her neck. He watched goosebumps spread across her skin and anticipated the passionate love they were about to make.

"Oh, how I love you, Levi," she softly moaned.

SOMETIME AFTER MIDNIGHT, Samantha began to feel rather different. She didn't think much of it at first...just thought her stomach was upset from something she had eaten earlier. She sat up, feeling rather nauseous.

"Are you alright, darlin'?" Levi asked as he sat up and put his arm around her. "What's wrong, beautiful?"

Samantha shook her head. "My stomach is feeling mighty peculiar. I reckon it ain't agreein' with that peach pie we had at dinner."

"Shall we head on back so you can rest?"

Samantha didn't want Levi to worry. "No, my love, it's nothin' to be alarmed of, I'm sure. Come over here and kiss me." She lay back down and Levi leaned over and kissed her. She could tell he was worried about her.

"Alright, darlin', I'm gonna get you on back now. You need to rest...besides, I feel a chill in the air. It's fixin' to get mighty chilly tonight."

Samantha held her stomach as he helped her to her feet. Levi began to dress, and Samantha hunkered over, not feeling herself at all. He walked over to her after he dressed and put his arm around her. "What is it, darlin'?"

Samantha grew pale and felt like she was going to be sick. She kept holding her stomach. "Nothin', my love...it's nothin' really, I'm sure of it."

"Nonsense, darlin', I'm gettin' you home now!" He helped her dress and got her on her horse.

As they headed for the ranch, she looked into Levi's eyes and smiled. She had never had anyone care for her and love her the way he did. That was plain to see. Just before they reached the ranch, she could feel Levi watching her as she rubbed her chest and throat. They were sore from throwing up, and every few minutes she would reach for her stomach with a strange sense of worry that she couldn't quite put her finger on.

After putting the horses up for the night, Levi helped her up the stairs and into bed. "Please, Levi, I'm fine. I can manage myself. Don't go frettin' yourself over li'l ol' me. I'm fine." She crawled into bed, feeling his gaze on her as she drifted off to sleep.

Just before sunrise, Samantha awoke and felt her stomach cramping. She began to get really nauseated and broke out in a hot flash. She quietly jumped up out of bed without waking Levi and rushed out to the privy. As soon as she made it to the outhouse, she dropped to her knees and began vomiting.

After what seemed like an eternity, Samantha wiped her face with her dress and pushed her hair back from her face and snuck back inside. A couple hours passed, and she began to feel much better. She kept getting sudden hot flashes, but the nausea had subsided.

Levi rolled over and open his eyes. "Well, mornin', darlin'. How ya feelin'?"

Samantha smiled. "Much better, my love. Just needed rest, as you said. How did you sleep?" She hated to lie to him, but a part of her felt like if she didn't admit something was wrong, it would go away.

Levi rubbed his eyes. "Honestly, I could use a couple more hours of shut-eye myself, but I gotta ride into town after breakfast and fetch a couple bags of oats and some nails. Gonna need some kerosene 'fore long, so I reckon I just as well grab some while I'm there." He sat up and stretched. "Would ya care to ride along?"

"I think I'll stay here and get to mending that favorite shirt of yours that has begun tearing under the armpit, if that's alright," Samantha said quietly.

Levi kissed her on the forehead and then on her lips. "I reckon I'll be headed out here shortly then. I love you, darlin'." He headed out and Samantha got up and walked to the window and watched him ride off. She held her stomach as it cramped something almost unbearable. She rushed to the privy again and spent the remainder of the morning performing the same agonizing routine. Samantha had always been a healthy young woman. She rarely even got the sniffles as a child. Something was definitely wrong, but she wasn't sure what it could be.

THE NEXT FEW weeks, Samantha would awake in the middle of the night and rush to the privy. The hot flashes and cramping had become more frequent. She had done her best to keep her illness from Levi and the boys.

The morning of Thanksgiving Day, she felt mighty poorly, and she decided to take a walk along the creek while Levi and the boys were out tending to the herd. As she walked along the prairie, she wondered what exactly it was that she had come down with. Was it life-threatening? Was it contagious? She wondered if she should tell Levi or if she should see a doctor. She didn't want Levi to worry, so she decided to try to keep it quiet as long as she could. She had hoped and prayed she would wake up one day and her illness would all be gone and that things would go back to normal. Unfortunately, she continued to remain ill without any sign of relief. She had heard of various diseases that had struck across the territory the past few years: typhoid fever, cholera, dysentery, diphtheria.

She stopped dead in her tracks and threw her hand over her mouth. "Oh, heavens, no…" Her heart beat wildly, and she broke out in a sweat and began shaking uncontrollably. She fell to her knees and covered her face with her hands. "What do I do?" she cried. "Oh no…what do I do?"

After she had herself a good cry, she walked over to the creek and leaned down and splashed her face with the cool clear water. She shook her head. She knew just what she had to do. She walked back to the cabin and sat on the porch swing and waited for Levi to return, fearing the outcome.

"HOWDY, DARLIN'," LEVI called out as his rode up to the yard. He jumped from Star and came hopping up on the porch, grabbing her in his arms and kissing her.

She smiled up at him. "Welcome home, love."

Levi held her and looked deep into her blue eyes. "I missed you, darlin'. I couldn't wait to get home so I could hold you and do this to you…" He pressed his lips to hers again.

"Should we take a li'l ride?" Samantha asked.

Levi looked at her, confused. "Well, darlin', I just got home."

Samantha lowered her head. He hated to disappoint her. "I reckon we can go for a li'l ride iffen ya want. Where we ridin' to?"

Samantha looked across the prairie. "Anywhere…I just feel like ridin' for a bit."

Levi grinned. "Well, let's go get your horse saddled."

After they had saddled Lightning and set out across the ranch, Levi rambled on about things he would like to get done around the ranch before the first snow would fall. He wanted to build a tack shed and put in a windmill for sure, and he had a few other things in mind.

The wind had switched from the south and was now blowing from the north. "Winter's comin'," Levi said. "I can feel it in my bones." He looked at Samantha. "Darlin'? Is everything alright? You seem awfully quiet today. Forgive me for sayin' so, but you just don't seem to be yourself."

Samantha pulled her horse to a stop. "Shall we walk?"

Levi looked at her, confused. "Alright, darlin', if you wish."

Samantha took Levi by the hand and together they walked through the buffalo grass. He watched her bite her lip several times, seeming to struggle to say something. Finally, she stopped and turned to Levi and looked him dead in the eye.

"Alright, darlin', now I want you to tell me just what's goin' on here. You've never once acted in this manner. Somethin' is wrong, and I expect you don't wanna tell me, but I reckon ya probably should."

She stood there looking into his eyes for several minutes. It was as if she hadn't even heard him.

"What is it, darlin'? You can tell me anything."

Samantha took him by both of the hands. "I've been ill for some time now, Levi. Every mornin' and night I've been wakin' up sweatin' like the dickens and runnin' to the privy. I've been feelin' mighty poorly for some time."

"What do you mean? Is it a fever?"

Samantha shook her head. "No, Levi, it is not."

"I don't understand, darlin'."

She gently squeezed his hand as a tear trickled its way down her cheek and fell to the ground.

"What could it be?" he asked, his voice catching. What was wrong? Was he going to lose her?

She took a deep breath in and let it out. "I ain't had my flow in three months, Levi."

Levi scratched his head. "Your flow?"

She gave him a serious look and then looked down at her stomach.

He looked down, and it dawned on him. Could it be? "You're joshin' me, right?" His heart began to race. "Are you sure?"

She nodded. "I'm purt near sure. I reckon it might not hurt to see a doctor, but I ain't never missed a flow. That could explain the stomach cramps and being sick."

His jaw dropped and he felt tears in his eyes. "What's this mean, darlin'?"

Samantha reached up and wiped a tear away from his cheek. "You're gonna be a father, Levi."

Tears flowed from his eyes as he stood there in complete shock. He wrapped his arms around her and held her tightly. "Oh, darlin', I love you so much. I don't reckon I know the first thing about bein' a pa, but I know in my heart that you will be a beautiful and wonderful mother. I reckon we'll just have to learn as we go along." Levi was trying his best to be supportive and excited, but deep down inside he was terrified. He was scared to death of failing as a father. He wiped the tears from his eyes and then looked down at Samantha's stomach. He softly placed his hand on her belly and then looked her in the eyes. "I'm gonna be a pa?"

"Yes, Levi."

"I just can't believe it." Levi took off his hat and shook his head. "A baby...unbelievable. I sure weren't expectin' that for a spell."

Samantha looked away. "Neither was I, Levi. It sure has come as a surprise to both of us, that's for sure."

Levi tried to think of something to say but fought for words. This was so unexpected. He had never really pondered the idea much about being a father. It had crossed his mind on occasion over the years, but he never truly gave it much thought. He loved Samantha more than any cowboy had ever loved a lady, but a baby? That was a mighty big responsibility, much more than raising cattle or thoroughbred horses. Horses and cattle came and went with the seasons, but a real baby? A child of God? That was a lifelong commitment.

Levi felt the tears welling up once again and Samantha wrapped her arms around him. "We will get through this. Just remember, Levi, you must stay strong for this child."

The north breeze began to pick up and a chill in the air was coming on strong now.

"I reckon we oughta' be gettin' back 'fore long, darlin'. Hate for you to catch a chill out here."

Samantha agreed and they set out for the cabin. The entire ride back, neither one of them spoke a single word. It was the quietest ride that Levi had ever experienced in all of his life.

That night, in their warm and cozy feather bed, Levi held Samantha a little tighter than before. He felt something growing between them that he had not expected. Something was changing for sure. He was sure of it. Levi rolled on his side and softly rubbed Samantha's stomach as she stared at the ceiling as if disappearing into her own mind. It was obvious something was on her mind, as she seemed distracted and caught up in herself as they blew out the lamps. All throughout the night Levi held her closely and never let her go. He was in and out of sleep, noticing that most of the night she lay facing away from him so that he could only make out her back in the moonlight. He wrapped his arm around her and rested his hand on her stomach, offering what little comfort he could.

THE NEXT MORNING, Levi awoke with a smile plastered on his face. They hadn't spread the news to Bud and the boys yet, and he was excited to do just that just as soon as he dressed and headed outside to assist them with the morning's chores.

As he slipped on his hat and boots, Samantha sat up in the bed. "Levi?"

Levi slid his pocket watch in his vest pocket. "Yes, darlin'?" He looked back at her and noticed something different about her. Her usual natural smile had been replaced with a look of fear and confusion. Her eyes no longer sparkled, nor did they hold that unique form of magnetism that had stolen Levi's heart. Instead, her baby blue eyes had the look of a young child who had just lost their best friend. Levi stood there, and his heart seemed to stop beating. "What is it, darlin'?"

Samantha looked him in the eye. "Can we hold off on spreadin' the news for a spell?"

Levi got an uneasy feeling. "Is everything alright, my love?"

"Yes. I would just like to see a doctor 'fore we go tellin' folks. I hope ya understand."

Levi nodded, even though he really did not understand why she wanted to keep it a secret. Wasn't she excited? He walked over to the bed and knelt to kiss her good morning. She leaned up and kissed him, but when their lips met, something was missing. The spark they had shared since that very first kiss back on Elm Creek seemed to have gone out. Levi's stomach tightened and his anxiety went crazy. He always feared the worst in damn near any situation, and now he could tell that Samantha was not herself. He could see the fear in her eyes and hear it in her voice. He hated to see her that way. He would do anything to bring back the smile that had won his heart. Whatever it took, he would die trying to make her happy once again. She must be extremely worried and scared. He was deathly afraid himself, but he knew he had to be strong not only for the baby, but for Samantha as well. She needed him…more than ever.

"Alright." He leaned down and kissed her forehead. "Samantha, darlin', I love you with all my heart and soul. I'll do whatever I can to give you and this child the very best life. I know times will get hard, and I know that I may not always be the easiest fella to get along with. There'll be times that you'll wanna clobber me upside the damn head with an old fryin' pan. But I promise ya, darlin', I aim to marry you and make you an honest woman and do my best by you as long as I'm still suckin' air."

Samantha gave him a smile, but he could see it was only an attempt for his sake. She reached and took his hand and placed it to her lips and softly kissed it. He leaned over and kissed her forehead once again, then headed out to the barn to saddle Star and take himself a little ride to clear his head.

He headed west, toward Wilmington. He couldn't get the image of Samantha's face out of his mind. He had never once seen that look on her face that he had seen that morning. It tugged at his heart and made a cold and lonesome feeling come over him. He needed to bring that smile back and bring joy into her life and assure her that everything was going to be just fine and that he would take care of her and their child. But how? It was a life-changing event for sure.

His mind wandered like crazy, wondering if he would make a good father like his father was to him. Would they have a son or a daughter? Would he have the patience to raise a child properly? He had a lot of patience and it showed when he was working with that filly. However, a child was much more different than a horse. He thought of all the things he would teach their child as they grew up on the ranch. How to hunt and fish and trap, and how to tend to cattle and ride. He'd also teach them how to stand up for what they believed in and how to love with all their heart and soul. And last, but not least by all means, he'd teach them to never be ashamed of who they were or of their family name. As he rode along daydreaming of what was to come, he began to smile.

He looked across the prairie and spotted a patch of flowers still growing along a rocky slope in the limestone soil. He decided to stop and pick a bouquet for Samantha in hopes of bringing some joy to her day. He spent the next couple of hours or so just browsing the countryside, picking anything he thought she might like. He wanted to pick her a good-sized bouquet because he knew that soon all the prairie flowers would freeze and die off till next spring. Winter was on its way, and every day the north winds would bring a chill, just a touch colder than the day before.

As he strolled across the prairie, Star grazed along in the grass. He heard a crack and looked up to see a cow elk standing up from a small ditch where it had been bedded until catching wind of Levi. She stared him down and watched him closely, and he slowly continued picking wildflowers in hopes she wouldn't realize he had spotted her. Thank heavens it was only an elk and not an Indian looking to have his scalp, because he hadn't been paying attention at all. As he passed by, the elk turned and snuck over the hill and out of sight. He watched her go and continued gathering a few more pretty flowers to take home to Samantha.

After saddling up, he carefully stuck the bouquet of flowers in his saddlebags and decided to turn and head north and circle back toward the ranch. As he passed by a small ditch that had a crystal-clear stream flowing right out of the ground, he saw a rabbit run into a brushy plum thicket. He had left his Winchester behind, or else he would have tried to shoot him for supper. A fresh rabbit sounded mighty good, too. He rode along the edge of the thicket, until, suddenly, all hell broke loose. A rooster pheasant came cackling and causing a ruckus out of a patch of coralberry. Star was startled and reared up and threw Levi hard to the ground, knocking him out cold.

When Levi came to, his vision was extremely blurry, and his head was spinning something awful. He closed his eyes for a minute or two and then tried to open them again in hopes that his vision would clear up. As he did, he saw a blurry view of the Kansas sky. He was lying on his back, and he reached up and rubbed the back of his head and then tried to blink his eyes a few times. Slowly but surely, his vision began to improve each time he blinked. He attempted to sit up and get to his feet, but whenever he tried to move, his head would begin to spin and throb. He decided to lie back down for a few minutes and see if his head would stop spinning. He looked around and saw no sign of Star. It was unlike her to leave him behind.

BACK AT THE ranch, Samantha was out in the barn cleaning out the stalls while Bud trimmed the horses' feet and put new shoes on them. The old gray calico cat that had randomly appeared some time back and then was never seen again had shown back up to pay them a visit. Bud watched as it headed for Samantha.

"Well, hello there," Samantha said as she leaned down to pet the cat. "You're a cute li'l fella, ain't ya?"

The cat brushed against her leg and began to meow and purr, wanting attention. Samantha continued shoveling horse manure out of the stalls as the cat laid down on the floor to watch. A pair of swallows flew in the door and started chattering as they flew circles around their nest before finally landing. The cat sat up and closely watched them, trying to plan a method of attack. Bud chuckled to himself, then resumed his work.

Shortly after Bud had finished shoeing the horses, he led his horse out of the barn and was headed to turn it out in the corral when something caught his eye. It was a horse on a run headed straight toward the barn. As he looked closer, he could tell it was Star. But where in the hell was Levi? "Miss Samantha!" he shouted at the top of his lungs. "Samantha, hurry, come here!"

Samantha came rushing out the door, looking to where Levi's horse was panting.

"Whoa, girl, easy there," Bud called out. "Easy now." He picked up her reins and tried to calm her down as Samantha looked her over. Bud handed her the reins and looked at Levi's saddlebags. On one side was his canteen and in the other side was a fresh wildflower bouquet. He carefully pulled the flowers out and looked at Samantha. She covered her mouth and gasped. Something was wrong for sure. They had no idea where exactly Levi had gone, so finding him was not going to be easy.

"Bud!" Samantha hollered. "Go fetch my horse and get her saddled, then round up Mike and the boys quickly. We gotta find him before dark."

Bud took off running for the barn. It took him a bit to gather all the boys, but at last they were set to go search for Levi. By the time he was ready, he noticed Samantha had turned Star in with the other horses in the corral and had tied his horse up. As she took Lightning from him, his eyes fell on Levi's Winchester and a handful of cartridges that she had in her hands.

BACK ACROSS THE prairie, Levi had finally gotten his vision to adjust but couldn't seem to stay on his feet long without his head beginning to spin horribly. Levi had quite a goose egg on the back of his head where he had smacked the ground. He looked around but couldn't see Star anywhere in sight. "Damn horse," he mumbled to himself. "Never gave me another reason to cuss her…now the damn nag has left me to walk." Levi let out a small chuckle. He hadn't told anyone where he was headed, so he wasn't sure if they would be able to find him. Honestly, he hadn't paid much attention to where he was going and didn't rightly know where he was.

Suddenly, he felt something kicking his boot, and as he opened his eyes, he was startled to see a colored man in a blue army jacket standing over him. He was over six feet tall and probably weighed less than two hundred pounds soaked and wet. He was as dark as night and had a thick gray mustache and long gray sideburns. His breath was as strong as the coffee that Levi had brewed for his morning breakfast.

As Levi sat up slowly, he recognized the man to be another Buffalo Soldier from Fort Leavenworth. The man looked at him. "I might regret askin' this, pardner, but did you lose your horse?"

Levi looked the man over. "Yes sir, ya might say that. A daggum pheasant jumped up and liked to scare my horse right out from under the saddle."

The man took Levi by hand and helped to his feet. "Where ya headed, stranger?"

Levi pointed south toward the ranch. "I got a spread just south of here a piece."

The man looked across the prairie. "I reckon you'll be needin' a ride, huh?"

Levi knew he must be a few miles from the cabin. He tried to walk a few steps but didn't seem to have much strength. He knew it was going to be quite an interesting hike back to the ranch. The man led his horse over to Levi. "Here, stranger, you take my horse and I'll follow along behind."

Levi looked at the horse, which was a tall, stout, black Morgan. He turned to the gentleman. "I can't take your horse, soldier."

The man handed him the reins. "Nonsense, stranger, get your ass up on that gelding."

Levi gave the gentleman a crooked smile. "I'm in debt to ya, soldier." Levi had fought for the Confederacy during the War against colored folks like the soldier, but he had never really gotten the chance to get to know one himself. Lots of folks didn't cotton much to the idea of colored folks living amongst them. They held onto a great deal of hate for them, just as they did the Indians. Levi may have fought for the South, but he never did agree with other folks' beliefs on any specific man or woman just for the tone of their skin. They were all children of God in his eyes and in his heart. Every race and culture of folks had their own breed of bad men, whether they were white, African American, Indian, or Chinese.

As Levi attempted to mount the soldier's horse, he realized he was weaker than he had expected. He had gotten thrown mighty hard and was still dazed quite a bit. The gentleman walked over and took Levi by the bootheel and helped him get his foot in the stirrup.

"There ya go now, stranger," the soldier said as he handed Levi the reins.

"The name's Levi, sir. I'm sure obliged to ya, soldier."

"I'm Private Chandler," the soldier said, offering his hand.

Levi shook his hand and then started the horse for the ranch. The soldier followed along on foot, carrying a Calvary-issued 1860 Spencer carbine.

As Levi spotted the cabin, he looked back and said, "Just ahead there, Private Chandler."

Private Chandler looked ahead. "Mighty nice lookin' place ya got there."

"Thank ya kindly. We're rather fond of it ourselves."

As they rode up to the cabin, Levi noticed Star was in the corral with the other horses. "Damned ol' horse musta decided to come on home without me, I reckon," Levi said as he shook his head.

Several of the horses were missing, and he figured the others must be out looking for him. Trying to find them out on the prairie would be hard, though, and he figured it would be just as easy to stay put rather than have them chasing each other in opposite directions. He rode up to the hitching post out front of the cabin and Private Chandler tied his horse up and helped Levi out of the saddle.

"Much obliged," Levi said as he got to the ground. He took off his hat and felt the goose egg on the back of his head. "Come on in for a cup of coffee, soldier. I'm in debt to ya."

Private Chandler took his hat off. "Well, now, I don't mind iffen I do."

Levi eased his way up the stairs and opened the door. "Samantha, darlin', I'm home." He waited for an answer as he prepared the coffee and was curious when Samantha didn't respond. He had expected her to be in the cabin. Had she gone with the others? "Well, soldier, when my lady comes down, I'll introduce ya. She'd love to meet ya."

Private Chandler looked around the cabin as he sat down in one of the wooden rockers. "I do have to say, sir, you have a right beautiful home here."

Levi poured him a cup of coffee. "Thank ya, Mr. Chandler. Tell me, what brings you out here this time of year?"

Chandler held his hand over the tin cup before he pressed it to his lips. "I was sent out here in search of a snowbird and his murderin' wife."

"Snowbird, sir?"

The man nodded. "Yes sir, a deserter, of the sort. In the United States Calvary, men often join the army to see themselves through the winter season, then desert in summer. We call them snowbirds."

Levi raised his eyebrows. "Ah…I see."

Chandler sipped his coffee. "This particular one was last seen in the Ottawa area sometime back. Rumor has it he boarded a stage with his wife and was seen headed west toward Dodge City."

Levi sat down in his rocker. "So this fella deserted the Calvary and took off, huh?"

"Yes sir, but that's not the half of it. He deserted the army in Lawrence and was caught and arrested in Pomona sometime back and was taken to Fort Leavenworth to a prison camp. He was to be sentenced that following Tuesday, and on Sunday night, his wife had come to pay him a visit. Unfortunately, the guard at the time was a young kid fresh off his momma's tit. Didn't have a lick of sense. That night, the fella's wife asked to visit and bring her husband supper. When the soldier turned his back to unlock the cell door, the woman pulled a knife from her dress and stabbed him in the back numerous times. The dying soldier fell to the ground and gasped for air as the woman grabbed the keys and unlocked the cell door. As the man rushed out of the cell, he reached down and grabbed the soldier's sidearm and took out across the yard, disappearing in the darkness. The soldier died shortly thereafter. Another snowbird prisoner in the next cell witnessed the whole incident."

Levi shook his head. "What happened to the other prisoner?"

Private Chandler looked him in the eye. "He was hanged the followin' mornin'."

Levi swallowed hard as the soldier went on. "Rumor has it the prisoner and his wife had been seen in Osage City sometime back but were said to be headed to Dodge for a honeymoon. I wired the marshal out there to keep a close eye out until I got there, but when I arrived, he said he hadn't seen or heard anything. I searched around for a few weeks out there with no sign so I decided to ride back this way for a spell and see iffen I could round up anything."

Levi's stomach tightened. He remembered when they had encountered the odd couple, Cody and Christine. He wasn't sure, but he thought he recalled them mentioning going to Dodge City for a honeymoon. He bit his lip and didn't say a thing. He hadn't seen or heard anything from them since dropping them off in Wilmington.

As Chandler continued, the sound of horses approaching caught Levi's attention. He guessed that it was everyone returning from their search. Samantha came rushing in the door. "Oh, Levi, thank heavens you're alright. I was worried sick."

Levi stood up from his chair. "I'm fine, darlin'…just took a li'l bit of a fall, but I'll be alright."

The soldier rose from his chair and took Samantha by the hand and gently kissed it. "Ma'am, my name is Private Chandler."

"Howdy, Mr. Chandler, my name is Samantha." She looked at the soldier and then looked at Levi curiously.

After Levi told her what had happened, she nodded. "Thank ya kindly, sir, for seein' Levi home here. You must stay for supper, I insist."

Private Chandler smiled. "I couldn't impose, ma'am, but thank you just the same."

"Nonsense. You'll be stayin', and I won't hear anything about it. Ya hear?"

Private Chandler turned to Levi and raised his eyebrows.

Levi chuckled. "I wouldn't cotton too much to arguin' with her. The odds will surely be against ya."

Private Chandler smiled. "Well, then, I reckon I could use a good home-cooked meal. Gettin' rather tired of opossum and muskrat."

A few minutes later, Bud and Mike and the rest of the cowhands came in to see what had happened. Levi filled them in and introduced everyone. When Private Chandler told them about his assignment to find the deserter and his murdering wife, Bud looked at Mike and his eyes widened.

Mike looked at Private Chandler. "These folks you're lookin' for? You say they was headed toward Dodge City?"

"Yes sir," Private Chandler answered.

Samantha looked at Levi and didn't say a word.

Bud turned toward Chandler. "You say that woman stabbed the man in the back?"

Private Chandler nodded, and Bud's jaw dropped. He sat down at the kitchen table. "What do these folks look like?"

Private Chandler brushed his mustache with his fingers. "The man is about five-nine and weighs about a hundred and ninety pounds. He's got green eyes and sandy brown hair that is balding. He's known to wear a mustache, and is much quieter than his wife. Now that woman is a whole other story in itself."

Bud looked at Levi and then at Samantha. Mike ran his fingers through his beard. "I'm curious 'bout this woman…was she a fine-lookin' gal?"

Bud looked at Mike and shook his head.

Private Chandler looked Mike in the eye. "Son, this damn woman is as nasty as a mangy coy dog that has been kicked away from its own pack. Even your cousin's girlfriend's neighbor's dog wouldn't even give her a humpin' iffen she was to come into heat."

Samantha got a look of disgust on her face as she covered her mouth.

Levi grinned. "Well, Mike, that sounds about like your kinda gal now, don't it?"

"Go to hell," Mike cussed with a grin.

Bud looked at Private Chandler. "Go on, soldier. This is a heap more interestin' than punchin' cows."

Private Chandler looked at Levi. "Another cup of that coffee sounds about nice." Samantha poured him another cup as he went on. "This woman has brown hair that comes down around her shoulders and has green eyes that show sign of her wicked and evil character. She walks with a limp at times and talks rather louder than most folks. She has a foul mouth that never stops. She tends to get right up in your face when talkin' to ya and likes to put her hands all over ya when she does so." Private Chandler had everyone's full attention. He sipped his coffee. "Damn, that's mighty tasty. Anyhow, as I was sayin', this woman is flat loco. Folks in Ottawa call her the crazy tobaccy chewin' lady."

Bud's face went pale. "Tobaccy chewin', you say?"

"Yes sir, this woman chews a heap more tobacco than ten men in the Kansas territory."

Levi's jaw dropped. Samantha looked at Levi and he crossed his arms and gave her a look. "Hmm…murderin' crazy woman, ya say?"

Private Chandler looked up from his coffee. "Yes sir, she's mighty capable of just about anything when she's desperate. She's not a woman to be trusted or to turn your back on."

A hush surrounded the cabin for several minutes and then Samantha said, "Well, boys, I should start preparin' supper." She began to clean up and prepare supper and Levi looked at Bud and Mike and shook his head. Not a word was said by any of them about Cody or Christine or their whereabouts. For all they knew, they could be long out of the territory. It had been several months since they had left them in Wilmington.

For the next hour, Levi visited with Private Chandler about the Santa Fe Trail and Fort Leavenworth's intentions to settle the Indian activity once and for all along the trail throughout the Flint Hills.

After supper, Levi said, "Private, you're more than welcome to set your bedroll in our barn iffen you'd like for the night. Only thing that might bother ya up there would be that ol' cat we call Sage."

Private Chandler chuckled. "I reckon I might just take ya up on that offer. Cold prairie ground makes these old bones mighty stiff this time of year."

Levi put on his hat and walked Private Chandler out to the barn and showed him where he could bed down for the night. As Private Chandler settled in, he said, "That was a fine supper. I thank you, sir."

Levi reached out his hand. "I'm in debt to ya, soldier."

Private Chandler shook Levi's hand. "Go have your lady check on that head now."

As Levi began to walk across the yard, Private Chandler hollered out, "Stranger, one other thing…"

Levi turned around. "Yes sir?"

Private Chandler looked him dead in the eye. "You introduced me to your lady and the hands, but you never did tell me your last name."

Levi stood there for a second, contemplating whether or not to tell the soldier his name. He remembered the fear he felt before when he had encountered the Buffalo Soldiers at the gravesite. However, something was different about this fellow. Levi looked the man in the eye. "My name is Cord, Levi Cord."

Private Chandler nodded, and uneasiness overtook Levi for a moment. For a second it had almost seemed that recognition glinted in his eyes, but surely not. Maybe he was just paranoid.

The soldier looked down at Levi's hips, and instinctively Levi went to touch the ivory grips of the Colt with his left hand. He was met with nothing but air, though, and quickly placed his hand on his hip for cover. Chandler's eyes rose back to Levi's, and the two held each other's gaze for a moment. Levi felt like he was seeing his own life of hardships reflected back at him in the eyes of the soldier...as if they weren't too different themselves.

After a few seconds, Private Chandler nodded and smiled at Levi. "Good night to ya, Mr. Cord." He walked back into the barn.

Levi stood outside for a minute and looked up at the moon, then turned around and headed for the cabin.

When he went inside, Samantha warmed a wet cloth from a pot of water and cleaned Levi's wound. He had quite a headache but was feeling much better than before. "Thank ya, darlin'. You're quite a cook, and a sawbones to boot." Levi pinched Samantha on the butt. She leaned over and kissed him, and he reached out and rubbed her stomach and then leaned down and kissed it. "I love you, Samantha, darlin'."

"I love you, Levi."

Chapter 23

Shortly after sunup, Levi rolled over and kissed Samantha on the forehead and whispered, "Good mornin', beautiful."

Samantha awoke and wiped the sleep from her eyes. "Mornin'."

Levi began to dress. "I reckon I'll go out and invite our guest to breakfast. He was kind enough to lend me his horse and see to it that I got home alright. I reckon he deserves a hot meal 'fore he rides on."

"I reckon that'd be nice," Samantha said as she slowly dressed. "I'll go fetch some eggs from the henhouse and prepare enough for y'all."

Levi noticed she wasn't quite acting like herself. "Everything alright, darlin'?"

Samantha looked up at him and then stared out the window as if she were a million miles away. Levi feared something was wrong but didn't want to pressure her. He knew folks sometimes just needed their own time to work out things going on in their minds and in their hearts. He knew becoming a mother was an unexpected surprise to her and that she was still likely in shock because of it.

Samantha shook her head. "Yes, love, just sleepy is all."

Levi leaned over and kissed her on the cheek. "Alright, darlin', iffen ya say so. Just worried, is all. I love ya with all my heart and soul. I'd rope the moon for ya iffen I had a long enough rope and a strong enough saddle to dally to."

Samantha looked up at him and gave him a crooked smile, then began to brush her wavy blonde hair.

Levi checked his pocket watch and gazed at the likeness of Samantha that he still kept inside. He headed out to greet Private Chandler.

As he walked outside, a crisp northern wind blew across his face, and he pulled up the collar on his wool coat to block the wind from going down the back of his neck. "Brr…" he mumbled as he headed for the barn. A hard frost had crystalized everything across the ranch. A turkey gobbled from its roost, and a mallard hen quacked faintly in the distance. As he looked across the yard, he noticed Private Chandler's horse was gone from where it had been left tied to graze in the yard.

Levi gave a knock, then opened the barn door. "Mr. Chandler? Samantha and I wanted to be sure ya had yourself a good home-cooked hot breakfast 'fore ya set out this morning." He looked around and saw no sign of Private Chandler anywhere. "Well, I'll be damned," he muttered. Sage came meandering her way over to Levi and began brushing up against his boots, meowing and purring. "Well, good mornin', Sage. Keepin' the mice down, are we?"

Levi heard something rustling through the hay on a wooden shelf in the barn and turned his head to see what was stirring around. A mouse quickly took off across the floor and disappeared into the hay. Levi turned to the cat. "I reckon not." He shook his head and turned to walk out the door just as something caught his eye. On the shelf next to a wooden box full of horseshoes was a folded, faded piece of paper. He carefully opened the paper and read the words inscribed in ink.

Blessed journeys, stranger. Stay fervent and vigorous and protect your lovely family. I bid you farewell.

PVT. Chandler

As Levi went to fold the piece of paper back up, he turned it over and his breath caught. Barely audibly, he read, "1864, wanted dead or alive. Fifteen hundred dollars for the arrest or capture of one Levi Cord. Wanted for suspicions of robbery and murder. Standing around five feet, seven inches and weighing near one hundred and seventy pounds. Blue eyes and clean-shaven face." Levi's heart raced wildly as he flipped the paper back over and read the words Private Chandler had written. The poster was just over ten years old. Levi had had no idea that Private Chandler had known who he was or that he had been previously searching for him. Why he had kept a wanted poster with him that long was unknown. Nevertheless, Levi felt a peaceful feeling of contentment as he folded the paper back up and put it in his jacket pocket. He sure didn't want anyone to get word of this possible reward even if it was ten years old. Chances are they had forgotten all about him by now, but he could not afford to live life on a game of chance…especially with a child on the way. Some folks would do just about anything to earn a dollar, let alone fifteen hundred of them. He found himself feeling grateful to the man that he knew barely anything about. Levi could have been swinging from the end of a rope if it weren't for Private Chandler…and he would have never found his happiness with Samantha.

Levi walked out of the barn and strolled over to the corral. He leaned on the wooden fence and gazed across the ranch. He watched the wind blow through the switchgrass and form a wave of blowing grass that danced across the Kansas prairie. His mind drifted back in time to all the things he had seen and done throughout his life. He thought about all the places he had been in his now thirty years, and where he was today. He gazed to the west along the Santa Fe Trail and recalled his journey to return to Council Grove to fetch Samantha. He felt as if his life had finally worked itself together and everything was finally falling into place for him. He had spent many a cold night alone, wondering what would ever come of his life. Many things flowed through his memory as he stood there gazing across the prairie.

A stiff cold wind picked up and came drifting across the ranch, causing Levi's coattails to flap in the breeze. Winter was approaching quickly. Soon the rippling water in the streams would be frozen and there would be no fishing in the creek until spring. Bud and the cowboys were already out working that morning. Bud had said last night they would set out east along the creek in the buckboard in search of brush they could cut for firewood. Off to the north, Levi could see the sky beginning to turn dark blue as winter clouds formed across the horizon. He had better ride out and give the boys a hand with the wood. They needed to make sure they had plenty on hand for the winter months to come.

Samantha's voice broke his train of thought as she called for him to come inside for a moment. Quickly he strode to the house, the smell of breakfast greeting him.

"I noticed Private Chandler's horse was gone, so I just packed this for you. Biscuits, jam, and some bacon for you and the boys," Samantha said, handing him a covered basket. Her smile was warm, and he leaned forward, giving her a quick soft kiss.

"Thank ya, darlin'. I'm sure they'll be mighty happy to see me ridin' in bringing gifts." Levi chuckled, then quickly walked to Star and mounted up. He needed to move fast before their breakfast got cold.

As he rode across the open prairie to the east, he rode along Soldier Creek in search of Bud and the boys. The temperature was dropping rather quickly, and he dreaded what was to come in the next couple weeks. The winter would mean more chores for the hands in the bitter cold months. Breaking frozen water tanks for the livestock with an ax and a hay fork was dreaded by all the hands.

A few miles up the creek, Levi spotted the cowboys sawing on a hedge tree that had fallen down and died some time back. He rode over and jumped down, letting Star graze on the prairie grass nearby. "How's it comin', boys?"

Bud rolled up his shirtsleeves. "Boss, we got near a half a wagon cut by now. I reckon we'll get a wagonload by dinner time, iffen that storm holds out long enough."

Levi looked to the north. "I reckon it'll be here 'fore we know it…a might quicker than we want, too." He walked over and relieved one of the cowboys and took one side of the saw and nodded toward the basket. "Miss Samantha made y'all something for breakfast. She figured this way maybe y'all would be able to get this done, seein' how you will have full bellies." Levi chuckled. He and Bud began sawing the tree while the other cowboys quickly ate the food Levi had brought and began stacking logs into the wagon.

For the next few hours, they cut trees and chopped logs, and by dinner they had a wagon loaded down.

"Ya reckon we'll have time to take this back to the cabin and get us a quick bit of grub and come back for another load 'fore that storm hits, Boss?" Bud asked.

They all turned their heads and watched the clouds as they continued to slowly head their way.

Levi shrugged. "I can't quite say, pard, but we gotta get to stackin' as much as we can. I reckon we're gonna be in for it this winter. I feel it in my bones." Levi saddled up and Bud jumped on the wagon while the rest of the cowboys climbed in the back and sat on the load of wood. They set out back for the cabin in hopes to find a hot meal waiting for them.

AS THEY SAT around the kitchen table enjoying the delicious meal Samantha had prepared for them, Levi said, "Y'all know that winter is gonna be amongst us quickly. And once the snow hits, it's gonna make it that much more difficult, on top of all the regular chores needin' tendin' to. I don't reckon we have nearly enough wood to heat the cabin here, let alone the bunkhouse as well. I just don't figure we'll have nearly enough time to stock up what we need. You boys are doin' a fine job 'round here, but there's just not enough hours in the day to accomplish all that needs to be done. Iffen we had another hand or two 'round here we might get lucky."

They all discussed the matter for several minutes and then Bud said, "You want me to ride into town later and see iffen I can round up a couple hands?"

Levi thought a moment. "Bud, I need you here. You're one of my top hands. No offense to you other boys. I just need someone in charge, and Bud has done a heap of good 'round here. I reckon after dinner here I'll ride on over to Wilmington and see iffen I can round up a hand or town. We could sure use another strong back to help with choppin' wood."

After dinner, Levi saddled up and set out for Wilmington while the cowboys headed back to try to cut another load before dark. The storm was getting closer, but it was taking a slow route, thankfully.

Levi rode up to the saloon and tied Star up to the hitching post out front. As he walked up the boardwalk, he stopped at the swinging doors and looked around the saloon. It had been quite some time since he had entered such a place, and most of the time, the outcome was never good. He reached down to undo the tie downs on his Colts, only to remember he wasn't carrying them. He had gotten used to moving around the ranch without them, but now an eerie feeling came over him. He was hesitant to enter the saloon unarmed, especially knowing about the reward that was on his head, even though it was some ten years old. He had changed his whole life around nowadays, however, not everyone would respect that.

As he cautiously walked into the saloon, he stood tall and walked up to the bar. "Howdy, barkeep," he said as he took off his hat and ran his fingers through his hair.

"Howdy, Mr. Cord, how's things over at your spread?"

Levi dug in his pocket for a silver dollar. "Busy, mighty busy. Just tryin' to prepare for this winter shit comin' on."

The barkeep chuckled. "I hear ya there."

Levi asked for a glass of sarsaparilla, then said, "I come to town to see iffen I could round up myself a couple good hands to join our outfit for a spell."

The barkeep scratched his head and began to wipe the counter with a white cotton cloth. "Hmm…" he said as he cleaned the beautiful walnut bar. "You can ask around here, but I ain't seen too many new folks in town, leastwise, not any lookin' for work."

Levi shook his head, then took a drink. He turned around and said loudly, "Alright, y'all, my name's Cord. I'm the ramrod over on a spread just east of here a couple miles on the creek. I've come to town here to hire me a couple good men to join our outfit through the winter. We got a good batch of wood to get cut and chopped and hauled back to the cabin. I'm needin' a couple boys with strong backs and a notion to work a day's work and earn a day's wages. Anybody in here lookin' for a decent job?"

A couple men sitting at a corner table chuckled, and one said, "Good luck findin' help here, pardner. Ain't nobody in here wanna get out and chop no damn wood. You're barkin' up the wrong tree. Go bark up another somewheres else."

Levi grinned and stared the man in the eyes for a moment. "Well, I reckon thirty dollars a week ain't good enough for your kind then, is it?"

The man's jaw dropped. "Thirty dollars a week? Well, now, mister, I was only foolin'. I'd help ya for thirty dollars a week, sir."

Levi looked at the man and grinned again. "I appreciate the offer, kind sir, but I reckon I'll have to pass." He turned to walk out the saloon doors and the man hollered out, "What's a matter, mister? You figure I ain't good enough to ride for ya?"

Levi heard a chair scrape, and he turned around to see the man standing and reaching down for his Navy Colt hanging at his hip. Levi looked the man dead in the eyes. "Pardner, now you're barkin' up the wrong tree. Why don't you go back to your daddy's farm and bark up another damn tree?"

The man looked down to where Levi's pistols would have been. When he looked back up, fear crossed his face.

Levi grinned. "Good day, now." He turned his back and walked out.

As he walked down the street, he heard a commotion coming from across the street in front of the store. He looked up and saw the hotel clerk holding a shotgun on a man and a woman and cussing profusely. "I told you time and time again that I will not allow you to stay here without pay. I was kind enough to let you make payments last month, and you failed to comply with the agreement. If you don't leave my property this instant, I will call for the marshal. You owe me forty-two dollars and sixty-seven cents, and you have failed to pay me. Yet you continue to stay and trash my hotel."

The woman yelled out, "I will not pay to stay somewhere that is infested with bed bugs!"

As Levi got closer, he recognized the man and woman, and he smiled and shook his head.

The hotel clerk's eyes widened, and his face turned red. "Bed bugs? Woman, your crazy ass likely brought them yourself. I run the cleanest rooms in all Wilmington, if not the whole damn county. If you refuse to pay me what you owe me this instant, I will have you removed, do you understand me?"

She grabbed her husband by the arm. "Do somethin', Cody!"

He turned to her. "Damn it, Christine, pay the man the money."

Christine looked back at the clerk holding the shotgun on them. "But…we ain't got the money now. You drank it all up over at the saloon."

Cody shook his head. "That's horseshit, Christine. Iffen you didn't chew so damn much tobaccy maybe we'd still have money."

Levi looked to the hotel clerk, who stole a glance at him while Cody and Christine fought. The anger on the clerk's face seemed to fade just for a moment as it traded for a look of disbelief. Levi shrugged his shoulders at the man. It seemed this pair hadn't changed a bit since he had last seen them.

Christine grabbed him by the arm. "Damn it, Cody, all you do is drink, drink, drink. You've spent all our money at every damn saloon we come to since Lawrence."

Cody grabbed her by the arm and shook her. "Shut the hell up, Christine! Don't you ever speak of that again, do you understand me?"

Levi recalled the first time he had met these two. It seemed they were always arguing like fools. He almost couldn't believe that they were going on and acting like this while the hotel clerk had a shotgun trained on them, but then again, he could.

Christine's face boiled with anger. "It ain't my damn fault you decided to desert and get yourself locked up and—"

Cody grabbed her by the face and put his hand over her mouth. "Another word outta you, Christine, and I will leave your crazy ass right here in this godforsaken town and ride on without you." He slowly pulled his hand away from her mouth and instantly she started yelling. He quickly covered her mouth.

"Marshal!" the hotel clerk screamed at the top of his lungs. "Marshal! Help!"

The marshal came running over, looking like he'd just woken from a nap. "What in tarnation is goin' on over here?"

"Marshal, these two damn beggars have been stayin' here for two months with no damn pay. They owe me for back rent, and they refuse to pay up."

The marshal turned to Cody. "Is that true? You refusin' to pay the man what you owe?"

Cody scratched his head. "Truth is, Marshal, we ain't got no money right now, but I got myself a job in Burlingame. I start tomorrow."

The hotel clerk clenched his teeth. "You're a damn cotton-pickin' lowdown liar. You've been sayin' that for the past two months and you ain't never left town once. Marshal, these two have been scroungin' around town here goin' from door to door and beggin' for anything that anyone will give them."

The marshal nodded. "Yes sir, I am aware of that. I've had several reports on my desk from folks in town 'bout you two. Tell me, son, what's your handle?"

Cody began to shake. Christine pulled on his shirt sleeve and said, "Allen. His last name is Allen, Marshal."

The marshal looked at her. "And what's your name, ma'am?"

Christine looked at Cody and didn't say a word.

Levi recalled what Private Chandler had said about his hunt for Cody and Christine for desertion and the murder in Lawrence. For some reason he couldn't even understand, he decided he had better step in. Sighing, he made his way across the street, calling out, "By God, Allen, where the hell have you been? I hired you on more than two weeks ago and you never showed back up. The boys and I searched for you for days thinkin' maybe Indians had got y'all somewheres."

Cody and Christine looked at each other, confused, and the hotel clerk shook his head and said, "I beg your damn pardon?"

Levi looked at him. "Excuse me?" He pointed at Cody. "I hired Allen here on over at the ranch and have been lookin' for him for a spell."

The marshal shook his head. "Well, then, I reckon since you are still refusin' to pay the man Mr...?"

Cody and Levi both answered the marshal at the same time. "Allen."

The marshal looked at them both strangely. "Since you're refusin' to pay your debt, I am placing you under arrest."

"You can't arrest my husband!" Christine hollered. "I can't make it without him."

The marshal grinned. "That's fine. Just fine, ma'am. You won't have to fret none 'bout bein' alone." Christine smiled, but then the marshal said, "You don't have to fret none at all, ma'am, cuz I'm placing you under arrest as well."

Her face went pale, and Levi's mind raced. He knew everyone back at the ranch would go off the deep end if he brought them home with him, especially Samantha. However, he couldn't stand the thought of the marshal finding out who Cody really was. Just the mere thought of Cody being hanged was unbearable to him, even though he was a bit of an unusual character and had a crazy wife to boot. Private Chandler had given him a second chance at life without him even knowing it. Why shouldn't he do the same for Cody?

As the marshal was about to cuff Cody, Levi pulled out some money from his money belt and said, "Hold it there, Marshal, hold on just a minute."

The marshal stopped just before putting the second cuff on and looked at Levi. "Now what in the hell?"

"Just hold your horses there, Marshal," Levi said as he counted his money. "How much does Allen owe ya here?"

The marshal looked at the hotel clerk. "How much did ya say these squatters owe you again, Mr. Harrison?"

Harrison cocked his head to the side. "Forty-two dollars and sixty-seven cents, to be exact. Why do you ask?"

"Well," Levi said. "Say I was to pay off Allen's debt to ya here, would ya turn him loose and allow him to come work for me?"

Harrison turned to the marshal and shrugged his shoulders. The marshal looked at Levi. "Are you sure about that, pardner? I mean, it ain't none of my affair really, but forty-two dollars, now, that's quite a heap of money."

Harrison cleared his throat. "That's forty-two dollars and sixty-seven cents, Marshal."

Levi counted out the money. "Allen here has hired on as a hand on our ranch and he's needed directly. I'll pay his debt and you release him to my care and there'll be no further questions."

The marshal looked at the clerk. "Do you object to that, Mr. Harrison?"

Harrison thought for a second and then rolled his eyes. "I reckon not."

The marshal looked at Levi. "Well, sir, I reckon iffen he don't object, then you got yourself a deal here, fella."

As Levi handed the Harrison the money, Christine said, "There! Take your damn money and shove it up your lazy ass, you sorry piece of scum." Cody tried to shut her up, but she continued. "We shouldn't of paid you a damn cent since your rooms are full of roaches and bed bugs!"

Harrison looked at the marshal. "Marshal, that crazy woman is insane. I run the cleanest rooms this side of Kansas City."

The marshal crossed his arms. "Yeah, not to mention the priciest damn rooms north of Wichita."

Levi chuckled, then tapped Cody on the arm. "Pardner, get that damn woman to walkin' 'fore someone clobbers her ass." He leaned his head in the direction of the crowd of town folks that had gathered to watch.

As Levi saddled up and proceeded to lead them to the ranch, Christine continued screaming at the top of her lungs, "You lowdown carpetbaggin' son of a horse's ass! You no good worthless Indian-lovin' pile of buffalo shit! You sorry piece of trash don't deserve our money!"

"Excuse me, ma'am?" Levi said bluntly. "Whose money are ya talkin' 'bout? Iffen I recall, if it wasn't for me, you'd be settin' over yonder in that cold and dirty calaboose. Now shut your damn mouth 'fore I shut it for ya. Is that understood?"

Christine turned to Cody. "Are you just gonna stand there and let him talk to me like that?"

Cody rolled his eyes. "Damn it, woman, shut your damn mouth for once, would ya? Least you could do is thank the man. I didn't cotton too much to spendin' another night in jail. 'Bout had all I can muster in that place." He looked up at Levi. "I'm obliged to ya, Mr. Cord, sir. I'll pay ya back as soon as I can."

Levi nodded. "I got a mess of firewood needin' cut and hauled to the ranch. You can work it off."

Cody smiled. "I'm in debt to ya."

As they headed for the ranch, Christine looked at Cody. "Cody, hand me the tobaccy, will ya?" Cody threw her a bag of leaf tobacco, and she took herself a plug. Levi's stomach turned as he watched her spit on the prairie ground. Spit ran down her lips and dripped off her chin and caught itself on her shirt.

Levi shook his head. "We better put a hitch in our giddy up or we're liable to get crosswise of this storm."

The storm was just overhead now and brewing something big. The air had turned colder, and the breeze had picked up to a straight north bitter cold wind. Tumbleweeds bounced across the trail and a swarm of blackbirds fought hard to fly to the nearest cover.

"Brr," Cody said as he walked along behind Levi's horse. Christine and Cody's ears were beet red from the cold, and Levi was sure his were, too. They continued onward, picking up their speed to try to reach the ranch before it began to cut loose.

As they reached the ranch, Bud and the cowboys were outside stacking a wagon load of wood alongside the bunkhouse. One of the cowboys saw Levi and said, "Boss is back. Looks like he got a couple new hands."

Bud turned around. "Aw, hell."

Levi dismounted and introduced the cowboys to Cody and Christine. "Boys, I want y'all to make them feel welcome and help them get settled in the bunkhouse. They'll be joinin' us for a spell."

Levi unsaddled Star and turned her in the corral as the sky began to drop little white snowflakes across the prairie. Levi rushed to the cabin, and as he walked in the door, Samantha said, "Well, hello there, I was wonderin' iffen ya was gonna make it back before the storm."

Levi walked over and gave her a kiss. "Well, I rounded up a couple new hands in town, darlin'."

"Oh?"

Levi was hesitant to tell her of Cody and Christine, but he went on and told her and got the exact expression that he had figured she'd give him. "You've got to be kiddin' me, right?"

Levi smiled and kissed her again. "We really need all the hands we can get right now, darlin', and seein's how he was out of a job, I figured we give them a chance and then as soon as winter is over and the spring is here we'll send them on their way."

Samantha shook her head. "What about Christine?"

Levi grinned. "She'll be workin' right alongside him."

"But Levi, she's a woman."

Levi scratched his cheek. "She is?"

Samantha threw a wet rag at him and smacked him in the face and they both laughed. "Now, Levi Cord, you be polite."

"Yes ma'am. I figure she'll be an extra hand just the same. God knows we could use the help, and they could use the work."

Samantha shook her head. "But what about that soldier, Private Chandler? He said he was searchin' for them."

Levi poured himself a cup of coffee. "I know, darlin', but he's already passed on now, and they'll only be here through the winter."

Samantha walked over to the window. "Whatever you say, my love."

THE DAYS BROUGHT much colder temperatures and more snow than Levi had seen in many years. Every morning, their daily routine would start out by breaking ice in the water tanks for the livestock. They would have to continue this chore all throughout the day. By the end of each day, the cowboys were whupped from swinging an ax and breaking the ice and then having to rake out the ice chunks with a hay fork. It was a never-ending chore. Due to all the snow covering the prairie, they would often have to go out and clear spots in the snow for the stock to have a clear spot to bed down. The bitter temperatures and going from wet one day and dry the next caused a lot of calves and older cows to get sick so they would have to bring them in and doctor them and try to warm them in the barn. If they were to get a calf that needed quick assistance, they would often bring them right into the bunkhouse and lay them on a blanket next to the potbellied stove to warm it up and keep it from getting pneumonia.

BEFORE THEY KNEW it, it was the day before Christmas Eve. Levi had decided that everyone would take the day off after their morning chores to go hunting for their Christmas dinner. His plan was to split up across the ranch and see if any of them could harvest a wild turkey for Samantha to prepare for supper. Turkeys were rather scarce in that part of the territory, but on occasion a flock would venture west along the creek and hang out for a couple weeks, then move on down the creek. They had seen some turkeys on the ranch a month or so back, and recently spotted a small flock foraging in the snow. Mike had been busy trapping for the last few weeks, especially since the cold weather had brought fur onto the game, and he had told Levi he had seen fresh turkey sign up the creek.

They awoke earlier than usual that morning, well before sunrise, and set out to break the ice in the water tanks so they could get an early start on their hunt. Levi grabbed his Greener 12-gauge double-barrel shotgun and a box of buckshot and loaded his saddlebags with some jerky for a snack. Bud and the rest of the boys grabbed their trusty Winchester carbines and enough cartridges to start a small war. Levi chuckled. "By God, boys, you're packin' enough shells to take Vicksburg."

The cowboys all grinned and Bud said, "Ya damn right, Boss. We ain't comin' back empty-handed. Too damn cold for that."

Levi chuckled and then kissed Samantha goodbye and walked out to saddle the horses. "Alright, boys, I'm gonna head due east. I reckon I'll take a look-see around the creek there and see iffen I can rustle up anything. Mike saw a flock of birds down that direction a few days ago."

Bud saddled up. "I reckon I'll head west and check the creek north of Wilmington. Saw some sign up the creek 'bout a week ago. Surely if we split up one of us has got to come across that flock sooner or later."

The rest of the boys split up across the ranch, going different directions. Christine and Samantha stayed home to take care of things around the ranch. They would have to bundle up and go outside and break the ice in the water tanks while the men folk were gone.

The snow had started to come down just after sunup. Levi figured that if the turkeys were in the area, he would have no problem picking up their tracks in the snow. He rode quite a spell along Soldier Creek before finding any sign of any game at all. He had expected to come across something by now, but nothing seemed to be moving anywhere.

"Where are those daggum birds?"

BUD HAD CROSSED the creek just north of Wilmington and spotted several fresh deer tracks, but there was no sign of the flock of turkeys anywhere. Mike had ridden south with the other cowboys, and Bud hoped he was having better luck.

Just after noon, Bud spotted something moving in the brush along the creek in front of him. He got down from the saddle and tied his horse to a nearby walnut tree and began to sneak down the draw and find a place to set up and see if he could get a shot at something. As he quietly crept along the creek, he picked a spot in the rocks where he could set up and seclude himself from and game that were to come into view. He tucked himself back in the brush, using the rocks to break up his outline, then sat and waited to see what was stirring in the woods up ahead. He prayed that whatever it was, it would head his direction. Snowflakes gently fell, making a fresh new blanket of snow on the ground. It wasn't coming down hard, but it was coming down nice and steady. It was rather pretty as he overlooked the draw. The creek was mostly frozen, but there was a small trickle of water flowing along a sandbar that kept that spot from freezing. Bud could see fresh tracks where a big coyote had crossed across the ice just before he had arrived.

About an hour passed, and Bud hadn't got a shot at anything. Every so often, he would catch something stirring in the brush ahead but never could make out just what it was. He expected that if it was turkeys, he would have heard a cluck or yelp of some sort after an hour of patiently waiting. He decided to get up and try to sneak down the draw a little way, when he heard something crashing in the brush. As he looked up, he saw a barred owl come flying down the creek and land on a branch of a sycamore just above him. Within seconds, Bud decided a nice fat owl would taste mighty good after sitting out there in the cold all morning. He carefully picked up his rifle and went to take aim, but the owl took off.

"Damn." He watched the owl land on a cedar branch, and he hesitated for a second, wondering if the owl was out of range or not. If he chanced the shot and missed, it was very possible that the echo of the shot would scare off any game within hearing distance.

He studied the owl for several minutes in hopes that he would get curious and come flying back within shooting range. He sat as still as he possibly could and watched the owl as he stared him down, never once taking his eyes off of him. It was a staring match for what seemed like an eternity.

All of a sudden, Bud heard a twig snap off to his left, and at that very second the owl jumped from his perch and landed on a branch about fifty yards in front of Bud. He slowly raised his trusty Winchester and took careful aim. The owl studied him cautiously and made the fatal mistake of looking behind him just long enough for Bud to put his sight right on his neck. Bud carefully pulled the hammer back on his rifle and squeezed the trigger, and the shot rang out and echoed down the creek. The owl tumbled to the snowy ground below and feathers slowly drifted across the creek.

"Got him," Bud whispered. He got to his feet and dusted the snow off his trousers and walked over to his kill. As he picked up the owl, he smiled. He was proud of his shot placement. He had made a good clean shot. The owl was dead before he hit the ground. He saddled up and pressed forward in search of the turkeys.

BACK TO THE east, Levi had finally come across some fresh tracks in the snow that followed the creek bed. "Lookie there, ol' girl," he said softly to Star. "Finally found them slick ol' birds." He pulled Star to a stop and looked around and studied the tracks for a minute. "Looks like there's five or six of them critters head down the creek."

He gently kicked Star and began to walk along just a bit further to see if he could ride to the top of the bluff and get a good vantage point to see a good distance down the creek. Star snorted and breathed heavily as he pushed her to the top of the ridge.

As they reached the top, he stopped and glanced at the creek bottom below, hoping to spot the flock of turkeys held up somewhere. Just ahead stood several tall cottonwood and sycamore trees that made the perfect spot for the turkeys to roost.

There wasn't a bird to be seen, but he heard a cluck and a yelp. He stopped for a second and looked around to see if he could pinpoint where the sound had come from. Once again, he heard a yelp, and he realized the flock was just over the ridge in front of him.

He quickly dismounted and walked Star over to the side of the hill and out of sight, then pulled his shotgun out of the scabbard and ran over and took cover next to a large oak tree at the base of the hill. He sat down with the tree against his back and commenced to waiting patiently to see if the flock would come over the rise and into shooting range. Every few minutes a hen would let out a yelp, and Levi could tell after a while that the turkeys were not moving at all. They were just hanging out on the ridge in the snow.

After about a half an hour, Levi decided to try something different…something he had never done before. He began trying to imitate a hen turkey clucking and yelping with his mouth. As he did, a sudden hush came over the whole prairie. The turkeys went dead silent, and Levi was sure he had just messed up his whole hunt.

A couple minutes later, though, the flock of turkeys appeared at the top of the hill. They had heard his call and decided to investigate. For several minutes, they stood at the top of the hill and looked around to see what had made the call. The boss hen raised her head and stretched her neck tall and gave out three single yelps, trying to get Levi to answer her.

Levi stayed as still as he could, his heart racing. He could see two large toms with three hens, all with their heads up high and staring down the hill.

They were just out of range for his shotgun, so he sat still and waited, praying they would come down the hill. He wished he had brought his Winchester.

After several minutes had gone by, the turkeys began to get wise. They had stood atop the hill and overlooked the whole creek bottom and could not see what had made the call. They started getting spooked and had begun to go back over the ridge when they spotted Star. Levi watched carefully as they threw their heads up and started clucking and fixing to take off. He carefully raised his shotgun and prepared to take aim if they turned back and came down the hill.

Suddenly, the boss hen tucked her head down and quickly headed down the hill straight past Levi. Levi took careful aim and placed the bead on the hen's head and readied himself for a shot. Just as he did, he saw the other two hens coming quickly, waddling their way through the snow. As Levi readied himself, he saw the two toms following along behind the hens. Each one of them supported a long coarse beard and had the prettiest red, white, and blue head. The snow was up to their bellies almost, and they struggled to walk down the hill.

Levi placed the bead of his shotgun right on one of the tom's heads and slowly cocked the hammers back. As the hens passed by not five feet in front of him, he began to breathe heavily, and his heart raced something fierce. Just as the first tom walked right in front of him, he squeezed the trigger and the tom began flopping in the snow. The hens took off flying, and the second tom took off running as quickly as he could through the snow. Levi jumped up and swung his shotgun around and pulled the second trigger, knocking the tom to the ground. He quickly jacked open the shotgun and kicked the empty shells out and replaced them with new ones. He ran over and grabbed the second bird and picked him up by the feet.

"By golly." The tom had spurs that were easily an inch and a half long, and his beard was pushing twelve inches long. He had to weigh near twenty pounds. He walked over and set the tom on the ground and inspected the other bird. This bird was just about the same size.

Levi smiled and picked the birds up and walked over to Star. "Well, now, what ya think of that, ol' girl?" He tied the turkeys over the saddle and mounted up and set out for the ranch.

LATER THAT EVENING, everyone finally arrived back at the cabin and Samantha helped the boys clean their harvest. Bud had brought home the owl along with a cottontail rabbit, and Mike had brought home two squirrels, one that was shot to pieces. The rest of the boys had come home with nothing more than a crow. It was quite a feast.

Chapter 24

Levi woke Samantha with a smile. "Good mornin', darlin'. It's Christmas Eve."

Samantha wiped the sleep from her eyes. "Good mornin', Levi. You're up awful early."

Levi sat up. "What do you say we get dressed and head out and find us the perfect tree for our first Christmas? We can cut a tree and bring it back and decorate it up and hang stockings over the fireplace for Saint Nick."

Samantha gave a small grin. "If you wish, my love."

Levi was excited to be spending their first Christmas together. He hadn't gotten the chance to spend the holidays with anyone besides Star in a long, long time. Samantha didn't seem so excited, though. "What's wrong, darlin'?"

"Nothing, my love…just tired is all."

He could tell something was the matter but figured that some fresh air and holiday spirit would be just the trick for her to really smile again, the kind of smile that reached her eyes and made them sparkle.

After breakfast, they put on their coats, gloves, and scarves and grabbed the saw and set out in the buckboard. Levi was all smiles. It was bitter cold out, and Samantha's nose was cherry red as he leaned over and kissed it gently. They pressed on along the creek looking over several different cedar trees, but none of them seemed to fit Levi's expectations. After a couple hours of searching what seemed danged near every single cedar tree on the whole entire ranch, Levi pointed at a big cedar along the creek bank. "There it is, darlin'. It's simply perfect. What do ya think?"

Samantha looked the tree over. "If you wish. It seems rather big, don't it?"

Levi looked up the tree. "Nonsense. I aim to find you the perfect tree, and, by golly, I reckon this here tree is the best danged tree on the whole ranch. Hell, it's probably the best damn tree in the whole territory."

Samantha smiled as Levi walked over and took the saw from the wagon and began to cut the tree down.

After they had loaded the tree in the wagon, they headed back to the cabin. Levi dragged the tree up the porch, then struggled to fit it through the front door. "Damnation, it's a bit bigger than I had figured," Levi said as he wedged it in the doorway.

Samantha chuckled. "Hmm…told ya it was awfully big, didn't I?" She helped him squeeze it through the door and place it in the corner. After they got it set up, Levi trimmed it the best that he could, making quite a mess of needles on the wood floor. Samantha swept them up with a broom and threw them off the porch.

Later that day, Levi decorated the tree while Samantha sat in her rocker staring off into space. She hadn't acted quite the same for the past month. Levi worried about her every day. He tried everything he knew to make her smile. She just seemed like her mind was a million miles away some days.

That night in bed, Levi held her in a tight embrace. He kissed her on the forehead and said softly, "Darlin', I don't know where I'd be without you. You're my everything, Samantha. I hope you know that. I love you with all my heart and soul. God surely blessed me the day he sent you to me. You truly saved me."

Samantha rolled over and kissed him and they made love until they finally fell asleep.

THE NEXT MORNING was Christmas morning, and Levi woke Samantha with a gentle kiss upon the forehead. "Mornin', sunshine," he said as she opened her eyes. Levi had gotten up early to prepare breakfast for her and the boys, and the whole cabin smelled of the finest feast of fresh eggs and buttermilk biscuits with homemade blackberry jam and fresh cut ham. The smell of kerosene burning from a lamp in the kitchen drifted through the house. The winter breeze blew across the yard and whistled through a crack in the door. It caused the porch swing to swing and creak. A rooster crowed from the henhouse.

As Samantha dressed, Levi put on his coat and went outside to fetch the boys for breakfast. Dally rushed out the door and took off to visit her friend Sage. After breakfast, Samantha and Christine began to prepare Christmas dinner while the men went out to tend to the chores. As Bud and Mike took the boys out to check on the herd, Levi asked Cody to come along with him and help chop ice on water tanks and feed the horses. He hadn't really gotten a chance to talk with him without Christine around. Seemed like she was always right on his shirttails and never let the poor fellow breathe on his own.

"Cody, you know, that's quite a wife ya got there, pardner," Levi said as he began to work on the ice.

Cody raked it out while Levi chopped it. "Yeah, she's a regular pain in the ass sometimes."

Levi chuckled. "So tell me somethin', pard. How come y'all decided to stay in Wilmington instead of returning home?"

Cody hesitated before he spoke. "Didn't really have much to go home to. I've been out of a job for some time now, and Christine well...that's another story. We never really stayed in one place too long. We always seem to move on from town to town and never settle down. I tell ya, Levi, it gets mighty old not havin' a place to call your own. Lots of times we have to sleep on the cold ground in the alley somewhere and eat scraps from behind the café."

Levi looked into Cody's eyes and felt sorrow for this man. He seemed like a decent man that had been dealt a cheater's hand. He may not have been the sharpest fellow in the territory, but he was friendly.

Levi continued chopping ice. "Tell me, Cody, what's the story behind Lawrence?"

Cody instantly stopped raking out the ice. "Whatever do you mean, Levi? Lawrence, you say? I don't recall ever bein' there before."

Levi set his ax down and got right in Cody's face. He looked him dead in the eye, but Cody's eyes kept darting away. "You lie to me again, pardner," Levi said in a hard voice, "and I'll fire your ass right here and now and send you on your way down the trail, you understand me?"

Cody looked at him and then looked down at the water tank. Levi put his finger under Cody's chin and pushed his face up. "Boy, you look at me when I'm talkin' to ya. When someone speaks to ya, ya look them in the eyes and stand up tall, ya hear? You got nothin' to be ashamed of. You're no less of a man than the next fella."

Cody looked Levi in the eyes and gritted his teeth. "Yes sir, Levi." He stood up tall.

"Now, that's better," Levi said. "Now, tell me about Lawrence."

Cody hesitated. "Lawrence, huh?"

Levi shook his head. "I ran into a Buffalo Soldier sometime back and he said that he was trailin' a fella that had deserted the Calvary and was arrested in Lawrence. This fella said that the man's wife helped him escape and murdered a guard."

Cody's eyes widened.

Levi looked him dead in the eye. "Pard, desertion was a hangin' offense last time I recalled."

Cody's eyes filled with tears.

"Wipe your eyes, pardner. Not everyone is perfect. Hell, I've seen and done things in my life most folks would just assume my neck be stretched for. I don't hold anything against ya. Your secret is safe with me." He reached out his hand, and Cody shook it.

"I'm right obliged to ya, Levi, sir, for everything. I won't let you down. I can assure you that."

"I appreciate all your hard work around here. Iffen weren't for you joinin' up with us, I don't reckon we'd make it through the winter."

Cody smiled. "I'll be here until ya give us the boot or shoot us."

They both shared a laugh and then continued with their chores.

After Cody and Levi had finished chopping ice, Levi turned to Cody. "Pardner, I gotta make a quick run into town. Care to join me?"

Cody smiled. "You bet. I'll go fetch the wagon."

Levi stopped him. "Hold it, pard. Instead of takin' the wagon, I got somethin' else in mind, seein' how it's Christmas and all. Follow me for a minute. I could use a hand here." Levi headed to the barn, and Cody followed.

When they walked inside, Levi said, "See that saddle over there in the corner?"

Cody turned. "Yes sir."

"Go fetch it, will ya?" Levi walked into a stall and put a bridle on the blue roan filly that he had spent countless days working that past summer.

Cody walked over and grabbed the saddle. "This is a right nice piece of leather, Levi. Fine work, I'd say."

Levi led the filly out of the stall. "Alright, throw that saddle on her and see how she fits."

Cody walked over and swung the saddle on the filly. As he tightened the cinch, he said, "Decide to give Star a break for the day, did ya?"

Levi shook his head and grinned. "No sir."

Cody turned around. "Then why did ya have me throw a saddle on this filly here?"

"Take a look under there, pard." Levi pointed at the bottom side of the gullet on the saddle.

Cody walked around the filly and looked under the gullet. "It says 'C.S.' I don't understand, Levi."

Levi looked him in the eye. "I spent a lot of time with this here filly. She's still got a ways to go and needs a lot of miles under her hooves, but I reckon she'll turn out to be the best companion you'll ever have."

Cody looked at Levi with a confused look on his face. "What are ya gettin' at, Levi?"

Levi handed him the reins. "I'm makin' you a gift of this here horse and saddle. You deserve a second chance at life, and this here horse is a fresh start."

Cody stood there for a moment, clearly in shock. He looked over the horse and saddle and with tear-filled eyes said, "I can't pay you for all this, Levi."

Levi smiled. "I'm not askin' ya to. It's Christmas, friend. Now get your ass in that saddle and let's get to town."

Cody reached his hand out to Levi and shook his hand. "Thank ya kindly, Levi. I'm right proud to have met ya and made your acquaintance. I never had a friend like you."

The two saddled up and set out for Wilmington. As they rode into town, they headed for the mercantile. Levi wanted to pick something nice up for Samantha and the boys for Christmas, but he wasn't sure just what to get. He knew it was awfully late to be getting his gifts, but ranch life had seemed to have gotten the best of him and it wasn't till now that he had been able to make it over there. Many of the businesses weren't open this close to the holiday, but the storekeeper's wife had passed several weeks ago, so he didn't have anyone to take off and spend the time with. They tied their horses up at the hitching post out front and then walked inside.

As they entered, a bell that hung over the door rang out and the storekeeper walked out from the back. "Well, Merry Christmas to ya, lads, what brings you out on this holiday afternoon?" A picture of his wife now hung behind the counter, in place of where she had often greeted customers in the past.

Cody browsed around that store and Levi said, "Howdy, Merry Christmas. I'm lookin' for somethin' for my gal and wanted to get a gift for my ranch hands but ain't too sure what to get. Any ideas?"

The storekeeper walked him over to a glass case and showed Levi some of the latest jewelry fashions he had. "These are beautiful mother of pearl earrings that come all the way from Sweden. They are a lovely piece that I'm sure your lady would admire."

Levi looked through the various pieces of jewelry and pointed a pair of earrings that stood out to him. "What about these?"

The storekeeper pulled them out. "Ah…these are a delicacy, son. These are of the finest quality. Genuine opal and silver earrings, and they come with this beautiful matching opal and silver necklace as well." The man reached down in the case and pulled out a lovely necklace and placed it on the counter.

Levi picked it up and looked at its beauty for several minutes. He imagined what it might look like on Samantha's neck. He smiled. "I'll take it."

The storekeeper looked up and shook his head. "I didn't even tell you how much they cost, sir."

Levi grinned. "No, you didn't now, did ya?"

Cody was admiring all the different styles of hats they carried in stock. Levi looked around and had trouble deciding what to buy the boys for Christmas. The storekeeper walked around showing him various watches and boots, but Levi wanted to get each one something special to show them his appreciation for all their hard work and devotion to him and the ranch. "What do you got in stock for coats and gloves?"

The storekeeper walked him over to a rack in the corner and showed him several various wool coats of all different sizes. Levi looked them over and thought to himself just how many coats he would need. He counted the coats on the rack and noticed that there were two short of what he needed. "Damn. Iffen ya had a couple more of these I reckon they'd do just fine."

The storekeeper raised his hand. "Hold that thought, you may be in luck. I may just happen to have some in the back. Wait here and I'll check."

As he walked to the back, Levi walked back to the case with the jewelry in it and admired the opal necklace and earrings. He was sure Samantha would love them.

The storekeeper came out and laid two wool coats on the counter. "Mister, you're in luck. I just happened to have these last two in stock."

Levi grinned. "Well, looks like it's my lucky day. I'll take them and ten sets of gloves iffen ya got 'em."

The storekeeper gathered the coats and gloves together. "Anything else for you today, sir?"

Levi smiled. "As a matter of fact, there is. I'm still waitin' on you to tell me a price on those earrings and necklace…"

The storekeeper chuckled. "Certainly. That set will run fourteen dollars and ninety cents, and you won't find a better deal around."

Levi didn't hesitate. "I'll take it."

The storekeeper smiled. "Splendid, sir."

As the man was figuring up the total cost, Cody walked over. Seeing him eye the tobacco, Levi said, "Might as well throw in a few things of that tobaccy too." The storekeeper added it to the bill and Levi paid the man. "I thank ya kindly, sir. Have yourself a Merry Christmas."

As they left, Levi spotted something in the corner that caught his attention. "Well, now," he said curiously. "What do we have here?" He closed the door and walked to the front window. There was a six-string guitar, and many a good memory he held close to his heart came rushing back. He walked over and carefully picked it up and gently strummed it to hear its old familiar sound. Boy, did it sound pretty.

The storekeeper walked over. "That's a genuine 1869 Brazilian Rosewood six-string."

"I see that," Levi replied as he strummed the strings and made a beautiful little tune. "Where did ya come by it?"

"To tell ya the truth, son, we ordered it outta Springfield, Missouri, but ain't had anyone show any interest but yourself."

Levi admired the wood finish and the way the neck felt in his hands. "How much ya askin' for it?"

"Fifteen even."

Levi loved music and really enjoyed sitting around the fire after supper and playing the guitar and singing songs with the other cowboys on the drives north. He'd often thought about buying himself an old guitar but had not come across one in quite some time. He inspected the guitar once more. "I'll give you ten dollars flat."

The storekeeper didn't bat an eye. "You play that thing mighty purty. I never learned myself, but always wanted to. I'd like that guitar to go to someone who will appreciate it, and I reckon that person just might be yourself. Ten, you say? You got yourself a deal, son."

THAT EVENING, THEY all shared one of the most enjoyable Christmas dinners they had ever had. The house smelled of smoke from the fireplace and kerosene from the oil lamps and fresh cooked turkey and beans and biscuits with homemade jam, potatoes, ham, and green beans that Samantha had canned. As they sat around the table enjoying the wonderful food and good company, they shared many cherished stories, most of which were probably a bit far-fetched, but nobody seemed to mind, and everyone got a kick out of listening. Laughter echoed through the cabin and brought a sense of peace and joy to the ranch that cold night.

After supper, everyone gathered around the fireplace and told stories of Christmases past. Then Levi walked out and, with the help of Cody, brought in all the gifts for everyone. First, he passed out all the coats and gloves to all the cowboys and then reached into his saddlebags and pulled out a bag of tobacco and tossed it to Christine. "Merry Christmas, y'all."

He gave Samantha her gift, and she teared up. "Oh, Levi, it's beautiful."

"Do you really like it, darlin'?"

Samantha turned around for Levi to help her put the necklace on and then put on the earrings. "How do they look?"

Everyone smiled and whistled and hollered as Samantha blushed. Levi looked her in the eyes. "Darlin', you look just...amazingly beautiful."

He walked over and grabbed the guitar, then sat down on the floor in front of the fireplace and began to strum and sing a few old familiar Christmas songs. Soon everyone that knew the words joined in, and before long even Dally was howling along. It was the perfect Christmas. Levi wouldn't ask for anything different. He was with the woman of his dreams and his true friends. He was quite content.

JANUARY ARRIVED, BRINGING another foot of snow across the ranch. The cowboys had their work cut out for them the next few weeks now that calving season was beginning. Everyone was mighty busy, and each hand prayed for an early spring. The past couple days, everyone had been worn down from many restless and sleepless nights tending to several calving mothers that were expected to deliver anytime. It was easy to say that everyone was dog-tired and ready for warmer weather.

On the second of January, Samantha came to Levi in the kitchen and said, "I don't reckon we have enough meat left in the icehouse to get by another week."

Levi took off his hat and ran his fingers through his hair and scratched his head. "We really went through that much already?"

Samantha nodded and wiped her face with her apron. "Since you took on Cody and Christine, our rations ain't been keepin' us that long. That damn woman can put away food."

Levi chuckled. "Well, I reckon I'll have to go out in the mornin' and see if I can fetch me a deer or two. I'd send Mike out, but I can't afford to spare him right now with all these first-time cows ready to drop anytime." He looked out the window at the snow-covered prairie. "I reckon I'll set out at first light and see what I can round up. I saw a good buck with a bunch of does just north of the creek yesterday mornin'. No tellin' where he'll be tomorrow, but I reckon I'll just have to see if I can pick up his track."

Levi grabbed his saddlebags and proceeded to prepare for the next day's hunt. He loaded a box of cartridges and some jerky and his skinning knife and grabbed his rope and settled down for the night.

The next morning, he put on his coat and gloves and kissed Samantha goodbye and set out for the barn to saddle up Star and throw a pack saddle on one of the other horses. After he saddled up and rode out of the barn, Bud met him in the yard. "You want me to ride along, Boss?"

Levi looked down at him. "I can't afford to spare ya this mornin', Bud. I need ya here tendin' to the herd. I'll be back to help as soon as I can round somethin' up."

Bud reached up and shook Levi's hand. "Good luck to ya, Boss."

Levi nodded. "Much obliged, pard, I'll need it."

He set out along the creek headed west for a piece, then cut north to where he had seen the whitetail buck the other day. It hadn't snowed since the morning before, so it would be a bit easier to track a deer if he were to come across any fresh signs.

A couple hours passed, and Levi still had not seen any sign of the buck. He had come across several fresh coyote tracks and some rabbit, but not a single deer. He pressed on, venturing northwest and watching the snow for any sign that he could find. The sky was gray and cloudy, and the wind was bitter cold. Every so often, the sun would pop out behind the clouds but would only stay for a couple minutes before disappearing again.

Levi finally came across a set of tracks in the snow. "There he is!" he whispered to Star. "I knew he had to be out here somewhere." Levi studied the tracks for several minutes and spotted a spot in the snow in a ditch where the buck had bedded down about an hour before. "Mighty fresh, ol' girl. Looks like he was here not long ago, takin' himself a li'l nap." He studied the area closely, trying to pick up his tracks and figure out which way he had gone from the ditch. There were three other sets of fresh tracks with him, so Levi expected there were does traveling with the buck.

After several minutes, he finally picked up the buck's tracks and figured they had headed north. He gave Star a gentle kick and cautiously rode along leading his packhorse, trying to spot the deer before they spotted him. As he rode along, he kept watching the tracks and could tell they were getting fresher. He figured they were not far ahead of him at all. Quietly, he pressed on until he saw a small grove of trees. He got down from the saddle and carefully examined the trees ahead, then looked at the tracks below, and he knew for sure the deer had to be bedded up in the ditch just ahead. He could see for a good distance all the way around the ditch, and the tracks were fresh enough that he could tell they had to be held up there.

He pulled his Winchester from its scabbard and quietly jacked a shell into the chamber and carefully released the hammer. He got down on his knee and studied the tracks one last time, deciding where he should set up to watch the ditch in hopes the buck would show himself sooner or later. He snuck around downwind, along the south side of the ditch, and tried to ease his way through the brush to get within shooting range of where he expected the deer to be bedded up. He walked about forty yards before deciding he had better set up behind an old fallen cottonwood tree. If he went much further up the ditch, he knew he would spook the deer for sure. He tied Star and his packhorse up to a stump over the ditch out of sight, and quietly crept forward to the cottonwood, trying to walk as quietly as possible. His boots crunched in the snow, and he eased his way to the tree, then sat down and prepared to wait.

The wind picked up and began to howl across the prairie. A tumbleweed broke loose from its roots and commenced to bouncing across the prairie, picking up speed the further it went. A red-tailed hawk fought to glide overhead as it searched for its afternoon snack. Levi pulled his collar up on his jacket and blocked his face with his wild rag and tucked himself down behind the tree, trying to block himself from the bitter cold northern wind.

A couple hours passed, and Levi didn't see any sign of the deer. He was certain they were bedded up in the ditch but had seen no movement since he had arrived. He reached into his pocket and pulled out a strip of buffalo jerky. When he looked up, he saw a flash of something just ahead of him about sixty yards in the brush. He slowly took a bite of the jerky and placed the rest back into his pocket and studied the spot where he had seen movement. As he watched carefully, he saw a flash again. It was the flicker of a white tail.

Levi's blood began to flow, and excitement filled his heart. As he looked harder, he spotted a deer standing on the side of the ditch under a patch of cedars. He couldn't make out if it was a buck or doe, but he could tell it was a deer. Every few minutes, the deer would flicker its tail. Levi patiently waited for it to step out of the brush. For the next half hour or so, the deer stood there feeding along the ditch. Levi continued waiting in hopes that the buck would stand up and walk out into the open and present him a fine shot.

About an hour later, he was getting restless. Where he was set up, he could see every way in and out of the draw, so he knew the deer were still held up in the ditch, and they were not in any hurry to show themselves. Several times, Levi contemplated the idea of crawling up the ditch and seeing if he could get lucky enough to spot the buck and get a shot off before he spotted him. If it hadn't had been for the snow, he probably would have tried a stalk, but he knew that the chances were slim to none of him sneaking up on this mature buck without being seen or heard.

The wind suddenly died down to a complete standstill, and not a sound was heard across the prairie for several minutes. The silence broke when Levi looked up to the spot where he had seen the last movement and caught a flicker of something out of the corner of his eye. He froze, still not wanting to be seen. He looked ahead and caught a second flicker of movement from his left and slowly turned his head to see what it was. As he did, his heart sank in his chest. He started to shake all over and began to breathe heavily. About forty yards to his left stood the massive whitetail buck staring him in the eye, frozen like a statue. Somehow the buck had snuck out of the brush without making a sound and had pinpointed Levi but wasn't sure just what he was. The buck raised his head high and locked his ears forward, listening for any sound that would alarm him and the does and send them running off across the prairie in search of a new hiding spot.

Levi's heart raced as he looked out of the corner of his eye and saw his rifle lying on the ground beside him. He had set it down briefly so he could grab the jerky and hadn't had the chance to pick it back up. Now he was caught dead to rights and had no idea just how he would be able to pick up the rifle and take aim without being seen by the buck. As he looked back at the buck, he saw him begin to stomp his feet in the snow and blow, alarming the does that there was possible danger in the area. The does began to blow from the brush, and, though Levi couldn't see them, he could hear them in the cedars.

Still focused on the buck, he inched his hand toward his rifle, the buck watching his every move. He lowered his head, then threw it back up, snorting and blowing and making all sorts of racket. About that time, a big doe stepped out behind him and stared Levi down as well. They had him busted. Levi felt the stock of his rifle in his fingertips and knew it wasn't going to be easy picking it up without spooking everything out of the county.

Out of nowhere, two does came barging out of the cedars and stopped atop the hill to look back toward Levi. As they did, the buck jumped and turned his head to look toward them. Levi quickly picked up his rifle and took aim. Just then, the buck turned his head back and went to bolt out of the ditch. Levi cocked the hammer back and placed the sight right on the buck's shoulder. The doe that had spotted him took off running and blowing up the hill, and the buck threw up his tail and turned his head to run. Levi carefully squeezed the trigger, sending a bullet deep into the buck right behind his front shoulder. The buck kicked his back legs up high and took off up the hill, through the cedars and out of sight. Levi jumped up and jacked another shell into the chamber and waited for the buck to run out the other side of the draw, but he never did. Levi began to shake uncontrollably.

After waiting about twenty minutes, Levi got up and quietly snuck up to where the buck was standing when he shot him. He spotted blood in the snow and began to track the blood trail. By the amount and color of the blood, Levi was sure he had made a good clean heart shot. He slowly continued on, working his way through the hillside covered with cedars. He saw a spot where the buck had stopped briefly on the edge of the brush and had searched for a place to hide. Blood had poured all over the snow where the buck had stood. Levi was sure he wouldn't travel much further. He pressed on and came to the top of the small ridge and looked down and noticed the blood trail venturing back to the north toward a nearby pond. As he looked down the ditch below the pond, he spotted the buck lying in the snow.

Relief and contentment overcame him. By harvesting this buck, they would be able to get by for a while longer. Levi walked up to the buck and carefully tapped him on the hindquarter with his boot. Once he was sure the animal was dead, he walked back to fetch the horses.

When he came back shortly after, he picked up the buck by his large antlers. He was a jim-dandy for sure, a big twelve-point brute with a long Roman nose and massive chocolate-colored antlers. Levi was sure proud of his harvest, and he knew Samantha would be thankful that he returned with fresh meat for the icehouse. He dressed the buck and loaded him onto his packhorse and then set out for the ranch. He was excited to return and show Bud and the boys his trophy buck and see the smile on Samantha's face when he brought her news of his success.

He felt the smile plastered across his face. He loved the thrill of a good hunt. The challenge and the reward and lessons learned always kept him pushing forward and gave him a certain kind of respect for the wildlife and the land. He enjoyed being outdoors, and he cherished his memories of his past hunts with his pa and his grandfather. Griz had taught him how to hunt and fish as a boy growing up in the Kansas territory. He often recalled when his pa would ride off to Topeka and leave him at his grandfather's homestead for a few days. Griz would load him down with a box of cartridges and send him out with a scattergun and tell him to shoot all the starlings and blackbirds that he could. When Levi arrived back at the cabin with a mess of birds, Griz would take him down to the creek or the pond and they would catch a mess of bass and bullheads for their supper. They would often catch a big old mean snapping turtle, and Griz would skin it and cook it up with some fresh cabbage from the garden. Levi couldn't stomach the smell of cabbage, but he loved the taste of turtle. He knew Griz would be right proud of him for harvesting this fine buck. He missed Griz something horrible. He missed being a little boy. He missed his family in general. He was excited to start a new family of his own with the love of his life, though. Just the thought of it brought a smile to his face.

As he rode along, mushing through the snow-covered prairie, he looked up and saw a large furry coyote. The coyote was sitting on a rock in the distance, watching him. A flock of snow geese flew overhead, headed south, and passed over the nearby pond since it was frozen. Levi sat tall in the saddle as he pushed the horses through the snow and back toward the ranch. It had begun to snow again, and Levi watched as big crystal-like snowflakes softly landed on the snowy ground. Levi was mighty thankful his hunt was over so he could return home and warm up in front of the fireplace and drink himself a hot cup of coffee. He loved a good hunt in the snow, but his arthritic body longed for a hot bath and hot coffee in front of the fire.

As he pushed on, he noticed the snow had covered up his tracks from before, leaving a fresh blanket of snow across the prairie. He spotted fresh bobcat tracks along the creek and knew Mike would be excited. Levi followed the tracks to the creek bank and watched where the cat had crossed the ice and met up with another bobcat. The price of bobcat hides was sky-high that year, and Levi scouted the area as he rode on back toward the ranch. There were a few thick brushy areas along Soldier Creek that looked mighty promising for trapping. All along the creek, Levi spotted several squirrel and rabbit tracks. They were both plentiful along the creek, and Levi thought a mess of rabbits would be right fine for supper later that week. He planned to return with Mike in the next couple of days to see what they could find.

Chapter 25

As Levi crossed the creek just west of the cabin, he saw a set of wagon tracks headed toward the south. He pulled Star to a stop and studied the tracks for a minute and then headed for the house. He couldn't figure out just who would be out in this cold in a wagon, but he didn't pay it any mind. As he rode across the pasture, he noticed the wagon tracks were coming from the cabin. He followed them all the way to the yard, wondering who had stopped by to pay a visit.

As he passed by the corral and rode up into the yard, he spotted Bud and Mike sitting on the porch steps in the cold. "Howdy, boys! Y'all missed quite a hunt!" Levi hollered out.

Bud and Mike looked at each other but didn't say a word. Levi grinned and shook his head. "Come take a look at this fine buck I shot."

Bud and Mike remained seated and Levi felt a chill run down his spine. Something wasn't right. "What in the hell's the matter with you girls? Am I workin' ya too hard?"

Bud looked at Mike and then looked at the ground. Levi's smile disappeared. He looked down at the wagon tracks and saw footprints going in and out of the cabin. He looked around. "It appears we had company."

Bud continued to stare at the ground. Levi studied the tracks. They came from the barn and led up to the house, then headed south across the creek. His heart seemed to beat more slowly than usual as he looked at the tracks leading in and out of the cabin again. "What in the hell is goin' on here, boys?"

Mike looked Levi in the eyes but didn't say a word. Bud continued staring at the ground and shook his head. A very uneasy feeling came over Levi. Levi looked up to the bedroom window in the cabin and then looked back at the wagon tracks leading across the creek. "No…" he said through gritted teeth. "Oh, God, no…" He jumped down from Star and rushed up the porch steps. As he placed his hand on the door handle, he looked back at the brothers. Bud's eyes never strayed from the ground, and Mike stared across the yard.

Levi walked inside and took his hat in his hand and stood in the doorway for a minute. He noticed right off that Samantha's boots were not sitting by the door where she usually left them. He called her name, and an old familiar feeling came over him when he heard nothing but the bitter cold wind blowing the shutters against the house. Without taking off his snowy boots, he slowly walked upstairs. Just before he opened the bedroom door, he whispered a prayer. "Oh, please, God…please, God." He opened the door and his heart sank as he looked around the room. The closet that had held Samantha's dresses was now empty and bare. "Oh, God, no…please, God, no." Levi's hands began to shake as he rushed downstairs.

He stood there for a moment, shaking uncontrollably. Everything of Samantha's was gone. He sat down in his wooden rocker for a minute to try to contain himself and figure out just what was going on. After a couple minutes, he looked across the room and noticed something sitting on the kitchen table. He got up and walked over and saw a folded piece of paper with Samantha's ring placed on top. His name was written on the outside of the paper. Levi's eyes instantly filled with tears. "Good God, no…" he cried. With shaking hands, he placed the ring on his pinkie finger while he slowly opened the folded paper. He couldn't seem to catch his breath. He was in a state of shock. Surely this wasn't happening. Maybe the letter would say she had just stepped out for a minute and would be back. Maybe she was worried about her ring getting caught on her rifle and that's why she'd had to take it off? He wiped the tears from his eyes as he began to read what she had written.

Dearest Levi,

I'm truly sorry to have done this while you were away. Truth is, I've been doing a lot of thinking and soul searching lately. A lot has been on my mind. As you must know by now, I am not happy. I feel as if we may have rushed into this love too quickly, and I deeply regret walking out on you. However, I believe that it is time for us to simply take a step back and simply humbly assess ourselves. I need to think about what is best for me and for this child, and being here is not what is best at this time. I ask for you to not come search for me. Please let me be, Levi.

Samantha Parker

Levi dropped the letter to the cabin floor and began to weep hysterically. His heart was shattered beyond imagining. He suddenly got the shakes so bad that he struck his knees and cried out loudly, "Oh, God, why? What in the hell did I do to deserve this? Why me?"

Levi buried his face in his hands and cried for several minutes, harder than he had in many years. Where did he go wrong? Should he try to go find her? Where would she go? Would she ever return? What about their child? He was devastated and broken and confused. Samantha and he had struck up a friendship and love that was truly hard to come by right from the start. There was much more than just a physical attraction between these two souls that made what they had more genuine and special, or so Levi thought. He had been in love before and felt the devastation of loss and heartache when she was taken from him. He swore off love and romance the day they laid her in the ground. Once he met Samantha, everything had suddenly changed. His whole life had changed with just one look. He had planned to spend the rest of his life being devoted and in love with her. He would have given everything he had just to make her smile. He could tell something had seemed different about Samantha since she found out that she was expecting a child. He had tried so hard to keep that unique and beautiful smile on her face. She would grin on occasion, but that genuine smile that stole Levi's heart that first day back in Council Grove had seemed to drift away.

As Levi sat there on his knees crying like a child in the kitchen, he heard Bud ask Mike, "Brother, why do you reckon Miss Samantha took off like that?"

"I don't rightly know, brother. Womenfolk have always been a mystery that I've yet to understand." Levi could hear frustration in his voice.

Levi sat there, clutching Samantha's letter tightly in his hand. Pain gripped his heart as he continued to listen.

"Boss loves her more than I've ever saw any man love a woman," Bud said.

"Love is a powerful thing there, brother. I know Levi loves her dearly, there's no arguin' that, and I'm damn sure that Miss Samantha knows that as well. However, for some womenfolk a man could break his back to try to give her everything under the sun to make her happy and win her love but that still won't ever be good enough. Now, don't get me wrong, Miss Samantha is a fine woman. However, you and I both have noticed a change the past couple of weeks, and I'm sure Levi has noticed it as well."

Levi felt himself grow agitated. They all were well aware of what had happened, so why the hell did they need to keep talking about it? He buried his face in his hands, debating whether to storm out there and get them to shut their gobs or to just stay in here away from everything and be alone with his thoughts.

"Should we go in and talk to him?" Bud asked.

Mike replied solemnly, "We must stay here now. He needs to let it all out first. All his feelin's and troubles. Iffen he holds that all in, it will only make the outcome that much worse. Let him cry it out. When he comes out, we'll be here for him. Just make sure he knows we'll always have his back through thick and thin."

A few minutes later, Levi wiped the tears from his eyes and stood. He looked down at the letter and read the words again and teared up once more. He took Samantha's ring from his finger and placed it on the table, then looked at Samantha's wooden rocker in the living room in front of the fireplace. He envisioned her sitting there, rocking away as she worked on her beadwork. A tear slowly dripped from his eye and ran down his cheek before falling to the hardwood floor. Levi placed the letter in his pocket and slowly walked over to the front door. He looked back at the stairs leading upstairs to the bedroom and lowered his head and walked out the door.

As he walked outside, he looked at Bud and Mike sitting on the porch. "She's gone boys, she's really gone."

Mike nodded. "We know, Levi, we know. Everything will work out, pardner, you just keep your head now and be strong. You've been through much worse than this, although right now it may not seem like it."

Levi looked down at Bud. "By God, Bud, she's really gone…"

Bud shook his head and stared at the ground, as if he couldn't stand to see his hurt. Levi's eyes continued to shed unstoppable tears of heartache no matter how hard he fought it. For several minutes Levi stood on the porch staring at the wagon tracks driving away from the ranch. He was lost for words. He never expected Samantha would leave him. He couldn't stomach the thought of losing her. He stood there staring across the prairie watching the wagon tracks as they slowly disappeared into the snow.

Levi sat down next to Bud on the steps. "Is she really gone, Bud? Ya reckon she'll come to her senses and come home soon?"

Bud looked at him, and Levi saw the look in his eyes. She was really gone, and he had no explanation as to why. He felt like a complete failure. At that moment he felt himself break again inside. "Oh, God…please, no!" he cried.

BUD LEANED OVER and put his arm around him, and Mike got up and sat on the other side of him and patted him on the back.

"Easy now, Boss," Bud said as he fought back the tears as well. He hated seeing Levi hurting the way he was. He didn't understand why Samantha had up and left without a word. He patted Levi on the back. "We're right here with ya, pard, we ain't goin' nowhere. We're gonna stand by ya through this. I mean it."

Mike lowered his head. "I'm truly sorry, Levi. I never figured Miss Samantha would run off and do such a thing. It just don't make sense."

Levi cried in Bud's arms for several minutes before Bud headed back to the bunkhouse. Inside, he saw Cody and Christine sitting with the other ranch hands.

Cody stood. "I reckon I better go find Miss Samantha and fetch her back."

Bud's started to stop him, but Christine grabbed him by the arm. "No, Cody, she needs to be left alone. As much as it's hurtin' Levi, he must let her go."

Cody looked at her. "But Levi is my friend. I must help him get her back."

Christine looked out the window at Levi. "Cody, Samantha has no intentions of returning, I assure you that."

Bud couldn't help but feel surprise. For once the crazy woman was actually making some sense.

Cody looked her in the eyes. "What on earth kinda hogwash is that, Christine? What in the hell do you mean she has no intentions of returning?"

"Intuition, I reckon. I've been expectin' her to leave for some time now. Honestly, I'm surprised she waited as long as she did."

Cody's jaw dropped. "What the hell, Christine? How did you know she was aimin' to leave?"

Christine shook her head. "When a gal gets a certain look in her eyes one day, like Samantha did, you can tell right off that she's a-waitin' the first stage to anywhere but where she's at."

Bud found himself thinking of Cheyenne. He assumed he had loved her almost as much as Levi had loved Samantha. Would she have left him too in time if the good Lord hadn't called her home? He wished that there was something he could do. He thought the world of Levi and really looked up to him and admired him. He felt helpless as they watched Levi's world slowly crashing down around him.

AS THE SUN went down, Levi got up and walked over to the porch swing. He turned his head and looked at his side and longed for Samantha something fierce. An empty feeling came over him as he realized she wouldn't sit there again. He looked out toward the barn where he watched Cody and Mike set to work on cleaning the buck he had shot.

Bud returned from the bunkhouse. "I reckon a pot of coffee would do us some good," Bud said before heading inside.

After a while, the temperature began to fall, yet Levi remained seated on the porch swing staring into the darkness. His hands cradled around the cup of coffee Bud had given him, but he still felt the cold creeping into his bones.

"Boss, you're gonna catch your death out here iffen ya ain't careful," Bud said. He must have noticed the goosebumps forming on Levi's arms as he went and grabbed a blanket and placed it on the swing next to Levi.

Levi just sat there staring at the creek crossing, praying that Samantha would return home. Bud was silent and as it grew later, he went inside, most likely to escape the chill.

THE NEXT MORNING, the sun broke its way through the clouds and cleared the skies for the day. Bud awoke with a stiff neck from falling asleep in the rocker. He got up and stretched and walked over to the window and looked outside. Levi was still sitting on the swing staring at the crossing. He looked like he hadn't slept a wink. Bud walked outside. "Damnation, Boss, you still alive out here? You're lucky you ain't caught your death of pneumonia out here all night." He looked down at the coffee cup he had brought Levi the night before and noticed Levi hadn't touched it at all. He walked over to Levi. "You alright, Boss?"

Levi turned his head and looked him in the eye. "Excuse me? Now what in the hell kinda damn question is that?"

Bud lowered his head. "I'm sorry, Boss. That was an ignorant question. I was just checkin' on ya, is all."

Levi shook his head. "Damn it. I'm sorry, Bud. I just can't…"

"I know, Boss," Bud said. "I know." Bud picked up the coffee cup and dumped it over the porch, then went inside to make a fresh pot.

For the better part of the day, Levi remained seated on the porch. He refused to go inside and face the cabin alone without Samantha there. Bud hung around the cabin with him while Mike and Cody and the rest of the hands and Christine set out to tend to the daily chores. Bud was afraid to leave Levi alone, for fear he might do something stupid. He knew in his heart just what Levi was feeling and he hated to see him go through it alone like he had himself once upon a time. He couldn't understand how he got through it alone himself when he had caught his sweetheart with the marshal. He also found himself thinking back to the devastation of coming upon the girl who had perished in the tornado and when he had watched Cheyenne take her last breath in his arms. It was a helpless and miserable feeling that he was sure he'd never overcome, and really couldn't expect Levi to either.

Later that afternoon, Bud walked out on the porch again. "Boss, why don't you and I take ourselves a li'l walk?"

Levi turned to him with tear-filled eyes. "If you wish, pardner."

Bud helped him off the swing and handed him a tin cup of hot coffee. This time Levi drank a few sips before setting the cup down. "Where we headed, Bud?"

Bud pointed toward the north. "Why don't we take a stroll up to that soldier feller's grave to the north?"

Levi agreed, and together they set out across the prairie. For the next few hours, Levi opened up to Bud about his feelings and his love for Samantha. As they reached Samuel Hunt's grave, the sun had gone down, and a full moon was shining bright over the snowy Kansas prairie. Levi gazed up to the moon and tears filled his tired eyes once again. He gritted his teeth and opened up to Bud about his past and told him stories that Bud had never heard before. Stories of his time in the War and the bloody and gruesome deeds that he had done while riding with Missouri guerillas. Stories of his childhood and how he had been abandoned by his own flesh and blood on the lone prairie when he was a boy and how he had grown mean and vengeful after that encounter. Some of the stories made Bud nauseous. He swallowed hard a few times to fight from vomiting.

Before they knew it, the night had drifted away in conversation and the sun was soon to rise. Bud was exhausted from not having slept worth a hoot for two nights, and he knew Levi's mind and body were physically and emotionally exhausted. Bud was sure Levi hadn't slept a wink since Samantha had left, and he knew he hadn't eaten anything at all.

AS THEY HEADED back to the cabin, Levi walked to the barn and opened the door and looked to see Lightning's stall empty. Levi felt as if he had a dagger stabbed right through the center of his broken heart. She had hitched Lightning to the buckboard and left without a single word of goodbye, with nothing more than a damn letter. Levi hit his knees and began crying once again as Bud walked over and put his hand on his shoulder. "Easy now, Boss. Everything will be alright. You really should try to get ya some rest, pardner."

Levi attempted to get to his feet but fell down, and Bud took him by the arm and helped him up. They walked over to the bunkhouse. "Come on, Boss," Bud said. "Come inside and take my bunk for a spell. Kick your feet up and rest some. I gotta tend to the horses, and then I'll be back to check on ya."

Levi walked inside and sat down on Bud's bunk and stared at the wall like a lost soul. Bud walked over and took his rope and chaps off the bunk. "Go on now, Boss, kick back and relax."

Levi stretched out and cried himself to sleep. He found himself dreaming of Council Grove and the days when he and Samantha had first met and courted along Elm Creek. He could see her face and her smile so clearly in his dreams.

Levi awoke as he heard a scuffle, and he sat up and stared at the door, realizing he must have slept the entire day away. He watched the boys all walk outside and decided he couldn't sleep anymore. He had to get up and move around. He had no motivation to do anything and no appetite to eat, but he just had to do something. He walked to the door and opened it and stared outside for several minutes. What he was going to do now? What was the purpose of living this life without her? He had built his entire ranch just for her, and now he couldn't bear to think of her never returning. He couldn't even stand the thought of going inside the cabin, knowing she'd never be coming home. He had taken so many little things for granted, and he deeply regretted every bit of it now.

He watched everyone saddling up to check on the herd, and he walked over to them. "Boys...I reckon I'm gonna take myself a little ride."

Cody turned to him. "Where to, Boss?"

Levi shrugged. "Not exactly sure, Cody, but anywhere is better than here for a spell."

Bud saddled his horse. "You want me to ride along, Boss?"

Levi shook his head. "No sir, I gotta spend some time alone. I hope ya understand, Bud."

Bud nodded. Levi went to saddle Star, then he set out across the prairie with no destination in mind.

BUD WATCHED LEVI as he slowly drifted over the hill to the west. He prayed for his safe return.

Later that evening, Bud and Mike sat on the steps with Cody and Christine and the other hands and waited for Levi to return. A couple hours after sundown, Cody said, "You reckon Levi run into some trouble?"

Bud looked into the darkness. "Nah, I reckon he's just tryin' to find himself and make sense of it all." He felt himself worrying over Levi but knew he needed space.

Christine turned to Cody. "I bet the Indians got him. If they did, I'm movin' into the house."

Bud turned to her and got up in her face. "The hell you are. Iffen you say another word like that, I'll remove your tobaccy-spittin' ass off this ranch immediately. Do you understand me?"

Christine swallowed her tobacco spit. "I...I...I was just sayin'."

Cody looked at her. "Damn it, Christine, shut your damn mouth, would ya?"

Mike looked at Bud. "Where do ya reckon he's run off to, brother?"

Bud looked into the darkness. "I don't know, but I reckon he'll be just fine. He can handle himself better than all of us together."

Mike looked him in the eye. "He didn't even take his rifle with him."

Bud felt a bit of worry, but said, "I'm sure he'll be just fine."

A couple hours later, everyone headed to the bunkhouse for the night. Bud sat up awhile waiting for Levi to return but drifted off to sleep shortly after laying down.

The next morning, he realized Levi had not returned and started to get a bit worried. He knew Levi wanted to be left alone, so he forced himself to stay and tend to the chores. He figured Levi would come home when he was ready. However, he was worried because he had gone off in the middle of winter with more than a foot of snow on the ground.

After the third day with no sign of Levi, Mike walked up to Bud. "Brother, I know Levi said he needed time, but I'm startin' to get a bit worried. You reckon we oughta go find him?"

Bud had wanted to go find Levi for quite a while, but he knew he had to work through this difficult time in his life on his own time and in his own way. After the fifth day with still no sign of Levi, though, Bud called a brief meeting with the hands during dinner time. He told them he was concerned for Levi's safety and that he planned to ride out to the surrounding settlements and see if he could find him or any information on his whereabouts. "Mike, I'm leavin' you in charge till I get back. We'll be needin' those new calves looked after directly. Cody, I want you and Christine to ride out and round up any mavericks you should come across. We can't afford to have 'em gettin' kilt by damn coyotes. Bring 'em in, and we'll keep 'em in the barn for a spell. I aim to find Boss and bring him home. I'll be back directly. Until then, y'all know what to do. No lollygaggin', ya hear?"

Everyone agreed, but Cody said, "Maybe I should go instead."

Bud turned to him. "I need you here, Cody. You've become quite a hand 'round here."

Cody nodded. "Alright, we'll be waitin' for ya. I wish you the best of luck, Bud." He reached out and shook Bud's hand.

After Bud had saddled up, he honestly hadn't the slightest idea where to begin searching. He had recalled his and Levi's conversation at Samuel Hunt's grave and tried to think of anything that Levi had said that would give him some kind of hint as to where he would have gone. Nothing came to his mind, which made tracking him very difficult. Difficult as it may be, however, Bud was a very determined hand when he had a mind to be. He had gone in search for Levi once before and finally tracked him down and he knew he could do it once again. He decided he would ride on over to Burlingame and see if he could find him there first, and then to Wilmington, then further if he had to. He planned to search the surrounding settlements and then he would hit every damn town between there and the Rocky Mountains if he had to. He wasn't about to give up on what had become his truest and best friend and partner.

When Bud finally reached Burlingame, he rode down the snowy street and watched as a storekeeper shoveled snow off the boardwalk in front of his little general store. An orange tomcat followed the old man down the boardwalk, rubbing against his legs every time he stopped. "Damn nuisance, run on now!" he heard the storekeeper yell.

Bud rode over to the saloon and looked around but didn't see Levi's horse tied anywhere. He looked through the windows to see if he could spot Levi inside, but only saw a few of the local cowboys from the Hinck spread and a few strangers he hadn't recalled seeing in the area before. He rode over past the livery and looked around to see if he could spot Star anywhere, but still no sign. As he peeked in the stalls and around the corral, a man's voice hollered out, and he heard the sound that most men feared the most. It was the sound of a double-barrel scattergun being cocked.

"Hold it right there, sonny!" a man hollered out. Bud slowly turned around. "What in the Sam Hill do ya think you're doin' sneakin' 'round here, boy? I oughta fill your belly with buckshot right now."

Bud looked the man in the eye and swallowed hard. "Apologies, sir, I was just lookin' for my boss's palomino mare."

The man glared him down. "Uh huh…the hell you were! You tell me another bold lie like that, boy, and I'll cut you in half!"

Bud stared the man in the eye as his fingers twitched slightly at the butt of his Colt. "That's the gospel truth, sir. You see, my boss's gal run out on him suddenly, and he kinda took off a few days back, and, well, sir, I just gotta find him. That gal was his whole world, and I can't stand to think of him out there alone somewhere bearin' all that hurt and pain inside. A pain like that can kill a man. I took off to find him and let him know that he's not alone, but I ain't the slightest notion of where he might be."

The man lowered his shotgun. "I apologize. I figured you to be one of them damn thievin' halfwits from over at the home, come to steal another horse."

Bud shook his head. "No sir, I ain't. I didn't aim to alarm ya, sir. I'll be leavin' now." He walked over and crawled back in the saddle and headed on down the street. He rode around town trying to spot Levi's horse but had no luck, so he decided to head back west past the ranch a fair piece. There was a saloon there he thought Levi might visit if he passed by. He rode up the street and saw no sign of Star anywhere. He rode to the livery and spoke with the gentleman but was told no one new had been seen coming into town the past few days, just the local citizens. Something still felt mighty strange about this town, and Bud was uneasy as he left the livery and rode over to the saloon.

He hitched Star up and walked over and looked through the windows.

There were lots of folks inside drinking and gambling. Bud saw three dance hall gals making their rounds from table to table trying to make two dollars for a good time in the back room. Bud studied the faces of everyone inside but could not see Levi. He looked down the street, then gazed toward the west and saw the sun quickly disappearing from the Kansas sky. He pulled the collar up on his coat and decided to get a room at the hotel for the night and then ride over to Wilmington the next day and see what he could turn up. If he still found nothing he would ride over to Eskridge and try there, then maybe Osage City. He was bound and determined to find Levi even if it was the last thing he did.

THE NEXT MORNING, Bud awoke and walked over to the café for a hot breakfast before riding out. He had gotten a good night's rest and was anxious to hit the trail. Bud finished his breakfast and browsed around town for a bit, searching for any clue or anything that would lead him in the right direction. Once he left town, he was in the same boat he was when he had ridden into town. The morning had brought a much warmer breeze than the day before. The sun was starting to melt the snow across the prairie, and it made for a much more relaxing ride. A few miles to the south, he crossed the steep banks of Soldier Creek. Just ahead, he spotted the faint outline of buildings in Wilmington, and he prayed like hell that someone would have some kind of information.

As he rode into town, he noticed the townspeople watching from the windows in the general store and hotel. The children in the schoolhouse all rushed to the windows and watched as he passed by along the schoolyard. Bud could hear the teacher shouting inside the school, "Children, please take your seats." Across the street, the blacksmith watched as Bud rode up and said, "Howdy, got time to fix a shoe for me? My horse knocked a shoe loose back while crossing the creek."

"Sure thing. It's been rather slow round here the past couple days."

He handed the blacksmith the reins and headed down the street on foot.

As he walked along the boardwalk, he didn't see any sign of Levi's horse on the street, so he walked into the hotel to see if he had possibly gotten a room and was staying there for a spell. Just before he walked in the door, he turned his head around and looked up the street toward the livery but didn't see Star in the corral out back.

"Howdy," he said as he walked into the hotel.

"Howdy," the clerk answered back. "What can I do for ya, sir? Are ya lookin' for a room?"

Bud took his hat in his hand. "No sir, I'm looking for someone and was wonderin' if by chance he was here or if he had been here recently."

The hotel clerk looked at him and then grabbed his logbook. "Well, sir, who is this person you are speakin' of?"

Bud looked around. "My boss, Levi Cord. He took off some time back, and I've been tryin' to find him and bring him home."

The clerk looked at him curiously. "Took off where? I mean...did he say where he was goin'?"

Bud explained the story to the man, leaving out the in-depth details.

"Well, sir," said the clerk. "He hasn't been here, I can assure you. We run one of the finest hotels in the territory with some of the cleanest rooms this side of Missouri. Trust me, sir, Mr. Cord has not been here, and that's for sure."

"Now what in the hell do you mean by that?"

The clerk grinned. "We run a respectable hotel with respectable clientele."

Bud gritted his teeth. "Are you sayin' that Levi ain't fit to stay in this hotel here?" He reached down and tapped his fingers on the wood grips of his Colt while waiting for an answer.

The clerk swallowed hard. "That is not what I was saying at all, sir. It's just that—"

Before the man could finish, Bud turned around and walked out the door, mumbling, "Miserable Yankee bastard."

Bud stood on the boardwalk for a few minutes, gazing up the street. "Where in the hell are ya, Boss?" he whispered. He walked over and sat down on a bench in front of the general store. What if Levi had gotten hurt on the prairie somewhere? What if he had done something foolish? Bud knew just how bad Levi must have been hurting, and when a man was hurt that bad, it could make him do some of the craziest things, whether they made sense or not.

Around dinner time, he decided to walk over to the saloon and have himself a drink or two and ask around to see if anyone had seen Levi in town over the past few days. He wondered if he had ridden off to Council Grove to try to win Samantha back, but he highly doubted it. As he walked into the saloon, he strolled over to the bar and ordered a glass of rotgut whiskey before sitting down at a table. The saloon had filled up with lots of townsfolk all crowding around trying to stay in out of the cold and the mud. There were eight tables in this saloon with green felt tops, and Bud had heard that two local dealers ran about the most honest games in the area. There were four lovely women there that Bud bet made more money on a single day than most men would make in a month of hard-earned wages.

A commotion broke out in the corner. "You son of a bitch!" a man yelled out. "I oughta pistol whip your cheatin' ass, you low-down Rebel bitch!"

Bud turned around to see a man standing over a table screaming at the other men gathered around the table playing cards. He kept his eyes locked on the man screaming. "I'm talkin' to you, you drunken piece of trash."

Then a voice spoke up that Bud recognized right off. "You got an awful big mouth for such a scrawny prick, don't ya?" Bud looked at the other men sitting at the table and then realized that the one with his back toward him was Levi. He knew Levi was fixing to get himself in quite a scuffle, and he also knew he was unheeled.

Bud stood and walked over to the table. "Boys, sounds like y'all need a li'l fresh air. Why don't ya say I buy ya boys a drink and ya go get some air and then cool off."

The man looked him up and down. "Who in the fuck are you, and what business is this of yours?"

Bud looked the man in the eye. "Pardner, I'd suggest you calm yourself 'fore someone gives you a lickin' you won't soon forget." He handed the man a silver dollar. "Now, go get yourself a drink, pardner."

The man's face turned red with anger and he reached for his Colt quickly but not quick enough. Bud drew his knife and stabbed the man in the belly repeatedly, leaving him dying in a pool of blood on the saloon floor. He walked over to Levi. "Howdy, Boss, been lookin' for ya for a spell."

Levi looked up at him. "What in the hell for?"

Bud stood there for a moment. "Time to come home, Levi. Got cows needin' tendin' to."

Levi stared across the room with a lost look on his face. "What's the use? You go on back and tend to 'em yourself. I aim to sit right here and do what I've always done best."

Bud looked him deep in the eye. "Oh, yeah, and what is that?"

Levi grinned and picked up a bottle and pressed it to his lips. He was so drunk he spilled the whiskey all over his face and down his shirt. Bud shook his head. "Come on, Boss, I'm takin' you home."

Levi refused to get up, but Bud grabbed him by the arm and pulled him out of his chair.

Levi got up in his face. "Boy, you'd better remove your hands from me or I'm gonna send you to hell."

Bud began to pull him out the door. "Boss, come on now. Just stop."

Levi demanded for him to let him go at once, but Bud refused. Levi balled up his fist and punched Bud right in the cheek. Bud wiped the tears from his eyes and the blood from his nose and socked Levi in the face, dazing his drunken carcass enough to carry him out of the saloon.

As he got him to the boardwalk, Levi began to cuss and resist something awful. "Let go of me! I won't go back! She's gone! It won't ever be the same…"

Bud grabbed Levi by the collar of his jacket and pulled him right up close to his face. "You can't give up now! I won't let ya, Boss. Sober up and let's ride."

Bud began to lead Levi down the boardwalk and Levi turned to him. "You go to hell, Bud Christopher."

Bud grabbed him by the arm and swung him around and punched him right in the face and then grabbed him and swung him up over his shoulder and walked over to the horse trough and threw him headfirst into the freezing cold water. Levi came up screaming and cussing and Bud shoved his head under water a couple times until he quit resisting. He leaned over Levi and saw him open his eyes and Bud said, "Boss."

Levi looked him in the eyes. "Bud? Is that you, Bud?"

Bud could tell Levi was beyond drunk and had no idea what he was saying or what he was doing. He wouldn't remember any of it when he sobered up.

"Boss?" he said again.

"Yes, Bud?" Levi answered.

Bud leaned down and got right in Levi's face. Bud could tell he had been drunk for quite some time…the smell clung thickly to him. "I think the world of you, Levi. You're one of the best friends I've ever had. I've been honored to ride with ya this long, but I ain't ready to give up on ya just yet. I know you love Samantha, and I know how much you're hurtin'…I truly do, Boss. I've been there and never dreamed I'd see the day I would get over it. To tell ya the truth, Boss, I don't reckon I ever really got over it. I just learned to get on with life and move on from it the best that I could. It's not gonna be one damn bit easy, but you will get through this. You just gotta take it day by day, one step at a time. It'll be as if you're a newborn child learnin' how to walk again for the first time. I know you can do it, Levi. I have faith in you."

Levi sat there in the muddy street listening to Bud talk. After a moment, Levi said, "Bud I don't wanna live without her. I don't know what I'll do without her. I can't believe she's really gone." He began to tear up, and he reached for a bottle he had in his coat. "Where do I go from here, Bud?"

"Look at me, Boss. Look in my eyes." Levi looked him in the eyes, and he continued. "You gotta cowboy up, and I mean it. Lose that bottle and saddle up and let's ride. If you don't ride with me now, I'm puttin' in my resignation and will be leavin' the ranch immediately." Levi's eyes widened and his jaw dropped. "Cowboy up, and let's ride now."

Levi wiped his eyes. "I don't know how, Bud."

Bud grinned. "For starters, toss that bottle, just for today."

Levi tossed his bottle into the alley, then attempted to get to his feet but struggled. Bud helped him stand up and walked him to the livery. It took all he had to get Levi's drunken carcass in the saddle.

Once they arrived back at the ranch, everyone met them in the yard and Bud told Mike, "Help me get Levi here to the bunkhouse."

Cody grabbed Star's reins as Mike ran over and helped Levi down. Levi stood on his feet for a second, then commenced to vomiting, falling to his knees. His eyes rolled back in his head, and he passed out. Mike caught him before he hit the ground. They carried him to Bud's bunk and wrapped him in wool blankets. Christine stoked the fire.

"Christine," Bud said. "You tend to that fire and make sure he stays warm. He's drunker than a skunk, and I reckon he'll be out for quite a spell now. Poor soul has gone through quite a deal in his life. I don't reckon he'll be gettin' over Miss Samantha for quite a spell, iffen he ever does. When he comes to, make sure he has plenty of water and food."

LEVI AWOKE TO the worst headache and hangover he could remember. He groaned as he held his head. "What the hell happened?" He sat up on the bunk and looked around the bunkhouse and wondered how long he had been asleep. He slowly reached to the foot of the bunk and grabbed his boots and put them on, intending to find Bud. As he walked over to the door, he held his head as it pounded something fierce. He opened the door and squinted his eyes as the sunlight poured in. He shielded his eyes as he looked across the yard for everyone.

He saw Christine over at the corral chopping ice. She kept looking over to the barn, hollering words he couldn't hear, so he assumed Cody was in the barn. Levi walked over to the privy. After he finished his business, he walked over to the barn. "Mornin', Cody."

Cody turned around and smiled. "Mornin'? Hell, it's after dinnertime, Boss. How ya feelin'? I was startin' to wonder iffen you was ever gonna wake up."

Levi shook his head. "I feel like I've done drank up the whole Neosho River full of whiskey. How long was I asleep?"

Cody chuckled. "Hell, around two and a half days, I reckon."

Levi shook his head. "Damnation. I don't recall the last time I done such a thing."

"I'm awful sorry 'bout Samantha, Boss. Iffen there's anything I can do, speak up."

Levi lowered his head. "Could you saddle my horse?"

Cody nodded. "Sure thing, Boss."

Levi dug down into his pocket and pulled out the letter Samantha had written. As he read the words yet again, his eyes filled with tears and he wiped his eyes with his jacket sleeve.

After Cody had finished saddling Star, he said, "There ya go, Boss. Where ya headed?"

Levi looked across the snowy prairie. "I don't rightly know, but I can't stay here, and I sure's hell ain't goin' in the cabin." He led Star out of the barn and crawled into the saddle and set out across the ranch once again with no destination in mind. As he got out of sight from the cabin, he dug down inside his saddlebags and pulled out a bottle of whiskey. He opened the cork and pressed the bottle to his lips. The taste was strong and burned his weathered lips as he swallowed a bellyful. For the rest of the day, he rode across the ranch, trying to steer clear of the cabin. He wasn't strong enough or ready to face the cabin without Samantha, knowing she was never coming home again. A piece of him had died when she left. A piece he was sure would never be replaced.

FOR THE NEXT month or so, every day seemed to consist of the same thing for Levi. Everyone was busy tending to the herd, and spring was just around the corner. Every day was another day closer to warmer weather. Levi would help with the chores in the mornings and then ride off alone and drown himself in a bottle. Sometimes Bud would ride along and leave Mike in charge while they were gone. Levi tried to hide his drinking from everyone the best that he could for a while but was not successful in the least bit. When Bud would ride along, Levi would spill his heart out to him about Samantha, and not a day went by that he didn't ask if Samantha was ever coming home. Bud had spoken up and said how much it tore at his heart to watch Levi drink himself away, but Levi was past the point of caring. He had lost near thirty pounds and looked as if he hadn't eaten in months, which was almost the case. On a rare occasion, Levi would force down a biscuit or piece of jerky, but most days he just filled his belly with whiskey.

One night, while everyone was sitting around the bunkhouse after sundown, Christine asked Levi when he thought he would find himself another woman. It was clear by the look on her face that she instantly knew she should have left her mouth shut, but it was confirmed when Levi shot her a look that could have killed her.

Cody turned to Levi. "I saw this purty li'l gal over in Wilmington the other day at the saloon that had the finest set of tits this side of Dixie."

Levi looked at him and said nothing.

Mike's eyes widened. "Oh, really now?"

Cody smiled. "She had legs that could wrap all the way around a cowboy and hold on tight. I was tellin' her 'bout Boss here and she said she could show him how a real woman is supposed to treat a man."

Levi jumped up from the bunk and tackled Cody. He punched Cody right in the face and wrapped his hands around his neck. Levi was aware of Bud jumping up and running over. Levi punched Cody in the face repeatedly as Bud held him by the neck of the shirt. Levi spun around and tackled Bud, knocking him to the floor, and then Mike jumped up and grabbed Levi by the back of the arm and swung him around. As he did, Levi punched Mike right in the lip. Cody lay on the floor holding his bloody nose. Bud jumped up and grabbed Levi by the other arm, and Levi kicked him in the leg.

After several minutes of an all-out brawl, Mike grabbed Levi and held his arms behind his back.

"I'm played out, boys," Levi said as he spit blood on the wood floor. "I apologize to y'all. I don't know what's come over me. I just need…"

Mike let go of Levi. "Need what, Boss?"

Levi wiped the blood from his lip. "I just need a damn drink. I got the shakes so bad."

Mike looked over at Bud, and Bud walked up to Levi. "You've never given me a chance to cuss ya, Boss, or quarrel with ya, and I downright hate to have laid a hand on ya just now, but ya left me no choice."

Levi lowered his head. "Shoot. I'm sorry, boys. I reckon I've made quite a mess of myself 'round here lately."

Everyone shook their heads.

Levi looked at Cody. "My apologies, Cody. I shouldn't have acted the way I done just now. Weren't no call for it."

Cody wiped the blood from his nose on his shirt sleeve. "Shoot, Boss, that's alright. I reckon I'da done the same thing."

LEVI PUT ON his coat and walked out the door and pulled out his flask and drank a sip of whiskey. Bud followed him outside and watched him drink the last drop in the flask. "Boss…?"

"Yes sir?" Levi answered.

Bud walked up and looked him dead in the face. "Boss, I got something to say to you."

Levi looked him in the eye and then lowered his head in shame.

"Raise your head, Boss." Bud reached over and placed his hand on Levi's chin. "Raise your head and look at me." Levi looked him in the eye as Bud spoke. "Boss, why don't you quit drowning you sorrows in that bottle and put those sorrows on paper. Pick up that guitar and put a tune to it. Might help some with lettin' go."

Levi bit his lip and fought back the tears. "I don't wanna let go."

Bud put his hand on his shoulder. "I know, pard, I know. Sometimes life deals us a stacked deck. We don't know why it just happens that way at times. I ain't sayin' that you need to forget her, ain't sayin' that a'tall. I'm only sayin' that you need to take those feelin's that you're holdin' onto and let them go. I know you love her. I know you always will, but sometimes it's best to bite the bullet and accept the hand that God has dealt us, no matter if we like it or not. Take those fine memories that you two shared and put them in a li'l spot in the back of your heart. It's alright to bring them out from time to time, but you shouldn't dwell on 'em and let them get the better of ya. Just remember, pard, God has a reason for everything. Talk to him, he'll listen to ya."

Levi looked across the yard and into the darkness, then looked at the cabin. "Pardner, I talk to him all the time, but I don't reckon he wants to hear from me. I ain't what I'd call worthy of his love."

"Nonsense, you're one of his children and he'll wrap his everlasting loving arms around you as long as you accept him and welcome him to your heart."

Levi shook his head and looked back at the cabin. The same empty feeling came over him and he thought to himself for a moment and then handed Bud the flask. "Thank you, pardner. I'm in debt to ya."

As he turned to walk away, Bud hollered out, "Boss, remember, take those sorrows and put 'em on paper. You might be surprised what will come of it."

Levi gave him a half smile, nodded, and turned to walk away. As he began to walk toward the barn, Bud said, "Once last thing, Boss."

Levi turned around. "What's that, Bud?"

Bud looked him dead in the eye. "Cowboy up."

Chapter 26

March came after a long and dreadful winter. Snowstorms had parted way for the spring showers and thunderstorms. Levi was mighty thankful for the sunshine and warmer temperatures. His drinking had begun to slow down day by day, and he became more social and less agitated with everyone. He had been staying in the bunkhouse since Samantha had left and still had not faced the cabin without her. If he needed anything from inside, he would have Cody or Bud fetch it for him.

One day, Levi awoke in the bunkhouse and something caught his eye across the room. As he turned his head, he saw the guitar he had bought in Wilmington. He sat there for several minutes thinking about Samantha and what he was going to do without her. How was he ever going to get over her leaving? Would he ever be able to? He reached for his flask before remembering he had given it to Bud. He looked back at the guitar and knew just what he had to do.

Dally came up beside him, nudging his hand with her nose. Samantha hadn't taken her with her for some reason. Dally reminded Levi too much of Samantha, so he had done his best to ignore her. Levi went to push Dally away, but again she nudged him, this time pressing her head hard against his chest as if to comfort him. He gave in and rubbed her ears. "Thanks, ol' girl," he said, his voice solemn. "Want to go for a ride?"

He got dressed and put on his boots, then walked over and picked up the guitar. He sat down on the bunk and tuned the guitar to get that perfect sound he admired so well. After he finished tuning, he strapped it to his back and walked over and rounded up a few pieces of paper and a bottle of ink and a quill. He walked out to the barn and saddled up Star and prepared to set out to find himself on the prairie.

As he headed past the corral, Bud was working a new red roan colt. "Mornin', Boss, where ya off to today?"

Levi walked over. "Mornin', Bud. I figured I'd take me a ride for a couple days and see iffen I can find myself again."

Bud smiled. "Proud to hear it, Boss. We'll get along just fine here. Take your time and do what ya gotta do. We'll be here when ya get back."

Levi nodded and reached out to shake Bud's hand. As Bud grabbed his hand, Levi shook it with a firm grip and Bud smiled and nodded.

Levi crawled in the saddle and decided to head southwest toward Elm Creek to a spot where the Flint Hills began and carved a beautiful scene across the rolling hills of grassland and prairie. He was rather fond of this specific spot and thought he would find peace there away from everyone and have a chance to clear his mind and release some of his bottled-up emotions and put them to paper, as Bud had advised. As he rode across the open prairie, he spotted a covey of bobwhite quail running single file ahead of him in a nearby ditch. He smiled as he watched them race each other to safety. A red-tailed hawk let out a screech as it soared overhead. To the south, Levi could see big dark blue clouds forming as a thunderstorm brewed and headed across the prairie to the east. Thunder echoed across the plains as he rode on.

Late that afternoon, he reached the banks of Elm Creek where he and Samantha, along with Bud and Mike, had crossed through the rushing muddy water the spring before on their way back to the ranch. He stopped for a moment and looked around and recalled their journey from Council Grove. Boy, did he miss Samantha. Not a day went by that she wasn't heavy on his mind and heart. Every day that passed, he seemed to grow a bit stronger, but he never stopped missing her or wishing for her return.

Just ahead, he came to the spot he had been searching for. The switchgrass swayed from side to side as the Kansas breeze blew across the prairie. Thunder echoed to the south, and lightning crashed to the ground. The wind died down, and the prairie came to life with robins splashing in puddles searching for worms and other insects being flooded out of the ground. Every so often, a raindrop would find its way to Levi's hat brim. He spotted a dead tree standing all alone next to a natural waterhole and decided he had finally reached the perfect spot to sit down and find peace within himself. He had a couple hours left of daylight now, and the lighting across the prairie was spectacular…the green grass sprouting up under the yellow switchgrass and the dark blue skies turning orange and pink to the west. Off to the south, Levi spotted a double rainbow stretching down from the sky and landing somewhere across the prairie.

He climbed down out of the saddle and reached for his quill and paper.

He walked over to a ditch and sat down next to the tree. He began picking his guitar. He had to retune a couple of the strings after his ride, but once he got her sounding just right, he began to play a little tune he had been humming for the past five or six miles.

As he tried to think of what to write, he found himself struggling for the right words. He had so many things rushing through his head all at once, so he decided to lay back and close his eyes for a few minutes. As he did, his mind drifted off to the past, and a sad and lonesome feeling hit him hard.

He thought about Samantha and just how he had felt since she had gone, and when he opened his tear-filled eyes, he began to write.

> There's a full moon tonight on the prairie
> And the memory just rolled into view,
> Of a girl, a paint horse, and an old heeler dog
> In the hills where the sunflowers grew.
>
> I was deep in the heart of Kansas
> Just a cowboy, twenty-nine at the time,
> Runnin' wild through the Flint Hills
> The prairie grass along the old trail
> It's been years but you're still on my mind.
>
> No matter where I may wander
> There's a memory that I'll never lose,
> Her blue eyes shine bright
> In my heart tonight,
> And I've got the Council Grove blues.

As he sat there writing his feelings down, he continued humming the same tune to each line, and the memories came rushing in. Tears flooded his weary blue eyes. Before he knew it, he had the first and second verses as well as a chorus written down.

He stopped writing for a moment and stared across the prairie to the west and wondered where Samantha was at that very moment. He wondered if she ever thought of him at all and if she missed him. He looked west toward Council Grove and began to write again.

> I remember those warm summer evenings
> Dancin' out under the stars,
> Back then I never dreamed she'd ever be leavin',
> Ah, but I guess things just don't stay as they are.
>
> Well, the years and the miles came between us
> And tonight as I'm dreamin' of you,
> Once again, I'm a cowboy,
> In the sweet arms of Kansas
> And I've got the Council Grove blues.
>
> No matter where I may wander
> There's a memory that I'll never lose,
> Her blue eyes shine bright
> In my heart tonight,
> And I've got the Council Grove blues.

Levi paused for a minute and stared across the Kansas prairie toward Council Grove once more. A meadowlark called somewhere to the east as it splashed in a fresh puddle. A tear softly trickled its way down Levi's cheek as he felt a feeling of final contentment overcome his heart. He gazed into the sunset and admired the way that it painted the perfect and romantic picture of true life on the western frontier. He smiled for the first time in a long time as he softly wrote the final lines of his song.

> Her blue eyes shine bright
> In my heart tonight,
> And I've got the Council Grove blues.

After he wrote the last and final line, he gazed across the grasslands, and with tears in his eyes said, "It's time to say goodbye, darlin'." He stood and walked over to a nearby grassy knoll that was covered with lovely wildflowers. The colors were just simply beautiful, painting the prairie so beautiful it seemed to take your breath away. He leaned down and picked a bouquet of flowers and walked over to the dead tree standing all alone, looking just as lonesome as he did out there on the open prairie. He placed the flowers at the base of the tree and stood there for a moment, looking back at the gorgeous sunset as it slowly disappeared over the Kansas horizon. He saddled up and decided to head back toward the ranch. There was a gorgeous full moon glowing overhead, so Levi figured he'd spend the night in the saddle and enjoy a peaceful ride back home. Whippoorwills serenaded him as he sat a heap taller in the saddle that starry peaceful night. The thunderstorm had passed him by and left a cool and refreshing breeze behind.

Several miles up the trail, Levi spotted something to the north that he couldn't quite make out. The dark sky was lit up with a bright orange tint a few miles ahead over the hill. As he rode closer, he began to smell smoke and knew then that something ahead of him had caught fire. He spurred Star to a gallop and rode to the top of the hill to see if he could get a better look. When he reached the crest of the hill, his heart sank deep in his chest.

The smoke was coming from the ranch. The barn was engulfed in flames. He could hear the sound of voices screaming and others laughing loudly. Flames lit up the yard, and Levi could see a dozen figures on horseback surrounding the cabin and the bunkhouse. All of a sudden, he heard gunshots ring out. He spurred Star with all he had and took off at a dead run into the darkness across the creek.

Whatever was going on, he was prepared to meet it head on.

About the Author

The Flint Hills Cowboy, Levi "Doc" Hinck, is a native Kansas cowboy who prefers to spend most of his time in the saddle punching cows. He's been known across the state for his past rodeo career, riding bucking bulls and broncs on various circuits. At the age of fifteen, he began to portray legendary Western characters such as Doc Holliday, Jesse James, Billy the Kid, Bob Dalton, etc. He joined up with a Kansas Old West reenacting group and traveled the Midwest acting in gunfights every chance he could. At the age of seventeen, he was asked to take part in a film for the *Investigating History Series* on the History Channel called "The Hidden Battle". The film was to be based on the Battle of Mine Creek in Kansas during the Civil War. On the location of the film, Doc met with the executive producer and was invited to a second film in Coffeyville for the Dalton Gang Raid the following week. After that, his movie career began to take off throughout his high school years. He since then has taken part in several documentaries and films.

Doc is a real-life working ranch hand in the Kansas Flint Hills. He has always had a love for history and, as he says, "Right here in my own stomping grounds, the Flint Hills hold some of the most romantic and important history that has almost been forgotten over the years. History that they don't teach you in school. I'd give anything to preserve that history and keep it alive for generation after generation; however, one day I'll be just another speck of dust out on this lone prairie, same as those that settled this countryside before me. I hope that before I go, I'll be able to share some of that cherished history to others that will pass it on and keep it alive."

Doc is a living historian and also spends much of his free time performing his favorite country-western music at events across Kansas and the surrounding states when he's not robbing banks and trains in an Old West reenactment. He is a proud father of two cowboys, Lane and Rossen.

Made in the USA
Columbia, SC
25 June 2021